Memories from Cherry Harvest

Memories from Cherry Harvest

Amy Wachspress

a novel

SOFT SKULL PRESS | AN IMPRINT OF COUNTERPOINT

Library of Congress Cataloging-in-Publication Data is available.

ISBN: 978-1-59376-440-1

Cover design by Ann Weinstock
Interior design by Maria E. Torres, Neuwirth & Associates, Inc.

Soft Skull Press
An imprint of COUNTERPOINT
1919 Fifth Street
Berkeley, CA 94710
www.softskull.com

Distributed by Publishers Group West

10 9 8 7 6 5 4 3 2 1

For the Ancestors:
Yael and Joseph Wachspress
Jean and Sidney Wachspress
Mildred and Milton Gross
Natalie and Eugene Wachspress

and for Ron

Bless the gift of memory
that breaks unbidden, released
from a flower or a cup of tea
so the dead move like rain through the room.

Bless what forces us to invent
goodness every morning and what never frees
us from the cost of knowledge, which is
to act on what we know again and again.

—MARGE PIERCY

PART ONE

Rivka and Ruth

ONE

Rivka

WHEN I REMEMBER RUSSIA, I ache with longing for the village of my birth, where the beloved grandparents magically produced candy in a handshake and told stories of long ago when God spoke to humans and enchantments filled the world. On the day we left our village, Mama covered my face with a shawl to prevent me from seeing the heads of our elders mounted on spikes at the entrance. My grandmother's head stood on one of those spikes. Did I actually see the heads or merely imagine them? The images that remain with me from that leave-taking have a gauzy, grainy texture because of the shawl. Mama succeeded in protecting me and my sister, Ruth, from the details of the gruesome scene, a significant success since the details of life in turbulent times are the most poignant part of history.

Our village had experienced other pogroms, but none as brutal as the one that drove my family out. "This is no place to raise children," Mama said. Papa seized the moment and persuaded Mama to emigrate to Palestine, the ancient Jewish homeland, the land of milk and honey. Mama hoped to find richness and sweetness there. I think she did for a time, and then she didn't. Palestine was not exactly a safe place to raise children either. Now that I am a mother, I wonder if there is any such place on earth.

When our family fled to Palestine, it was a land largely inhabited by Arabic peoples reluctantly hosting the colonizing British, who believed they owned the land, as the British were apt to do in those days. A trickle of Jews from throughout Eastern Europe flowed into the region. We Jews called it the *aliyah*, or "ascent," which was our term for the return of the Jews to our ancient homeland. Upon our arrival, we set up a temporary home in a relocation camp. We were not there long before our family was transformed by the hand of an unlikely change agent.

The first time I saw Miriam, I was sitting on the step in front of our family's two-room living quarters. She was playing jump rope with the other children who gathered daily in the dusty road, jabbering at each other in a tangle of languages like the throng at Babel. Miriam was a bossy girl with a thick mane of curly dark brown hair. I had curly hair too, but mine was not as untamed as Miriam's. I watched her guardedly from my vantage point. Ever since we had left Russia, I had felt utterly uprooted. I was hesitant to enter our new life in Palestine because to do so felt like a betrayal of my beloved Russia. Unlike my parents, I did not blame Russia for the pogroms and persecution of my people and chose to remember my homeland with affection instead. Russia was the place where I had known everyone in my small world, and they had known me. After I left, the world was full of strangers.

My sister, Ruth, was eight years old, and I was six when we arrived in Palestine. She was less reserved than I and immediately began carving a place for herself among the children, her wavy brown hair flying up and down as she jumped rope with them, and her large hazel eyes flashing with the challenge of keeping the rhythm.

After her turn jumping, Ruth stepped aside as I heard Miriam ask her, "Why doesn't your sister play with us? What's wrong with her?"

Ruth shrugged and answered, "She's doesn't feel like it."

Apparently not satisfied with Ruth's answer, Miriam proceeded to investigate. She flounced over and drilled her little backside into the step next to me. My heart flip-flopped. At first, Miriam said nothing as we watched the others at their jump rope game. She was smaller than I, and younger. Her hair leapt wildly from her head, daring anyone to comb it into submission. I watched from the corner of my eye as she unwrapped a hard green candy with fingers that sported chipped red nail polish. I had never seen a girl my age wearing nail polish.

She offered me the candy and I took it hesitantly. As I put it into my mouth, I asked, "Your mama lets you wear nail polish?"

"My mama lets me do anything. She lives in heaven."

"I thought only dead people are in heaven."

"They die, then they go to heaven, then they live forever." She had a tone of authority in her voice that prevented me from doubting her and made me feel foolish, as if I should understand how heaven works. "Mama watches me from heaven and she'll never let anything bad happen to me. She's more powerful now than when she was here."

"How did she die?"

"In the Jewish and Russian War."

This answer made no sense to me since I was both Jewish and Russian. "If your mama lives in heaven, then who takes care of you?" I asked.

"Papa. He's working here in the camp. I come with him because my brother goes to school and there's no one to watch me. Papa builds things, so he goes wherever people need something built. Usually he works where there are no children around and I have to play by myself. I'm glad he is building things here because I have friends to play with. Do you live here?"

"Until we save enough money to move away from the camp."

"You're lucky. I wish I lived with these friends. Do you sleep over?"

"Sleep over?"

"You know, sleep over with your friends."

"I don't have any friends." I wondered where my cousins and play-mates from Russia were and what they were doing at that moment. I would wonder that forever.

Miriam cast me a look of surprise, then offered, "I'll be your friend."

"You already have friends," I said.

She shrugged. "I have a lot of friendship in me. I haven't used it all up yet. Do you think your mama would let me sleep over?"

Miriam's proposition shocked me.

"Go ask her," she commanded.

I didn't know if I wanted this girl to sleep over. Her aggressively cheer-ful and inquisitive style frightened me a little. I stood slowly and went inside. Maybe Mama would say no and that would settle it. Mama was busy taking up the hem in a dress that Ruth had outgrown so that I could wear it. "Mama, I met a girl named Miriam. She's outside. She asked if she can sleep over."

Mama looked surprised. "Who is she? Perhaps I should talk with her mother."

"Mama lives in heaven. You can talk to her but she can't talk back," Miriam's voice piped up behind me. I whirled around to find her standing in the doorway.

Mama scrutinized the self-assured child. "So. This is Miriam, I pre-sume? Let's have a look at you."

Miriam stepped into the room. "Papa is working nearby. I can bring him after work and we can ask him if I can sleep over."

"You bring him then and we'll talk about it," Mama told Miriam, with a touch of amusement in her voice.

"Come on," Miriam said, motioning me back outside with a wave of her hand. "I'll teach you a jump rope song that I just made up today." Miriam's vitality was contagious and made me want to learn a jump rope song. I wanted to watch those red fingernails swiftly turn a rope with absolute control.

That evening, a weary man appeared at our door. He crushed a limp cap in one muscular hand and held his daughter's hand in the other. Mama met him on the doorstep. "You must be the papa," she said.

He smiled and tiny crinkles appeared at the corners of his eyes. "Yes, that would be me. I am Meir," he introduced himself. "My daughter says that you have invited her to spend the night here with you." He raised an inquiring eyebrow. "She has made friends with your children?" He glanced from Mama to Miriam and back to Mama as Ruth and I peered at him from inside the doorway.

"My daughters played with Miriam today and Miriam asked if she could sleep over," Mama said.

Before Mama could continue, Meir turned to Miriam and, with a pronounced twinkle in his voice that belied the attempted sternness of his words, said, "So you invited yourself. You know that's not polite, sweet pea."

"I just gave them the idea," Miriam explained.

"I know how you are full of ideas," Meir responded.

I wondered what Miriam's papa meant by that. I glanced at Ruth, who was following the conversation intently and did not look in my direction.

"It's fine with me," Mama was quick to say. "She's welcome to stay if you don't mind leaving her with strangers." It seemed peculiar to hear Mama refer to us as strangers, but then I realized that to Meir we were.

"I trust her intuition. She can stay," he said. "I'll be back to work first thing in the morning. We're putting in a water system on the north corner. I can come by for her after work tomorrow, but if she causes any difficulty, then send her away. She knows where to find me."

"That's fine," Mama told him.

Miriam gave her papa a kiss good-bye and skipped over to me and Ruth. "Where are we going to sleep?" she asked eagerly.

Ruth and I took Miriam inside and showed her the little bed we shared. Miriam touched our worn yet brightly colored quilt with her fingertips as if memorizing every stitch.

"My grandma made this quilt for us from scraps of our baby clothes. She died in Russia," I told her.

"My mama died in Russia too," Miriam informed me, her eyes wide with astonishment, as if this was a coincidence that had solved a great mystery. "I bet Mama met your grandma in heaven and they decided to make us friends." The minute Miriam said it, I believed it.

The next evening, when Meir came to collect his daughter, Papa insisted that he stay for a cup of tea. Mama hastened to light the gas plate to heat some water.

"I can't stay long. I have to get home to my son," Meir said with a slight note of worry in his voice. "He is only ten years old."

"Who looks after him while you are at work?" Mama asked.

"Well, he goes to school most of the day, of course. And afterward he goes home. A neighbor checks in on him for me. I don't like to leave him alone for so much of the time, but I have no other choice. Thank goodness he is responsible." Meir sighed. "In Russia, I worked as a carpenter, but I seem to have a knack for building larger things than furniture. In Palestine, I have been fortunate to find work designing and building houses and other buildings, drainage systems, water systems, small bridges, anything at all. I have a good instinct for how much pressure something can bear before it will collapse." He paused and looked off into the distance. "Unfortunately, this instinct failed me when it came to my late wife. She did not have the temperament for life in Russia. She attacked a captain with a candlestick during a pogrom. It would have been a funny story about her bravery and spirit, I suppose, if he hadn't killed her. So now I am on my own with the children." I tried to imagine Miriam's mother, a heroine who had died bravely.

"Oh no," Mama responded, and it sounded as if all the breath had gone out of her. "I'm so sorry. We left after a particularly vicious pogrom in which my mother was murdered."

I thought about the ride past the wall of the village, my face wrapped in Mama's shawl.

There was an awkward pause in the conversation, which Miriam dispelled when she tugged at Meir's sleeve. "May I sleep over again?"

"You haven't been invited, sweet pea."

"She's welcome to stay," Mama offered. "She was no trouble at all. I would be happy to keep her anytime."

"See? They don't mind," Miriam pleaded.

"But I want to spend some time with you tonight. I miss you." Meir put his arm around Miriam's skinny waist. "Avram misses you too."

"No he doesn't," Miriam thrust out her lip. She turned to Mama. "Can I sleep over tomorrow?"

Mama laughed. "You must do as your father wishes," she said.

"You will wear out your welcome," Meir warned.

But she didn't. Miriam slept over most of the nights that week and the following week. On Friday, when Meir came to pick up Miriam, he informed us that he had completed the job for which he had been hired at the camp and he would be moving on to his next job. "You will have to say good-bye to your friends for now, sweet pea," Meir told his sorrowful daughter.

"I want Rivka and Ruth to come to my house," Miriam demanded. "Give them our address." She took a crumpled candy wrapper from her pocket. "Write it here." She pointed with a pink painted fingernail.

Mama handed Meir a piece of paper. "Yes, write down your address and we will come visit. Why don't we come on Sunday and I'll cook something for all of us for dinner? Something healthy. You let that child eat entirely too much candy," Mama scolded.

Meir looked sheepish as he replied, "I would love to have you cook something healthy for us on Sunday; are you sure it's no bother?"

"It would be my pleasure."

On Sunday, Papa raised his hand to knock on the door just as Miriam flung it open. Her eyes sparkled and her crazy mane flopped about her shoulders. "I have a plan, I have a plan," she sang merrily, dancing on her tiptoes.

"Come in," Meir greeted. "Look at all this food you have brought. This is too expensive. You must let me pay for this food. My goodness."

Miriam's brother, Avram, immune to his sister's exuberance, did not budge from his nest in a heap of pillows where he sat with a book propped against his knee. I had the feeling that I had seen Avram somewhere before. I could tell that Ruth remained unimpressed by him. He examined us with a thinly veiled expression of irritation before returning to his book.

An impish smile played on Meir's lips as he informed us, "Miriam has a plan."

"So we hear," Papa laughed.

"It is an excellent plan," Meir added.

"It is an excellent plan," Miriam repeated, fit to burst with her idea. "I thought of it all by myself."

"We propose that you live with us until you establish yourselves in Palestine." Meir held up a hand. "Before you protest, let me say that the arrangement would serve us both. You will have a home and I will have someone to care for my children while I am at work. And to cook for us. We will pool our resources. We will be better off together than we are separately," Meir argued his point, anxious to win Mama and Papa over. I watched my parents to see if they were being convinced.

"Say yes. Say yes, yes, yes!" Miriam shouted. "Then I can show you your rooms! Every night will be a sleepover!"

"You must say yes," Meir pleaded. "You have no idea what a relief it would be for me."

Mama wagged an accusatory finger at Miriam. "You rascal."

"She dreamt this up, but there hasn't been such a good idea since the fulcrum was invented," Meir exclaimed.

Miriam skipped to a doorway and announced, "This will be your room. Come see."

Meir suggested that Mama and Papa sleep in the master bedroom, where Papa, who was building a business as a tailor, would have space to set up his sewing machine. We girls would share a large bedroom at the back of the house, and Avram would keep his smaller bedroom at the front. When Meir said he would sleep in the living room on the couch, Papa immediately protested, "It isn't right to put you out of your bed."

Meir assured him that he could sleep through anything and it was the most practical arrangement. "When your tailoring business takes off, then we will be in a position to look for a larger house for all of us," Meir said. "That is, if we get along together. But there is only one way to find out."

When we moved in with Miriam's family, my childhood, and Ruth's, became inextricably bound with the childhoods of Miriam and Avram. Mama so thoroughly adopted Miriam and Avram that we almost could not remember a time when she had not mothered them. Mama felt it was her duty to stand in as a surrogate mother for Meir's children because she identified so profoundly with the woman who had run screaming into the street waving her candlesticks in fury. I think Mama must have sometimes wondered how close she might have come to that end herself had we remained in Russia. Every now and then I caught her speaking aloud to the absent woman whose children she was raising. "Look at your Avram," she would say (when she thought no one was listening), "how tall he is and how well he does in school. You must be so proud."

Papa and Meir, as it turned out, were like twins who had been separated at birth and found each other again later in life. They shared a passion for chess, which they played nearly every evening, while they rubbed their respective chins, leaned back precariously in their chairs, and read the Yiddish newspaper aloud to each other between moves and sips of tea. Mama never failed to chide them about tipping back in the chairs. "You'll break the rungs out of those chairs," she would complain, and then mutter something barely audible about men and their failings.

It didn't take long for Avram to warm to our family, especially me. We soon became inseparable. Avid readers, we passed books back and forth to each other as frequently as passing the salt and pepper shakers at the dinner table. We invented an elaborate game with sticks and rocks and other found objects. We created a town, with people, houses, and public buildings. Everyone in the town had a job.

"This is Mr. Kaplan, the shopkeeper," I said as I moved a twig to a cinder block and put more twigs there to represent Mr. Kaplan's family. "He has a large family and goats and chickens, and his wife is beautiful even though she's a little fat. But the other people in the town consider her beautiful."

"This is Mr. Cohen," Avram said as he placed another twig. "He's a teacher who's pious and studious. He doesn't care much for Mr. Kaplan, who is too ostentatious for his tastes."

"What is ostentatious?" I asked.

"It means he is sloppy with his money and a show-off and he buys a lot of things he doesn't need just to prove he can do it."

"OK, but he's also generous," I added, hoping to improve Mr. Kaplan's character.

"All right, he can be generous," Avram conceded. "We can make Mr. Cohen miserly if you want."

"Oh yes, let's." I clapped my hands gleefully. "And then Mr. Cohen has an argument with Mr. Kaplan over a goat that Mr. Kaplan sells him." I moved a rock from Mr. Kaplan's house to Mr. Cohen's. "There's the goat. This goat doesn't produce milk. Mr. Cohen wants to return it and get his money back."

Avram threw me an admiring glance. "How do you think up such things?" he asked.

"I don't know. They just pop into my head. So, Mr. Kaplan says the goat won't produce milk because Mr. Cohen allowed her to dry up because he was too lazy to milk her every day and now he has to breed her to start her milk up again. He doesn't want to go to all that trouble." I picked up the Mr. Cohen twig and made him speak in a gruff, angry voice, "She wasn't producing milk when you sold her to me. You said she would give milk but she was dry as a bone, dry as dust on the road." I changed my voice to a high squeaky one and replied as Mr. Kaplan, "I milked her on that very morning that I sold her to you and got plenty of milk out of her, a river of milk, a land flowing with milk."

Avram grabbed Mr. Cohen and a boisterous argument ensued. Some of the neighbors got involved and gave advice. Then Avram made the people drag Mr. Cohen and Mr. Kaplan to Judge Avimelech. They brought the goat. What a scene we had in the courtroom. It was the first of many times that Judge Avimelech would have to intervene and issue orders to Mr. Kaplan and Mr. Cohen about how to conduct their business.

Just as Mr. Kaplan and Mr. Cohen turned to go home, grumbling over Judge Avimelech's decree, Mama called us in for dinner, so we left our village reluctantly on that night, as we did on many nights.

We loved to think up real stumpers for Judge Avimelech to resolve and then we would spend days coming up with suitable judgments that resolved the conflicts satisfactorily for all the parties involved. The more convoluted the challenge posed by the conflict, the more we enjoyed examining all the angles and working out an approach to meet it.

Our families had only been living together in Meir's house for a few months when, one night at the dinner table, Mama announced, "Well, children, we are going to have a new addition to our household soon."

"A dog?" Avram glanced at Meir with excitement.

"No, not a dog," Meir answered. "That's all we need."

"A baby," Mama informed us. "I'm expecting a baby."

"I want a girl," Miriam demanded instantly. "I'll take care of her and dress her up. She can wear my favorite clothes when I grow out of them."

"I think a boy would make a better balance," Meir teased his daughter. "Look how many girls are at this table already. How about another boy to back Avram up?" Avram grunted in appreciation. "Have you thought of a name?" Meir asked.

Before Mama or Papa could answer, Avram blurted, "Benjy." We turned to him in surprise.

"What?" he asked innocently. "I think you should call him Benjy. I used to pretend I had a brother named Benjamin when I came home from school by myself and no one was here. I imagined what we would do together until Papa and Miriam arrived."

"Benjamin," Papa repeated. "It's a good name for the youngest."

"And how do you know he will be the youngest?" Mama asked coyly.

Papa clutched his head in mock dismay, "Oy, yoy, yoy."

"How many do you want?" Meir asked, with a mischievous twinkle.

"At least enough for our own football team," Mama answered, as she pinched Papa's arm.

"Oy, yoy, *yoy*," Papa said louder. We nearly fell off our chairs laughing at his expression.

Avram's name stuck. We referred to the baby as Benjy for the rest of Mama's pregnancy. If she had given birth to a girl, we probably would have called her Benjy. Luckily, the baby was a boy.

"He's so tiny," Miriam marveled, bending over to peer into the swaddling blankets, where Benjy's soft face was the picture of repose under a shock of dark hair.

Miriam sat cross-legged in the bed next to Mama, and I leaned on her shoulder for a better look. "When will he wake up?" Miriam asked. "What color are his eyes?"

"His eyes are gray," Papa told us. "But they might change color when he gets older. A lot of babies have gray eyes. And babies sleep a lot," he explained.

"I think he needs his hat. He looks chilly," Miriam said. She ran to the bureau to fetch a tiny blue hat that Mama had crocheted for him. Miriam put the hat ceremoniously on Benjy's head. I wished I had thought of getting Benjy his hat.

"Now he's ready to *davven*," Papa commented, which set Meir laughing.

"Don't make fun of my baby," Mama warned.

"We're not making fun of the baby," Papa told her, his eyes dancing, "we're making fun of the hat." Meir roared with laughter.

"What a fool I was to agree to live under the same roof with two men." Mama rolled her eyes and chuckled.

"He looks good in the hat," Ruth said, defending Mama. I shared Papa's opinion about the hat, but I didn't say so.

"Thank you," said Mama. "And it is common knowledge that Ruth has impeccable taste in clothing."

"Can't argue with that," Papa said as he patted Ruth on the shoulder. I wondered exactly what it meant to have impeccable taste and wished that I had it too.

"Can I feed him?" Miriam begged.

"You're not equipped," Meir said with a chuckle. Mama threw him a disapproving look.

"He won't eat grown-up food for quite a while," she told Miriam. "He just sucks milk from my breast. Like kittens or puppies suck milk from their mothers."

That fat baby boy, healthy and with the future rolling out before him like uncut fields of wheat, was the crowning gift of Mama and Papa's escape to the holy land. With the birth of Benjamin, gently the tight coil of Mama's spirit unwound as she lowered the defensive guard she had carried with her out of the land of oppression from which we came. Benjy's birth heralded the best years of Mama's life, when she and Papa thrived in the land of milk and honey. So did we, the children they raised in that house spilling over with sunshine, where Mama gave us the gift of an enchanted childhood.

That gift was never more pronounced than during our annual summer vacations to the beach, which was the place I loved most in the world. When I was eight years old, Mama discovered she had a cousin, with half a dozen children, who lived less than a mile from the Mediterranean Sea. Mama and her cousin wrote vigorously to each other for months, and the cousin invited us to her house for a visit. We eagerly accepted her invitation. After that first time, Mama took us children to stay with her cousin every summer while the papas remained behind to work. Her house was not quite close enough for us to see the water from it, but we could smell the sea and hear it in the distance, and we could taste it in the air.

When Benjy was a chuckling toddler with soft dark curls, Mama would strip him naked by the water's edge and he would slap his chubby thighs and smack his feet in the wet sand, while Mama stood guard over her precious gem. Meanwhile, Miriam, Avram, Ruth, our cousins, and I sculpted elaborate sand castles with turrets, walls, and hedged pathways complete with ferocious sea creatures to defend them against marauders. We collected shells, stones, and feathers to decorate our constructions. Avram and I stretched out on towels on the sand and read aloud to each other. Mama bought us lollipops from a little shop up the road from the beach and Benjy shamelessly begged Mama for those lollipops. "Just one?" he would say, holding up one fat finger next to his face, his earnest, expressive eyes turned upward toward Mama. But one was never enough for him. He would chew it instead of sucking on it and it would be gone in an instant; then he would beg for another.

Sometimes, in the evening, we gathered driftwood for a campfire and then Mama and her cousin cooked plump potatoes and chicken for us on a metal grate placed over the red-hot wood, with roasted apples for dessert. As the cool evening breeze brushed our skin, we watched the sunset woo the sparkling water, hypnotized by the motion and the flush of colors fading from flame orange down to blue-black night. Always, at the end of a full day on the beach, we stumbled back to the house where we rinsed off at the pump in the yard and tumbled into bed, happy, exhausted, smelling of the campfire and the outdoors, dreaming of doing it all over again the next day.

After our glorious month at the beach, the papas joined us for a few days only, and then escorted us home on the bus. Every year we lugged several flats of deep amber apricots from our cousin's orchard back with us, and as soon as we arrived at home, Mama preserved the fruit with honey, boiling it in jars in her big metal vat on the stove. We ate those golden apricots throughout the long gray winter.

It was at about the same time that we started going to the beach each summer that Mama joined a community garden not far from our home. She took us children to it as often as possible. Avram and I did not care for gardening, but we liked to sit in the shade of the fruit trees and read. Ruth watched Benjy for Mama since she preferred not to soil her clothes or ruin her fingernails with gardening. So it was mostly Miriam who planted, weeded, watered, and harvested; helped prune and trim in the winter; and prepared the garden beds in the spring. Miriam was never happier than when she was digging in the garden soil, and she had a passion for the fruit trees. She gave them names and talked to them, in particular a large old cherry tree she dubbed "Elijah." She spoke about Elijah as if he was a cherished stuffed animal or an imaginary friend. Ruth and Avram begged Mama to make her stop talking to the tree. But I understood how a tree might become a good friend. You could open your heart to a tree and it would never tell your secrets.

One of Miriam's frequent chores was gathering warm eggs from the chickens. She claimed that she could smell the eggs and cooed over how wonderful the scent was. The garden was often radiant at the day's end, when the young golden-green plants glowed as if with an eerie inner power. Miriam said she had seen a fairy under a squash leaf once, and after that she, Ruth, and I always looked for garden sprites and spirits during the magic hour when the sun was going down. Perhaps another mother would have chastised her children for talking about fairies in the squash plants, but Mama valued imagination and cultivated it in us. I think imagination had rescued Mama from any number of difficult situations.

One of the ways in which she encouraged our creativity was during our bedtime storytelling ritual. Mama would put Benjy to bed early with his own little story and a Yiddish lullaby, always the same one about a child being lulled to sleep by the sound of a flowing river, a remnant of Russia. Then, when we girls settled down in our room and Avram sprawled across the foot of Miriam's bed, Mama joined us in inventing our own stories. They weren't different distinct stories, but part of one ongoing story that continued down a never-ending road. In our story, a group of children traveled the world together. As coincidence would have it, the traveling children were one boy, three girls, and a baby. Sometimes the children met people on their adventures, like the good and powerful wizard Dimitri who had given them the magic crystal when they saved his life in Siberia. They could use the crystal to call him if they needed help. And sometimes they met creatures, like the shy elephant Matilda, the parrot with the power of invisibility, or the evil python named Pythagoras by Ruth, who hated math. And sometimes wonderful things happened, like festivals and celebrations and expeditions under the ocean, and sometimes terrible things befell them, like pogroms and being imprisoned in Pythagoras's caves in the underworld. Whether at a cliffhanger moment or a temporary resolution, the story always ended "to be continued."

Inevitably, the latest book that I had been reading would influence my contribution to the development of the bedtime stories. Sometimes, all Avram had to do was cast me a look, and I knew that I had been caught overlaying something I had recently read onto our bedtime tale. I don't remember exactly when we outgrew the bedtime stories, but we were well into our teen years before we gave up that ritual.

I continued to share my ideas about the world around me with Avram, and as we matured we often discussed politics. Mama didn't give politics much thought, and the papas were far too opinionated to carry on a civilized conversation with me about politics. They could gang up on me and then I felt as if they were foisting their own beliefs on me before I had a chance to decide what I believed. Avram and I valued our freedom to share whatever was on our minds when we talked with each other about political systems, economic systems, social justice, and utopian communities. Talking about our ideas helped us to formulate them. Avram and I agreed that people had to learn to live together, and that if we couldn't develop an inclusive social system, an economically stable and democratic political system, a framework of mutual respect within which conflicts both large and small were resolved, then we would be lost as a species. Just as we had contemplated the judgments meted out by Avimelech in our imaginary village as children, we agonized over who should control Palestine and whether or not a Jewish state was viable. Our Zionistic papas would not have taken kindly to this discussion; however, as Avram often reminded me, we had not lived as many years as our fathers had in a country where persecuting Jews was a longstanding national sport.

Once, when I was fifteen, Avram and I snuck off to a demonstration to oppose the construction of a housing development on a traditional wintering site for some of the nomadic tribes that traveled through the region. The tribes had been barred from their winter home, where they usually settled for several months each year, by the British who had begun constructing apartments for European immigrants there. We simply stood in witness at the fence that surrounded the construction site, along with a group of about thirty people Avram knew but whom I had not seen before. Our short vigil had no impact and I wondered why we had bothered to do it at all.

"Because it's better than doing nothing," Avram insisted. "The British should at least see that someone disapproves."

"It would have been better to do something that really made a difference," I said.

"How do we know what will make a difference? Maybe we did make a difference," Avram suggested.

"I doubt it."

"What do you think would make a difference?" he asked.

"Maybe we should have brought some metal cutters and cut the fence down, or something." I didn't believe this myself, but I also didn't want to admit that I couldn't think of anything. I wondered what it would take for the British to stop building and leave the site to the nomads who had used it for hundreds of years.

"Then you would have been arrested and you still would not have made much of a difference," Avram said.

It was in the context of our ongoing dialogue, Avram's and mine, about how to improve the world, that, at the age of sixteen, I was introduced in an unanticipated manner to the allure of taking action to make positive change.

The course of my life might have been so different had I passed that young man at the schoolyard gate without taking the paper he thrust into my hands. I glanced at it long enough to see that it was, surprisingly, written in Russian, then I slid it between the pages of my notebook, intending to read it later. Once seated in class, my classmates and I were subjected to a seething tirade by my teacher against the man at the gate and the evils of Communism. My agitated teacher paused from her diatribe to ask if anyone had taken a paper from "that Communist vermin" at the gate. When I confessed that I had, the teacher confiscated the paper and tore it to shreds.

At seventeen, I had a reputation as a fastidious student. I was not shy about raising my hand in class and offering my opinion or answering a question the teacher posed. I was outspoken but polite. I am certain that my teacher was as stunned as I when I uncharacteristically shouted at her, "How do you know what that paper says? You can't even read Russian!"

Later that day, a girl in my class named Tamar, whom I knew of but had never spoken to, took me aside. "What do you know about communism?" she asked me where no one could overhear.

"I have read about it," I replied. "And I was born in Russia, so I am fluent in Russian."

"And what do you think about Communism?" Tamar asked hesitantly.

I did not know as much about Communism as I had implied, but now I was interested. "I would like to learn more about it," I answered. "I'm always open to new ideas."

Tamar eyed me curiously and then offered in a quiet voice, "If you really want to learn more, then I can introduce you to some people. Meet me at the school tonight at seven. Tell no one that I approached you about this."

I was startled and much too curious to pass up the invitation. I agreed to meet her. That evening, I began to live in half-truths. I told my parents that I was going out with a new friend. Tamar and I threaded our way through narrow streets to a small walk-up apartment. She knocked twice on the door, paused with her hand upraised, and knocked twice again. A man with thick glasses opened the door cautiously and peered out. When he saw Tamar, his face broke into a smile. He opened the door wider, saw me standing behind Tamar in the hallway, and looked back at Tamar anxiously.

"She's all right," Tamar assured him. "Let us in." I was surprised that our brief conversation in the schoolyard had been enough to convince Tamar that I was all right.

We entered a dimly lit room furnished with a sagging couch and metal chairs that looked as though they had been dragged back into service from the trash against their will. The furniture was populated by a small cluster of people, most of whom looked to be in their twenties (certainly older than I), in the midst of a heated discussion about the ramifications of the hypothetical spread of communism in Europe. When Tamar and I entered the room, the others fell silent.

"What?" Tamar challenged. "What?"

"Don't ask 'what,'" chided a young man who, with his straight dark hair and piercing brown eyes, was a male version of Tamar. "We didn't agree to this. We're supposed to agree on someone. Who is she?"

"A friend from school. I *had* to bring her. You should have heard her in class today. The way she stood up to the teacher," Tamar replied, embarrassing me. "She's fearless. Don't be rude to her."

"The teacher made me angry," I said by way of explanation, mostly for Tamar's benefit.

"Just what we need around here, another hothead," said the man who resembled Tamar, appearing more amused than disappointed. He offered me an unexpectedly deep smile that was as rich as good coffee, while the others looked me up and down as if deciding whether or not to purchase me.

"Rivka, may I introduce my suspicious and paranoid comrades; suspicious and paranoid comrades, Rivka." The others laughed as they introduced themselves. Coffee-smile was Tamar's older brother, Yakov.

After the introductions, the fellow with the thick glasses launched back into the heated discussion that Tamar and I had interrupted with our arrival. "As long as people remain ignorant, they can be manipulated by corrupt leaders," he said. "Once they know the truth, then they will act on it."

"That is assuming that they themselves are not corrupt as well," a woman with a ponytail and blue eyes responded.

"We have to assume that the people are not corrupt," Yakov said. "Nothing works unless people are basically good and want to do the right thing. If we can't assume that, then why bother at all? We're all lost."

The woman with the ponytail crossed her arms against her stomach and shot Yakov a skeptical look. I filed away in my mind that she was a cynic and Yakov an idealist.

Then the fellow with the thick glasses said, "Knowledge empowers people against oppression. It equips them with the tools to see the truth and to fight injustice."

Although I had just joined the group, I was not one to keep my thoughts to myself and I was bursting to contribute to the discussion, so I spoke up. "Knowledge is necessary for people to see the truth, but I think that it's memory that empowers people and it's memory that will inspire people to resist oppression." I was thinking about our village, how we were forced to flee, and the anger and hurt that stayed with me from that removal.

"Memory?" Yakov asked, with a puzzled expression. "What do you mean?"

"Physical memory of what has been lost, including loss of place. Cultural memory of longstanding persecution. Deep memory of one's birthright and the injustice that has robbed one of access to it. There are many kinds of memory. Separating people from their memories is a direct route to forcing them to submit to domination." After I had spoken, the others studied me, a new and unknown entity within their field of activity. I hoped that I was beginning to prove myself to be one of their equals, capable of contributing value to the group discussion.

"She's right. We learn from history. Forgetting what has happened is dangerous," Tamar said.

"Forgetting is a form of complicity with the oppressor," the woman with the ponytail added.

"Exactly," I agreed with satisfaction.

The conversation then turned to discussion of an upcoming clandestine organizing meeting that would bring together Arab workers and Jewish workers. As far as I could understand, the animosity between the Arabs and the Jews was being exacerbated by the British authorities because they did not wish for them to join forces and establish a united labor presence in the territory. If they could keep the Arabs and Jews arguing with each other, then they wouldn't be likely to form an alliance against the British. I agreed to help set up the hall for the meeting, which consisted mainly of opening folding chairs and making coffee. Even so, for me it was the beginning of my efforts to take concrete action.

Before we parted ways, the group repeatedly impressed on me the importance of secrecy. The comrades warned me that I was in danger if I continued to meet with them, and assured me that they would understand if I chose not to return, but I was young and consequently thought I was invincible, and the danger was more an attraction than a repellant. I wondered how I would keep my new association a secret from Avram, who I imagined would smell my involvement with the Communists on me the second I came in the door of our house. Yet, I kept my secret. I wasn't sure how he would respond if I told him about the Communists, and I was worried he might tell our parents if he thought I was doing something dangerous.

The following week, I arrived early for the organizing meeting. Yakov and I set up chairs together and then talked for a couple of minutes as we sipped coffee, until people began to trickle into the room. As it turned out, few of the other youths I had met through Tamar could speak Arabic, as I could. I was able to greet the Arab workers who arrived for the meeting in their native tongue, which earned me more than one sidelong glance of admiration from my new political activist friends. After the meeting, and after we folded the chairs back up and put them away, Tamar followed me out into the night. She linked her arm through mine as we walked together.

"My brother likes you."

I considered her words for a minute before I said, "I like him too."

"No, I mean he seriously likes you," Tamar said.

"I don't know," I said, shrugging, as I tried to conceal my delight at this news. I wanted to hear more. "He just seems interested in explaining his ideas to me."

"Trust me," Tamar said. "The way he talks about politics with you is his version of flirtation."

"Well, I seriously like him too," I told her, with a slow smile, realizing that I had just tipped my hand.

"I'll be sure to let him know," she said. I felt a surge of fear at having admitted that I had feelings for Yakov.

"How old is he?" I asked.

"He just turned twenty-one a few weeks ago."

"So I guess he doesn't have a girlfriend?" I asked.

"Not yet," Tamar answered. Then she released my arm and we wished each other a good night.

As I became more involved with my Communist friends in Palestine, I worried that Papa would find out about my activities because I knew he would be furious with me. The Communists were outspoken against Zionism and did not support the establishment of a Jewish state as Papa did. They envisioned a brotherhood of Arabs and Jews with equal rights in a jointly owned country ruled by the workers, that stripped the land-owners of their dominance. The more I learned about this vision, the more I came to perceive Zionism as socially unjust. I wanted a safe home for Jews as much as Papa did, but I didn't want to build it on the disen-franchisement of the Arabs. The Communist approach seemed to me as if it had a greater chance of resulting in the safety of the Jews than a vision that was likely to transform potential allies (the Arabs) into dangerous enemies. Papa and I both wanted a Jewish homeland and an end to our people's exile, but we had different ideas about how to go about that. I would never be able to convince him to change his mind, and I became fearful that he would find out what I was doing, not because he would punish me for it, but because he would be deeply hurt by it. I was not sure I could trust Avram to keep this secret for me, and so I avoided any type of discussion that might give him a clue as to what I was doing.

Yakov had started to walk me home from the meetings that I was now attending a couple of times each week. We parted ways before he would have been visible from my house. Eventually, I talked to Yakov about my fear of being discovered by my family.

"My father brought us here when my sister and I were little girls because he is passionate about a Jewish homeland," I told Yakov as we walked. "I try to imagine what he would say if I told him I no longer believe a country run completely by Jews is viable in Palestine."

"That's a hard dream to abandon," Yakov said. "We Jews so desperately seek a safe haven in the world. It's hard to imagine that such a haven is possible in a country that is not run by Jews."

"Do your parents know that you and Tamar are Communists?" I asked.

He paused before responding, and I wondered if I had asked a question that was too personal. I could almost see him make the decision to open a window into his life for me before he replied. "We live with my aunt and uncle. Our mother died of pneumonia six years ago. Her sister, my aunt, was about to make *aliyah* to Palestine. She begged my father for permission to take me and Tamar with her. We have three older brothers who remained behind in Poland with our father. I'm not sure why he agreed to let my aunt take us. Maybe he thought Tamar needed a surrogate mother and sent me so she wouldn't be alone. Maybe he was simply overcome with grief and couldn't face raising us on his own. So I am without parents, as it were."

"Well your aunt and uncle, then," I said. "Do they know?"

"No, but they actually wouldn't understand what it means," he replied.

I cast him a quizzical look.

"They are old-fashioned and they never think about politics," he said. "They have other concerns, everyday sorts of concerns." He left it at that and I didn't pursue it.

We had known each other for a few weeks when Yakov suggested that we take a walk in an olive grove near my house after one of the group's meetings, and, before long, it became our habit to walk there together, not just on evenings when the group met, but on other evenings as well. Only Tamar knew that we were seeing each other outside the meetings.

One evening, after I had known Yakov for a couple of months, we went for our usual walk in the olive grove and then sat down on the hillside beneath the outstretched arms of the ancient trees. The beauty of the setting sun, which ignited the gathering storm clouds with amber light, distracted us from our conversation about the future of Palestine. "It looks like something ferocious is on its way in," Yakov observed.

"I'm not afraid of getting wet, are you?" I asked.

"Of course not."

"I forgot, you're not afraid of anything," I teased.

"Not true," he replied with surprising seriousness.

A roll of thunder rumbled as giant drops of rain began to pelt us, swiftly gaining momentum. I pointed to a small wooden shelter on the hillside and we clambered up to it. Yakov gave me a hand up into the shelter and put his arm around me. We were breathing heavily from our run and from being so close to each other. I tilted my face to his, water dripping off my hair and clinging to my eyelashes. The scent of fresh rain rose from Yakov's shirt, and the raindrops tapped loudly on the roof of the structure in which we stood. I wanted to kiss him more than anything, and I could tell he felt the same way, but I didn't know if he would do it. So I kissed him first, right on the lips, and he pulled me to him, his arm tightening around my waist, and kissed me back. Oh, that sweet first kiss. And then again and again, breathless, giddy.

"I'm falling in love with you," he said, his voice muffled in my hair.

"I'm already in love with you," I replied.

We kissed over and over again in our tiny shelter. Those kisses seemed so simple compared to the complex fury of the world, which we were bent on trying to remake and rescue.

Before we parted on that rainy evening, I invited him to meet my family, and he agreed to introduce me to his aunt and uncle.

Yakov's appearance in my life was helpful because it explained my evening absences more believably than the explanations I had been giving about getting together with my "new friend Tamar." Ruth and Miriam wanted to know every detail about Yakov and could not get enough information about our romance. Avram appreciated Yakov's interest in politics and social issues, and they took to one another immediately. Papa, to my amusement, approved of Yakov because he was learning carpentry, a good trade. Little did Papa know that he was a Communist revolutionary. A Jewish carpenter revolutionary in the holy land, how clichéd was that? Meir discussed Yakov's work with him, and Mama seemed under the impression that she had a professional obligation to feed him. Fortunately, he was dutifully appreciative of her marvelous cooking. I was young and in love and teetering on the edge of a precipice, but I didn't see it until I tumbled over the side.

A spectacular rose and orange sunset graced the hills on the evening that I was arrested. The spring air was fresh and herbal with the scent of young tomato plants, peppermint, and geraniums. All of us were sitting in front of the house. Benjy, who had just turned ten, was playing a game of chess with Papa on the porch. Ruth and Miriam were looking through a sheaf of dress patterns. Ruth had recently started a job as a clerk in a clothing store and she wanted to make a couple of new dresses to wear to work. Mama spooned out plump apricots from the last two jars that she had put up the previous summer and set a bowl before each of us. Avram had a book open on his lap where he sat, a step above Meir and I, who sat on the bottom step and discussed Tolstoy's portrayal of women in his fiction, since I was rereading *Anna Karenina*.

The taste of the apricots held a promise of the coming season's bounty. I felt wealthy. I drank deeply of the tangy air, rolled the apricot taste in my mouth, and took a mental snapshot of the family, savoring our contentment. Then I called to Mama up on the porch, "The last jar always tastes the best."

It was then that the British officers drove up the road, stopped, and emerged from the car. They walked slowly, as deliberate as fate, toward my family. I knew why they had come. As the officers approached, Papa and I both stood and I gestured for him to stay, but he followed a few paces behind me.

"What is it?" Mama called in panic from the porch. "What do they want?" Mama's face haunts me still. The hard-won tranquility of her years in the holy land shattered in an instant. The appearance of these officers confirmed her dread that something crouched just around the corner to swallow her up along with her loved ones, though she could not comprehend exactly the form of that crouching danger.

The officers offered no information about why I was being arrested, but I knew it was because of my Communist activities. What else could it possibly be? I didn't want to make things worse by aggravating the officers, and so I suppressed my anger and went quietly, steadily, with them, my heart pounding loudly in my ears. Mama, on the other hand, shrieked and tore at their arms so that it took both Papa and Meir to haul her off of them in an effort to prevent her from being arrested along with me.

I was transported to a jail, where I was put in a holding cell with other Communist women, and I learned from them that the British had conducted a sweep, arresting many known and suspected Communists at once throughout the region. We women posed a logistical problem for them because there was no women's prison in Palestine. They isolated a portion of the men's prison to house us temporarily. I had no idea whether or not I would be tried, and if so, what sentence I might receive. I was not even sure of what I was being accused. I wondered if Tamar, Yakov, and my other comrades had been arrested as well and who had betrayed us. I shakily asked my cellmates if the British would torture us to get the names of other Communists and a gray-haired woman with an authoritative air reassured me that the British were not torturing Communists in the holy land. I wondered how long I would be held. Being in jail was not compatible with being young and in love. I had been seeing Yakov nearly every day for almost six months, and now I would not see him at all. He had probably been arrested also. How long would it be before we saw each other again?

My arrest and imprisonment had an abstract cast to it. It seemed to me as if the British officers had arrested someone else while I observed from a distance, detached. My first night in jail had a surreal edge, so that I felt feverish, and simple objects, like a spoon or comb, appeared shiny, their colors too intense, their shapes vaguely unfamiliar. There were five of us in one small cell and we each received a blanket on which to sleep. There was no bed in the cell, so we spread our blankets on the floor. The lights glared brightly throughout the night. The guards talked, laughed, and smoked cigarettes. I slept little and the fatigue heightened my anxiety.

Before noon the next day, they loaded us onto army convoy trucks and drove us out of the prison. As the open trucks rolled through the gate, I saw Ruth running alongside them, searching for my face. "Here, over here!" I shouted.

She ran with her arms outstretched, as if about to catch me should I attempt to jump from the truck. "Where are they taking you?" she cried.

"We don't know," I called back.

The trucks whirred off, leaving Ruth in a storm of dust. I imagined my charming sister brushing the dust from her skirt, turning to the officers, and flashing a dimpled and mildly flirtatious smile. "Excuse me, sirs," she would say, "please kindly tell me the destination of those trucks." She would find out where I was being taken. My family would come for me. They were resourceful. I had faith that they would help me somehow. And then I realized that Papa was about to discover that I had been arrested for becoming involved with the Communists. I wished I could talk to him, to explain, to spare him the pain and anger he would certainly feel on my account. But I did not even have the means to write him a letter.

I later learned from Avram that when Ruth came home and informed my family that I had been taken to a women's prison in Lebanon, Mama immediately sat down and wrote a letter to her brother Romek. He had emigrated to America when our family had come to Palestine. I had only the vaguest memory of him as a man with a loud voice who smelled of wood shavings and cinnamon. He had done rather well in America and he owned a hardware store. Mama wrote to ask him to take me in if she could find some way to extract me from prison.

We were transported over the border to a women's prison in Lebanon because there was no women's prison in Palestine. In the shuffle, I was reunited with Tamar. We hugged each other and wept, relieved to see a familiar face. We were assigned to the same cell, which we shared with two other women. The prison was damp and infested with rodents and lice. The food was usually edible but neither appetizing nor nourishing. I was wary of the meat and therefore often went to bed hungry. I never felt completely rested. The British guards treated us decently but with indifference. We were nothing more than a problem that needed to be solved. There was no mention of a trial or charges. My cellmates were outraged that no due process of justice was being observed. I could not seem to muster similar rage and instead feared for my future and secretly questioned my involvement with the Communists in the first place. I did not discuss my doubts with anyone, not even Tamar. I felt as though I was somehow betraying Yakov by having doubts at all. I missed him and wondered where he had wound up.

Despite the physical deprivations, I lived in a heightened state of awareness both because of primal self-preservation instincts and because of the company of the extraordinary women with whom I shared my imprisonment. We met in the exercise yard and at mealtimes and talked quietly in our cells. Because I spoke Hebrew, Russian, Yiddish, some Arabic, and a substantial amount of English, I often translated as we swapped stories, giving each other glimpses into one another's hearts, as if we bent over an imaginary quilt made of the patterns of our lives. I pumped Tamar for stories of her childhood because they were the stories of Yakov's childhood as well, and because it passed the time. We confided our fears in each other.

An old woman from Morocco spoke one night about the places she had lived, the various struggles for freedom in which she had participated, and the many times that her actions had landed her in jail. "I feel hopeful when I see you young people here. I need to know that others will carry on after me, that others will pursue our ideals when I become too tired to continue." Her words made me feel self-righteous for having been arrested as a result of my convictions and I was less inclined to perceive my involvement with the Communists as a mistake after that.

I missed Mama dreadfully in that Lebanese prison. I often spoke to her silently before falling asleep. I rehearsed what I would say by way of apology for the pain I had caused her and Papa. But how could a girl possibly apologize to her parents for such a thing?

One afternoon, without warning or explanation, two guards appeared in my cell and removed me. Flanked by the guards, I walked on wobbly legs as we marched down several corridors, past many closed doors, and into a small room with chairs and a table. They seated me and, leaving an armed guard just inside the door, disappeared. My hands trembled and I forced myself to remember that the elders imprisoned with me had assured me I would not be tortured. Despite their assurances, when the door opened a few minutes later, I half expected to see a Spanish Inquisition–style interrogator. Instead, Avram and Ruth entered the room, and tears of relief ran down my cheeks.

"How are you?" Ruth asked anxiously. "Are you getting enough to eat? Are you safe? They haven't hurt you, have they? Do they let you wash? You look thin."

"Speak in Yiddish," Avram instructed softly.

"I am fine. They treat us decently. Some of the other women have taken ill from the poor food and unsanitary conditions, but I remain well. My spirit . . ." I hesitated. How could I explain the ways in which my physical well-being had become less important to me than my spiritual well-being in prison?

"Your spirit?" Ruth raised an eyebrow.

I looked at Avram. His deep brown eyes did not flinch from my gaze. He had been able to read me better than anyone else for as long as I could remember, but now I had gone beyond his grasp and I could not find the words to express how I felt. "I can't explain," I whispered.

"Never mind," Avram spoke urgently. "We haven't much time. Listen carefully. They will deport you. You and the others."

"Deport me? To where?" I asked incredulously.

"Russia. They send Communists back to their country of origin," he said.

"Ridiculous! That's absurd," I blurted.

"Nevertheless, it's what they do. We don't know when, but soon, they will put you on a train and we have made arrangements."

"We?" I interrupted, confused. "Who? Mama and Papa?"

"It isn't safe to speak here," he whispered as a pleading tone crept into his voice. I searched his face. Then it dawned on me.

"You too?" I formed the words with my lips and released them with no audible sound. Avram nodded almost imperceptibly.

He was a Communist too! How could we have failed to guess about each other? I had to repress a bizarre urge to laugh. In that moment, Avram's face, formerly as familiar to me as my own, appeared strange and extraordinarily beautiful. A confusing rush of desire filled me, so that I had to work to concentrate on Avram's instructions rather than the beauty of his lips as they formed the words with which to deliver them.

"The British will ferry you by boat to Greece to connect to your train to Russia. Do not board the train in Athens. When you reach the train station in Athens, proceed to the ticket counter and wait. Someone will meet you there with the appropriate papers and will guide you safely to France."

"How will I know this person?"

"The person will know you."

"And if I am watched?"

"Not likely. Once the Brits send you over the water, they are through with you. They expect you to remain on the train."

"What about Yakov? Do you know where he is? And what about Tamar? She is here with me. Did you know? Will they send her back to Poland?"

"Tamar goes with you," Avram rushed on. "Tell her what I have told you. You will both be met in Athens. Yakov is held in Jerusalem. He is someone else's responsibility."

I wondered who was responsible for Yakov and where he would be sent. How could we arrange to meet in France? What if he was not sent to France? Would I ever see him again? I had a million questions that I could not ask, and so instead I asked, "How did Papa take it when he discovered that I was working with the . . . you know," I lowered my voice and was afraid to say the word *Communists*, but Avram understood exactly what I meant.

"He said to tell you that perhaps one day he will be able to talk with you about it, but for now, and under the circumstances, he wants you to know that he is more concerned about your safety than anything else and that he loves you," Avram told me.

The combination of my anxiety about the possibility of losing Yakov forever and my relief at the kindness of Papa's message, the forgiveness inherent in his response, caused my eyes to fill with tears. "And how is Mama?" I asked quickly.

"She is not taking it well," Ruth answered. "She is terrified that you will be harmed. She has written to the authorities. She is not sleeping well." I did not even know half of what Mama had lived through in Russia, the terrible things she had seen. I could not possibly comprehend the depth of her fear for my safety.

The door opened and an official in a crisp uniform entered and spoke to the armed guard at the door. Then he turned to us and announced in English, "Visit is over. Let's go."

"Tell her that I am fine and that I think of her every day. And tell Papa that his kind words mean everything in the world to me. Give them kisses and hugs from me," I said hurriedly.

Ruth embraced me. "None of us love you any the less for it," she assured me.

Avram squeezed my arm. I did not know when I would see him again, my dearest friend. I flung my arms around him, burying my face in his neck and pressing my lips against his soft skin, kissing my family good-bye in the valley of Avram's shoulder. I felt his body tense as he whispered in my ear in Yiddish, "I have always loved you. More than you know. I will find you wherever you go."

Then they were gone.

I did not know what to make of Avram's words or the odd attraction I had felt for him during our conversation and when we parted. I was in love with Yakov, wasn't I? I had to admit that my feelings for Avram during our meeting were not exactly the feelings of a sister for a brother. But he was not really my brother. He was my closest friend and confidant. I began to think back over the years that he and I had spent growing up together and more recently as young adults living in the same house. Innocent moments, such as eating oatmeal in the kitchen at dawn or lying side by side on our towels at the beach while reading aloud to one another, took on new dimensions and suddenly did not seem quite so innocent. I felt confused and a bit frightened. How could what I had felt at our meeting change the nature of our relationship in the past? Could I possibly love two men at once?

That night I had trouble sleeping, and to unwind, I conjured memories of our summers at the Mediterranean. There was never anything better than that first day on the beach. We tumbled like puppies onto the welcoming sand, drunk with the wide-open freedom of the endless blue waves stretching to the horizon. I remembered Benjy as a toddler sitting with a splat at the water's edge and then scrambling back up onto his dimpled feet to run back and forth in the shallow surf. I could almost taste those roasted potatoes smothered in butter, and the fire-baked apples. I saw in my mind's eye one of the many sand castles I had built with Benjy, and I pictured Avram on his beach towel, with the sun caught up in his hair, reading aloud to me from the original Russian version of *The Brothers Karamazov*. I recalled the many nights lying awake to gossip and giggle with my cousins, Ruth, and Miriam. I was sure that our vacations at the Mediterranean would stay with me always, a shout of joy calling out down the corridor of my memory. Recalling our vacations by the sea calmed me, and I was able to finally drift off to sleep.

Only days after Avram and Ruth's visit to the prison, the British provided me, Tamar, and a dozen other women with a one-way ticket to our respective countries of origin, just as Avram had predicted. British soldiers accompanied us to the Mediterranean Sea, where they herded us onto a boat before abandoning us with only cursory instructions. I wondered how this sea, which held such happy memories for me, could have become part of the geographic barrier that would divide me from my family. British soldiers met us in Greece and put us on a train to Athens. From there, we were to connect with trains that would carry each of us to our country of origin.

When I worried that no one would meet me in Athens and that I would be forced to return alone to Russia without a plan for my survival, I thought about Avram's words and repeated to myself his instructions. The train wheels struck a rhythm in my head. *Someone-will-meet-you-in-Athens, someone-will-meet-you-in-Athens, someone-will-meet-you-in-Athens*, they hammered as I gazed at the fields beyond fields of wild poppies that smeared a vibrant red blur across the landscape.

As Tamar and I disembarked from the train in Athens and entered the station, a woman appeared and matched her stride to ours. She introduced herself as Thérèse and commanded us softly in rapid English to follow her. We were relieved to oblige. Thérèse hurriedly led us through winding streets to a place she referred to as "a safe house." It seemed to be a temporary shelter for displaced Communists. "I have a few more trains to meet and then I will take you to Paris," she informed us.

The stress of our journey had rendered Tamar physically ill. She stayed in her room at the safe house and slept while Thérèse, who spoke Greek fluently, took me for a walk in Athens so that I could see a little bit of the city. I wrote a letter to Mama and the family, reassuring them that I was doing well. I imagined Avram reading the letter and plotting to leave home so he could follow me into the wide world.

Thérèse met at least one train every day and brought back deportees from the train station, cramming us into that little safe house like tomatoes in a canning jar. Tamar and I slept together on a mattress on the floor of a tiny room. After sleeping for nearly two whole days, Tamar felt better, and we discussed our options, thinking ahead to our arrival in Paris.

Finally, at the end of the week, Thérèse told us, "Only one more train." She had been speaking French in the safe house constantly to help me and the other deportees begin to learn the language.

On our last night in Athens, Thérèse burst into our room in a frenzy of excitement and rushed Tamar and me down the narrow staircase into the living room where a man stood blinking as if recently awakened to a flood of bright light. We ran to him at once and hung on his neck like children, knocking him off balance so that the three of us would have tumbled to the floor if Yakov had not righted himself against a doorframe.

I rounded on Thérèse with feigned anger. "Why didn't you tell me Yakov was one of your deportees?"

"I didn't know he was yours," Thérèse laughed, "until he started asking so many questions."

Of course Yakov, Tamar, and I sat down immediately like crows to an ear of corn and compared our experiences since we had last seen each other. I was overjoyed to be reunited with Yakov, and the new life that awaited me in Paris instantly seemed bursting with possibility. I was so excited that I kept Tamar awake late that night, whispering to her until she asked me to leave her alone so she could sleep, even if I couldn't.

The next morning, as I hurtled northward to a country far from the land of the Olympian gods, I imagined whispers emanating from the sun-lit streets, rushing around corners, sweeping past the train, whispers of a people long gone who had walked those sunbaked ancient streets. I regretted the brevity of my stay in Athens and hoped I would be able to return one day for a longer visit.

At each station where the train stopped, I worried that a British officer would appear to detain me. But as we passed more and more stations and nothing of the sort happened, I became increasingly relieved and finally exhilarated at having escaped. I was no longer a prisoner, I had been reunited with Yakov, and I was on an adventure of vast proportions. I gazed curiously out the train window at the unfamiliar countryside. Once, while the train was still in Greece, I purchased goat yogurt and salty brine-cured olives from young boys who walked the station platform. After two days of poppy field carpets rolling out from the train tracks to the edge of the world, we entered Italy, where the train stopped for a few hours and we disembarked to walk through the streets, admiring the colorful tile roofs and the exquisite architectural detail of the houses. Yakov bought a necklace of plump figs from a street vendor and we popped the fruit open to reveal the sweet pink flesh foaming with an abundance of tiny seeds. By the time we arrived in Paris, we were longing for a hot bath, so Thérèse obliged by taking us to the public baths where we dunked and swam like wild ducks. It was such a relief to have regained control of our lives.

Along with several other young people who had been deported from Palestine, we slept on the floor in a communal apartment owned by a young Communist couple who worked as schoolteachers. Tamar had a stroke of luck and quickly found a job as a nanny for a Jewish family with a large house overlooking the Seine. She immediately had her hands full with the twin girls in her charge.

I was fed and sheltered for the time being, but I needed to find work, as did all of us in that apartment. I wrote to Mama and Papa and sent them my address. I wondered when I would see them again and how I would manage to return to Palestine. Since return was not an option at the moment, I focused my attention instead on the positive aspects of my situation: I was young, in love, and in Paris. For Yakov and me, the most pressing concerns were to find a means of earning a living and avoiding the authorities so that we would not be deported yet again; however, the latter was not as worrisome as it at first seemed. The French had little interest in rooting out Communists; neither were they aggressively seeking out illegal immigrants at that time. Even so, we felt obligated to exercise caution and keep a low profile. Yakov had his heart set on attending the Sorbonne one day to study political theory. But it was only a dream because he had no money with which to pay his tuition and he did not speak much French yet. I was picking up the language a lot faster than he was.

Each night, Yakov and I slept next to each other, fully clothed, on the floor, beside other deportees. We were still both virgins and in retrospect I wondered what on earth had kept us from correcting that situation back in Palestine. I should have been more courageous, but I wasn't; he should have been more forthright, but he wasn't; and so there we were.

The first few nights in Paris, we were careful not to touch one another at all, but it was quite impossible to maintain this chaste arrangement as our feelings for each other grew stronger with each passing day. After a few nights, Yakov began to throw an arm across my shoulders and to kiss my neck when no one was watching. Sometimes I would lie with my head on his chest and listen to the thrum of his heart. We drew apart to sleep but almost always awoke during the night entangled in each other, and poor Yakov could not hide the evidence of his desire. We were becoming quite desperate to move out of that overcrowded apartment.

Then Yakov found work at an airplane engine parts factory, which was a huge step toward our independence. The day he started there, I stopped in at a little pharmacy down the street from our living quarters to buy soap. As I chewed my lip and studied the choices, I heard the short balding man behind the counter speaking with a customer in Russian.

When the customer left the store, I spoke to the man behind the counter. "I notice that you speak Russian," I said, tentatively.

"And you too?" He raised one bushy eyebrow.

"I was born in Russia and I love the language still."

"Are you new in Paris?" he asked.

"That is a long story."

"I am Russian; I love long stories," he chuckled. He reminded me of those long-ago grandparents in the village of my birth, and I was inclined to trust him.

"Well, I am not Tolstoy," I said, as I considered how much I wanted to reveal about myself to this stranger, even though I liked him. "The short version is that my family left Russia and emigrated to Palestine when I was a child. I grew up there and I recently moved to Paris with my boyfriend."

"Jewish?" he asked.

I hesitated, and hated myself for it. I understood all too well that I had to protect myself, but must I distrust everyone? "Yes," I replied firmly, at last.

"I too," he said softly. He sandwiched my hand between the two of his and said, "My name is Vladimir, but my friends call me Vladi. My dear wife recently passed away and my sons are not interested in working in a little corner pharmacy. I need someone to help me at the counter and with the bookkeeping. I have been considering selling candy. With a dark-haired beauty like you at my counter, I will make enough money selling candy to allow me to retire. Would you like a job?"

I almost said a prayer of thanks out loud on the spot.

So I went to work for Vladi, who opened his new candy counter and soon dubbed me "The Sweets Department." He would recommend that his pharmacy customers check in with The Sweets Department for additional over-the-counter medicine. Although I was not earning much money, it seemed like a lot to me. I felt extraordinarily fortunate to have stumbled upon Vladi, who felt a bit like family.

When we agreed that we could afford to rent an apartment, Yakov put a hand under my chin, tipped my face to look me in the eye, and asked me if I wanted to marry him before we moved in together. I did not immediately answer, and he said, "You are worrying me, Rivka. A man makes a proposal of marriage and the woman does not reply?"

"I'm thinking," I said. "I'm worried that if we apply for a marriage license, the authorities might discover that we are not citizens and then we could be deported, quite possibly separated. I don't want to risk it. I would not mind living with you without getting married. Convention is of no concern to me."

"You're right, of course," he said.

"Then let's not take the risk of going to city hall," I told him.

"Agreed. So what do you want to do?" he asked.

"I don't need to prove my feelings with an official document," I assured him, as I put my arms around his neck and kissed him on the lips. I had already decided in my heart that I was his wife. I didn't need a piece of paper to prove it.

"You don't mind?" He ran his fingers gently up and down my back.

"Not at all." And so it was settled.

Vladi had a son who worked as a property manager and he offered us a small apartment not far from the pharmacy. When we moved into that first apartment, we owned nothing. We needed towels, blankets, a clock.

"We are true Communists," Yakov boasted.

"But surely Communists need to sleep somewhere and need a pot in which to boil water," I pointed out. Fortunately, our new friends from the apartment we had stayed in upon our arrival in Paris brought us a mattress, a few kitchen items, towels, a couple of lamps, and a radio. Thérèse presented us with a pair of ladder-back chairs and a small wooden table for the kitchen. Tamar brought us used bedding that she had purchased at the open-air market.

On our first evening in the new apartment, some of our friends filled the tiny living room, sitting about on the floor and passing bottles of wine from mouth to mouth since we had few glasses. We had pooled our money and bought long doughy baguettes, Brie, and apples. Tamar was the only one who knew that Yakov and I had never spent the night alone together. She eventually shooed everyone out, and when she kissed me good-bye in the doorway, on both cheeks in the French fashion, she whispered in my ear in Hebrew, "Have a good night, sister-in-law."

I shut the door behind Tamar and leaned my back against it. In the soft amber light cast down the hallway by numerous candles, I discerned the solid shape of Yakov's broad muscular shoulders as he slowly approached. He kissed me, pressing my back against the door, and placed his hands on the nape of my neck, which glowed like hot coals beneath his touch. He cupped my face between his hands and brushed his thumbs across my lips, kissed my throat, my neck, my ear. I whispered to him, "I will never desire anyone or anything more than I desire you at this moment." But time would prove me wrong. I would desire him beyond endurance in years to come.

Soon after we moved into our apartment, Yakov left his job at the airplane factory to work as a carpenter's assistant. "In a few years, maybe I can save enough money to pay for my tuition at the Sorbonne," he told me with his usual enthusiasm.

I wrote to my family in Palestine about our jobs and how we were settling into living in Paris. There were tremendous opportunities for young people in Paris and we had many plans for the future. I too imagined that I would have a chance to study at the college level once I had learned French well enough. We had made friends, we loved the food, we were listening to terrific music. Out of respect for Papa and the spirit in which he had forgiven me for my radical politics, I did not mention the fact that Communists were more welcome in France than in Palestine (or in England) and that we did not need to hide our political beliefs.

I spent a long time agonizing over whether or not to inform them that I was living with Yakov. I was mostly worried about how my parents would react to the news that I was living with him when we hadn't married, but I was also concerned about Avram's response. I was falling more in love with Yakov with each passing day; even so, I had no desire to hurt Avram, and although I was not sure exactly how he felt about me, I did know that his feelings were not entirely brotherly and that they were not entirely unreciprocated. Well, I couldn't marry two men, could I? I was more than happy with the choice I had made, so I decided to tell the family that we had moved in together.

It was Tamar, who attended synagogue regularly with her employers, who suggested that we have a rabbi marry us. "Have a religious ceremony to tide you over until you can manage a civil ceremony," she urged.

Yakov made the sour face he reserved for the mention of celery. He did not believe in God and had as much use for rabbis as he did for the vegetable he so disliked.

"Oh, for goodness' sake, Yakov, you're marrying Rivka, not the rabbi," Tamar reminded him in exasperation.

"But where will we find a rabbi to marry a pair of strangers? And Communists to boot?" I asked Tamar.

"My rabbi might do it. You don't have to say that you're Communists," Tamar answered.

"Tell that to the groom," I said, pointing at Yakov with my thumb.

"The atheist groom," Yakov muttered.

"I rest my case," I said.

"Not to worry," Tamar assured me. "You don't know Rabbi Kaplan."

"As soon as Yakov opens his mouth," I told Tamar, pessimistically, "the rabbi will start spitting in a circle to protect himself from the evil eye."

"He's not that kind of rabbi," Tamar said with a laugh. "Besides, he's hard of hearing."

"That's helpful. If Yakov says he's a Communist, then perhaps the rabbi will think he said he's a botanist or an arsonist instead," I said with grim humor.

The rabbi's hearing difficulty presented no barrier to Yakov when Tamar introduced us to him several weeks later. Yakov held out his hand, and as the rabbi shook it, Yakov announced loudly, "I am Yakov; I am an agnostic."

"That's very Jewish," the rabbi responded quietly with a cunning smile. "So tell me, Yakov, an agnostic, how do you explain all of this that surrounds us? How do you explain the spirit?"

"Science," Yakov answered.

"And what makes you think science has nothing to do with the spirit?"

"What do you mean?" Yakov asked, taken aback.

"All spirit is connected, is one, as is said in the *Shema* prayer. Spirit moves in many dimensions, including the perceived world, your 'scientific' world. These many dimensions are all part of God's intent. Just because you, in your limited understanding, cannot fathom something doesn't mean it doesn't exist."

"If I must go on faith, I prefer to place my faith in the human spirit than in a hocus-pocus divine spirit," Yakov told Rabbi Kaplan.

"It's not that we want proof of God's existence in order to believe," I explained. "It's just that we don't expect God to bail us out. We believe that we have the responsibility to do it ourselves."

"And what makes you think that I, or any other pious man, believes that God intends to bail us out?" the rabbi asked.

"Isn't that how the pious interpret the Bible?" Yakov asked.

The rabbi clucked his tongue. "If we look to the Bible, we find a tangle of contradictions."

Thus began our conversation with Rabbi Kaplan.

An hour later, the rabbi informed us that he had another matter to which he needed to attend.

"But we haven't spoken about our marriage," I reminded him.

"That's so," the rabbi agreed as he rubbed his bearded chin. "One does not enter lightly into the sacred covenant of marriage." He looked at us with his penetrating eyes. "If this young man engages your heart half as well as he engages your mind, my dear, then he will make you a fine husband. Bring your witnesses a week from Sunday at ten o'clock and we'll draw up the wedding contract. It has been a pleasure to meet you." He shook Yakov's hand. He shook my hand. This was some rabbi.

The week after Rabbi Kaplan married us, I received a letter from Mama. As I read, I filled Yakov in on the news: "Benjy is doing well in school; he is learning to play the piano. And, you will never believe this, Ruth has gone to America to live with Uncle Romek. And . . ." My news report stopped short.

"What is it?" Yakov asked

I looked up with eyes full of tears. "Avram and Miriam are coming to Paris."

"When?" he asked.

"In the spring. I can't wait to show them Paris. They will love it."

"I'm happy that you'll have your family near you," he said, as he pulled me to him and brushed his lips against my neck. "But I don't want to give up those lovely nights of having you to myself."

"Then we will find a bigger apartment," I said.

"Not until they get work," he said, kissing my neck. "They arrive in the spring?" he whispered. "That leaves me time to do some damage." He kissed me on the lips.

In April, Avram and Miriam stepped off the train into a city bursting with color, its gardens drenched in pinks and purples. Paris, which had welcomed Yakov and me when we had nowhere else to go, shouted its verdant spring awakening from the rooftops. In the evenings, a fresh, herbal fragrance permeated the streets as the scents of an explosion of blossoms clung to the air. Showing the city to Avram and Miriam was like reading a favorite book aloud to someone who has never read it. As I shared my favorite places with them and introduced them to the many diversions that Paris had to offer, even to those (like us) who had limited financial resources, I discovered that I had grown remarkably fond of the city in the short time that I had lived there.

Avram slipped into our circle of friends like a bright fish slipping into a silver pond. He found work immediately at the airplane factory where

Yakov had worked when we first arrived. I didn't think he would last a week, but he surprised me. He took pride in being a "common working man," as he referred to himself. I think he believed that it gave him the necessary credentials to talk about Marxist theory with us and our Communist friends in the cafés late at night.

As much as life in Paris suited Avram, it did not suit Miriam. She discovered that she did not care for city living as much as she had thought she would and began to regret her decision to travel to France. She said that she needed more open space and that the buildings were crowded too close together. I took her walking to see the architecture and she admired the detailed stonework and the clever gargoyles but commented on how dirty the buildings were. She assured me that she was glad to spend time with me but qualified this assurance by saying that she was homesick for our parents and the life she had left behind in Palestine. She took a job in a garment factory, which lasted exactly forty-five minutes before she had an argument with her supervisor because she had taken her shoes off. After that she worked in a pastry shop for a couple of weeks as a sales clerk before she was fired from that job too. She had never worked before in her life and it was beginning to look as if she lacked the subservient and flexible temperament of a good employee.

Her employment misadventures irritated Avram. "You have to compromise like the rest of us," he told her. "Few people work at a job they love. We work for the bosses who own the means of production. What makes you think you are better than any of the other common folk who must work for a living?"

Miriam did not deign to reply. She tossed her curls over her shoulder and stomped barefoot through the house.

"Why can't Miriam stay home and do the housework and the cooking?" Yakov suggested. "She could be our collective wife, since Rivka works too."

"We don't need four incomes," I pointed out to Avram. I hated to see Miriam so miserable.

"She should learn how to hold down a job," Avram grumbled.

"Why?" Miriam asked as she bit into a peach. "I like Yakov's idea. Avram sounds like Papa, doesn't he?" Miriam said to me.

Avram reluctantly agreed to the arrangement.

Soon after that, Vladi's son offered us an apartment with two bedrooms. It was small, but the layout was better for us. Yakov and I took one bedroom, Miriam the other, and Avram slept on the couch in the living room. "The acorn does not fall far from the tree," I teased, referring to Meir's years on the couch.

On our first Sunday in the new apartment, I rose early and slipped out to buy the morning newspapers at a nearby tobacco shop. When I returned, Miriam was flipping pancakes in the cast iron skillet. I spread out the papers on the kitchen table and read her the news. She set out raspberry jam and yogurt. When the strong scent of coffee permeated the apartment, the men were charmed out of sleep and glided into the kitchen like snakes to a swami. They sat at the table, hair uncombed, buried their noses in deep cups of café au lait, and read the papers.

"I think it would be a good day for the Tuileries," I told Miriam. The Tuileries Garden, adjacent to the Sorbonne, was filled with a wonderful array of flowers.

"I can pack us a little lunch to take," Miriam offered.

"Lunch? I think I'm going to be full of pancakes until next Tuesday. Where did you get this jam? It's great. Tastes like Mama's," I said. The men grunted in agreement.

"I made it," Miriam informed us with a note of pride.

"Hey," Avram said, beginning to show some sign of life, "they've staged a revival of Hauptmann's *The Weavers* over at the Odéon. I think I'll go tonight. Upper-balcony seats cost next to nothing. Anyone else?"

"I'll go," I said.

"Which one is that?" Yakov asked.

"First came out, what? Thirty, forty years ago?" I answered, with a glance at Avram for verification.

"Something like that," Avram said. "It's about the working poor rising up against industrialization."

"Against the dehumanization of industrialization," I qualified.

"Sounds like a real knee-slapper," Miriam said with a tone of amusement. Avram frowned. Yakov struggled to keep from snorting his coffee through his nose. "I'll pass on the show but I'll meet you at the café afterward. I love to watch you plot the revolution into the wee hours. That's better entertainment than the theater."

"You just like Yakov's entourage," Avram teased.

"Maybe I do. So what?" Miriam threw him a coy smile.

"Yakov's entourage?" I asked.

"You know," Avram told me, "all those serious fellows who read his weekly editorial in that Yiddish newspaper and follow him around discussing it."

"Oh, them," I said. "They're friends of ours. Of course they read his editorials."

"They like it when he holds court at that café," Avram insisted.

"I do not hold court," Yakov responded curtly. "So when do you begin tutoring Vladi's granddaughters?" Yakov asked me, blatantly changing the subject.

"Wednesday. I'm still trying to figure out where to start. They understand a little Russian, but not much." I wanted to do well for Vladi, who had offered to pay me to teach the girls, and I was excited about it. I couldn't wait to get started.

"Have them write letters to Mama in Russian for practice," Miriam suggested.

"Great idea," I said, with a rush of affection for our resourceful Miriam. I hoped I could coax her into enjoying Paris so that she would stay. It was delicious having her with me.

I looked around that breakfast table and admired my Paris family. Miriam's beautiful, long hands shaped her words in mime before she said them. Yakov's deep eyes flashed, as if a spark might jump from them and ignite his open newspaper with flame. The auburn tint of Avram's hair created a halo of reddish light about his head, almost like a visible electrical energy field surrounding him.

However, while I was feeling content in the presence of my family and beginning to allow myself to become attached to Paris, a wicked beast was creeping toward the heart of Europe. It lurked in the shadows, where I could ignore it for a while longer, but eventually it would step out into the light. Hitler was gaining more strength with each passing day. I missed Ruth at our breakfast table, but a time would soon come when I would be grateful that she was not there, that she had escaped to America, a safe place overflowing with possibilities, far beyond Hitler's grasp.

TWO

Ruth

WHEN MAMA CUT OPEN the pale-blue letter from Uncle Romek with a butter knife, a ticket for a berth on a ship sailing to Manhattan slid out onto the kitchen table. I had to restrain my impulse to snatch it up and claim it. Uncle Romek had sent it for Rivka, of course.

Later that evening, Miriam and I sat barefoot on the back steps, eating cherries and spitting the pits into Mama's flower bed.

"You know I love her," Miriam said, "but it's not fair that she gets mixed up in that foolish politics and then she's the one who gets to go to America."

"Hush," I replied. "Rivka is in prison and we are free to sit here and eat cherries." I watched Benjy bounce his red rubber ball against the back wall of the house.

"Whose fault is it that Rivka is in prison? I wish I had a rich Uncle Romek in America."

"He's not rich," I corrected, "just successful." I stood briskly and went into the kitchen, where Mama and Papa were discussing Rivka's situation with Meir and Avram. Miriam followed on my heels.

"The British will deport her," Avram explained patiently. "It is arranged that she will go to France. These people know about these things and they have done this before. I trust them to deal with it successfully." I had already heard this part of the plan, but I had never heard what Avram said next. "Besides, I want to go to France in the spring to join her and keep an eye on her. Paris is the center of the world. That is the place for a young man to be right now."

"Take me with you. Take me!" Miriam begged. "I want to see the world too."

I was not convinced that Paris was the center of the world. I would cast my vote for New York instead. I wondered if Miriam, who was never happier than when she was up to her ankles in mud, would enjoy city life. Then I looked at my mother, and I saw her in a way that I had not seen her before. When had her hair gone so gray and her face become so lined with wrinkles? And how was it that I had not noticed? It would be hard for her and the papas if we all flew from the nest at once, but I was not willing to pass up an opportunity that might not come around again just for Mama's sake. So, with my heart beating so loudly in my throat that I almost feared it would jump out of my mouth if I spoke, I asked, "Since Rivka can't use it, may I use the ticket to America?" Slowly, the way the taste of apples and the scent of wood smoke creep up to signal autumn closing in on the end of summer, the incredulous faces of my family turned toward me.

"Suddenly everyone has to go somewhere?" Mama complained as she brushed the tears off her cheeks and patted her hair into place.

I picked the ticket up. It felt so light.

When I sailed to America on the wings of my sister's misfortune, I fully expected to be reunited with my family in the near future. Whether or not I would live in Palestine again was unclear to me. But if I did not return, perhaps I could convince my family to come to America if it confirmed its reputation as the land of opportunity. I wondered if I could ever break up my father's stubborn love affair with Zionism. In the end, whatever my parents did or did not do, I had to live my own life, and America beckoned.

Two months later, I stood at the railing and watched the Statue of Liberty rising from the electric-blue water of New York Harbor, showered in a tumble of golden morning light. The sight of the giant metal lady, welcoming the weary to America, caused goose bumps to rise on my arms.

I stood in one long line, and then another, feeling ashamed that my English was so mediocre. A practiced patience had taken me this far through the ocean voyage and I was determined to maintain it through the entry process. In the early evening, the labyrinth of immigration spit me out into the swarming crowd of waiting relatives. I was spared the challenge of recognizing my uncle based on my memory of a faded picture Mama kept on her dresser when I saw a cardboard sign that read (in Russian) ROMEK WELCOMES RUTH TO AMERICA. Laughing and crying at once, I threw my arms around my uncle in relief and excitement.

"You look exactly like your mother," he repeated over and over as he patted my arm and then my face.

He took me home to his roomy apartment over his hardware store, where Aunt Netya placed an enormous plate of food in front of me. "Eat, eat, my child," she insisted. Netya wore her hair on top of her head in a bun in such a way that it puffed out all around like the underside of a mushroom. I liked the style and wondered if it would work with my wavy hair.

As Netya bustled around the kitchen, children of all ages flew in and out. "I need a potato for my project for school," "Where is the button hook?" "Mitzi is wearing my sweater, tell her to give it back," "Can I go to the movies with Howard on Thursday?" "Can we eat those cookies?" So many children. Some of the children spoke Russian and some spoke Yiddish and they all spoke English. Which ones were my cousins and which ones belonged to some other family?

Romek pulled up a chair while I ate the fried cabbage, chicken, and noodles Netya put on my plate. "Netya is especially delighted that you are here because it means she can finally get out of the hardware store," my uncle told me.

"Because of me?" I asked.

"Yes! If you will help in the store, then Netya will not have to do it," Romek explained.

"I am happy to help in any way that I can, except I don't know anything about hardware," I said.

"We'll teach you," Romek assured me. "Netya knew nothing about it either when she started, and now she knows everything."

Netya waved a hand in our direction and said, "No, no, I am just good at pretending."

"When you have improved your English enough," Romek continued, "then I would like to offer to send you to teacher's college. Teaching is a good profession for a young woman."

"That sounds wonderful," I told him, overwhelmed by his generosity, although the thought of becoming a teacher had never occurred to me.

"When you finish eating, I will show you your room," Romek said.

He had squeaked a little bed into a corner next to a large double bed in a back bedroom. That night I discovered that three of Romek's daughters shared the double bed, all tumbled together. I could barely turn around in the crowded room and missed the spacious, sunny room in Palestine that I had shared with Rivka and Miriam. But I planned to keep so busy that I would barely notice where I slept. I couldn't wait to write to Rivka about our American family and the completely different world that I had stepped into.

On my first Saturday in America, Romek and Netya took me to their synagogue, which overflowed with activity. I felt self-conscious because our family had never gone to synagogue in Palestine. We had observed the Jewish holidays and had lit candles and said blessings every Friday night to welcome the Sabbath. Papa and Meir studied the Torah portion together each week on Saturday morning, and Mama kept her kitchen kosher. But we had not belonged to a synagogue community after we left Russia. The religious rituals of Judaism were something we did in private. I was not used to such a public experience of our culture.

I spent the whole day at the synagogue with Romek's family, returning home in the evening for a light meal and the Havdalah ritual that separated the Sabbath from the workweek. I soon discovered that my cousins' lives revolved around the synagogue. Romek's children went to Hebrew School more days than not, Netya belonged to a Jewish women's group, and Romek regularly studied Torah with some of the other men in his congregation. He went to early-morning prayer before work on Mondays and Thursdays.

When Netya asked me what I thought of their synagogue, I replied, "The people are friendly. And everyone wears such beautiful clothes to Sabbath services. I love to look at the dresses and hats. Even the children look stylish."

Netya laughed as she shook her finger at me. "You are missing the point."

She was right. The religious services were lost on me. My mind was elsewhere. I had come to America looking for something and I was beginning to find it in the fashionable clothing, hats, shoes, and accessories that the women wore. Compared to the serviceable clothing worn in Palestine, the clothing in America was rich with creativity and beauty. I couldn't get enough of it. As often as possible, I took the train into New York City on a Sunday to go window-shopping. I adored looking at the clothing in the store windows and the styles people wore as they hurried through the streets, busy with their important lives. It was said that Paris was the fashion capital of the world, but I could hardly believe that the dresses, blouses, skirts, hats, shoes, and handbags in Paris could be more modern or visually pleasing than those I saw in New York. I wondered if my intellectual sister even noticed the clothing that the women in Paris wore.

Despite my lack of connection to the religious core of the synagogue, I enjoyed attending services and participating in the community. I felt most at home among other Jews and was welcomed warmly by members of the synagogue. One Sabbath, when I had been in America for a few weeks, I stood in the synagogue social hall listening with amusement as Uncle Romek told a funny story. After the story, he pointed to a man near the door who was watching us with a tentative smile playing on his lips. "That's our Big Nate," Uncle Romek informed me, and he beckoned to the man.

As Big Nate approached, Uncle Romek said, "Let me introduce you to my niece Ruth, who has recently arrived from Palestine."

"My pleasure." Nate shook my hand, and as he did so, he pressed a caramel candy wrapped in waxed paper into my palm. The gesture transported me back to the lost village of my childhood in Russia so swiftly that it took my breath away. Tears sprung to my eyes.

Romek gently touched my arm. "Are you all right?" he asked.

"I'm sorry," Nate apologized with concern and confusion. "Did I do something wrong?"

I wiped the tears with the back of my hand. "Yes, yes. Thank you. Yes. I mean no. No. Nothing wrong. You uncovered a buried memory, that's all."

"A memory?" Romek asked.

"The grandmothers and grandfathers in our village used to leave candy in our hands with a handshake when I was a little girl. Did they do that for you when you were little, Uncle Romek?" I asked.

He screwed up his brow with the effort of looking back that far. "Yes, they did. I had forgotten."

"Most of the elders in our village were killed in a pogrom the night before our family fled Russia, and no one has pressed candy into a handshake for me since," I explained wistfully. Nate watched intently as I unwrapped the candy and popped it into my mouth.

"Your niece is charming," Nate told Romek. "May I be so bold as to invite her for a game of cards with me, Izzie, and Ida?"

"You must ask her," Uncle Romek replied with a glint in his eye.

"Yes, yes, I'd love to," I said. "Who are Izzie and Ida?"

"Izzie is my brother and Ida is his girlfriend. Wednesday evening? I'll come for you around six."

When Nate retreated, I quietly said to Uncle Romek, "He's lovely."

"I thought you would like him."

"What is his family like?" I asked.

"His father owns a delicatessen. His mother died several years ago of breast cancer. Izzie, whom he mentioned, is his older brother. They nearly lost Izzie to polio when he was a child. He still wears a brace on his leg. There's a younger sister in the family too, named Malka. They work in the deli with their father. And, Nate is a bachelor, by the way," he informed me.

"No doubt that is why you introduced us," I responded. "Why is he called Big Nate?"

"He has a younger cousin who is also named Nate. He's Big Nate, and the cousin is Little Nate. The nickname suits him because he has a big heart. He keeps those caramels in his pockets for the children. And sometimes for widows or anyone in need of cheering up. He is also generous with his time. If someone requires a hand repairing their roof or building a fence, they can count on Big Nate to help. He can fix practically anything."

I didn't need fixing, but I would have pretended I did to see more of Big Nate. As it turned out, there was no need for pretending. Later that week, Nate came around to Uncle Romek's house to take me home with him for a game of bridge after dinner. We lived in the same neighborhood, and so we walked the few blocks to his father's house, where he introduced me to Izzie and Ida, with whom I would soon become fast friends. After the others taught me how to play bridge, we established a regular Thursday evening card game. Nate would come by for me after dinner and walk me to his house, weather permitting. Ida usually baked a coffee cake or pie for us to share for dessert before we started to play. I liked to make popcorn on the stovetop halfway through the evening and we nibbled at it until we finished up for the night.

One of my favorite times in the whole week was when Nate walked or drove me back home after our card game. I began to confide in him more and more. "I was sad to leave my family behind when I came to America," I told him, "but it was such an adventure and I had such big dreams for my new life here that I never imagined how much I would miss them. Sometimes I feel as though things are not real if I can't tell my sisters about them. And our letters take so long to travel back and forth across the ocean that the news I get is not really news. It's history."

"Do you regret coming to America?" Nate asked.

"Absolutely not," I replied emphatically. "Palestine is a land of hard manual labor. People there have little time for the more refined aspects of life. I don't want to live such a physically challenging life. I want a more creative life and access to more cultural resources. I just wish that my family would also come to America."

"Have they considered it?" Nate asked.

"I very much doubt it. My father is a Zionist, and Mama goes where Papa goes. They could emigrate, you know. It wouldn't be too difficult. Papa is a tailor and I think Uncle Romek could help my parents start a new life here. Papa has many good years of work left in him. But I would probably have to move heaven and earth to entice them to leave Palestine."

"What about your sisters? Perhaps they would join you?" Nate asked.

"I'm working on that," I said. "Believe me."

When I was with Nate, I felt like a grown woman, not like the girl who had left Palestine to see what life in America might bring. I wrote to Mama about him at length and Mama wrote that Miriam had nicknamed him "Mr. Perfect." Miriam wrote to me and shamelessly asked me if Mr. Perfect had kissed me yet. I put off writing back to her because, in fact, Nate had not kissed me yet and I was beginning to wonder if the feelings I had for him were perhaps not entirely reciprocated.

When he helped me on with my coat or put his hand on my arm to guide me down the sidewalk, I nearly shivered under his touch. I wondered if I was normal or if I would soon discover that I had some kind of psychological disorder. I desperately wanted him to kiss me, not just because a kiss would confirm that he had feelings for me, but also because I wanted to feel his lips on mine. I feared that if I voiced my feelings to anyone, I would jinx the relationship. I couldn't bring myself to write about it in a letter. If only Rivka were nearby, I think I could have told her about it. She wouldn't have laughed at me.

Ida rescued me from myself. She took me aside and said, "I can't help but see how you feel about Nate, so let me give you a word of advice: be patient. Izzie and I have been together a long time and I know from experience that he and his brother take their time with this kind of thing. It might be a little while before he admits how he feels, first to himself and then to you, and even longer before he has the courage to act on it."

"I thought I was losing my mind," I told her. "Thanks so much for saying something."

"Don't worry," Ida reassured me. "He's crazy about you. Everyone can see it but him."

I resolved to wait as long as necessary. As it turned out, that was not much longer after Ida offered her advice. The next week, when Nate walked me home from the Thursday card game, he paused under a streetlamp and turned me toward him. I tipped my head back and looked up into his eyes that always penetrated mine with such intensity. He put his arms around me and brushed his lips against mine. I locked my hands behind his neck and, trembling, closed my eyes, hoping for more. I was not disappointed. He gave me a real kiss, unhurried and searching. I had never kissed a man before. An unfamiliar, powerful, and disquieting yearning rushed through my blood. I no longer recognized myself. As we stood under the streetlamp kissing, I imagined I could feel my future life swirling out of the sky and flying down to meet me. I didn't want him to let me go, but after a while he did. As we drew apart and continued walking, Nate said, "I've been wanting to do that for a long time."

"I wondered when you would," I said.

"I was wondering that myself," he admitted with a quick laugh.

"I'm glad we have stopped wondering," I replied.

It was shortly after our first kiss that Nate discovered that I liked to take the train into New York to window-shop. I had gotten into the habit of going in on a Sunday morning, walking slowly past my favorite stores, and buying a sandwich at a little restaurant I had discovered down the street from Macy's. Then I would walk around some more before returning on the late afternoon train. I was always home well before dark. Nate asked if he could accompany me when I went into the city.

"If you have the patience to wait for me to look in all the shop windows at the dresses and shoes, then you're welcome to come anytime," I said. "And if you don't mind eating lunch at Jill's Sandwich Shop. They have a terrific Swiss on rye."

"I love Swiss on rye. It's the official food of all families who own a deli," he informed me with a chuckle.

So Nate and I started going into the city together a couple of Sundays every month. He insisted on paying for my train ticket and my lunch and he usually treated me to a show or live music in the evening. We went to hear swing in the many little clubs that were springing up all over the city. Nate was a good dancer and we often went to dance clubs. We weren't as flamboyant as a lot of the other couples, but we danced well together. I memorized the feel of his hand around my waist and reconstructed it in my imagination as I daydreamed about him behind the counter in Romek's hardware store.

The ride in and out on the train afforded us plenty of time to talk and I loved to tell him stories about my family because it made me feel as though they weren't so far away. It was not as if I did all the talking, though. He told me stories too. He especially liked to talk about his childhood. I wished that I had gotten to meet his mother. Thinking about that made me wonder how long it would be before I saw my own mother again.

Romek and Netya were delighted that I was dating Big Nate. They had known him his whole life and they thoroughly approved. I was so preoccupied with my romance that I was completely blindsided when Romek handed me a piece of paper one evening and announced with satisfaction, "I think your English is good enough for you to go to school. So I've enrolled you in teacher's college for the coming semester, which begins in the fall."

"Isn't it wonderful?" Netya added enthusiastically. "I wanted to go to teacher's college when I was young and I was never able to do it, what with the children and the store. But you can do it. I'll help you if you have trouble with the English."

"And when you complete the course, you'll have a useful profession," Romek said. "We wanted to surprise you."

"Well, yes, thank you," I stammered. "It is quite a surprise." I was stunned. I couldn't quite believe that they had gone forward with this plan without consulting me. And I did not want to go to teacher's college, but I had no idea how to extricate myself from Romek's grand plan gracefully.

On a Sunday as fresh and clean as new soap, I sat staring out the window of the train to New York.

"You have something on your mind, don't you?" Nate asked me.

"You know me too well," I answered.

"It's obvious. A stranger would be able to figure out that you are lost in your thoughts. So what is it?" Nate took my hand in his.

I squeezed his fingers, thankful for his companionship. "Uncle Romek enrolled me at teacher's college for the fall. He's so generous, and he and Aunt Netya are so excited for me to go, but I don't want to do it. I mean, I like children, and I want my own eventually, it's not that; it's just that I don't relish the idea of spending the whole day with someone else's children. My interests lie elsewhere. For instance, Ida and I draw pictures for each other of our ideas for dresses, shoes, handbags, and other clothing. That interests me. Uncle Romek has this fantasy of what I'm going to do with my life or who I will be, and the person he imagines is not me."

"You have to tell him that his plans aren't right for you," Nate advised.

"How can I do that when he has given me so much already? I don't want to seem ungrateful."

"He'll understand."

"He completely sprang it on me. I knew that he had this idea that he wanted to send me to teacher's college, but I thought he would discuss it with me before actually enrolling me. Why didn't he ask me first?" I sighed. "He means well. I can't think how to get out of it without hurting his feelings. I don't want to be a teacher," I said adamantly.

"Then what would you rather do?" he asked as he gently stroked the back of my hand with his thumb.

"I might like to decorate the interior of houses or design clothing. I could set up the displays in store windows or develop patterns for dresses. I would love to do something in the fashion field, to make beautiful things that can also be of use. Do people go to college to study that? I mean, do people study such a thing, or do they just do it?" I looked down at my hand, nested so comfortably in his, while I flushed with confusion because I longed for something abstract and perhaps unattainable.

"You could study interior design," Nate suggested.

I felt a rush of excitement. "Interior design? Is that something people study?"

"Absolutely," he said. "Or they just do it, as you said. One or the other."

I thought about this for a moment, while Nate turned to stare through the window at the scenery. I had been talking too much about myself. I asked Nate what he was thinking.

"Half-baked thoughts." He flashed a mischievous smile and I wondered what those thoughts would look like when they finished baking.

In the end, Ida rescued me from Uncle Romek's ambitions for me. She convinced Uncle Romek that perhaps my talents and interests lay outside the classroom. The next day after Ida spoke to him, Uncle Romek took me by the elbow and steered me into the well-groomed gardens surrounding the synagogue. "Come walk with me," he said. I glanced at him curiously as I fell into step alongside him.

"I must get that cash register fixed this week. That drawer still won't close properly," Uncle Romek told me.

"I'll ask Nate to look at it," I offered. Certainly he hadn't taken me aside to discuss the cash register drawer.

Uncle Romek studied me. "Ida tells me you don't want to attend teacher's college."

I thought carefully before replying and then confessed, "I didn't know how to tell you. I don't want to seem ungrateful. I'm more grateful than I can say, for everything that you and Netya have done for me."

"So if you don't want to be a teacher, what interests you instead?"

"I'm interested in visual design, such as designing women's clothing or the décor in a house. Nate suggested that if I want to go to college, I should study interior design. Do you know a school where they teach that?" I asked tentatively.

"No, I don't," Uncle Romek said.

"But I'm not so sure I even want to go to college. I may want to just start doing it."

"Do you know how to sew?" Uncle Romek asked.

"Do I know how to sew? My father is a tailor!"

"Why don't you and Ida try making some dresses together? Who knows? Perhaps you can sell some of them. I'm sure Netya would let you use her sewing machine."

"That would be brilliant." I was so relieved that Uncle Romek was not angry with me for rejecting his generosity that I kissed him.

"Perhaps if I had had an Uncle Romek when I was growing up, then I would not be peddling hardware," he said wistfully, and then, kissing the tip of his finger, he touched my nose with it. "Start simple."

We walked back through the garden. When we reached the doors to the social hall, Uncle Romek said, "We'll get that cash register drawer fixed this week," as if that had been the reason for our conversation all along.

On the first Sunday that felt like summer, Nate and I went into the city together. We planned to go to a club to hear some music, but beforehand we went for a stroll in Central Park. I wore an ensemble of my own design that consisted of a white cotton dress with pink and gray trim and a gray pinafore. My hat had a pink cloth flower on it and a thin gray ribbon around the band, so it matched my dress. Nate wore an excellent white suit and gray vest, which complemented my outfit. He bought me an Italian ice from a cart. I felt as though I was inside a movie scene carefully orchestrated by a practiced hand. We sat on a bench and made short work of our ices.

"You chose a pink ice to match your dress, didn't you?" Nate teased.

"And what if I did?" I defended myself.

"I think you're adorable."

I went absolutely crimson.

"Don't blush too deeply; you'll turn a color that clashes with your out-fit," Nate warned, tapping my arm.

"Oh, stop." I laughed as I peeked at him from under the brim of my hat.

Nate's face became serious and he swallowed hard as he withdrew a small box from his pocket. I held my breath for a minute as I covered his hand with mine. "Let's just sit here, forever, and hold on to this exquisite moment for the rest of our lives," I said.

He carefully tipped my hat back on my head, put his arms around me, and kissed me. Then he dropped to one knee on the grass before me and opened the box. "I love you, Ruth," Nate said softly, "and I would like to marry you, if you will have me."

He had done it flawlessly; exactly, precisely right. Only Nate would do it so exactly right. Until that moment I had not known how irrevocably I had fallen in love with him. I took the ring and studied it closely, a dainty gold ring with a diamond chip nestled in a circlet of tiny emeralds, and then I looked at Nate, kneeling at my feet, his face upturned expectantly.

His eyes were shining with the hope that we would make a home together that would last a lifetime. I whispered, "I do."

He eased the ring onto my finger.

"It's superb," I said. "It's the most beautiful thing anyone has ever given me." Then Nate kissed me deeply. I felt as though my life was starting right then and there.

When Nate released me, I asked breathlessly, "When shall we have the wedding?"

"That depends," Nate answered. "If you're willing to wait a little while, I have this idea."

"What is your idea?" I was thinking that I didn't want to wait another second.

"I want to build you a house first. My father hoped I would go to college and he saved money for me. But I'm not the college-going sort. Izzie and I plan to start a fuel business. Father has agreed to let me use the money to build a house and to start the business. If you don't mind, I would like to do both of those things before we get married."

"So I will be able to help you design the house?" I was beginning to understand my role in the plan that he had laid before me.

"That's a big part of the idea."

"And we'll move in and live happily ever after," I said, a bit giddily.

"From your mouth to God's ears."

"I suppose we'll have to decide how many children we want," I pointed out.

"How's that?" Nate asked in puzzlement.

"You know, to plan how many bedrooms." That got a laugh out of him. "So what exactly is a fuel business and why is that a promising business to start right now?"

"We'll sell oil for heating and cooking, and we'll also have a gas station for automobile drivers. Fuel is about to take off. More and more people are converting from coal to oil to heat their homes. And the day will come when most people will own their own automobile. You'll see; gas stations will be sprouting up everywhere. As our business grows, and I have increased investment capital, I plan to buy stock in fuel. That's where the big money will be in the years ahead."

"If you and Izzie start your own business, who will help your father with the deli?"

"Malka," he replied. "She lives to prepare food. That deli is her passion. But as for Izzie and me, we don't care if we never see another pickle as long as we live. We want to do something modern and exciting. We should call our company Sick of Pickles." Nate glanced at his watch. "We ought to head out if we want to be on time for the show."

I jumped off the bench and twirled around. "I will always remember this bench and that tree and this day and you in your lovely suit looking so handsome."

Upon our return to Uncle Romek's house, I waited in the kitchen, where Netya and my cousins admired the ring. Meanwhile, Nate went into Romek's study to formally ask for his consent, which was not required, but we had decided it would be a respectful gesture.

That night, after Nate had disappeared down the street, I wondered if I could actually wait until he had built a whole house before I would be able to sleep with him. He had looked so handsome as he strode into the darkness. Marriage seemed such a long way off and I wanted him to touch me now in ways that made me blush at the thought.

The next day, after the hardware store closed, I went around to Ida's house to show her the ring and that's when we discovered the joke was on us. Izzie had proposed to Ida over the weekend as well. Ida and Izzie had already set a date for their wedding in November, after the Jewish High Holidays.

"That's a magnificent time of year for a wedding," I told Ida. "Think of those autumn colors!"

"Exactly," Ida said. "We can do gold and burnt orange. We can use dried flowers and pinecones in the centerpieces."

"Your bridesmaids can wear pumpkin-colored dresses, with Izzie in a black suit and gold tie." I was getting carried away.

"You're giving me goose bumps," Ida said, pointing to her arm. "Imagine pumpkin-colored trim on my dress and an orange, gold, and red bouquet."

"We'll serve butternut squash soup and pumpkin pie for dessert. Malka will love it."

"She's going to cater of course," Ida said.

"Does she know how?" I asked.

"I don't think she has actually catered an event before, but she's a natural."

The idea of Malka catering a wedding set my mind moving so fast that I almost had to run to catch up with it. "I think I'm having a brainstorm," I exclaimed.

"Tell me quickly," Ida said. "Because you're scaring me with that there's-a-Martian-in-the-garage look."

"Why don't we start a catering business? You and Malka could oversee the menus and preparation while I handle the presentation of the food. For instance, we can arrange cheeses and breads on wooden boards and pile the fruit into baskets and pottery bowls. Maybe use dried flowers and natural objects, like shells, to decorate the food tables. We'll have to see what we can afford. I don't have much of a business sense, but Malka is good at that. Maybe she can teach us how to run a business."

Ida's eyes twinkled. "We'll call it the Babushka Catering Company."

THREE

Rivka

"EVERY WEEK YOU WRITE in the newspaper urging Jews and Communists to leave Europe before Hitler's long, cruel arm reaches them, so what about us? Shouldn't we leave?" My head rested on Yakov's chest, which rose and fell, like the swells of waves, with his even breathing.

"I have wandered from one country to another my whole life. I have finally come home and I will not be bullied out," he said adamantly. "France is mine. I choose to stand my ground here."

"Do you want to know what I imagine about you sometimes?" I asked.

"Will I like this?"

"I imagine you like one of those superheroes in the American comic books, with a shiny red and blue superhero outfit, a puffed-up chest, and a mission to defend the rights of decent people everywhere."

He snorted with laughter.

I lifted my head off his chest and leaned my chin on my hand so I could see his face. "It's comical but it also scares me to death because I know how easily I might lose you to the courage of your convictions."

He took my hand and placed a kiss in the palm. "You will never lose me."

I got up and went into the kitchen for an apple. Miriam sat at the table writing.

"More letters to Mama?" I inquired.

"Uh-huh," she answered absently.

"What are you telling her?" I asked.

Miriam looked up at me, and then she placed her pen on the table and read aloud from the letter: "Rivka has Yakov, but I have no one to keep me here. I have taken a job at the greengrocer's around the corner to earn enough money to return home. If this adventure has taught me anything of real importance about myself, it is that I don't care for city living. Dimly lit rooms of cigarette-smoking intellectuals discussing political theory. Avram can have it. I miss your vegetable garden and the beach. These cramped, dirty buildings of Paris remind me of drunken old men in drab overcoats huddling together to stay warm. Rivka expounds on the spectacular architecture suffused with centuries of history. She can have the history. I would much rather run through the fields or stand ankle-deep in mud, picking raspberries. You will laugh out loud to hear me say it, but I miss digging in the dirt with you and putting up jam, even in the heat. I would gladly trade these historic buildings for a cherry orchard or a field of sunflowers any day." She looked up. "That's as far as I got."

"I'm sorry you're so miserable."

"I wouldn't exactly characterize myself as being miserable; after all, here I am with you and Yakov and that pill of a brother of mine," she said, the note of affection in her voice belying her description of Avram. "I expect that the minute I leave I will miss all of you terribly. It's just that living here doesn't feel real to me. I feel as if I am playing house. I need to feel real again. Oh, it's impossible to explain!"

"Let's go to Versailles on Sunday," I suggested. "The gardens are spectacular. It will cheer you up. Maybe it will make you feel real."

"Versailles sounds terrific."

We got up early on Sunday to catch the bus. As we arrived on the palace grounds, Miriam brightened visibly. I was glad I had thought of taking her on the outing. We seemed to get stuck in our familiar routine too often and it was important to do something different sometimes. We walked the paths arm in arm at our leisure. At the herb beds, Miriam examined every detail and marveled over every choice the gardeners had made. She knelt down and rubbed a sprig of lavender between her fingers and then breathed in the tangy fragrance of the oily residue. Slightly intoxicated from her brush with the lavender, she turned to a perfect stranger passing by and commented, "I live for this, not all those lofty ideals, but simply the scent of lavender. It's heavenly." The startled expression on the man's face was priceless.

"I agree," he replied, seriously, as he quickly recovered from his surprise. "I have a theory that the scent of lavender stimulates the brain and causes one to feel joyous." He bent over and pinched a flower himself and drew in a long, sensual sniff. "Oh, that takes me home," he whispered, contentedly.

"Precisely," Miriam agreed brightly. "It takes me home too."

"Now that everyone's gone home, I guess I'll have to eat lunch by myself," I quipped, pretending to pout.

"May I introduce myself?" the man requested, with old-fashioned courtesy. "I am Robert LeFleur." He pronounced *Robert* in the French with a long, fluid *r* sound on the end and no *t* sound to close it up. *Ro-bairrr*. The way he said it made him sound open for comment. "May I have the pleasure of accompanying you lovely ladies through the gardens? I am a horticulturalist and perhaps can answer any questions you may have."

"How did you become a horticulturalist?" Miriam asked.

"Do you really want to know? I wouldn't want to bore you," he said.

"Absolutely. Tell me," Miriam commanded with a toss of her curls.

He tilted his head and raised an eyebrow, and then he complied. "I have a farm in the south of France, in a small town called Crevecoeur."

"You own a farm?" Miriam asked.

"I inherited it from my parents. I was an only child and a late-life baby." We continued to wend our way through the herb garden while Robert spoke. "I have spent my life managing my father's vineyards, orchards, and wheat fields, while dreaming of studying modern agricultural techniques in Paris. I lost my parents when I was young and they left me to care for the farm. Recently I had the good fortune of employing a reliable overseer in whose care I was able to leave the farm so that I could come to Paris to study horticulture at the Sorbonne."

We had arrived at the fruit trees. Miriam pointed out an apple tree and commented, "Unless they thin that fruit, they will have tiny apples with no flavor."

"I am sure they will get to it," Robert said. "The gardeners of Versailles are among the best in the world."

"Well, then they should have pruned the top down harder in the winter," she pointed out.

"True," Robert agreed.

I had no idea Miriam knew so much about fruit trees.

After Miriam and Robert discussed the pruning and grafting of fruit trees at length, he invited us to join him for lunch. We had brought bread and cheese with us, but Robert offered to treat us to a meal at a café. Miriam accepted without hesitation for both of us, and I didn't protest, since Miriam seemed to be enjoying the day more than she had enjoyed anything in a while.

We sat in filigreed green-black metal chairs at a café table in the dappled light filtering through the leaves. I felt as if I had tumbled into a Renoir painting. We sipped carbonated water infused with cherry syrup while Miriam interrogated Robert about grape growing and elicited from him a full description of the French countryside. She seemed to have dropped the disgruntled Parisian Miriam persona and was so much more like the naturally inquisitive Palestinian Miriam of our childhood that I thoroughly enjoyed watching her converse with our new acquaintance. The clarity of the afternoon put the world in focus. Miriam was in her element among the trees and flowers in a way that she never would be in the heart of a city.

When Robert discovered that we had never ventured inside Versailles, he offered to pay the admission fee so we could enter, and we accepted the offer. What a spectacle! The multitude of windows cast sunlight throughout the spacious rooms and arched hallways. Viewing such an abundance of beautifully crafted artwork, furniture, and tapestries was like eating too much of an incredibly rich dessert. And to think that this belonged to royalty once, and now anyone, for the fee of admission, could enjoy the beauty. That was as it should be. Such beauty ought to be more available to the masses. I moved more slowly through the rooms than Miriam and Robert, who went on ahead. When I met up with them on the front terrace, I took a moment to observe them unseen. They made a handsome pair, even though Robert had to be at least ten years older than Miriam. He also had a pronounced orthopedic impairment. When he walked, he swung his legs forward from the hip, rotating his body from side to side, like a duck. Of course it would have been terribly impolite to ask him the nature of his disability, so, though curious, I refrained.

On the bus ride home, I asked, "You liked Robert, didn't you?"

"Very much," Miriam replied.

"Are you going to see him again?"

"I hope so. We exchanged addresses."

"Maybe you will find something to keep you in France," I suggested.

"Or not. I barely know him," she responded tartly.

I said nothing further and rested my head on Miriam's shoulder as she hummed to herself softly, lulling me to sleep.

On Monday and Tuesday, Robert met Miriam after work and went for a walk with her. She solved the mystery of Robert's limp by asking him about it and she told me that from childhood he had suffered from arthritis in his knees and hips. He had had it for as long as he could remember and he claimed it didn't prevent him from doing any of the many physical activities that his farming required.

On Wednesday he took her out for dinner.

On Thursday they picnicked on the wall beside the Seine.

On Friday he took her to see the ballet.

On Saturday morning, we stumbled into the kitchen for coffee and found Miriam cheerfully preparing one of her oversized pancake breakfasts, at which she announced that Robert would be joining us for dinner that evening and she expected everyone to be at home and on our best behavior. Miriam apparently intended to cook a dinner of vast proportions.

Avram scowled.

"Take that disapproval elsewhere," I told him. "Robert is marvelous."

When Miriam headed off to the farmer's market with her basket on her arm, Avram called after her, "Remember we have to eat for the rest of the week, too. Don't spend our entire weekly food budget on one gourmet meal."

"You can eat noodles for the rest of the week," she taunted Avram as she disappeared down the stairs.

When Robert turned up that evening wearing a suit, I winced inwardly, hoping that Avram and Yakov would have the good sense not to make fun of his formality in front of Miriam later, after he left. But the dinner went well and no one mentioned the suit afterward. Robert's accounts of rural living captivated Yakov almost as much as they did Miriam. Avram spoke little at the table, but he confessed to me later while we washed the dishes that he thought Robert was a "decent country gentleman."

"So you approve?" I asked.

"I suppose," he admitted grudgingly. "Putting up plums, tending the goats, watching the grapes ripen from her kitchen window; it makes her mouth water. She has romanticized the lot of it."

I searched for the plug at the bottom of the soapy sink of water. "Do you think she'll marry him?" I asked.

"She's known him for only a week." He smiled that subtle Avram half smile, and the little peaks in the center of his eyebrows caught the mischief from his mouth. I felt a rush of affection for him. Since I had married Yakov, my brief physical attraction to Avram had subsided and my feelings for him were sisterly. For his part, he had shown interest in several different women who came to our habitual café, most recently a lively redhead who worked with him at the airplane factory, which led me to believe that he had accepted my marriage to Yakov and moved on with his own life. Perhaps I had imagined that there was ever anything else between us.

"What are you thinking about?" he asked.

"That we'll have a better chance of seeing her again in the French countryside than we would if she returned to Palestine." I imagined Miriam happily installed in a rural home with goats and lavender, not too far from Paris. My thoughts turned to Ruth, so far away, and I remembered that I owed her a letter. I would have plenty to write to her about now that Miriam had met Robert.

"Or if she went to America," Avram said softly. He had practiced intuiting me in our childhood and had mastered the art of it.

Miriam stuck with her job at the greengrocer's and continued to save money for her passage back to Palestine, while seeing Robert nearly every day. Whenever I broached the subject of her future, she grew reticent. All she would say was "My plans are undecided for now."

In early summer, Robert invited Miriam to accompany him on a visit to his farm. "Nothing improper," Robert hastened to say. "You will stay with my overseer's family." Miriam accepted the invitation, and then, rather than requesting a vacation from her job, she quit. So much for her plan to save up enough money to return to Palestine. While she was at Robert's farm, I half expected to receive a letter from her announcing that she would not be returning to Paris. But she did return, and when she did she finally opened up and shared her more private thoughts with me again. She related the highlights of her time in Crevecoeur, where she stayed with Robert's overseer, Christian, and his wife, Babette, in a large, stone farmhouse bubbling over with children. Miriam had arrived during cherry harvest and Babette needed help, so Miriam had pitched in and together they had furiously preserved an avalanche of cherries. Robert had given her the full tour of his orchards, she had received a formal introduction to his goats and horses, and she spent hours discussing the finer points of the cultivation of grapes with him. To Robert's delight, she fully appreciated the work that had gone into his spectacular herb and flower gardens surrounding the house. It was in the flower garden, Miriam told me, that Robert proposed, surrounded by the sensual, bright blue-purple delphiniums, blazingly orange nasturtiums, and abundant lavender, which was buzzing with honeybees.

By the time Miriam and Robert returned to Paris, she had already written to Mama, Papa, and Meir to deliver the news that she was to be married and would be living on a farm in Crevecoeur. I wondered if her marriage to a landowner would entice our parents to come to France one day to visit us. Avram and I were to be the witnesses for Miriam and Robert's civil wedding in Paris. Miriam said that the village of Crevecoeur was in the process of planning a large reception for them upon their return.

On her wedding day, Miriam was radiant in a purple and red flowered dress and a broad-brimmed hat. Robert arrived at our apartment mid-morning in a taxi and picked up Miriam, Avram, Yakov, and me to ride together to city hall. There were papers to be signed and then we were taken into a small chapel. The ceremony would have been entirely practical and unromantic if not for the unrestrained joy of the bride and groom, who appeared to be oblivious to their surroundings. Robert choked up when it came time for him to recite his vows, and Miriam took his hand in hers and placed his palm against her cheek. It took Robert several tries to get the words right, and by the time he had mastered them, Miriam's eyes were shining with tears. I thought back to Avram's comment about Miriam perhaps being more taken by the farm than by Robert and wondered if he had changed his mind about that yet. After the ceremony, we went to a sidewalk café for lunch. Following lunch, Yakov needed to return to work, but Avram and I took the bus with the bride and groom to Versailles to stroll in the gardens.

As we trailed the newlyweds down a manicured walkway, Avram was distant and uncommunicative. "What is it?" I asked finally in exasperation.

"I would have preferred to see her return to the safety of Palestine. I think that it will not be long before Germany forces France into war. Now she will be right here in the thick of it. People are carrying on with their lives, as of course they must, but they are in denial about the Nazi threat across the border. It's there. It's real. And I am worried about my sister's safety here in France."

"Even if the Nazis manage to infiltrate France, surely they will be far more interested in conquering Paris than invading a little country town like Crevecoeur," I suggested.

"I agree that they will focus on seizing Paris, but why would they confine their activities to Paris if they have the capacity to expand throughout the country?"

A chill ran through me. "Do you think Palestine is any safer, with its own hostile factions and the opposition to a Jewish state?"

Avram shrugged. "You know how oblivious Miriam can be to political events. I just wish she was not remaining in Europe."

"Perhaps we should all think about leaving," I replied, "although I doubt I could pry my husband out of Paris. He loves it here, and so do I. What about you? What keeps you in France?"

"This is where I want to be right now as well," he said, which was far from a complete answer, but I chose not to press him to explain himself further.

That evening, back at our apartment, I watched Miriam pack her few belongings. She and Robert were to spend the night in a hotel near the train station.

"I suppose that next there will be little Roberts and little Miriams," I teased.

"Don't badger me about children when you and Yakov won't take the plunge," she said as she wagged an accusatory finger at me.

Touché. "It's not a good time for us to start a family."

"It's never a good time," Miriam pointed out. "If people waited until it was a good time, then hardly anyone would have children."

"I meant with the political situation," I qualified.

"Why do you assume that's not what I meant?"

"Because I know it isn't," I told her.

"I have a lot to learn about farming before I start raising children," she said, with a sense of practicality that reminded me that despite the haste with which she had married, she knew what she wanted and had no doubts about her feelings for Robert or the life she would live with him. "Anyway, I'm still too young for babies," she continued. When we parted, I hugged Miriam close and her eyes sparkled with tears when we drew apart. I thought of something Avram had said once about Miriam marrying a farm. We women think we are marrying a man and in fact we are marrying a way of life.

Despite the fact that Miriam had not cared much for Paris, I would always think back to the days and nights I spent in that apartment in Paris as a golden time. My life in those days was like a lovingly constructed sand castle that was doomed to crumble when the war drove up to our doorstep and crushed the beauty of Paris to dust.

FOUR

Ruth

IDA CHOSE ME FOR her maid of honor, and of course Big
Nate stood up as best man for Izzie at a stunning autumn wedding. Ida
and I designed and sewed the dresses for the wedding party. Her parents hired a professional tailor to make her gown. I felt wealthy participating in the planning and execution of such an elaborate event. Her parents
bought yards of marvelous material for us to work with for the dresses.
Ida chose the invitations from a thick album provided by the stationery
company and she selected her flowers from a neighborhood florist who
specialized in weddings. Malka kept calling us over to the deli to taste one
thing or another that she wanted to prepare for the wedding dinner, while
I lay awake at night imagining how best to present the food on the serving
tables. I wondered why on earth Mama and Papa chose to carve out a mea-
ger life in Palestine when this abundance lay just across the glittering water.

The week after the wedding, Nate and his workmen broke ground on
our house, on a lot that was on the same street as Izzie and Ida's house.
A brand new elementary school, with brightly painted doors and shiny
doorknobs, winked in the sun only two blocks away. Izzie and Nate's
office for their new company was within walking distance from the neighborhood, on a busier thoroughfare.

A few days after he finished the foundation on the house, Nate appeared
at the hardware store with an unwieldy object wrapped in newspaper.

"What's this, what's this?" Romek asked.

"An engagement gift for my Ruth," Nate said with a grin.

When I tore back the paper, I discovered an electric sewing machine.

"I thought this would come in handy to get you started," Nate told me.

I flung my arms around his neck and kissed him.

"You can set it up at Ida's until our house is finished. It's all arranged."

Between Babushka Catering, the work on the house, and the dress-making business I started after becoming the proud owner of an electric sewing machine, I didn't have time to sell nuts and bolts anymore in Uncle Romek's store. My life was opening up around me like the sails on a ship. I had a heart-to-heart with Uncle Romek and we came to an agreement about how much I would contribute to the household financially with some of my earnings from my new business ventures. Predicated on our agreement, he released me from my job at the store and hired the eager son of a friend to take my place.

Nate consulted me on every feature of our house. I chose the moldings and the doors, the banisters for the staircase, and the brick for the facade. We pored over the architectural drawings together and considered wall-paper patterns, wood stains, and fixtures. Once, when Nate and I were walking in the city together, I saw an arresting painting of a Chinese woman in the window of an Asian import store and I insisted on enter-ing to talk with the owner about it. He explained that the woman was wearing a traditional *qipao* with overjacket typical of the Manchu Qing dynasty and that the Chinese characters in the upper left-hand corner of the painting meant "grace" and "beauty." I asked why the woman's feet weren't bound, and the shop owner explained that the Manchu women didn't bind their feet but instead wore elevated shoes. The painting made me feel like laughing and crying at the same time. I wished that the woman would turn and smile at me in recognition like an old friend. I had to have that painting to hang above the fireplace in the living room in our house, and I made a down payment on it with some of my earnings from my dressmaking business. It would be several months before I made all the payments on the painting, but eventually it would be mine and it would hang in my living room for the rest of my life.

I drew little pictures in my letters to the family in Palestine to show them some of the details of the house, and once I drew a diagram of the floor plans for both the ground floor and the second floor. While Nate was building the house, I was building a clientele for my dressmaking business from among the women in our synagogue and their referrals to their friends. Nate joked that my business was "bursting at the seams," which was not entirely true, but it was certainly doing well, and his pun always elicited a laugh.

That winter, I didn't see as much of Nate as I would have liked because I was busy with my sewing and with Babushka. Nate worked at his fledg-ling fuel business during the day, and when he was not at his office, he worked on the house as if driven forward by wolves in pursuit. Then one day I looked up from the sewing machine and realized it was spring. I had been engaged to Nate for nearly a year. That evening, when Nate stopped in at Ida's to see me before going home, I suggested, "Let's do something special. Maybe go away somewhere. I feel like I have barely seen you all winter."

"Barely seen me? We're building a house together," Nate exclaimed.

"You know what I mean."

He thought for a moment and then said, "We could go up to the race-track at Saratoga for a weekend."

"That sounds good, but I can't go unchaperoned," I reminded him.

He laughed. "Of course not. I bet Ida and Izzie would be more than happy to chaperone you."

Ida, who was expecting a baby in September, was enthusiastic about a trip to Saratoga. I made hats for myself and Ida and I bought a little suit-case with a matching toiletries kit. The four of us would look wonderfully smart.

On a sunny Friday morning in late June, we boarded the train. We ordered smoked turkey sandwiches in the dining car for lunch, and I could hardly bear to ruin mine by eating the lovely little triangles arranged so attractively on my plate. The verdant scenery of Upstate tumbled over in abundance. I drank it like nectar.

I had barely left my neighborhood, except to go into New York, since I had arrived in America, and the train journey reminded me that a whole wide world existed beyond the small circle of my concerns. I adored the delicate pointed leaves of the maple trees. In the lush, leafy countryside, neat little rows of greens marched out to the horizon. Baby cornstalks hinted at their potential for height and the tomato plants were dotted with yellow blossoms. I wondered what Mama would think about this farmland here in Upstate New York, and I smiled as I imagined her figur-ing out what would grow well in this climate and then starting a summer garden. I looked off into the distance where the purple mountains stood guard.

At Saratoga I basked in the luxury of having a hotel room to myself. I had been sharing my bedroom at Uncle Romek's house with two of my cousins, and before that I had shared with my sisters in Palestine. I could hardly imagine growing up in a house where a girl could have her own bedroom, which would be the case for my children one day in the house that Nate was building. After dinner we went for a stroll, returning to sit on the verandah in large wicker chairs to watch the flame-orange stream-ers of sunset and the flicker of fireflies dancing in the darkening air.

After Ida and Izzie retired, I walked with Nate under the trees, where he kissed me hard and a little wildly. "You had better hurry up and finish that house, Nathan," I whispered, my broad-brimmed hat slightly askew.

Nate put his hands on my neck, his thumbs gently resting on the front of my throat. "As fast as I can, darling," he replied.

The next morning dawned sunny and clear, and the thoroughbred horses on the racetrack pranced with superb grace. I felt quite elegant in a yellow and white dress with coffee-brown trim. After seating me and Ida, Nate and Izzie went to place their bets. I hadn't imagined that Nate would actually bet on the horses, and it disturbed me. I was raised to consider gambling a vice, and betting on horses fell squarely into that category. When I voiced my concern to Ida, she counseled me to hold my tongue. "That's why men go to the racetrack," Ida said, with a touch of incredulity. "They would think you've gone stark raving mad if you complained about them betting on the horses, Ruth."

I took Ida's advice and kept my thoughts to myself. I went for a walk through the stables, and when I returned, Ida suggested we go into town. We left the men and headed off on our own, talking about babies and dresses, which restored my sense of balance. We returned to the hotel in the late afternoon to freshen up before meeting the men on the verandah. Izzie had invited a distinguished-looking, middle-aged gentleman he had met at the racetrack to join us for dinner. Mr. Conrad managed a newspaper in Boston and had traveled all over the world. I surreptitiously whispered to Ida that he looked to me like a vagabond wizard, with that goatee and his baggy pants.

We sat at a table overlooking a well-tended lawn framed by sprawling, blue-green cedars of Lebanon. A summer storm interrupted the spill of sunshine, creating a rainbow over the distant mountains. I was intoxicated with the rain-scented air drifting in through the window screens.

Mr. Conrad told us that he had recently returned from Europe, so I asked him if he had gone to Paris, hoping to hear something about life in the city where Rivka, Avram, and Miriam lived, but Mr. Conrad had been in Switzerland, not France. He described a Europe teetering on the edge of chaos and destruction. Mr. Conrad was not Jewish, yet when he discovered that we were, he was quick to tell us that he had long admired Jewish culture. He had a childhood friend who was Jewish and he had learned about many of our customs when he was young. Leaning so close that the smell of his cigar made me dizzy, he warned us that European Jewry was in grave danger. My throat constricted and I completely lost my appetite. In fact, I thought perhaps my dinner would come back up as I listened to Mr. Conrad's dire predictions about the possibility of the Nazis spreading their hatred beyond their borders.

Ida could see from my expression that I was not doing well with the conversation. "Surely France and Britain will remain beyond his grasp," Ida said hopefully.

"No telling," Mr. Conrad responded grimly, "no telling what could happen if the United States does not wake up soon and act. I have made for myself a personal mission to inform the public, and our blind politicians, about the course of events in Europe. We live in dangerous times. We have arrived at a turning point in history, if only our leaders would recognize it."

Nate, who could also see my distress, took my hand. "My fiancée has family in France. You alarm her," he told Mr. Conrad.

Mr. Conrad leaned uncomfortably close to Nate. "I mean to alarm her. She should get her family out of France as soon as possible. Anyone with family in Europe, Jewish or otherwise, should get them out." Mr. Conrad sat back in his chair, fished around in his pocket, and handed Nate his business card. "If you need assistance bringing your family out of Europe, do not hesitate to contact me. I have a friend who is rescuing Jews as we speak."

Nate's mouth set in a firm line as he took Mr. Conrad's card. "Thank you for the warning," he said evenly. Miraculously, Izzie then managed to steer Mr. Conrad toward the subject of his many travels, and Mr. Conrad proved to be an excellent storyteller, capable of giving the listener a flavor of life in foreign lands. But his words had already opened a door to a world of worry, and I had stepped through. His warning would rob me of peace from that day onward. Rivka's letters painted a picture of Paris as a city brimming with opportunities to experience all manner of cultural events, such as dance, theater, art, and music. She rarely shared information about the political climate or the proximity of Germany to her home. After the conversation with Mr. Conrad, I could no longer picture her and the others safe at night.

The return trip on the train lacked the gaiety of the trip out. We ate the same lovely triangular sandwiches in the same dining car, but my thoughts were elsewhere and I did not delight in the attractive presentation of the sandwiches as I had the first time I saw them. Ida was tired and slept most of the way. Nate and I worked a crossword puzzle together, but I was distracted. The moment I arrived at home, I wrote to Rivka and begged her, begged all of them, to emigrate. I told them what Mr. Conrad had said about the danger in Europe.

Rivka wrote in reply that Yakov refused to leave. They continued to hope that France would not fall to the Nazis, but if it came down to a battle, she informed me that both Yakov and Avram intended to stand and fight. They were prepared to draw their line in the dirt, and Rivka would not leave them. In any event, Rivka wrote, it was not as if she and Yakov could return to Palestine even if they wanted to, and they had no interest in traveling to America. As for Miriam, she had married her farmer the week before and moved to some ridiculously tiny village in the French countryside. Rivka assured me that Miriam would write soon with all her news, and she did. I received a letter from her a few days later with details about her new home. She was learning how to grow grapes for wine making and she catalogued the animals that her husband kept on his farm.

I was infuriated. They were too foolish or too stubborn to protect themselves. Yakov and Avram's crazy principles would get them killed. And there did not seem to be anything that I could do about it.

In the fall, Ida gave birth to her son, Gary, a delicious little fellow who brought a smile to the lips of everyone who crossed his path. His uncle Nate doted on him. "I want one of these as soon as we get married," he told me. I carefully held my peace and evaded this topic. Truthfully, I was not so eager to have children as soon as we were married. I wanted more time to pursue my clothing design business and to build Babushka. I kept my opinion on this subject to myself, thinking we would have plenty of time to discuss children after we were married, and I remained confident that we could agree on a plan, for I certainly did want children eventually. Nate had almost completed the house and I had picked out a heavy, ornate dining room set and a gaily striped sofa. We set our wedding date and I wrote to Mama and Papa, Rivka, and Miriam to let them know. How I wished that I had Mama and my sisters with me to help me plan and to celebrate with me on my big day. In my fantasy, both Papa and Meir would walk me down the aisle, one on either side; Rivka and Miriam would be my matrons of honor. Maybe Benjy would have played the piano at the reception. I wondered what type of music he liked to play. I would have to ask Mama about that in my next letter to her.

As it was, I had Ida, Aunt Netya, and my cousins to help me plan. I chose rose and periwinkle as the wedding colors. Our wedding would not be anything as lavish as Ida's had been. Nate's father paid for most of the expenses, and Uncle Romek bought my dress. A few weeks before the wedding, I received a parcel from Mama. She sent me the lace veil that she wore when she lit the Sabbath candles on Friday evenings. I knew that it had been in the family since my great-grandmother had made it for herself and it was one of the few things that Mama had brought with her from Russia. I was so deeply moved that she had given it to me as a wedding gift that I decided to wear it as my wedding veil.

As the date drew near, Nate became less physically demonstrative of his affection and I was grateful for it. I knew that he was having difficulty containing his desire for me, as I was for him. The long engagement had worn on both of us. The touch of his hand on the small of my back as he guided me through a crowd could make me feel nearly faint with wanting him. I could not imagine what it was like for him, a man, with needs of his own.

The wedding took place in the synagogue social hall, and it was modest but elegant. There was not a dry eye in the house when Romek walked me, his immigrant niece, down the aisle with a lavender rosebud in his buttonhole. Nate's father blew his nose noisily into a large white handkerchief as Nate stomped on the glass to end the ceremony and begin the festivities. During the reception we opened the glass doors leading out to the gardens. It was a fairly simple community gathering in a synagogue, but I felt like the belle at a southern cotillion.

On our wedding night, we bade farewell to our guests and went home together at last. As we approached the house, exhausted yet excited to finally be alone, we were greeted by light pouring from the windows. We glanced at each other in surprise. Upon entering the house, we discovered bouquets of red, pink, and peach roses (my favorite flower) in vases, jars, and glasses throughout the house. Nate swore that it wasn't his doing. When I later learned that Ida, Malka, and my cousins had snuck into the house during the afternoon, while Nate and I were already at the synagogue, I was touched by their gesture of love and their wish to make our wedding night as romantic as possible.

The instant we came in the door, Nate began trembling. He lifted me in his arms and carried me up the staircase, step by step that he had hammered in place with his own two hands to bring him to this day. I lost my shoes along the way. In the bedroom, he undid the long row of tiny buttons that marched down the back of my dress. By then I was trembling as well. Calmly, deliberately, he undressed me, touched me, kissed me, and finally entered me, there, in the bedroom he had built, in the bed I had chosen, spinning beneath the forest-green wallpaper spattered with an effusion of enormous pink lilies. There I definitely took Nate to be my lawfully wedded husband. Afterward I wept with relief, and excitement, and the miracle of it.

"Are you all right?" Nate asked.

I nestled into his broad, sturdy chest and ran my fingertips up and down his side, from the curve of his pelvis to the edge of his collarbone. "I'm fine," I reassured him. I pointed to a scar on his thigh, a jagged mark that ran for several inches. "What is this?" I asked.

"A bad memory," he said.

"Oh?"

"My father gave me a beating with his belt for stealing money from his cash register when I was ten years old. I deserved it."

I could not imagine Nate's father doing such a thing to a ten-year-old child. Even more than that, I had difficulty imagining Nate stealing money. "I can't picture you doing something like that," I said, thinking of how much more I had yet to learn about him.

"It was complicated," he replied.

"Well, no bad memories tonight," I told him. "I'm too happy for that. Nathan, why did we wait so long?" Nate laughed and I could feel the vibration of the laugh as it rose from deep down inside him.

By the end of our first week of marriage, we had worn each other out. We came home from synagogue right after the service on Saturday and fell asleep. Nate would have kept at it, but I had learned from Aunt Netya how a woman can tell her cycles and her fertile days. When my fertile time of the month arrived, I tried to explain to Nate as gently as possible that I was not ready to have children yet, that I wanted more time. He nearly blew a gasket.

"What do you mean you don't want to get pregnant? I want a house full of children."

"So do I," I reassured him. "Just not yet. We are barely married. I want to have some time alone with you before we start a family," I pleaded. This seemed to appease Nate, even though it wasn't my real reason. I wanted the time to continue designing and making clothing a little longer before focusing on children, and I also loved working with Malka and Ida at Babushka. I wondered how long I could keep Nate's passionate desire to have children at bay. The deteriorating political situation in Europe worked in my favor in this regard because Nate became preoccupied with rescuing Jews from Hitler. We both felt strongly about doing something to help our people who were trapped in the eye of the storm in Europe. If I could not convince my own family to flee, then at least I could help others who were less stubborn than my siblings.

Nate had a congenital heart murmur, for which he took medication, that would prevent him from serving in the military should America eventually declare war on Germany. Although I never said a word about it out loud, I was deeply grateful to have a husband who would remain out of harm's way. Nate, of course, hated the flaw that prevented him from enlisting. He didn't want to talk about it, but I realized that he might feel like less of a man because of his defect, and that rescuing Jews from Europe was probably his way of doing his part.

We never forgot Mr. Conrad's grim words at Saratoga, and we dug up the business card that Mr. Conrad had pressed on Nate at the dinner table and contacted him. Mr. Conrad introduced Nate to his friend Ira who lived in New York. At that time, the American government had immigration quotas in place to limit the number of immigrants entering the country from Europe, but Ira was a genius at finding ways to get around the immigration quotas in his efforts to transport European Jews to safety. He took personal responsibility for many individuals whom he had never met until they stepped off the boat in New York Harbor. We began helping Ira raise funds and find housing for immigrants. I never forgot that I myself had made a new start because of Uncle Romek's generosity and now I was in a position to help others. We owned a house with three empty bedrooms. Nate and I agreed that we wanted to open our doors.

I had but a small window within which to enjoy my privacy with my husband and the precise order of my home before the first in a long stream of immigrants came to stay. Shmuel was a tall man in a black overcoat with a withdrawn wife and two timid daughters. These people had never hungered for a life in America the way I had. Thrown into exile as their only choice for survival, they missed the community they had left behind as well as their accustomed way of doing things. Shmuel's wife burst into tears if she burned the toast in the toaster or whenever a fire engine drove past the house. The two little girls sniffled and whined miserably. These people, our first immigrants, required my constant attention, and nothing I did seemed to please them. They refused to eat almost everything because it wasn't kosher. They would not even eat off my plates. They considered our synagogue liberal virtually to the point of heathenism and preferred to worship at home rather than set foot in it. We could have been practicing pagan fertility rituals and it would have been the same to

Shmuel and his wife. I finally took him into New York on the train to help him find an ultra-orthodox community.

Nate was glad to have been able to rescue Shmuel's family, and we never regretted taking them in; nonetheless, we admitted to each other that we had been disappointed. Nate had imagined we would receive a family who would delight in everything about America. Instead, Shmuel sincerely thanked Nate for saving his life and the lives of his wife and children, and then he took his family to live in the Hasidic ghetto I had ferreted out in the city. We were gratified that they were safe and in a community with which they felt comfortable. Undaunted by our first experience, however, Nate proceeded with his plans to assist in bringing more of Ira's refugees to safety. This time, he handpicked refugees he believed would be more compatible with our lifestyle. That is how we had the good fortune to meet Chaya and Dave.

Chaya had lost her husband to an episode of anti-Semitic violence she refused to speak about. Her seventeen-year-old son, Dave, wanted to start fresh in America. Nate hired Dave to work in his gas station, which was adjacent to the office for his fuel business, and he paid the tuition for Dave to attend night school to study accounting. Chaya and I understood each other's Yiddish and we shared a passion for cooking. Within a month of her arrival, Chaya began to line up work for herself cleaning houses for women who belonged to our synagogue. Occasionally we were able to pay her to work as a server when Babushka catered an event.

At breakfast one morning, I found Nate explaining to Dave how to read the stock market prices in the newspaper. Nate said, "For instance, I bought these at seven cents only a few months ago, and look, today they have gone up to fifteen cents. So I've doubled my money already. I could sell now or I could hang on to this for a while, which I choose to do." He went on with the lesson, but I had already been gripped by the cold realization that he was risking our savings with his dabbling. That night, in the privacy of our bedroom, I asked, "How long have you been gambling in the stock market?"

"It's not gambling; it's business speculation."

"That could cost everything you've worked so hard to build."

"Hardly. I've invested a fraction of our assets."

"I don't like it, Nate. I think it's dangerous. In Russia, only the most dissipated young men gambled. Decent men earned money legitimately."

"Oh, for goodness' sake! The stock market is legitimate, and whether you like it or not, I plan to make a great deal of money on it so that I can spoil my beautiful wife with the finer things in life." He pulled me toward him and kissed my neck, as if sex would solve everything.

"It's not a good time of the month," I said, as I gently shrugged him off.

"It's never a good time of the month," he said sharply.

"That's not true. And you know I want to as much as you do. There are other things we can do, besides, you know . . ." I trailed off, embarrassed.

"I don't want to do other things. Other things don't make babies, Ruth. I want children. You've always known that."

Tremulously, I confessed, "I want children too, but I want more time to myself before I have to give all my attention to a baby. I want the freedom to pursue my passion for dressmaking and clothing design for just a little longer."

"Ruth, be reasonable; you can have a baby and make dresses too. The one does not preclude the other. Especially with Chaya here to help you. I'm a patient man, but I have waited years to marry you and to have children with you. I had thought we were in agreement about this."

Nate was right of course. And I owed him so much. Hopefully I could find a way to make time to design and sew clothing while raising children. But never again like this, with a whole day stretching before me like a promise. I struggled unsuccessfully to fight back my tears.

"Now don't start crying," Nate said, drawing me to him and putting his arms around me. "I hate it when you cry."

"No, you're right. You're completely right. You deserve children, and those children deserve a wonderful father like you." But even as I capitulated, there was a private part of me that felt betrayed. I was afraid that there would come a day many years in the future when I would regret my failure to follow the longings of my heart while in my youth.

I noticed a subtle change in Nate after I agreed to try to get pregnant. I doubt that anyone else would have seen it, but I saw it. He had a certain contentment that had been missing before, and I felt guilty for having withheld from him something he wanted so badly. The possibility that he might at any time be siring his child excited Nate so much that his lovemaking rose to a new level. He knew exactly where and how to kiss me and touch me to make me crazy with wanting him. I daydreamed about him while he was at work and had to laugh at myself, sitting at my sewing machine, fantasizing about making love to my husband.

I am convinced that I knew precisely the moment when I became pregnant, when that egg that would become my first child was actually fertilized by Nate's sperm. I was peeling potatoes in the kitchen and I became light-headed. Overcome by dizziness, I stretched out on the sofa in the living room and promptly fell asleep. Chaya threw an afghan over me and finished preparing dinner for the family on her own. Nate arrived from work to find me sleeping. When he woke me for dinner, the dizziness had subsided, but somehow I could not clear my mind. That feeling of fogginess never quite went away for the entire pregnancy. I did absentminded things like putting a pot holder in the refrigerator, or going into the bathroom to wash my hands, forgetting to wash my hands, but taking the bar of soap with me and leaving it on the bedroom windowsill. Fortunately, Chaya often kept track of these fractured comings and goings and usually straightened things out.

Even though I knew from that first dizzy moment peeling potatoes, I said nothing to Nate until nature confirmed the truth. Finally, one night, as I lay in his arms, I whispered the news to him, "You got your wish."

"My big wish?"

"Your biggest wish."

Nate leapt out of bed and danced around the room.

Within twenty-four hours, Nate embarrassed me by telling everyone in the community. I was only six weeks along and I hadn't even gone to the doctor yet. I forgave Nate for the indiscretion of revealing my condition so early in my pregnancy because he was obviously too overcome with anticipation to restrain himself.

After my first visit to the doctor, Nate started with the baby toys. Stuffed animals. Brightly colored wooden blocks. Rattles. A blindingly red truck. Then baby furniture. By the time I could feel the baby kick and wheel inside me, Nate had fully equipped a nursery, moved a cradle into the bedroom, and brought home a high chair with exquisitely turned little bars running around the back. He was besotted with the idea of becoming a father.

I had written to Rivka, Miriam, and Mama to let them know I was expecting. I wished that Mama could be with me for my labor and delivery. I couldn't imagine having a child who would not know my parents. I sometimes wondered why I had traveled so far from my family and then gotten married in a foreign country. The distance felt more overwhelming than ever. I had been blessed with sisters and I had chosen to settle in a country on the other side of the world from them. At times, I wondered if I had been foolish to think that I would be happy in America, but then Nate would wrap me in his arms, bury his face in my hair, and whisper in my ear, so that my heart leapt with joy at his presence, and I had no doubt that marrying him was the best decision that I had ever made.

Nate declared that I had never been more beautiful than I was with my ripe belly. He put his ear to my stomach every night, listening for messages from his long-awaited son or daughter. He talked and sang to the baby, until, from the time I was six months along, the baby often moved when it heard Nate's voice. Then, one morning, a couple of weeks before the baby was due, Nate said he had a special surprise that he would bring home at the end of the day. I tried to coax it out of him but had no luck.

That afternoon, I had dozed off on the sofa and awoke when I heard the door open and close. Nate was home early. As I swam to consciousness, I realized that he had brought someone home with him, and then, with a rush, I recognized the woman. It was Mama! Like a reflex, my eyes flew behind her to see if Papa was there too, and Benjy, Meir, or any of the others. But it was only Mama, which was certainly enough. More than enough.

Mama's hair had gone entirely silver white and it seemed as if she had shrunk since I last saw her. The skin on her face and her hands was even more worn than I remembered and revealed the hard life she had led. She caught me in her arms and stroked my hair with trembling hands.

"Ruth, Ruth, Ruth, I didn't know if I would ever see you again," she said.

"Of course you would," I replied, laughing through my tears. "Of course. You will see all of us again."

While Mama and I embraced and wept, and while I attempted to recover from the shock of my mother appearing suddenly and miraculously in my own living room, Nate awkwardly shifted from one foot to the other, turning his hat around in his hands and asking, "You're not angry at me, are you?"

"Angry?" I shouted. "Why would I be angry?"

"That I didn't tell you beforehand. I've known she was on the ship for almost two weeks, and I kept it a secret."

"Well, when I get over the shock, I might be." I laughed, wiping away my tears with the back of my hand. "You didn't even give me warning so I could clean the house!"

"Chaya did that part for me," Nate admitted sheepishly.

"Does Romek know? And Netya?" I asked.

"Yes," Mama answered. "They met me at the pier with Nate."

"Everyone knew but me," I lamented. "I would have liked to meet the ship too."

"That would have ruined the surprise, though, wouldn't it?" Nate said.

"Let me look at you," Mama exclaimed in Hebrew, patting my full belly. "And such a handsome husband, also a good provider. Very good, it's very good."

"How is Papa? And Benjy and Meir? I wish they could have come with you. I wish you would all come, that you would move here. Papa would love it in America, I just know it." The words poured out of me like a river rushing over its banks. I had so much to share with Mama, so much to show her in America, so many people for her to meet. I didn't know where to start.

"Papa is Papa. I doubt you could pry him out of Palestine with anything short of a plague of pogroms. He is committed to the new Jewish homeland. I brought you pictures of Benjamin. Now that he has finished school, he is learning about farming, but his great love is music. He plays the piano beautifully."

"You must be exhausted from your trip," Chaya said, in Yiddish.

"Oh my goodness, I am so excited I forgot my manners," I apologized. "Mama, this is Chaya. She and her son, Dave, live with us. They have come over from the old country." Mama and Chaya nodded to one another and greeted one another warmly.

"I am not that tired," Mama said, switching from Hebrew to Yiddish so that Nate and Chaya could understand her. "I had more time to rest on that ship than I have had in my entire life so far. So, where is the kitchen?"

I laughed so hard at her question, so typical of Mama, that I started to cry all over again. I flung my arms around Nate's neck and told him, "You take such good care of me."

He tangled his large hands in my hair and spoke close to my ear, "Because I love you so much."

FIVE

Rivka

FOR ME, THE INVASION of France was personal. I even lost my sense of smell because of it. The world stank and my nose refused to smell it. My sense of smell returned during the second trimester of my pregnancy. I had not meant to become pregnant. It was about the worst possible time to have a baby. But the stress of the war changed my cycles and threw off my contraception. Yakov, with his indomitable sense of humor, claimed that Hitler gave him a baby. Hitler also dissolved our family.

As the Nazi army advanced across France, for my safety and that of the baby, it became imperative that I leave Paris. I made arrangements to join Miriam in Crevecoeur and to assume a gentile identity. As clearly as we knew that I would have to leave, Yakov and I knew that he would stay behind. Yakov, and Avram as well, had no question in their minds that they would go to the front to fight, but in the three weeks that it took me to buy my train ticket and make my arrangements to depart, the front had come to us. The invading army hovered like plague on the outskirts of our beautiful Paris.

While Yakov went to try to convince Tamar to leave the city, Avram and I sat in silence, pretending to read. I had wrapped myself in an afghan and curled up on our threadbare couch. Avram sat across the room in the reading chair, where he had not turned a page in fifteen minutes.

"What are you brooding over?" I finally asked.

"I'm not brooding. Hens brood."

"Then don't be a chicken and talk to me."

After a pause, which I took care not to step into with words, he said in a husky voice, "You know that I love you."

"I love you too, Avram."

"Not that way. Not the way you love me. I love you more than that. I don't know what these events will bring," he waved his hand in a broad stroke, as if he could erase the war like chalk on a blackboard. He looked me in the eye as I realized with horror that he was saying what he wanted me to know in case we never saw each other again. "I have always loved you. Your happiness means more than anything to me. So you have my word that my mission, for the duration of the war, will be to protect Yakov and to bring him back to you, because I know what it would mean for you to lose him." He choked on his words and was forced to pause before he could continue. "I wish things had gone differently. That many things had gone differently." Avram searched my face, catching me in the headlights of his gaze. Then he rose, awkwardly, and held me while I sobbed.

I had thought that these feelings were behind us, that perhaps they had never really existed. Yet he was still in love with me, even after my marriage to Yakov, and despite the fact that I had never solicited or encouraged his love in that way. At least, I thought I hadn't. Had I somehow misled him? Unconsciously given him a sign that under other circumstances I might have had those kinds of feelings for him? No, no. I was in love with Yakov, my husband, and only him. It might be possible to be in love with two men at once, but I couldn't imagine how it would be workable. I was thankful that I had not headed in that direction.

I wiped my eyes on my sleeve, released Avram from my embrace, and went to put the kettle on for tea. While I waited for the water to boil, I thought about Mama bundling up two small daughters and leaving her village to travel all the way to Palestine from Russia. If she could manage to do that to protect her children, then I could take a train to Crevecoeur to protect my baby.

SIX

Ruth

I SAT ON THE sofa, sipping a cup of tea, while Mama, ensconced in my comfy overstuffed easy chair, knitted a sweater for the baby. She had her own cup of tea in front of her, but it was growing cold as she clicked and clacked her knitting needles.

"Your house is so beautiful," she said, "that I can't quite believe I am here. I keep expecting to wake up in my own tiny kitchen back home. Sometimes I think I might wake up in the past, back in Russia with our village burning down. I can hardly believe that my grandchild is about to enter the world amid such luxury and that I am here to see it. If I am dreaming, then don't wake me up."

"You could live in this luxury too, Mama," I reminded her. "You could emigrate to America. Nate knows how to get the proper papers and we would sponsor you. You, Papa, and Benjy. Meir too. I wish you would do it."

"Your papa would never agree to it." Mama sighed. "He and Meir talk incessantly about a Jewish state, about the need for a Jewish homeland, where our people can be free of the persecution we have suffered in the Diaspora."

"There is a thriving Jewish community in America too, Mama. Palestine is not the only place in the world for Jews to live safely," I pointed out.

Mama paused from her knitting and peered at me over her glasses. "If you really believe that, then you are fooling yourself. The only place that Jews will ever be safe is in a country that Jews own and Jews govern."

I couldn't imagine a pogrom occurring in my neighborhood, but I had to remind myself of the life my mother had experienced in Russia. A person does not just forget that kind of trauma. I chose not to voice my disagreement.

"I think your papa is right about that, and I'm grateful to him for not being harder on Rivka when he discovered that she was working with the Communists," Mama continued. "It was difficult for both of us to accept that our own daughter was opposed to Zionism and had gotten mixed up with those troublemakers. It's challenging enough for Jews to convince the rest of the world that a Jewish homeland is necessary, without our own kind working against the idea."

I sipped my tea in silence as Mama continued, "Your papa and I, and Meir too, were pretty sure that Avram was involved with those Communists as well. Otherwise, how would he have managed to contact them so quickly after Rivka was arrested and then figure out how to get her out of jail? But Avram never brought it up and we chose not to ask. We wanted to pretend we didn't know. Meir had no idea how else to cope with it. Soon you will be a parent and you will see what it means to love a child. Papa struggled to reconcile his love for your sister and his hurt over what she had done. I remember once during that time when he said that if he had to choose between having a Jewish homeland in Palestine tomorrow and saving the life of his daughter, he would choose Rivka. That's why we are not true revolutionaries, your papa and I, because we're not willing to sacrifice everything for a cause."

I drank the last of my tea and then I said, "A Jewish state that truly provides justice for all would be a marvelous thing. It could be a beacon for the world by providing a model for a country that is not built on persecution and genocide. When you go back to Palestine, tell Papa that I believe in Zionism and I think there should be a Jewish state." I wanted to send him a message showing that I supported his ideals, despite the different life choices that I had made.

"He'll be happy to hear that," Mama replied, with satisfaction.

"But I don't want to live there, in that Jewish homeland. It's just too much work," I added.

"That's the truth," Mama agreed. "We do not have an easy life, but it is the life we have chosen. We work hard on our kibbutz on the Galilee. Your Papa and Meir have built many homes on that kibbutz board by board. My friends and I feed the whole community from our garden. Your brother Benjamin has lived in Palestine for all his life, so he is a genuine sabra," Mama said proudly. I had only recently learned of this term, which referred to native-born Jews in Palestine, Jews not born in exile but in the homeland of the ancient Hebrew tribes. Mama continued, "I already fled one country; I'm not prepared to flee another. I am not a young woman who can pack her things and go like I once did, like you and the others have done. It was difficult enough for me to get on a ship and sail across the ocean to see my grandchild be born."

"I hope you know how grateful I am that you came," I said.

She patted my knee. "Of course I do, Ruth. I did not mean to imply that you are ungrateful."

"I almost don't want to have the baby so that you don't have to ever go home," I told her.

"Now that would never do. I came all this way to see my grandchild, not to see that big belly," she teased.

In those final days of my pregnancy, I often nodded off to sleep on the sofa, as cozy as a well-cared-for little girl, listening to the lullaby of Mama and Chaya speaking to each other in Yiddish. Then one April morning, early, before the sun came up, I surfaced from a deep sleep to realize that the rhythmic cramps I was feeling must be labor. Listening to Nate breathing softly beside me, I wished the whole thing was over already. Imagining what I would have to endure to bring this baby into the world, I didn't think I could stand Nate's enthusiasm. I quietly slipped out of bed and woke Mama and we crept down to the kitchen together for our habitual cup of tea.

Chaya soon joined us. "Don't be frightened," she told me. "Just remember the purpose for the pain. Focus on the baby." But as the pain intensified, I drifted away into a land inhabited by nothing more than the unadulterated bright light of terror. When Nate came down for breakfast and discovered I was in labor, he exploded with excitement, asking questions about my condition faster than Chaya could answer them and offering to rub my back or call the doctor. His excitement irritated me. Like a cat that has jubilantly brought in a dead bird as a gift only to find his master yelling in response, poor Nate could not figure out why I failed to share in his delight.

"Go to work," Mama told Nate in Yiddish. "I'll send for you when we go to the hospital."

"I want to go to the hospital now," I demanded. The instant that Mama had mentioned the hospital, I wanted to be there already. They would take care of me there and I would be safe. They would make sure I was not in too much pain.

Mama rolled her eyes. "They would send you home again. It's much too soon," she told me, putting her arms around me. I began to cry. Nate hurriedly ate breakfast and went to work.

Ida left Gary with Malka and came over to help. But I was beyond help. I screamed and pleaded to see my doctor, whom I hoped would give me a large dose of painkillers. I wanted nothing more than to go to sleep and skip the whole labor and delivery. The rest of my labor was surreal, the events and images jumbled like puzzle pieces tossed out randomly on a table. I remembered that Nate came back home and took me, Mama, and Ida to the hospital. As I was admitted, I wondered for a moment what Mama was doing in America, but then I remembered that Nate had brought her over to be with me, and I was so glad that she was there that I clung to her and wept, without being able to explain to her exactly why I was weeping. Mama told me afterward that I insisted that demons had possessed my body. I vaguely remembered being caught in the waxy grip of those demons. I knelt on the floor and banged my head against the metal bed. I tore at my hair until I pulled out a clump.

Apparently after I tore out my hair, the doctor banished Mama to the waiting room, administered an injection of something that gave me the vague sensation that I had left my body, and restrained me by strapping my arms to the bed. I lay in a drugged stupor, the pain distant and unrelated to me. I was eventually moved to a delivery room where they strapped me firmly to a table. A nurse ordered me to push, but I had no idea what she meant because I was thoroughly disconnected from the experience. The baby's head came down far enough for the doctor to grab it with forceps and pull it out. That I felt. The agony of the forceps delivery, which tore me badly, knocked me unconscious. They must have kept me unconscious with medication because by the time I came around I had been stitched up and deposited in a regular hospital room on the maternity ward.

When she saw that I was awake, a nurse placed a soft bundle in the crook of my arm. "It's a girl," she told me. "A healthy little girl with everything in its proper place." She kindly brushed my hair as she informed me, "Your husband is on his way in."

"I know what that means," I said with a weak smile.

We had agreed to name her Sophie after Nate's mother if she was a girl.

I looked at my Sophie's sleeping face. Her perfect hands. Her perfect mouth. Nate and I had somehow miraculously made this little person who possessed a spirit all her own, a spirit I would get to know intimately in the many years that lay ahead for us. My world and everything in it transformed.

Then, like fireworks, Nate burst through the doorway, with Mama close behind. The moment he saw us, his face softened. He uttered only one word, "Sophie." As he tenderly reached to touch Sophie, she wrapped her little hand around his finger in her sleep. Tears welled in Big Nate's eyes. Mama was at his elbow, also crying, as she peered eagerly into the face of her brand-new granddaughter. Nate extricated his finger from Sophie's grip and placed his large, callused hands on either side of my face as he bent to kiss my forehead. "Thank you, thank you."

"Nathan, take her," I told him, and he lifted the bundle from my arms. He and Mama, who wiped her eyes with the hem of her dress, leaned their heads together and admired our baby.

Because I had torn so badly during the delivery, they kept me at the hospital for nearly a week. The nurses were wonderful and took such good care of me and my baby girl. I felt like a queen. I loved it and I thought I could have stayed there forever. A steady stream of friends and well-wishers visited us each day, beginning with Nate's father and Malka, then Izzie and Ida, who arrived shortly after Sophie was born. Aunt Netya and Uncle Romek came almost every afternoon and brought with them pictures that their daughters drew to hang on the walls. My room filled with flowers. Mama arrived the moment visiting hours started and sat by the sunlit window in the afternoons, knitting a small blanket for her new granddaughter. Malka came to visit in the evenings after the deli had closed, and she brought Nate's father, who liked to sit quietly and hold our baby girl named after his wife. Ida paid a baby-sitter to watch Gary so that she could stop by in the late morning every day.

Nate brought a photographer into the hospital to take pictures and we mailed them to Papa and the family in Palestine and also to the family in France. I had never missed Rivka and Miriam more than I did right after Sophie was born. I insisted that Sophie looked like Rivka, but Mama said it was impossible to tell with a newborn and I would have to wait a few months before I would have a better idea.

When I finally went home from the hospital, Mama took expert care of me and little Sophie. She made soup, cleaned the house, shopped for groceries with Chaya's help, did the laundry, and took the baby so I could sleep. In the evenings, she, Chaya, and I slowly sipped our tea together. Netya and Romek came to the house often in order to visit with Mama as much as possible while she was still in America. Those first few weeks after Sophie's birth were a magical, golden time. But finally, Mama announced that she had better return home to Papa and Benjamin and her life on the kibbutz on the Galilee, a life that I had chosen to leave behind. Nate made the travel arrangements. I dreaded Mama's departure. It could be a long time before I would see her again, and by then Sophie would be so much bigger, and unable to recognize her grandmother.

Wrapped in the cocoon of our small world, intently focused on the needs of a new baby, Mama, Chaya, and I had not read the newspaper or listened to the radio. But Nate read the newspaper, and he knew that the trouble in Europe had intensified. A few days before Mama's scheduled departure, Nate brought home the grim news that Hitler had invaded France. When Mama finally stood at the ship's rail waving good-bye to me and baby Sophie, we wept bitterly, not just with the sadness of parting from one another, but also with the sadness of being separated from Rivka, Miriam, and Avram, compounded by the anxiety we felt for their safety. I wondered if I would ever see any of my family again. I would not have traded places with any of them, and I felt grateful every day to live in America, but I wished that we were near one another and I hated Papa's Zionism and Rivka's communism, because these "isms" separated both our family and, on a larger scale, our nations. Politics suddenly seemed to me to be the root of all the suffering in the world, and I wondered why people, even people in my own family, couldn't see that there were more important things in life than political movements.

After Mama left, I struggled to regain that first flush of joy I had experienced right after Sophie's birth. Whenever Sophie delighted me with her delicate yawn or I watched her sleeping peacefully, I wished that Mama was there to share these moments with me. I could not begin to keep up with the housework as Mama had done, and every day brought more compromises that affected the orderliness of my home. I was constantly tired. Nate tried to be patient, but he had difficulty understanding how I could have lost all my energy as rapidly as a burst balloon. Sophie's night feedings disrupted my sleep pattern, and during the day she never slept for more than half an hour, not long enough for me to get anything done or to take a restful nap. It seemed that she wanted to nurse all the time. She liked to be held and she complained when I put her down. I hated to hear her cry even for a moment, so I carried her all day long.

Most baffling to me was that I had difficulty enjoying sex. When Nate touched me in that way, I became uncomfortable and unresponsive. My breasts were sore from nursing the baby and I was in a constant state of exhaustion. Nate was certainly as physically attractive to me as ever. But my body refused to cooperate. I couldn't adequately explain to Nate my complicated feelings. I couldn't even explain them to myself. I asked my doctor about it and was relieved to hear that my experience was not unusual and that it would likely pass when I began to wean the baby. When I told Nate what the doctor had said, he took my hands in his and assured me, "I can be patient. Sophie needs you more than I do right now."

Meanwhile, Nate redoubled his efforts to assist Ira in rescuing Eastern European refugees. I would have helped him more if I wasn't so busy with Sophie. He had to do the work for both of us, and he threw himself into writing letters, raising money in the community and sending it to European contacts, and arranging for travel papers. Just the day before the Nazis invaded Paris, we had written yet another letter to Rivka begging her to leave. The letter was later returned to us. My sisters had both been engulfed by the war and I no longer knew how to find them.

SEVEN

Rivka

 I THOUGHT I UNDERSTOOD the meaning of exile, that I had learned that hard lesson in childhood. But exile redefined itself when I left Paris, which had become my home. I did not fully realize how emotionally attached I was to the city until forced to leave it. How could it be that Paris would not protect me and keep me and my unborn child safe? My pregnancy in that place and time was a cruel twist of fate. War is the antithesis of pregnancy.

As for Yakov, he had a convert's passion for France. His loyalty to the country had exceeded even his loyalty to the Communist Party. "Decent people must say that enough is enough and take a stand," he asserted. Yakov and Avram intended to join the Resistance as soon as they had seen me safely on the train to Crevecoeur. So it happened that, five months pregnant, I stared into a suitcase containing a handful of my possessions, all my money, and a bundle of letters from Miriam, Ruth, and Mama, as I prepared to flee Paris and send my husband and brother underground to fight a war. Ruth had mailed me a photograph of her and Mama with her new baby. I looked at it for a long time before tucking it into my suitcase. It seemed like a picture of someone else's family and I felt horribly removed from them. Would I ever see little Sophie in person?

At dusk, I crawled into bed. My eyes traveled over the modest room as I savored my last moments in this cozy apartment in which my daily living had brought me such pleasure, this home that I would never see again. I had felt a pristine contentment in this bed on many a night. I would always remember the delicious taste of a strong cup of coffee on a sunlit morning in the kitchen, warming to a conversation with Yakov and Avram about an article we had read in the newspaper, and Miriam's Sunday pancake breakfasts. I would miss Vladi and my job at the pharmacy where

I had enjoyed seeing each bright-eyed child choose sweet treats. And I would miss those late-night conversations in the cafés, Saturday afternoon visits to the museums, and Sunday matinee performances viewed from high up in the cheapest balcony seats.

Yakov came into the room and sat on the edge of the bed as he took my hand in his.

"I'm fixing it in my mind to take with me," I told him.

"You carry within you that which is most important to me," he said, tapping my belly.

Yakov gathered me in his arms as I wept, caressing my hair with his steady, gentle hands, those hands that I might never feel again. His broad, strong shoulders were a fortress that protected me from the evils of the world. How could I live through this war without the ability to curl up on his chest at night? What if I would have to live the rest of my life without him?

I touched him desperately, trying to hold every detail in memory. I read his body like Braille. If these were my last moments with him, I wanted to love every inch of him, the well-worn path of him, of which I never tired. We made love that evening as if our lives depended on it. Dusk grew dark. I slept briefly and then woke, still in Yakov's arms.

"I refuse to lose you. I promise I will live. No matter what. This is my resolve," he pledged.

Yakov and Avram put me on the early-morning train. Through the grimy window I watched them grow small on the platform. I wondered, with apprehension, about the probability of our seeing each other again alive, undamaged by the war. I imagined a shield of energy emanating from my spirit and surrounding them in silver light, preserving them from harm. I resolved to keep this shield around them in my mind for as long as it took. I would protect them with a mother's love, this new variety of love that was opening slowly within me, petal by petal, like a rose.

The train was packed with fleeing Parisians, but a kind gentleman, seeing that I was pregnant, gave me his seat by a window, and I accepted his kindness. From this vantage point, I witnessed the disintegration of Paris. It appeared that the city had gone mad. People ran through the streets carrying odd objects, such as bedsprings or a large framed painting, and doing inexplicable things, such as sitting in a bathtub that was set out on the sidewalk. Groups of women and children huddled together in fright. I imagined lifelong friends parting with hasty farewells. The Nazis were soon to be right here, in our homes. Our daily lives had degenerated into chaos. A woman sat cross-legged at the edge of a cobblestone sidewalk beneath the blossoming chestnut trees that perfumed the air. I would forever afterward associate the scent of chestnut blossoms with the invasion of Paris. Clothed in a faded flowery dress, the woman held a baby to her breast and rocked forward and back. She wore no shoes. Her hair stood out from her head in disarray. Her eyes stared vacantly. She wept silently. The image of that woman became the personification of occupied France for me.

By noon the train had left the turmoil of the city in its wake. The beauty and serenity of the countryside offered a sharp contrast to the Paris we had left behind. I opened the window and drank the fresh air like a medicinal tea. An elderly lady wearing a wool hat reached into her basket of food and offered me bread and cheese. Sensing that she wanted to share her journey with someone, I accepted a small portion. She introduced herself as Madeline and asked my name. I didn't want to tell it to her; what if sharing my name could result in my capture by the Nazis? I was a Jewess in a country now controlled by men who wished me dead. The war entered my soul and squatted down, feet planted. The acrid smell of smoke filled my nose, though nothing burned. It was my mind playing tricks on me, invoking the smoke of the Russian village of my childhood as it went up in flames.

"My name is Michelle," I lied, in my most authentic French accent. I would have to listen carefully to the country dialect in Crevecoeur and force my tongue to duplicate it. I could do it. I had a talent for linguistics, and I would use it to protect myself and my baby. Perhaps it would be a good idea to wear a small crucifix around my neck. I would see if I could secure one in Crevecoeur.

"Did you leave the baby's father behind?" Madeline asked, chewing her doughy bread.

"Yes," I answered.

"That's a shame. He should be with you," Madeline said as she shook her head and tsk-tsked. "Such difficult times."

"He can't leave his business in Paris," I lied.

"Paris is no place to have a baby right now," Madeline sighed. "So where are you going?"

"To my sister's farm in the countryside," I said, as I wondered how to extricate myself from this conversation. Must I be suspicious of everyone?

"I see," Madeline said absently as she searched for something in a purple string bag.

"Do you have children?" I asked. It turned out to be the right question. Madeline chattered on about her children for quite some time while requiring nothing more from me than an occasional sympathetic nod or murmur of affirmation. After a while I leaned against the window and slept. In the evening, when we pulled into the station in Crevecoeur, I was one of the last passengers on the once-crowded train. I carried a small suitcase, my handbag, a string bag of food, my hat, and my heavy wool coat. The weather was warm, but I would need the coat come winter. If I was still alive then, I thought, with a shudder. I could not help but wonder if we should have heeded Ruth's warning and tried to escape to America. I wished I was with her in that house, with all the rooms, that her husband had built, even as I knew in my heart that Yakov would never have gone and that I would not have left him so far behind in France.

Robert winced as he swung his bad hips up into the train car to help me down. He gave me an awkward hug as he took my suitcase. "Where is Miriam?" I asked.

"The cart only fits two people up front. Besides, she's busy cooking up a storm to feed you." I groaned as I imagined the huge country meal she would have waiting for me. I had no appetite.

Robert put my things in the wagon bed on a green and white checkered tablecloth. He offered me a hand up onto the worn wooden seat and then climbed up beside me as he clucked to the horse. The cart lurched forward.

"The cherries just came ripe, so we're up to our eyeballs," he commented. "Miriam has put up at least forty jars already. And the pies . . ." Robert rolled his eyes. "This time of year we have an abundance of fruit." He spoke about the fruit, the trees, Miriam in the kitchen, and the farm. His country news soothed my battered spirit.

As we pulled up to the stone farmhouse, Miriam emerged with several dogs of assorted sizes bounding alongside her. She shooed the chickens out from underfoot with a wave of her hand. She wore a long gingham apron over her flowered dress. The apron bore the stains of many a gutted cherry. A blue ribbon attempted to corral her curls.

"That's my girl," Robert murmured under his breath, so that I barely caught it. The affection in his voice caused a wave of longing for Yakov to wash over me.

Flashing her infectious smile, Miriam reached up to help me down from the wagon seat. She embraced me with strong, sure arms, and the comfort they afforded caused me to begin to cry. When I regained control, she held me out away from her for a better look at my belly. "How far along are you?" she asked. "About five months?"

"Almost," I said.

"You must be starved; come in, come in and eat dinner."

"I'll take your bag to your room," Robert said as he hurried past us.

I inhaled the scent of young tomatoes, rosemary, and lavender.

Furnished with rough-hewn wooden furniture, the house spread out generously into many rooms, each containing its own secretive nooks and crannies. Colorful hooked rugs sprawled on the wide-planked wooden floorboards. The accoutrements of country living overflowed into the kitchen and hallways. Tools that had wandered in from the barns and fields leaned against the walls. Handmade furniture stood on solid legs. A spinning wheel squatted near the living room hearth next to baskets loaded with freshly carded wool. The kitchen brimmed with cherries and strawberries.

"I baked bread," Miriam said. "Usually I bake on Thursdays, but for you, today. The invasion is awful, but, selfishly, I am happy that you are here."

I sat down heavily at the oak table. I had drowsed all day on the train, yet I was exhausted. Miriam served me an enormous chunk of warm brown bread with butter, a bowl of carrot soup, and a plate of chicken, potatoes, and collard greens. She set a basket overflowing with blueberry muffins at my elbow and put a glass of wine in my hand. I found my appetite and ate more than I had imagined I would before Miriam filled my plate. She sat down with me and sipped a glass of Burgundy. "What in heaven's name are Yakov and Avram doing in Paris? Why didn't they come with you?"

"They joined the Resistance, Miriam. They will fight." I took her hand in mine. "Dear, dear Miriam, please understand that it is dangerous for you, for us, to know this. You must be careful. One slip of your tongue could be a death sentence for Yakov and Avram, and for me and you as well." Miriam's eyes flickered with fear as I continued. "I doubt we will see anything of them for a long time, since their coming here would endanger us."

"I want you to stay here with us, to have the baby on our farm, but Robert says you mustn't," she said regretfully.

"He's right. You and I together? We would be too obvious. We must blend in and become invisible."

"I must tell you my news," Miriam said, with a secretive smile. "I'm expecting one too." She patted her stomach.

"Oh, Miriam! How far along are you?"

"Only a couple of months, but how exciting, both of us pregnant at the same time, isn't it? Anyway, we've arranged for you to stay with a good friend of Robert's. She lives not far from here, so I can visit with you often. Her name is Catherine Nance. She has a new baby herself, named Isabel, and Catherine is a midwife. So how convenient, eh? There is a well-to-do family here in Crevecoeur, the de la Reines, who own many vineyards and wheat fields. They'll see to it that Catherine receives the means to feed you and care for you and the baby if, in exchange, you work in their vineyards. The de la Reines have sent their sons to the war and they are shorthanded. They are decent people. Monsieur de la Reine is the mayor of Crevecoeur. Many of the villagers work for his family."

"Do you think we are safe here?" I asked.

"This is a Catholic community of good country folks who despise Hitler. I go to the church on Sundays with everyone else. It is a house of worship, for anyone who chooses to pray, and I say my own words there. I believe that divine spirit surrounds us, permeates everything, and that we can commune with it anywhere. The priest spoke about the German Occupation in church and said that the parishioners can defend France by hiding those whom the Nazis seek, such as Jews and Resistance fighters. There are people from this village who are away fighting. Catherine Nance's own husband joined the Resistance several months ago and she has received no word about his well-being since he left. She is on her own with a little daughter and looks forward to your companionship."

"Why would she agree to hide me at such risk to herself?"

"It's not just Catherine; it's the whole village that is committed to hiding you, and me. Our priest, Father Charles, says that the Bible forbids the evil from which you flee. Jesus teaches compassion, mercy, and reverence for life. Hitler is the anti-Christ. You can trust the people of Crevecoeur. They are righteous gentiles. You are my sister, and they will protect you as they protect me. They will do it because it is the right thing to do. They believe it is God's will. Many men from Crevecoeur have joined the Resistance. Tomorrow I'll introduce you to Father Charles. He has arranged a believable identity for you and has created false but credible papers for both of us. He will inform you of the details. We have changed my name; I am now Marie. You will be called Vivian," Miriam announced.

It reminded me of playing make-believe as children, except this pretending was deadly serious. I wondered if Miriam comprehended just how serious it was. I looked at her sharply.

"What is it?" Miriam asked.

"I'm worried for your safety, that perhaps you don't take this seriously."

"You sound like Mama." Miriam sighed. "Of course I take this seriously. My brother and Yakov have gone off to fight," Miriam's voice quavered. She looked out the window for a moment and then turned her gaze back to me. "On such an exquisitely beautiful night, with the smell of the garden drifting in on a breeze through the window, and forty jars of cherries safely packed away for the winter, with the animals making their nighttime settling noises, the bugs buzzing and chirping, with you here under my roof, and both of us with babies on the way, with all these blessings, how dare a war rage on the outskirts of this circle of beauty? It isn't fair. I don't want to believe it."

"But you must believe it," I said, even as I realized that Miriam would fight against the reality of the war by protecting the reality she and Robert had created on their farm.

That night I slept at Miriam and Robert's farm, and the next day I moved into my new home. I had a small room to myself in Catherine's house, which was located close to the village center. Catherine had, for many years, worked in the vineyards, but more recently, since her baby girl was born, she stayed at home and took in laundry for the de la Reine household. Catherine had served as midwife at the births of the de la Reine grandchildren, so the family had a strong attachment to her and her baby Isabel.

Every day but Sunday, I rose at dawn. A large wagon came by and I climbed in with other women from the village to ride to the vineyards. I had trouble standing all day at first, but soon I grew accustomed to the physical demands of the work. The many vines needed to be fastened to wires so that they grew in the flat, espaliered pattern required. The vineyards had to be weeded constantly, treated with foul-smelling soil amendments created from manure, and checked for insects that ate leaves and fruit. The grapevines stretched for acres. One day in the vineyards followed the next on through the summer.

Catherine and I sat by the hearth after she put Isabel to sleep in the evening, drinking cups of raspberry-leaf tea and talking. She claimed that the raspberry leaves would strengthen my uterus and help me to have an easy delivery when my time came. We shared the bittersweet experience of having our first child in the absence of our husbands, for her baby had been born after her husband had gone to fight the Germans. Catherine and I both accepted the reality of our daily lives under Nazi Occupation in a similar resigned and practical fashion. We followed the unfolding of events as best we could, seeking the latest news from any reliable source available. And so we made a life together in wartime.

The air had the crisp edge of autumn clinging to it as I rose to meet the wagon for work. I had barely stood in the field an hour when my waters broke. As I looked up from the grapevines at the scene before me, it became two-dimensional and I had the strange sensation that I was inside a page in a book. The woman standing next to me said my name and touched my shoulder in concern. A contraction seized me and I moaned in pain. The news that I had gone into labor rippled swiftly down the vineyard row.

Madame de la Reine sent her buggy to take me back to Catherine's house. Two men lifted me gently up onto the buckboard. By the time I arrived, Catherine had put a pot of water on to boil. "So today is the day," she exclaimed. The buggy driver hurried off to fetch Miriam. Catherine made raspberry-leaf tea. I paced around the little house, turning inward as I struggled to manage the intensity of the contractions. Catherine showed me how to pull sound from deep within, breathing into the pain. "High-pitched sounds will take you away from the labor," Catherine warned. "Low sounds will speed the delivery."

I thought of Ruth, who had recently gone through labor and delivery, and I envied her for having had Mama with her. I imagined Mama stroking my hair and telling me it would be all right and that I could do this. Then I thought of Yakov and became furious at him for abandoning me to give birth to this baby without him. Soon my fury dissolved into grief at his absence and pity for myself, delivering my baby alone in a foreign place. I lost any real sense of time. When Miriam arrived, full and round with her own pregnancy, I was overcome with joy at seeing her, and for a brief moment, in the altered state of labor, I imagined that she could conjure Yakov. I seized Miriam by the shoulders and demanded, "Where is Yakov? Where is he? Where is my Yakov?" I wanted more than anything for my husband to be present at the birth of our child. How could events have spiraled out of control so drastically and left me in a little village far from my parents and my husband for one of the most important events of my life?

Miriam stroked my hair as I sobbed. "I'm right here," she repeated over and over. "I'm not going anywhere. I'm here."

At least I had Miriam, who paced the room with me for what seemed like days as the pain grew more and more intense.

Every once in a while Catherine would ask me to lie down on the bed, and she would check my progress, until finally she said, "Here we go. Your baby is right there. On your next contraction, I want you to push. Don't make any sound; just put all your energy into a good hard push."

I pushed for all I was worth and the pain receded. Catherine instructed me to push through several more contractions and then she said, "Now on your next contraction, I want you to resist the urge to push. Try your best not to push, and that will help prevent you from tearing." I concentrated on following Catherine's instructions. I crushed Miriam's hands in mine with such force that the blood drained out of the tips of her fingers.

"Here it comes," Catherine announced. "I have the head, and the shoulders will arrive on the next contraction. No pushing now; you're doing a terrific job. Yes. Yes. Here she is. A girl. And look at that head of hair!"

Catherine placed the baby on my chest and covered her with a warm blanket. I gazed eagerly into my daughter's face and could not remember what the world was like just a moment before, and all the moments before that, without her spirit in it. My entire life before her arrival became no more than the promise of this child. Every fingernail, every eyelash exquisite. What a complete and miraculous creature Yakov and I had made, her face luminous, haloed in dark hair. The delicate lips, the tiny nose. She peered at me in wonder, as if startled to have arrived in the world, amazed to see what her mother looked like. I brushed the damp hair with my fingertips and whispered "*shayna*," the Yiddish word for "beautiful," and that is what I named her.

In the evening, people stopped in to see the new arrival. Monsieur and Madame de la Reine brought baby clothes, preserves, and cheese. Father Charles poked his head in for a few minutes to admire my Shayna. I was grateful to have given birth to my baby in such a caring community. Catherine fed me mulled wine, which warmed me through and through as I curled up in bed with Shayna like a mother bird nesting down with her fledgling.

When Shayna woke during the night to nurse, I tended to her in the surreal candlelit glow of my first night as a mother, and in that privacy I wept for the absence of my husband and from fear for his safety. I would have liked to live a life with few regrets, and yet Yakov had not been with me for the birth of our child. I wondered if he would ever see his daughter. I tried to banish these thoughts. My anxiety would do nothing to keep him safe. I imagined that silver shield of light protecting him. That was all I could think of to do.

Miriam had never been present at a birth before and she wanted to talk about it over and over again with anyone who would listen, especially me. I was happy to oblige. Although I did not subscribe to religious dogma, I believed that a spiritual energy pervaded our lives. "How could anyone who has ever experienced the birth of a baby deny that each person has a spirit?" I asked Miriam, who heartily agreed with me.

Because a Nazi invasion of Crevecoeur did not seem imminent, we agreed it would be safe for me to stay with Miriam until I recovered from the delivery. Staying in Miriam's house, I was swiftly reminded of the boundless energy of the girl I had met long ago in a Palestinian relocation camp. Miriam hardly slept. She beat the sun to the barn every morning, rising before first light to tend to her animals and gardens. She baked bread, spun wool, sewed quilts, canned pumpkin, as busy as the day was long. In spite of her many chores, she would drop everything to take the baby when I needed to catch up on sleep with a daytime nap. Shayna thrived, quickly growing plump and rosy.

We had been on the farm for a week when I woke in the night to find Miriam hovering over me, her face ringed with amber light emanating from the tall candle in her hand. "Wake up," she whispered, "we have visitors."

I looked past Miriam to the doorway and instantly flew out of the bed and into his arms. "Yakov, Yakov, Yakov." I kissed his face a dozen times.

"I came to see my daughter," Yakov said softly, holding me tightly.

"I came to see her too," another voice spoke from the hallway.

I released Yakov in order to embrace Avram, giddy with happiness. "If I had known that you would come if I had a baby, then I would have had one sooner," I told Yakov, as he lifted his daughter out of the bed. "I named her Shayna."

Tears shone in his eyes. "Shayna, Shayna, what a messy world we brought you into. Papa is trying to clean it up for you."

"He will do it too," Avram asserted. "He's modest. He will not tell you about it. In the Resistance they call him Philippe."

Yakov interrupted hastily, "Avram, hush."

Realizing his mistake in revealing Yakov's underground name, Avram blushed with embarrassment.

I climbed back into bed and hugged my knees like a child listening to a bedtime story. "Come sit; all of you come sit. Avram and Yakov must tell us what is going on out there; we receive only limited news."

Yakov sat next to me without taking his eyes from Shayna's face. Avram and Miriam perched on the end of the bed, while Robert settled in a chair by the window. I imagined that my bed was a boat and that I could sail us away to a safe island, like one of those that we had invented in our bedtime stories with Mama when we were children.

"How long can you stay?" I asked.

"I will leave tomorrow night," Yakov replied. "I had to see her. And you of course."

"Tomorrow?" The boat in my imagination dissolved into the water.

"We are lucky to be here at all," Yakov said. I shivered.

"The Nazis would dearly like to capture Yakov," Avram informed me.

"If they knew this village is harboring *the* Philippe's wife and child . . ." He stopped midsentence as Yakov shot him a cautionary glance.

In subdued voices we exchanged the news of our separate lives. After a while, the others excused themselves and left me alone with Yakov. Shayna woke and I changed her diaper, then nursed her until she drifted back to sleep in my arms. Yakov and I spoke softly in words filled with our longing. I described the baby's birth and my home with Catherine.

"This is a safe place for you," Yakov said with visible relief.

"Do you ever think of your own safety?" I asked.

"I do not intend to die in this war, if that's what you mean," Yakov insisted.

"No one intends to die in war," I said.

Yakov took me by the shoulders, his grip solid and certain. "I promised you when we left Paris that I would not die in this war."

"That is not a promise you can make." I wondered if I could forgive him for dying if it came to that.

"I can make such a promise. No matter what happens, stay alive. I will come back to you."

I wanted to remain awake to savor each sparkling drop of Yakov's visit, but exhaustion overcame me. As the sun rose, Shayna and I slept on Yakov's chest.

Meanwhile, and as Avram also slept, Miriam laid siege to the kitchen. She baked pie, roasted a couple of chickens, stewed vegetables, fried potatoes, and chopped fruit. By the time we came downstairs in the late morning, the mouth-watering scents of apricots, onions, fresh basil and rosemary, cherry pie, and chicken fat greeted us.

"You have enough food here to feed the entire French Underground for a week," Yakov remarked.

Miriam wiped her hands on her apron and smiled broadly. "So what if there is a war on. We will live a life of abundance just to spite those crazy warmongers." She tossed her dark curls defiantly. I wondered if my efforts at stoic acceptance served me as well as Miriam's defiance served her. Perhaps my approach was self-defeating and I needed to resist the Occupation more in my own heart. It seemed to me that maybe Miriam would be the ultimate victor in this war. If only I could follow her lead, keep my fears at bay, and enjoy life "just to spite the crazy warmongers." But my husband did not rest in the safety of my arms at night, as Miriam's did.

We enjoyed our midday feast and for one brief moment tasted what our lives would have been like in another place and time, a place of peace. Robert opened a fine bottle of aged wine. We drank and laughed and passed Shayna around. We sang several French drinking songs that we had learned in the cafés in Paris. Yakov put his arm around my waist.

"If only Ruth were here, this would be perfect," I said.

"Ah, yes," Yakov said. "About that. If you write her a letter, and one to your parents, I will see that your letters are smuggled out of France. If you have already given them this address for Miriam, be sure to tell them not to write to either of you here."

While Miriam fetched paper and pencils, Robert asked quietly, "What is going on out there?"

"Evil," Avram replied. "Evil is going on out there. Anti-life. Anti-humanity." We fell silent, as if waiting for Avram to assist each of us as we slipped back into the cloak of our wartime life, which we had shed briefly in the pleasure of one another's company.

"Have you received news of the camps?" Avram asked somberly.

Yakov gestured with his arm, as if to shield the baby daughter he held against his heart from Avram's words.

"The camps?" I replied, swallowing dryly in fear.

"I don't want to listen to this," Miriam announced before she rushed out to the hen yard, slapping the screen door rebelliously against its frame behind her.

"The word from Germany is that the Nazis have built elaborate death factories. They transport Jews from throughout Europe to these factories, called concentration camps. They systematically murder Jews there, while keeping a small number of prisoners alive to operate the camps. They have established these death factories at Bergen-Belsen, Dachau, Auschwitz. It's not only Jews; they murder others also, such as dissidents, gypsies, homosexuals. The Resistance helps smuggle people out of Europe to America, where they speak up about this genocide so that the world learns of the breadth of humanity being devoured in the belly of Germany." Avram's words made the hair on the back of my neck stand on end. Robert's knuckles turned white as he gripped the arms of his chair. Avram continued, "The truth about Germany must come out, and the more people who know it, the better. In the Resistance, we interfere with any Nazi activity in France. For instance, we sabotage their attempts to transport French citizens out of France to the camps and we destroy communication lines and do whatever we can to confuse the enemy and to assist in hiding and freeing agents working against the Nazis, especially those wanted by the Nazis. Yakov thinks up the most disruptive disasters to visit on the Nazis. He's terribly clever. They can't keep up."

"You must stay out of their reach," Robert said hoarsely.

I wanted to hear about Yakov's life away from me, but I was not sure I wanted to hear this account of my husband's dangerous exploits.

"Always careful," Yakov assured him.

My husband had become a warrior, a man of courage. I was proud of him while at the same time I felt as if I no longer knew him.

"Miriam refuses to know the truth of what is happening out there. Why?" Avram asked Robert, with a note of anxiety in his voice.

Robert shrugged. "It is how she copes. It is her method of resistance. She insists on enjoying life despite them."

"I fear she will suffer a deeper injury when she wakes up to the truth," Avram worried.

"Perhaps the war will end first. Why don't you speak to her of other things? She has missed you and worried about you," Robert suggested.

At that moment, Miriam appeared framed in sunlight in the kitchen doorway, carrying a large basket of berries, her flowery apron pulled tight over her pregnant belly. A rush of love for her flooded my heart and I was as proud of her as I was of the heroic activism of our men.

Yakov said, "I need a little time alone with my girls before we must go."

My throat tightened. In a few hours he would vanish. Would I ever see him again?

Upstairs, we shuttered the windows, closing out the hot, bright afternoon sun, the harsh brilliance of the world, and lay in bed where we held each other and our baby girl.

"I am making a memory," Yakov said softly. "I will keep the memory of this afternoon as a talisman to ward off calamity and to remind me of the reason I must live."

Once the protective cover of darkness fell, the men prepared to leave. We parted with no words unsaid, clear in our love for one another. Yakov gave Shayna his father's blessing, reciting the ancient Jewish benediction a parent gives to a child: "May God bless you and keep you and may God's countenance shine upon you and bring you peace."

The delivery of this benediction surprised me because Yakov did not believe in God. But the well-worn words had a potency that transcended belief. I recalled other words that were usually spoken on Yom Kippur, words taught to me by Papa: "Today God inscribes in the Book of Life who shall live and who shall die in the coming year."

Yakov and Avram followed their faint shadows into the moonlight. If only my love for them could keep them safe, then they would come to no harm. They became gray undefined shapes and then blended into the dark. After they disappeared, I turned and wept on Miriam's shoulder.

The next day I returned to Catherine's house. It seemed too dangerous for me to stay with Miriam, the two of us together. So far the Nazis had not arrived in Crevecoeur, but, according to Avram, they were working their way through the countryside, so it was only a matter of time. For this reason, Father Charles spoke with Monsieur de la Reine, who agreed with him that the parishioners should identify Father Charles as the town's mayor from then on, since Father Charles feared for the de la Reines' safety. He argued convincingly that the village could more easily do without him than without the de la Reine family, who provided a livelihood for the many people in their employ and who produced much of the food the community consumed.

I awoke one winter morning when Shayna was three months old to a knock at the kitchen door. I left Shayna sleeping and went into the kitchen to see what was going on. Catherine spoke quietly to the person outside before closing the door and turning to face me.

"The Nazis have arrived," she told me. We exchanged a frightened look. "You must go back to the vineyards for your protection. I'll look after Shayna. They're seeking information about Resistance fighters."

I hastily washed up, ate some bread and cheese, and prepared for work. I nursed Shayna while Catherine made me a lunch to take with me. "Madame de la Reine will send some goat milk for me to feed her while you're gone," Catherine said.

I rocked Shayna in my arms, watching her sleep, while I waited for the wagon to pick me up. It wasn't meant to be this way, I thought to myself, as I fought back tears at the thought of spending a whole day away from my baby. While I worked in the vineyards, my thoughts remained in that room with my tiny daughter. By evening my engorged breasts ached. I returned wearily to Catherine's house, where I nursed Shayna, barely able to keep my eyes open. Catherine insisted on going over the details of my alias with me. I was Vivian, wife of Catherine's brother who had gone to war and had not returned. In fact, Catherine's brother had died several years before the war, but Father Charles had falsified the records and removed the headstone from the graveyard. He had carefully assisted others in documenting fabrications in an effort to save their lives.

The Nazis remained in Crevecoeur for a week before leaving Father Charles "in charge" and departing. Being in charge meant they would hold him accountable for the activities of the village. At a community meeting in the church, the Nazis had announced that they expected us to report any knowledge of the whereabouts of Resistance fighters to Father Charles at once so that he could contact the appropriate Nazi authorities. The Nazi commanding officer made it clear that failure to inform the Nazis of activity connected with the Resistance would have deadly consequences. I could see why Father Charles had become the mayor to protect Monsieur de la Reine. If the Nazis thought that the village had defied their commands, they would blame Father Charles, and it would be his life that would be forfeit as a result.

After the Nazis left, I continued to work in the vineyards, seeing Shayna only in the evenings and on weekends. I missed her terribly. Shayna was fine with Catherine and I didn't worry about her well-being. I just wanted to be with her. It was sometimes difficult for me to see Catherine playing lap games with her fair-haired baby, singing to her and talking to her, when I knew that I had such limited time to do the same with Shayna.

Catherine liked to remind me that the villagers took pride in harboring me and Shayna. As stories of my husband's bravery and cunning traveled the countryside, his activities soon became the stuff of local legend. Miriam, on the other hand, did not need a famous husband to inspire love and devotion. She was a darling of Crevecoeur in her own right. She sent her magnificent soups and preserves to the sick and elderly, organized the women to make baby quilts for new arrivals, and assisted her neighbors by doctoring ill livestock.

In January, when Miriam had her baby, I could not keep from feeling jealous that she could stay at home with him. He was a big boy, and born so quickly that Catherine didn't even make it to the farm in time to deliver him. Robert caught the baby himself and he talked about it for months afterward, his face glowing with pride. Robert was Catholic; nevertheless he agreed to allow Miriam to name their son Akiva, after a great Hebrew sage, but to protect him from the danger of his Jewish heritage, they called him little Robert. If Miriam had radiated life and energy when pregnant, she did so twofold once she had a child. It was a wonder to me the way Miriam blossomed in such difficult times. But even as a child she had had a habit of inspiring joy in others and generating a pervasive sense of optimism in her wake.

When spring unfolded its glistening wings, it flew through the village bringing a sense of renewed hope. Often a mist hung on the land in the early morning, transforming the familiar landscape into a strangely enchanted place. Some mornings, as I stumbled sleepily into the vineyards, I left the war behind for an instant, and I felt pure delight. It was on just such a morning that a fellow vineyard worker named Nicole stopped me and asked me to read a letter that someone had sent her. I read her the letter and then asked why she had never learned to read.

"Many of us don't read," she explained in a voice that carried a tone of defensiveness. "We have no need."

"If you would ever like to learn, I would be happy to teach you," I offered. "It's not as difficult as it looks and it's handy to know how."

The next day, Nicole accepted my offer. I borrowed a primer from the schoolteacher and sat with Nicole when we broke for lunch at midday. Nicole's reading lesson soon took on a life of its own. Before long, several other vineyard workers and even a woman who worked at the de la Reine house approached me to teach them to read too. We borrowed more primers from the school and they joined my lunch-hour class. I couldn't teach everyone who wanted to join the class, so I promised those who expressed interest that I would get to them eventually. I intended to do it too. My newfound passion for teaching gave me something solid to hold on to, something constructive that I was doing to be truly useful. Every day I looked forward to the lunch-hour class, which took my mind off my longing to see my baby. As I worked the grapevines, I thought of ways to help my students progress. I daydreamed about a time when the war was over and I might have the opportunity to study the best methods for teaching adults to read. I imagined a different life, in the future, when I would work as a teacher. I had always been good at learning languages and I enjoyed it. Could I turn my passion for languages into a teaching career after the war? I longed, with a longing that ached like the bone-cold chill of winter, for the war to end so that we could get on with our interrupted lives.

The opportunity to teach gave me respite from my grindingly dull work and so rescued me from complete despair. Teaching offered me a welcome form of intellectual stimulation. I missed those late nights in the cafés in Paris, discussing politics, economics, and culture with our friends. No one in Crevecoeur had an interest in this type of conversation. The villagers could talk for hours about the weather, their dogs, and repairing chimneys. Catherine and I talked about babies, children, parenting, our husbands, and the relationships in our lives. She was a smart woman, but she had no interest in political or economic theory. I would have liked to talk with someone about fascism and to have shared my ideas on how it evolved and how it could be prevented or defeated. I wondered if there was a viable nonviolent approach to fighting Hitler. I heard a rumor that the king of Denmark had pinned a yellow star on his chest and that everyone else in the country had followed his lead, refusing to identify their Jews, and had saved the Jews of Denmark this way, but I didn't know if this was true. At any rate, there was no one in that little village with whom I could talk about philosophy or politics in the way that I had talked about these things with Yakov, Avram, and our friends in Paris before the war. My new diversion, teaching, helped to fill this void.

One evening I arrived at home to find the house dark and empty. A note from Catherine on the kitchen table said she had gone to deliver a baby for Babette, the wife of Robert's former overseer, Christian. A nearby neighbor had taken Shayna and Isabel. I brought the girls home, played with them, fed them, bathed them, and put them to bed. Still no Catherine. Miriam turned up in her wagon just after sunrise to collect the babies.

"It's Babette," she explained. "She's having complications with her labor."

Although Christian had left to join the Resistance, Babette still lived on Robert's farm in the overseer's house. She had four children under the age of twelve. She and Christian had their own vineyards and gardens on land that Robert had given to them, and Babette had maintained these as best she could with the help of her children in Christian's absence.

I was somewhat concerned, but Babette had already given birth to so many children that I thought it would turn out right in the end. I returned home from the vineyards that evening, expecting to find Catherine eager to launch into an elaborate description of the details of the birth, as she was inclined to do. But when the wagon dropped me off at the house, it appeared dark and cheerless. I entered to find the babies asleep and Catherine staring into the red glow of a dying fire.

"What happened?" I asked in alarm. "Tell me quickly. What's wrong?"

"Babette hemorrhaged. We couldn't stop the bleeding. We lost her."

"You lost her?"

"She's gone."

"And the baby?"

"He's fine. Miriam has him. Miriam has all the children. Virtually orphans now."

"But Christian . . . ?"

"If he lives, it would be suicide for him to return home. He is a known Resistance fighter."

"What will become of the children?"

As Miriam told it, on the first night after Babette's death, she put the children to bed in her house and sat down in the kitchen across the table from Robert, who asked, "What will become of these children?" And she replied, "We'll just have to keep them."

Babette's aging aunt, Renée, had lived with her and helped her care for her children. Renée moved in with Miriam, who breast-fed Babette's baby along with Akiva. The villagers helped Miriam in whatever ways they could, offering to milk her goats, bringing food to the house, and giving the family baby clothing. Overwhelmed by my simple life of working in the vineyards while caring for one baby, I wondered how Miriam had the energy to maintain that busy household full of children as well as the animals and gardens on the farm. I found my answer when I went to visit Miriam not long after Babette's death. As I entered the kitchen, I saw the babies kicking their fat legs where they lay on a blanket spread out on a braided rug. Suzette, Babette's oldest, kept an eye on them while she spun wool on the spinning wheel. Renée and the other children were busy baking cookies in the small oven while Miriam had breads rising on the table and pies in her big oven. The house smelled of yeast and swelled with the shrieks and giggles of the children.

"It's baking day," Miriam explained as she retied a bright-blue kerchief around her unruly hair.

"Come out and walk with me a little," I urged.

Miriam wiped her hands on her apron. "I'll only be a few minutes," she told Renée.

As soon as the screen door slammed behind us, I asked, "How are you doing all this? Are you all right? This is not too much?"

"I love too much. I love the instant family. Life gives us unexpected treasures," Miriam said, hugging herself and looking into the distance before turning to look at me. "If I stay busy, then the war stays far away. I will focus on the day-to-day details until one day, when I will look up from weeding and baking and reading aloud to the children, and the war will be over. And I'll say, thank goodness we've put that behind us, and pick up my mending where I left off."

"I hope that it happens just like you describe it."

Miriam smiled. "I'll tell you a secret. The truth is I'm happy. And I'm determined to give these children an enchanted childhood, like Mama gave to us, in spite of the war and the loss of their mother. Robert and I agree that they deserve better than what they've been dealt, and we're going to give them as much of it as we can."

For an instant, I imagined Miriam standing as if made of stone, immovable, impermeable, a charmed statue guarding the gate of the home that she was providing to those children.

Two months after our conversation, Miriam took in another child. Father Charles had visited a neighboring parish and when he returned he brought with him a mentally infirm Jewish boy who had been orphaned by the war. Because the boy could not take care of himself and had limited potential, he had been difficult to place in a foster home. Father Charles took Daniel to live with him. But as soon as Miriam got wind of the situation, she insisted on taking Daniel home with her. "Living in a church with a priest is no life for a nine-year-old boy," she insisted. She swiftly scooped Daniel up and absorbed him into her busy household.

The children thrived under Miriam's loving care while she thrived in the daily work of caring for them. Before Akiva had turned a year old, she took in two more Jewish orphans. Additional children soon followed. As fast as Father Charles found children, Miriam and Robert found beds for them. Without recognizing it as such, she and Robert created an orphanage filled with Jewish children and children of Resistance fighters. In the midst of the malevolent landscape of war, Miriam ensured with a furious determination that these orphaned children would not be robbed of the wonder of childhood. She inspired all of us in Crevecoeur to care for our children with all our hearts, as if in this way we defied the Nazis. I know for a fact that Miriam never once considered herself brave. Quite the opposite. She thought she was a coward, hiding in the safety of her farm.

EIGHT

Ruth

I RECEIVED ONLY ONE letter from Rivka and Miriam during the war. They wrote, months after the invasion of Paris, that Rivka had given birth to a baby girl and that Miriam expected a baby soon too. All three of us with new babies at once, yet so far apart. I would miss out on the tiny daily miracles of their babies' growth as they passed the milestones of cutting a first tooth, saying a first word, taking a first step. Would I ever see their babies? I imagined Mama, Papa, and Meir with our little ones underfoot, running through their house. And Benjy, an uncle to so many babies at once. It didn't seem likely that this scene would come to pass anywhere but in my imagination.

In the letter, Rivka cautioned that I should not expect them to write again and explained that I could not write to her, and that Yakov and Avram had joined the Resistance. This news made me sick with worry and I ate next to nothing for several days after the letter arrived. I so wanted to write back, but I heeded Rivka's warning and restrained myself. Forbidden to communicate with them with ink and paper, I often spoke to Rivka and Miriam in my head, and each week at synagogue I prayed for their safety and the safety of their husbands, children, and friends in Crevecoeur.

When America entered the war, I remained grateful for the good fortune that allowed Ida and me to keep our husbands at home, far from the fray. Izzie had survived polio as a child and wore a brace on his bad leg, while Nate had that heart murmur. Perhaps another woman would have considered these health problems bad luck, but I was an expert in bad luck. Bad luck was Miriam and Avram having their mother killed because she lost her temper during a pogrom. Bad luck was riding past my grandmother's head mounted on a stake as my family fled our village. Having a husband who could not fight in the war because of a heart defect was my idea of good fortune.

Izzie and Nate's fuel business was taking off like a horse out of the gate, with their customer base growing weekly. Dave was doing an excellent job managing the gas station for them, and they had expanded it so that they provided simple automobile repairs. Meanwhile, Nate pursued his rescue activities more aggressively. When Sophie was six months old, he brought a reserved and serious couple in their mid-fifties out of Europe. Chaya knew them from the old country, where this couple was prominent in their community. Less than two weeks after they arrived, Ira called Nate with the exciting news that he had the rare opportunity to rescue a Polish family. He had been thwarted in previous attempts to smuggle Polish Jews. This family had miraculously escaped to Belgium. We took them in without hesitation, as we did the others who followed, moving through our home in a steady stream as they fled the only life they had known and struggled to acclimate to a confusing, alien culture in America.

I was grateful for Chaya's companionship and help. If the house settled down for the night before I was too exhausted to move a finger, I would have a cup of tea with Chaya in the breakfast nook before bed. But our days started early, so we were often more inclined to go to sleep than to stay awake for that last cup of tea.

Each morning, I woke at five-thirty and nursed Sophie while Nate showered and dressed. Then I went downstairs and put the percolator on for coffee, which was ready by the time Nate finished his habitual bowl of cereal. Then he retired to his den with his coffee and the paper. Often the only moment he had to himself all day was his fifteen minutes in the morning in his den, his personal domain, which was a small room with no more than a couch, recliner, loaded built-in bookshelves on the upper walls, and a radio on a stand.

After his coffee, Nate left for work. If the weather was nice, he walked, and if it wasn't, then he rode the bus so that I could keep the car. While he read his paper, I toasted a pile of bread in the oven, then I buttered it and put it on a platter alongside a bowl of fruit. The refugees, whom we referred to as "our houseguests," would swiftly consume the toast and fruit down to the last crumb. At eight o'clock, Chaya took her leave and went off to work for the day, and Dave set out for the gas station either on foot or by bus, depending on the time of year and the weather.

After I made breakfast, I retrieved the newspaper from the den and set it on the work table in the middle of the kitchen with pencils and small pads of paper that I bought at the five-and-dime. Anyone looking for work would turn up soon afterward to comb the classified ads. If we had school-age children in the house, I sometimes helped get them off to school, if I was needed, and this included being sure they had something to take with them for lunch. Then I found someone to watch Sophie for a few minutes so that I could shower and dress. After that, we assessed the job offers and figured out how everyone would get to where they needed to go for the day. We set up a schedule, and usually I was needed to drive someone for an interview, although many times the job-seekers took the bus, as did those who were working already.

Most of the refugees had lived with physical deprivation in Europe and there was rarely a week that did not include one or more visits to doctors, dentists, or labs for tests. Somehow, in between driving to job interviews and medical appointments, I needed to take care of our laundry, grocery shopping, food preparation, cleaning, yard work, and attending to the inevitable repairs and maintenance needed for the house. I planned the meals for the week for the whole household, stretching our weekly food rations the best I could. If I allowed any of the refugees to accompany me to the grocery store, it took twice as long to shop and I spent more money than I intended, so I tried to go alone. I delegated the preparation of lunch to any adult who was to be home in the middle of the day, and the meal usually consisted of sandwiches. I almost always took charge of dinner myself. I certainly didn't do all the food preparation on my own, but I did a lot of it. Our meal was often soup or stew that involved the chopping of a great many vegetables. Nate looked after Sophie after dinner so that I could oversee the cleanup.

Our schoolchildren had to do their homework, in English, which often posed a huge challenge. Late in the evening, Sophie needed her bath and then to be nursed before bed, and only I could do that. Those of our houseguests who were attending night school came in late, found leftovers to eat, and cleaned up after themselves. I had high standards of cleanliness, and even though our houseguests tried their best, I was frequently frustrated with the results. I hated finding things (or not finding them, as it were) put away in the wrong spot. It drove me wild and, try as I might, I could not overcome this pet peeve. At least I managed to restrain myself from haranguing our houseguests about it most of the time.

Each day brought new challenges as Sophie grew and her needs changed. When she started eating solid food, I had to make time to feed her and clean her up after she ate. When she became mobile, she needed constant attention from me or someone else in the house, and certain doors had to be kept closed and certain items had to be moved to higher ground to keep Sophie out of mischief. I reserved part of each day to play with Sophie, and as often as possible I took her to the park so that she spent time outdoors in the fresh air. When she became old enough, I read stories to her before bed at night.

When Sophie was an infant, I remember locking myself in my bedroom in the middle of the day to nurse her and have a good cry more than a few times. I tried not to complain to Nate about the stresses of my daily life. It amazed me when women at the synagogue expressed their admiration for my ability to stay organized with a new baby and the refugees I was harboring in my house; in truth I did not feel competent at all and teetered on the verge of panic much of the time. I was pleasantly surprised when the sisterhood at our synagogue took up a collection and bought us a large coffee urn so that I could keep hot coffee going for our houseguests during the day. They also bought us coffee each week, and Ida stopped by to deliver it on Wednesday mornings. She stayed to have a cup with me, so I thought of Wednesday as "coffee day."

After I weaned Sophie, I had significantly more energy, plus my interest in sex returned, much to my relief (and Nate's delight of course). Sophie, our little star, was my greatest treasure. The houseguests adored her. She really was irresistible. In our linguistically diverse household, much of our communication occurred through her. I could not have predicted how much I would adore my daughter. It gave me great pleasure to dress her in precious outfits and curl her hair, threading ribbons into it. She was such a beautiful baby. I showed her off to everyone. Every day, when Nate came home from work, he crawled around on the floor with her. In bed at night, I filled him in on the details of Sophie's accomplishments, how she could hold a spoon, pull herself up to her feet in her crib, try to hum along when someone sang a song. Sophie was the center of our universe.

NINE

Rivka

BY THE FALL HARVEST, I had taught Nicole and my first cohort of students how to read. I "graduated" them and took on a new group. The challenge of having new students invigorated me. It was a great source of pride for me that I was able to teach these people to read French, which was not my first language. Nicole, meanwhile, began to write poetry, which was moving in its simplicity and insightful in its perceptions of the natural world.

We celebrated Shayna's first birthday and soon afterward she began walking. Shayna and Isabel loved to go to Miriam's, and I took them to visit as often as I dared. Autumn meant apple season and this translated into armloads of work in Miriam's kitchen. One Sunday when I took the girls to Miriam's, I arrived to find her children perched on ladders and branches in the apple trees with their baskets as they collected shiny fairy-tale apples. They shouted to one another from tree to tree.

"I can see the church from here."

"No, you can't."

"Look, over there is the steeple."

"That's just a weather vane on Monsieur Clou's barn."

"It is not."

"We have a lot of cows in the pasture, don't we?"

"Do you see Maggie the goat?"

"Is she there?"

"Are you picking apples or looking at goats?"

The children descended with their apple baskets slung over their arms and dumped the fruit into bushel baskets placed under the trees. Then they ascended again with a clatter and ferocious shaking of branches, like huge and gangly birds. Apples rained down onto the ground as the children scrambled around in the trees. They giggled, climbed, and picked the fruit for Miriam and Renée to press into cider, bake into pies, and preserve for the winter in sauces, jams, and butters. I called to the children in greeting and herded Shayna and Isabel into the kitchen, where Miriam had vats of applesauce bubbling on the stove. Akiva and Christian Jr. played in the corner with pots, pans, and wooden spoons, surrounded by pumpkins.

As I came through the door, Miriam greeted me with a twinkle in her eye. "I have a surprise for you." We left the babies with Renée, and Miriam led me upstairs to her bedroom. She opened a drawer and unwrapped a small, handmade rag doll. "I received this a few days ago," Miriam explained. "A Resistance fighter came through in the night. He didn't stay. I don't know his name. He said Yakov made this for Shayna."

I took the crude doll and examined it for any clue of Yakov's well-being. But it was simply a doll and I didn't blame Shayna for taking little interest in it when I first showed it to her. She was distracted by the older children who surrounded her. That night, I placed the doll next to our sleeping daughter and imagined myself tucking Yakov into bed with her, safe and sound. A belated birthday present for Shayna: proof that her father lived.

Catherine came up behind me as I gazed at Shayna and her handmade doll. She put her arm around my waist, offering silent comfort. I leaned my head on her shoulder and said, "If we get through this, I want to have another child right away so that Yakov can be there for everything."

"We'll make it through," Catherine replied with determination. "One way or another."

I wanted to believe her.

"Come," she continued, "I have a hot cup of tea waiting for you in the kitchen."

We went into the kitchen, where I sat down at the table and took a sip from the steaming cup. "Spearmint?" I asked.

"Peppermint and spearmint combined," Catherine answered. "I get that from my mother. She never made one without the other. She grew mint in her garden."

"Now that sounds like my mother in Palestine. She used to bind bunches of herbs together with string and hang them to dry on a rack she rigged in the kitchen. It was a good thing the ceiling was so high, or the papas would have brushed their heads on the leaves each time they walked across the room."

Catherine laughed. "You stay right there. I have to show you something." She went into her bedroom and emerged with a small album, which she placed on the table at my elbow. She leafed through it until she came to the photograph she wanted. "My mother," she said. Then she pointed over her mother's head to a thick row of drying herbs hanging on a wooden frame suspended from the ceiling. "She dried her herbs in the kitchen also."

But I was not looking at the row of drying leaves over Catherine's mother's head. I could not tear my eyes from her mother's face. "Catherine, have you ever noticed anything about Isabel that reminds you of your mother?" I asked.

"Oh my, I wouldn't know where to begin," Catherine replied cheerfully. "Isabel has inherited so many of my mother's traits that you would almost think they were the same person."

"They are," I told her.

"What do you mean?" She sounded startled and faintly anxious.

"This is hard to explain, and I know this must sound strange, but the instant I saw your mother's face in this photograph, I had a flash of recognition. I just knew, with a certainty that I can't describe, that Isabel has your mother's spirit," I said. "I'm not talking about an intuition or a vague feeling. I mean that I know this absolutely to be true."

"As in reincarnation?" Catherine asked cautiously.

"Yes, reincarnation," I confirmed.

"You believe in reincarnation?" Catherine shifted in her chair uncomfortably.

"I do," I replied.

"I thought that, even though you are Jewish," Catherine whispered, almost afraid to say the word aloud, "that you don't believe in God."

"I don't believe in one god, but I do believe that all beings have spirit and that a person's individual spirit can return to this world over and over again, housed in different bodies each time. I realize that I don't often discuss my spiritual beliefs, but forgive me, I had to say something when you showed me the picture of your mother. I had to tell you that I know. I'm sure. She's back in Isabel," I insisted.

"This must be an unusual batch of mint tea," Catherine joked uncertainly as she struggled to formulate an appropriate response to my words.

"That doll from Yakov set me off. I'm tangled up in deep thoughts this evening," I offered by way of an explanation. "I think I'm going to go to bed before I start seeing pixies in the potato bin."

Catherine smiled, visibly relieved to have an end to our strange conversation. We kissed each other on both cheeks and parted for the night.

Later, in my bed beside Shayna, I thought back to the first time I had seen Avram when I was a little girl, and how I had the feeling on that day that there was something familiar about him that I couldn't quite place. The memory made me wonder. When I had that perception about Isabel that night, it was the first time that I was definitively aware of experiencing recognition of a returned spirit.

In early summer, Miriam and Robert had a bumper crop of cherries. When Miriam first moved to the farm, she added more cherry trees to Robert's family orchard. Both the new cherry trees and the older ones were heavy with fruit. The de la Reines offered to loan me to Miriam for a week to help preserve the cherries. I was met with quite a sight when I arrived at the farm. Miriam's gaggle of children again swung from the trees, only this time they were covered in cherry juice. Even Suzette, the oldest, had cherry stains on her hands and mouth. The children's colorful clothing appeared between the tree branches like vivid plumage.

I beckoned to Suzette, who clambered down to talk to me. When we heard a large belch emerge from the tree next to us, Suzette called out, "Daniel, is that you up there?"

"It's me," Daniel answered from his perch in the branches.

"Don't eat too many cherries; you'll make yourself sick. Pick some for Maman to make us a pie, OK?" Suzette told him. She was becoming a young woman in her mother's absence. I imagined how proud Babette would have been of her firstborn and felt a wave of sadness that she was not there to see her children thriving.

Miriam and I washed and pitted the plump purple-red cherries, packed them into jars, prepared jam, and spread fruit on the drying racks. As we stood side by side, pitting cherries, our hands stained black with the juice, Miriam grew uncharacteristically pensive before asking, "Do you ever think about what you want to be remembered for after you die?"

"Of course," I answered, slowly, "I think everyone thinks about that, and more so during a time of war."

"I hope I live to be an old woman and that I see these children grow up, but if by some misfortune I don't, I've been thinking I want to leave something of value behind for them, and for others."

"And what have you been thinking that would be?"

"I would like it to be the love that I have made, my love for the children, Robert, you, the farm, Crevecoeur, all of this. I would leave that behind, and also my cherry orchards." She smiled faintly as she brushed a thick curl off her forehead and tucked it back into the purple kerchief on her head. "I must have enough cherries here to feed the whole village," she said. Then she paused before continuing. "When people look at my life, after I'm gone, I want them to say that I was grateful for my blessings, that I was appreciative, and that I was the sort of person who spread joy."

"I think they say that about you already," I assured her. "You have been like that as long as I have known you. I think it is what Mama loves the most about you."

Miriam's eyes filled with tears. "I sometimes wonder if we will ever see her again. She seems so far away now."

"And has never seen our children," I added, determined not to let Miriam's tears set me off crying as well. "I think Shayna looks a lot like Benjy. Do you think she will ever meet her grandparents or the rest of our family?"

"When the war is over, I think it is entirely possible," Miriam said.

"When the war is over," I echoed. "It seems like such a time will never come. And even if it does, as it must eventually, who will own France: the French or the Germans?"

"I don't think I can bear the thought of Germany having power over us for the rest of our lives. It can't happen. I refuse to think that way. It would be impossible for us to go on. We must keep thinking positive thoughts and putting a positive vision out into the world so that it will come true."

In the fall, Shayna began talking, and unlike Catherine's little Isabel (who was a child of few words), she relentlessly exercised and expanded her vocabulary by speaking in a steady stream to anyone who would listen, and often to no one in particular. As the girls grew older and more able to understand and listen, Catherine and I began making storybooks for them. The idea came to me because I recalled Mama's bedtime storytelling ritual from my childhood and how much we enjoyed inventing those stories when we were growing up. If I couldn't offer my daughter the experience of knowing her grandmother firsthand, at least I could offer her the legacy of her grandmother's creativity. So I wove characters from my childhood stories, like Dimitri the wizard and Pythagoras the python, into new stories that Catherine and I made up with the girls. I wrote down the stories and Catherine drew simple ink illustrations. We made storybooks about tropical islands, talking animals, the jungles of Africa, and the streets of America. In our stories, Catherine and I imagined ourselves everywhere but Crevecoeur in wartime. We imagined that we were not two single mothers, separated from our husbands, waiting for a war to end.

TEN

Ruth

THE MORE INFATUATED NATE became with our darling Sophie, the more he wanted to have another child. Although I feared going through childbirth again, I could resist neither the desire I had for him in our intimate moments nor his enthusiasm for trying to have another baby. Why had I married such a deliciously handsome man? He knew just what to do to dissolve my determination to stick to my safe times of the month. That is how I became pregnant again when Sophie was not quite two years old. In truth, I couldn't wait to discover the new little person who would join our family. Perhaps we would have a boy this time. I refused to return to that butcher of a doctor who had torn me so badly when I delivered Sophie, so I went instead to a woman doctor who had delivered Ida's second child.

The week that I told Nate I was pregnant again, he began a tradition that lasted for our entire marriage. On Tuesday evenings he brought home Chinese food from a restaurant called the Shanghai that had recently opened near his office. The owners had several restaurants, including two in New York near Jewish neighborhoods. The Shanghai had such a large Jewish clientele that they cooked kosher Chinese food. I couldn't get enough of it, and our houseguests loved it too. Tuesday night Chinese dinners became one of our favorite "family" times as we sat around the dining room table together and opened the little cardboard boxes to discover what delights they contained. Who would have guessed that these refugees from Eastern Europe would take to Chinese food so enthusiastically?

My second pregnancy was entirely different from the first one. Instead of draining all my energy, this pregnancy energized me. I cooked enormous meals for our houseguests. I did art projects with Sophie and took her on long walks in her pram. I didn't fall asleep early every night like when I was pregnant with Sophie but instead stayed awake to spend time with Nate, drink a cup of tea with Chaya and one or more of the other women living in my house, write letters to Mama and Papa, and sketch dresses, skirts, hats, and shoes in my drawing book. I even found time to do some sewing, and I made a few outfits for Sophie. In the spring, I enlisted a couple of the youngsters living with us to help me dig up part of the yard, and we planted green beans, squash, asparagus, collards, cabbage, potatoes, and tomatoes. I didn't know much about gardening, just the bits and pieces I had picked up from Mama in the garden in Palestine. There was a houseguest with us at the time who knew a great deal about how to grow vegetables. She helped me start the garden and taught me how to nurture the plants along. I wished I had taken more interest in Mama's gardening when I was a girl. Our little Victory garden did surprisingly well. We added some herb boxes, and I was excited the first time I cooked up our homegrown potatoes with homegrown rosemary.

During the summer, Chaya remarried, and she and Dave moved out of our house. I had come to depend on Chaya for so much that I missed her terribly, despite my pleasure that she had found happiness in a new marriage. She certainly deserved happiness. Our goal was always to assist our houseguests in establishing their own lives, but we had encouraged Chaya and Dave to stay with us and not to strike out on their own. When they finally moved out, Nate and I agreed that we wanted to have our house to ourselves when the new baby was born. We had only one family still living with us at that time, but they were a doozy. Yossel and his family had moved in over a year earlier. He and his wife refused to find work. I mean, they didn't blatantly refuse, but something always got in the way. If one or the other of them found a job, something inevitably came up so that it didn't pan out. They always had an excuse. If it weren't for the fact that they had four daughters, whom I had grown fond of, I would have probably lost all patience with Yossel and his wife and put them out in the street. Whenever Nate asked Yossel about work, he replied, "God will provide." In private I told Nate, "God and my husband will provide." Nate reckoned that Yossel and his wife tried to stay as invisible as possible so that maybe we would forget they were living in our house. I was half inclined to ask them to move out and to leave their children behind until they were settled and could take the girls to live with them. But it occurred to me that they might just disappear and leave me with their four girls to raise.

In the end, Nate rented an apartment for them and we personally packed their things, then Nate and Dave physically moved them into the apartment. My Nate. Some would say he was a soft touch, but I say he was compassionate. For years he gave Yossel's family a monthly allowance to help them get by, and for years the girls often popped in to see me after school. They sometimes helped me in the garden. I wondered how these well-mannered children could be so different from their sponging parents.

Once we had moved Yossel's family out, we were free of houseguests, and we intentionally kept it that way. I put all my energy into Sophie, who, at two years old, was as smart as a new suit. I wondered if I would ever love another child as much as I loved Sophie. Ida, who had two boys, assured me that I would fall in love with the second one as much as I had the first. "Remember what it was like before Sophie was born and you couldn't imagine who she would be, then she came and suddenly you couldn't remember the world without her?" Ida asked. "The most wonderful people, whom we haven't met, are waiting just around the corner to enter our lives."

When I went into labor, I panicked. I had warned my doctor that I could not handle labor, but I know she didn't believe me until she saw it for herself firsthand. I pleaded for drugs and she complied. In the end, I was so medicated for the pain that I became unresponsive. The doctor knocked me out and performed a Caesarian. Many women are upset if they must have a Caesarian, but not me. Knock me out. Take the baby. Wake me up when it's over. That suited me just fine.

When I woke up after the birth, I had a throbbing headache. I gingerly turned my head, and there sat Nate in a chair next to my bed, holding our baby. Nate brought the baby to me. With coloring darker than Sophie's, this little one had a lot of hair and long fingers.

"A boy?" I asked Nate.

"A girl," he replied.

"Did you have your heart set on a boy?" I asked softly.

"I had my heart set on this one, whoever she is," Nate said, with the deepest satisfaction and joy.

We had expected a boy, so we had no girls' names picked out. But a beautiful Russian name popped into my head the minute I saw the baby.

"Irina," I said. "What about Irina?"

"What do you think?" Nate asked our daughter.

Irina yawned.

On the night after Irina was born, I had, for the first time, what I began to think of ever after as "the Chinese dreams." Having Sophie had already changed me, but when I became the mother of two, I think my entire psyche shifted. That is the only explanation I could come up with for the timing of the onset of the recurring Chinese dreams. I had no idea why I dreamt of China, or how I even realized that it was China when I began to have that dream. I knew next to nothing about China, and yet these dreams contained vivid details of Chinese culture. In the dream I had that night, I stood next to my husband, who was and wasn't Nate, both at once. My head was bowed in submission. Tears ran down my cheeks and spattered the deep-blue silk jacket that I wore over my loosely fitting dress. I stared at the pattern of gold-embroidered flowers and birds on the jacket and tried to control myself. My husband was shouting at a young woman in a peach-colored jacket with large flowers embroidered across it. It was humid and the air was filled with the scent of flowers, strong as ripe melons. There were lush gardens somewhere nearby. I stole a glance at the young woman, whose eyes pleaded with me, but I remained silent. Then I saw her look through the open window at a gardener. His eyes met hers briefly before he hurried from the garden. I turned my gaze toward my feet after that and did not look up. I feared that if my husband saw me look up he would strike me. The young woman fell to the floor, weeping, and I was engulfed in her grief. When I woke from the dream I was terrified and I buzzed for the nurse. I asked her if she would bring my daughter to me from the nursery. I insisted on keeping Irina next to me in my own bed for the rest of my stay in the hospital.

Because of the Caesarian, I remained on the maternity ward for a couple of weeks. The nurses looked the other way when Nate pretended to put Sophie inside his overcoat and sneak her past the reception desk so she could see her new sister. She wanted to take care of Irina the way she took care of her stuffed animals and dollies.

When I left the hospital and returned home, I swiftly discovered that having two children was more than twice as complicated as having one. The work increased exponentially. Even though I chose not to breast-feed Irina in order to preserve more of my energy, I was still sleep deprived and I craved sleep the way a starving person craves food. I couldn't imagine what condition I would have been in had I breast-fed. I navigated the day in a haze of exhaustion, devoting all my energy to meeting the needs of my children. But I was content in my small and comfortable world. I would sometimes bury my nose in a laundry basket of clean fluffy diapers and savor the fresh scent. I often sat in the rocker in Irina's room while she slept, well cared for and safe in her crib. There I felt insulated from the anxieties of the war and was able to distract myself from my fear for the safety of my loved ones in Europe.

As Irina grew into a sturdy, active baby, Nate was in his element. This was what he had wished for: a happy family life, a wife and children to come home to from a long day at work. He played wildly with Sophie in the living room in the evenings, while the baby watched from a blanket spread out on the floor. As I washed the dinner dishes, I would listen to the girls shrieking and laughing in the next room with their doting daddy.

Irina was very different from her sister. She proved to be less easily entertained than Sophie. She was demanding and harder to please. When Irina began eating solid food, I had to work at finding food she liked. Then just when I thought I had her figured out, her tastes changed. For instance, she would happily eat puréed carrots for a few days and then suddenly start spitting them out, looking for a new flavor. She quickly lost interest in toys, even new ones, and wanted to move on to something else right away. She required constant attention, constant stimulation, constant entertainment. Fortunately, Sophie constituted a one-youngster entertainment center all by herself. In an effort to keep up with her active older sister, Irina began pulling herself around the floor like a lizard when she was only six months old. Once mobile, she tore up and ate magazines, sucked on Nate's boots, and swallowed anything she could fit down her throat. Sophie delighted in reporting the latest naughty thing Irina had done. "Mama, Irina knocked down Daddy's umbrella and now she's all wet"; "Irina is eating a worm"; "Irina took her poopy diaper off and put poo-poo in her hair." Sophie reported each infraction with the utmost seriousness, but I could tell that underneath her deadpan reportage, Sophie was gleefully amused by her sister's misdeeds.

Sophie had been the kind of baby who watched conversations intently and patted everyone's face. Irina, on the other hand, took greater interest in her physical world, exploring every inch of it. She took things apart. She saw objects she had to have and screamed if not allowed to examine them. Like scissors. Oh, what a loud ruckus when Irina caught a glimpse of scissors, which of course would have gone straight into her mouth, so they remained out of her reach. She got into everything and required constant vigilance. I was convinced that she was a genius and boasted to everyone about her latest exploits. "You will never guess," I told Ida. "Irina took my pots out of the cupboard and stacked three of them by size."

Although he continued to help bring refugees out of Europe, Nate had not invited any to live with us since we had moved Yossel's family out. One night he asked me how I felt about taking in Jews coming out of Europe again. I told him that if I had been in Europe with my family, and we were able to escape, I would have hoped that someone would have helped my family out. It was the least that I could do for other Jews. So after Irina's first birthday, we agreed that we were ready to open our home again.

It was extremely difficult to smuggle Jews out of Europe at that time, and even more difficult to get them into America because of the quotas in place. Nevertheless, Ira managed to arrange to rescue people, and Big Nate, with his big heart, found homes for them (with some help from me), not just in our house but with others in our community. Nate had formed a committee at the synagogue the year before to raise funds to support Ira's rescue work and to assist the refugees when they arrived. By the time Irina was born, Nate had enlisted many other members of our congregation to help with these efforts.

Soon after our agreement to open our home again, Simcha and Anna and their four-year-old son came to live with us. Simcha had worked in a factory, and the owner of the factory had smuggled him to America with money Ira sent. At night, with the children safely in bed out of earshot, Simcha and Anna told horrifying stories of the Nazis and the death camps they had constructed in Europe. I wept, while Nate became incensed and resolved to work even harder to bring people out. Simcha knew of other families desperate to leave. Nate's committee activated the community to gather donations of clothing and household items to help the refugees start over in America. We continued to place families in individual homes. Nate spoke out everywhere he went to make people aware of the horrifying events taking place in Europe under the Nazi Occupation. Although it was difficult for me to discuss without succumbing to panic, I spoke as often as I could manage about my sisters in France and my brother who was fighting in the Resistance. Mr. Conrad sent Nate clippings of his articles published in his newspaper in Boston. He reported atrocities so unbelievable that readers accused him of writing propaganda. "I could not fabricate such terrible acts from my own imagination," Mr. Conrad wrote to Nate. "God help those who invented such inhumanity."

Simcha, Anna, and their son were living in one of our bedrooms; a single mother, Ray, and her two children (a boy and a girl) had moved into another one of the bedrooms; and two Hungarian brothers slept on the couches in Nate's den and the living room. The Hungarians were noisy and untidy, and after one of them made an unsolicited sexually charged overture to Ray, she began to wage a battle with him, criticizing everything he did. Although it was not my job to sort out their animosity, I did wish to have a harmonious home, so I tried to smooth things over, but with little success.

I had good days and bad days, like everyone else.

On a good day, my girls were fed their meals on time and Irina took a long nap, so I could get some housework done; Ray's children did not come home from school in tears; Simcha, who had a college degree in physics, managed to keep his job as a plumber's assistant despite his poor English; the rabbi brought over a used but serviceable pair of shoes for Ray; I roasted chickens for dinner, which put everyone in a jolly mood; and the Hungarians didn't leave dirty plates with ketchup and fried potatoes stuck to them on the floor of Nate's den where they had been listening to the radio until late at night.

On a bad day, Irina kept me up half the night because she was teething; I sent Anna to the store to buy bread, eggs, and vegetables for dinner, but she let her little boy carry the grocery bag home and he dropped the eggs and broke them; I left Irina and Sophie with Ray so that I could run to the bank and when I returned I tripped over a pair of boots that Nate had left lying near the front door and I fell and smacked my knee hard on the floor, Ray's little boy came home from school with his eyeglasses broken in half at the bridge and refused to tell us how it happened; one of the Hungarians had been offered a job (thank goodness) but he needed clean clothes to wear for his first day and while Ray was showing him how to work the washer and dryer they got into a huge shouting match because (she said) he leaned too close to her to peer inside the machine (Nate had to separate them).

So it went, one foot in front of the other, one day at a time, solving each problem as it arose. And many of the problems, such as buying a new pair of glasses or keeping bread in the house, cost money. Nate's business was still doing well, but we spent the money he earned as quickly as he earned it and could not save much. It did not help that the cost of providing papers and passage and paying off the proper authorities had gone beyond all reason. But who can measure the cost of human life? Romek took out a mortgage on the hardware store to provide funds for Ira to help Jews escape. Feeling worn-out became my normal state, and, haunted by the frightening stories of extreme inhumanity in Europe that the people I sheltered had shared with me, I often felt defeated.

Always, at the back of my mind, ached the knowledge that my sisters lived in the heart of danger, trying to protect their babies. What if they were dead and I would not know for many years? What if I had a niece hidden in France with no living family? How would I find her? If Miriam and Rivka were no longer on the farm in Crevecoeur, then where would I begin to look for them after the war? I wondered how long this war could last and if I could hang on to my sanity for the duration.

When I awoke as exhausted as when I went to sleep, it took all my strength to get out of bed and begin to do the myriad everyday chores that needed doing, the chores that took me away from my children, that prevented me from firing up my sewing machine and using my creativity. I had not done a catering job with Malka since before Sophie was born and Babushka had folded when America entered the war, even before food rationing began. I resented Nate for going off to his job in the morning and leaving me to juggle everything that needed to be done to run the household and help our houseguests start a new life in a strange land.

The world often seemed filled with more evil than good. And just when I thought I could not possibly take on one more responsibility, felt as though I could not wash one more dirty cup or arrange for one more visit to the dentist, I discovered I was pregnant again. I loved Sophie and Irina, but I didn't need any more children. Two was plenty, especially when I had so many other people to look after and we were on a tight budget. I thought I was being careful, but my cycles had become irregular from the fatigue. I didn't tell Nate about the baby at first. If I told him, then I would have to admit that it was true. But one night in bed, Nate asked, "How long has it been since you had your time of the month?"

"It has been a while," I answered.

"Is everything all right?" he asked.

"I'm not sick."

"Then?"

Silence. Nate waited.

"Yes. I'm pregnant again."

Nate stroked my hair as I lay on his chest listening to his breathing. When I finally looked up at him, he was grinning like the Cheshire cat.

"Oh, Nathan! This is a terrible time to have a baby. Look at the state of the world that we are bringing this child into. And we can't afford it.

We're exhausted. Our house is full of refugees. We don't have time for Sophie and Irina, let alone another one. How can you be so disgracefully happy about it?"

"I love being a daddy," he replied unabashedly.

"I don't know how I will manage this, I just don't know," I said, close to tears.

"You are the eighth wonder of the world, Ruth. Everyone says so. You'll be just fine," he reassured me.

"I'm not fine now," I disagreed, "and I'll be even more not fine with a new baby."

"I have complete faith in your ability to deal with everything that needs to be dealt with."

"That is so easy for you to say, but you don't really understand what dealing with everything means. You go off to work every day and I stay at home and take care of this house full of traumatized and needy people. I mediate and negotiate and arrange, and by the end of the day I can't stand up. Then you come home for dinner. How much can I do? How much? I take care of everyone else, but who takes care of me?"

"I do," Nate said, stroking my cheek. "I'm here. I'm in this with you."

"Then would you please help more with the work."

"Honey, I'm trying to earn enough money to support all of this, and that's not as easy as you seem to imagine. I can't just pop home in the middle of the day to sort out lunch. I'm the one who foots the bill. It's my daily work that puts food on the table for all of you."

"You may earn the money to buy the food, but I shop for it and prepare it and I am the one who puts it on the table."

"Our work, saving the people we can manage to save, is my contribution to the war effort. You know I can't enlist to fight."

"And I'm grateful for that," I murmured. "I truly am."

"So this is something I can do instead of sitting at home while others are dying. Do you really want me to stop helping Ira to rescue these people?" Nate asked. "All these people would most likely be dead by now if we hadn't helped them escape Europe."

"Help them escape, Nate. Make your contribution to the war effort. But have them live with someone else. We've done our share. Every bed in the inn is full and I have reached my limit. Having another child right now is more than I can handle." I didn't know how to make him understand how overwhelmed I felt. I didn't know how I was going to continue to manage our household.

"The war is exhausting for all of us, but it can't go on forever. It's a small sacrifice on our part to share our home and our wealth with these people to save their lives."

"Don't give me your fund-raising speech. Listen to me. I have reached my limit." I began to cry, and once I started I couldn't stop. Nate attempted to comfort me, but I was inconsolable. I put on my robe and went outside to the garden. It was crisp and cool; the moon lit up the yard with a sur-real blue-white light. I sat down next to my asparagus and wept for the ordinary life I was living and the extraordinary life I had wanted to have. I had come to America with dreams. Where had I gone off track? All I wanted was enough time to devote to raising my beautiful daughters and a little time to spare so that I could work at this thing that I loved, to have the chance to enjoy some small success at designing clothing. Perhaps it seemed frivolous in the context of the political events that dominated our lives, but it mattered to me. My life consisted of one long string of mun-dane chores. Nate seemed incapable of putting his shoes in the closet. He left them lying on the kitchen floor where he took them off. Why was it left to me to put them away? To put everything away?

I knew I shouldn't complain about our houseguests. As Nate pointed out, we were saving lives. And I did not begrudge these unfortunate peo-ple the safety of our home. But I felt as if my dreams were falling through my fingers like water. I wondered if I could pick up one more dirty dish without turning from the sink and running away. I yearned to break free and go to a quiet place where I could sit peacefully at the sewing machine for a full afternoon, sewing until the faintly orange glow of evening threw slanted shafts of light across the wall as the day drew to a close.

I sat on the back steps until my tempest had passed and I had calmed myself enough to return to bed. Nate's even breathing told me that he had fallen asleep. I didn't think he would ever understand what was miss-ing for me from my life. I turned my back to him and thought about that pattern of slanted shafts of light at day's end. Golden evening light. I imagined myself in a peaceful room, sewing, looking up and smiling as I saw the light from the sunset. Nate threw his arm across my waist in his sleep, but I barely noticed. I was in a quiet room at sunset, sewing.

ELEVEN

Rivka

 "THE THIRD BIRTHDAY IS important because it's the first one a child might remember," Miriam said, and for this reason she insisted on throwing a party for Shayna. She invited the whole village. Everyone brought food to share and Miriam made a huge chocolate cake with fresh whipped cream. When I arrived, the trees quivered with Miriam's children as usual, but no fruit was in season that late in the fall. "What are you doing up there?" I called to them.

"We can see forever," a voice sang out.

"We can see past the war," another voice piped up.

I imagined those little hands and feet climbing into the sky to embrace the spirits of their lost parents, the children springing from the trees, finding their mothers and fathers, and then floating back down to Miriam's orchard.

Robert met me on the driveway.

"There's no fruit to harvest this late in the fall, but there they are," I commented.

"We only grow children in the trees at this time of year," Robert said with a chuckle.

Shayna let go of my skirt and broke into a run, shrieking with delight, "Look, Maman, a pony cart!" Miriam had decorated a donkey and a little cart with flowers and fabric, and the youngest children were taking rides around the yard in it.

We ate splendidly and I even drank a couple of glasses of wine. Miriam and I sang Russian songs from our youth while our French friends clapped along, goading us on. The villagers danced and sang drinking songs, of which they had an endless supply. I danced. Catherine danced. The children danced. Shayna made a spectacle of herself as she whirled and twirled and never fell down dizzy.

"Look at her," Catherine said, "she's a natural."

Robert had whittled an adorable giraffe out of beech wood for Shayna, and Father Charles gave her a real picture book from Russia. Trust a priest to produce a small miracle. Miriam gave Shayna a handmade dress with plump maroon quilted cherries on it.

Long after the children fell asleep in a heap in the beds upstairs, we adults continued to sing, converse, eat, and drink as we gathered around a bonfire. On the other side of midnight, as the festivities wound down, Miriam put her arm around my waist.

"We've done well under the circumstances, haven't we?"

"We have," I replied. We gazed up at the full moon together, and for a brief moment I felt at peace.

"If anything should happen to me, promise that you'll keep the children safe and take care of the orchards," Miriam said, shattering my moment of respite.

"What on earth does that mean?"

"I'm pregnant again, and lately I have episodes of foreboding that seize me at odd times, when I am least prepared to cope with them."

"You'll be fine," I reassured her. "You were made for childbearing." Perhaps she couldn't shake the memory of how Babette had died.

"I sometimes wake in the middle of the night in a panic."

"It's the war, the children, and now this pregnancy. You do so much." Miriam rubbed her forehead with her thumb and forefinger.

"Get more rest. Accept more help when it's offered," I pleaded.

"I'll try."

"Thank you for making this extraordinary birthday for Shayna."

"Shayna is an extraordinary child. So are they all. I am lucky to have the privilege of having these children in my life."

When we parted, Miriam laid her hands on my head and then ran them down to my shoulders, looked deeply into my eyes, then ran her hands down my arms and held my hands hard in a vaguely ritualistic series of gestures. "My sister, my friend, we are blessed," she said.

"We truly are blessed," I said.

Miriam turned and walked into her house.

A week later, the Gestapo arrived and set up a field office in Crevecoeur that we were told was temporary. We went about our business silently and quickly, heads bowed, praying for them to leave without incident. They systematically searched the forests surrounding the village and every barn, looking for members of the Resistance. They questioned those of us working in the de la Reine vineyards. They asked me who I was and where I lived. I responded with my best Crevecoeur dialect. I gave my alias and information about the bogus identity that Father Charles had invented for me. I prayed silently. I did not even know to whom I was praying, but the prayer unfolded on its own volition in my mind. That night Catherine and I sat late by the fire. I could not sleep. I was gripped by a cold terror.

In the morning the Gestapo had departed, taking with them Miriam, Robert, their children, and Father Charles.

According to Robert's field hands, the Nazis came to the farm after midnight, woke the children at gunpoint, tore them from their beds, and put them in the back of a truck with Robert and Miriam. Renée blocked the door and screamed at the soldiers. They shot her. Father Charles was already in the truck when it arrived. They could hear him reciting psalms aloud. The field hands watched in helpless terror from the shadows. They were outnumbered by Nazi soldiers with guns. If they had interfered, they would have been killed or seized.

No one knew where they took Miriam and Robert. No word came. With Father Charles gone, our link to the Resistance vanished. The village was left with no knowledge of what would happen to those who had disappeared and no knowledge of how the Nazis had discovered the orphanage. Had they uncovered Miriam's true identity? The identities of the children she harbored?

A numbness filled my soul. My body continued to function in its usual ways while my thoughts traveled to memories of my childhood, my life in Paris, and Miriam's family on the farm. I stumbled over my words and found it difficult to remember my French; only Yiddish came to me. I did not want to get out of bed. I heard Shayna ask Catherine, "What is wrong with Maman?"

"She feels sad because the war does not end," Catherine explained.

Over and over I recalled my last conversation with Miriam on the night of Shayna's party. I clung to the memory of the last time I had seen Miriam as she disappeared into her house so quietly under the full moon. I finally understood with agonizing clarity what my mother had suffered, the knowledge that those you loved most in the world were in constant danger and you had no power to protect them. And I could see why my father yearned for a Jewish homeland, governed by Jews, where we would be safe at last, our children protected from harm.

After remaining in bed for three days, I rose and returned to the vineyards. I craved the mindless work that exhausted me so that I could plummet down the deep well of sleep at night. Only in sleep could I escape my fear for the lives of Miriam, Robert, the children, and Father Charles. After a week of working like a mad bull, I got up in the middle of the night and walked all the way to Miriam's house. Catherine found me there at daybreak, making the beds, washing the clothes, cleaning up the mess the Gestapo had left behind. She had asked a neighbor to watch the girls and had gone looking for me. Without a word, she joined me, and the two of us worked silently side by side as we folded children's shirts and put them away in the drawers, swept the floors, picked up toys, set Robert's boots by the front door.

Robert's field hands stood watch around the property while we were there and would have told us if anyone approached, but no one did. For the time being, the Gestapo had caught their prey and were apparently no longer prowling.

As I cleaned up the house, I remembered Miriam and Ruth bowing their heads together on the back steps of our house in Palestine while they played with paper dolls, changing their outfits, coloring dresses and hats and cutting them out, while Avram sat in a wicker chair under the fig tree, reading a thick book, and Benjy perched on a wooden bench so he could reach the little outdoor table, where I helped him chop and mold play dough Mama had made from flour, water, and salt. I heard Papa's voice in my head, calling us to come wash up for dinner. "Give me a minute to cut out this hat," Miriam called back.

Catherine and I closed up the house together as best we could, not knowing how long it might be before someone lived in it again. Perhaps we took a risk doing so, but it was a risk I needed to take.

I returned to the house a few days later. I could not stay away. I wandered through the rooms, saying the children's names aloud, stroking their pillows, picking up their toys, and putting them down. Then I took the pruning shears from the shelf in the kitchen and went into Miriam's orchards. I could almost hear the gleeful shouts of the children who had so often swung from these trees. I began to snip back branches. But before long, one of Robert's field hands found me among the cherry trees.

"It is too dangerous for you to be here, Madame," he warned me anxiously.

"But Miriam's trees. I promised her I would take care of the orchard if anything, if she . . ." My voice faltered.

"Do not worry, Madame, we will tend to it," he told me gently.

Catherine was not so gentle. "Enough. You have to stop going to that house. If the Nazis find you there, they will capture you as well."

"I don't much care," I snapped.

"You have to care. You have a daughter to raise. She lives. Your husband is counting on you to survive."

For the first time, I caught myself wondering if survival was a good thing.

The third anniversary of Akiva's birth arrived in January and on that day I came to a complete standstill. I stayed in my bed in a darkened room with the shutters drawn. I remembered our conversation over the cherries, when Miriam said she wanted others to say of her that she was someone who was grateful for her blessings. She would certainly be remembered as such a person. And I wept. Miriam would have wanted me to keep hoping, to keep counting my blessings. She would have wanted me to fill Shayna's childhood with as much of that enchantment she had spoken about as possible, just as she had tried to do for her children. So I rose from my bed and went to work and when I came home on Akiva's third birthday, I played with Isabel and Shayna. I sang songs with them and read stories and played finger games.

After we put the girls to bed, Catherine made a pot of tea and we sat by the fire.

"Today is Akiva's third birthday," I said as I stared into the glowing embers.

Catherine nodded. "I know it."

"I dread hearing news," I said.

"They might be back," Catherine responded.

I could not remain so hopeful, perhaps because I was my mother's daughter, and painfully aware of the tragedies that were visited on our people without a thought by those who sought to destroy us.

During the first flutter of spring, I looked up early one morning to see the sun burning fire-gold just above the treetops, as if bent on setting them aflame. The air smelled fresh; the land smelled clean. We had just spent two weeks rewiring the lower vineyard with shiny new copper wire, and as the sun rose over the hill, it caught the waves of twisted copper in its glow, so that I looked out upon a field of glinting metal. I remembered Miriam's alleged sighting of garden sprites from our childhood and imagined that elves had planted some otherworldly fruit in the vineyards that gleamed with an unearthly glimmer. For a fleeting moment I succumbed to an unexpected rush of delight in the presence of beauty.

Then I saw him, a lone man, on the edge of the field adjoining the vineyard, with his back against the rising sun. A silhouette that looked familiar. I was certain he had come for me. I turned to Nicole, pointed to the figure, and said, "I think I have a visitor. Let the others know where I have gone."

He stood still and waited for me to approach. As I drew nearer, the familiarity of the man resolved itself into Avram, and I went to meet him on leaden feet. I did not want to know. When I stood before him, he reached out and took both my hands in his. He turned my palms up, then turned them down, then turned them up again. My hands were filthy and rough to the touch. Only after he had examined my hands did he look into my face.

"I hate to see your hands like this. This is a waste. You should be using that mind of yours for something useful."

"I have been teaching the villagers to read," I told him. Avram looked much the same physically, but his eyes, those doorways to the soul, betrayed him. His spirit was damaged. I could see it. I didn't want him to speak because I wanted to savor for just a moment the fact that at least he was still alive. I was grateful for that miracle. So I clenched him to me in a fierce hug and would not let him go. Like a warrior warding off danger, I encircled him in the iron fortress of my protective arms.

"Rivka, Rivka, Rivka."

"It is you," I replied.

"Yes, it is."

"Avram." At last I released him. "Come, I will make you a cup of tea." I began to turn, but Avram took my arm, looked into my eyes, changed my life forever.

"They are all dead. Miriam, Robert, the children."

My legs went weak and I could not breathe. I collapsed on the ground abruptly. "I already knew. I knew when I felt the world become smaller." I had been fighting this feeling ever since they had disappeared, but I knew it was true. My dread had been more than dread; it had been the sense that they were lost.

Avram sat next to me. "I must tell you what happened. Forgive me. I must tell," Avram pleaded.

"I'm listening," I whispered, although truly I did not want to hear. Not now. Not ever.

"This is the story Robert told me," Avram began.

"Robert? You saw him alive?"

"Let me tell you from the beginning. As Robert told me. He never learned who informed on them or how the Nazis discovered the orphanage. But the Nazis did discover it and they were furious that the children of Resistance fighters and Jews lived untouched right under their noses. They uncovered Miriam's Jewish identity. It incensed them that Robert, a Christian, with land, had chosen to marry a Jewess.

"The family was taken to a Nazi way station not far from Crevecoeur that first night. What became of Father Charles remains a mystery, as he was separated from the others there. The Nazis believed that Miriam knew the whereabouts of Resistance fighters since she cared for their children. After traveling for the entire next day in an open truck, she, Robert, and the children were taken to a prison. When the truck arrived, the children were thirsty, hungry, exhausted, and terrified. The family was thrown into a cell together. Then the Nazis took one child at a time away from Miriam over a period of two days. They started with the oldest and worked their way down. Miriam and the remaining children grew increasingly hysterical with horror, grief, and fright. Each time they came for another child, they asked Miriam to give names and locations of Resistance fighters. She could have given them you, I suppose, but it would have made no difference, and of course she never would. She rattled off anything she could make up, because she knew nothing to tell. And of course nothing she said made any sense, so they thought she was lying.

"For two days the family was gradually murdered. They pried Miriam's children from her arms, one by one, until, finally, they took the last, her own Akiva. Then Miriam and Robert were left alone in their cell for maybe a day or more. Robert could not recall how long. Miriam curled into the fetal position in a corner and did not move.

"When the Nazis returned, Robert beat at them with his fists, but his outrage was nothing more to them than an annoyance. They led the couple into a concrete room, where they had neatly lined up the naked bodies on the floor. They forced Miriam to look at the marks of torture on her murdered children. She could not walk. They dragged her. All her beloved little ones dead, with the blood from their wounds not yet dry, with the scars of their suffering crying out to her. What monsters could do such a thing? And finally, at the last, they came to Akiva, her own flesh and blood. One of his feet was missing. Miriam asked, 'What have you done with my baby's shoe? He had two shoes, my Akiva.' It was the last thing Robert ever heard her say."

"Please, no more," I sobbed, rocking back and forth on the ground and covering my ears.

"If I am killed, someone must know what happened. Someone has to know and live to tell it. To give testimony. You must bear witness. You must listen." So Avram continued. "Miriam went into a coma. They could not revive her, not even with electric shock. As Robert described it, her spirit simply left her body and went to the children. She had flown beyond the grasp of her persecutors. The last time Robert saw her, they took him to an infirmary room in a bizarre sort of hospital where Miriam lay in a tangle of plastic tubing. The 'doctors' were keeping her body alive. Robert could see that they wanted to keep torturing her but she had disappeared from the corporeal world. They commanded Robert to speak to her. He said her name, but not as a call to consciousness. He said her name as a farewell. She eluded their revival efforts. She shut down and willed herself dead. After she died, they released Robert in a village in the east of France where he knew no one. He was there for several months before I found him. He was in tatters, virtually unable to walk, and suffering from uncontrollable tremors. His hair had gone white. The village folk knew something terrible had happened to him and they fed him so he wouldn't starve and gave him shelter during the nights. I had looked hard, with the help of the Resistance network, to find him. After he told me all of this, he begged me to take pity on him and shoot him. He said he did not have the courage to commit suicide, but I think he simply respected the sanctity of life too much to take any life, even his own. After all, he was a Catholic. He was dead in every way except that his heart was still beating. His suffering was greater than any I have yet seen, and I have seen suffering, believe me. I honored his request."

By the time Avram had completed his account, we were flat on our backs next to one another and staring up into a blue sky so cheerful that it seemed to mock our grief. "You shot him?"

"And I buried him. And I marked his grave."

We said nothing for a long time. I listened to the birds calling to one another and felt the dampness of the surrounding grasses on my cheeks. Or perhaps it was my tears.

"What kind of human being can justify visiting such horror on children?"

"Are they human?" Avram replied. "Do they qualify as human?"

I trembled as I asked, "There is more, isn't there?" For Avram had come alone.

"No, that is all of it. The end." Avram clenched his jaw.

"No, I mean there is more news," I whispered. "They came here looking. I think they were looking for him, looking for me and the baby so they could bring him in on the hook of our capture."

Avram took my hand in his and I waited for the axe to fall.

"They won't come looking for Yakov anymore. They captured him last week while I was with Robert. If I had been there, maybe I could have prevented it. They took him to Auschwitz."

I had been prepared to lose Miriam, but Yakov? My Yakov? No, not my husband too. It was more than I could bear. "Do you know anyone who has ever come out of Auschwitz? They say that no one comes out of there. But maybe he will survive." I shivered and my teeth chattered despite the warmth of the sun on my face.

"I promised you I would protect him and that I would bring him back to you. I failed." Avram covered his face with his hands.

"You are not to blame. You must believe that."

He wrapped his arms around me in an effort to still my trembling.

"He only saw his daughter once," I wept.

"Be proud of him, Rivka," Avram said. "And when she is old enough to understand, tell his daughter to be proud. I would not know where to begin to tell you all he has done. Everyone who knew him, who came in contact with him, fought with him, was inspired by the flame that burned in him. The dreams we had when we were young, all the ideals: he kept them. In the midst of this insanity, he kept them. He never lost hope, never lost faith. He always believed that it was possible to build a country on those ideals. We just needed to get out of this mess first. Somehow, he never lost hope."

Avram held me through the late morning and we reminisced about our childhood, sharing remembrances about distant or dead loved ones. He told me stories about the things Yakov had done for the Resistance, like the time he engineered the derailment of an entire train of supplies, including food, releasing a train car full of pigs into the night. I described for him the life Miriam had made for her children on the farm. We wept and whispered and finally we slept. I woke to the blinding light of late afternoon and lay in the field for a long time, feeling the weight of my new grief settle on me like a stone too heavy to roll from my heart. I did not have the strength to stand.

As Avram slept, I wished myself transported to the future, past the duration of the war, to a place and time when I had grown accustomed to the tragedy of this moment and could live with it tucked away in a back passageway of my soul. In the distance I heard the crew finishing up in the vineyards for the day. Friends would worry and I knew I should go home to Catherine's, to care for my daughter, but I did not have the strength to move. I wondered how long Avram had gone without sleep. When he woke, the vineyards and fields were silent. He stroked my arm.

"I must go," he said.

"Please come have something to eat first," I begged. I had lost the feeling in my left leg and Avram had to haul me up off the ground. I limped badly, leaning heavily on him. We made our way slowly to Catherine's house. Soon I would have to tell Miriam's story to the villagers of Crevecoeur, who prayed for her safety daily and lit candles in the empty church. I did not relish the thought of being the one to break their hearts with this news.

When Catherine met us at the door, I told her right off, "Miriam, Robert, and the children are dead and Yakov is in Auschwitz. We must find something for Avram to eat quickly because he cannot stay."

Catherine made tea and set food on the table, crying softly. The girls wanted to play with us and tugged at my hands, begging for a song or a story. They were curious about Avram, and Shayna asked him if he had ever eaten a duck's egg. She had recently become fascinated by our neighbor's ducks. Avram told her that he had eaten duck eggs and asked her if she liked them. She replied with an emphatic yes. I read the girls a few stories so that they would leave Avram and Catherine to talk while Avram ate the simple meal that she had prepared.

I had taught the girls my mother's Russian lullaby about the lulling sound of the river, and I asked them to sing it for Avram before he left. I insisted on accompanying him to the edge of the forest, even though my leg was still not functioning right.

"Where are you going from here?" I asked.

"Better that you shouldn't know," Avram said.

I thought to myself that ignorance had not helped Miriam in the end.

"Now you must survive for all of us. To tell the world what happened here," he said.

But I resolved to tell as little as possible of the gruesome events. Perhaps the telling of it had been Avram's albatross, but it would not be mine. "You might make it through this war yet. Then you can tell your own story," I said.

Avram's voice became husky with emotion. "If I survive, and Yakov does not, I will come back for you and Shayna, if you will have me."

"Dear Avram," I said. "I will be here waiting for you." Avram grasped my shoulders and kissed me, fiercely, hungrily, full on the lips. Then he tore himself from my embrace and disappeared into the forest. I resisted imagining Yakov dead. I had to help him stay alive by keeping him alive in my thoughts. And to imagine both Yakov and Avram dead would be more than I could stand, especially now that Miriam was gone. "Take care of yourself, my love," I whispered after Avram.

That night, I overheard Catherine speaking to the girls as she tucked them into bed.

"Why are you crying so much tonight, Maman?" Isabel asked.

"Because I have heard that some good friends and many lovely children have died in the war," Catherine answered.

I held my breath, because the girls knew all the children who had died, but Catherine did not tell them who they were.

"Were the children three years old like us?" Shayna asked in a tremulous voice.

"Two of them were almost three years old," Catherine answered. "They have gone to Jesus. He will care for them now," she assured the children. Later, she apologized to me for saying such a thing to a Jewish child. She said she knew it was improper, but that saying it gave her comfort. I assured her that it was not at all improper in my opinion.

I could not bring myself to repeat the horrifying details of Miriam's death, so I told the villagers an abridged version of the story, which was difficult enough to relate. My leg, which had lost all feeling on that morning when Avram came to me with his news, never recovered. I continued to limp and was forced to favor my good right leg. Perhaps I had experienced some type of mini-stroke. I interpreted it as a sign that I was unable to stand on my own two feet without Miriam. Perhaps if something happened to Ruth in distant America, I would know because my legs would go out from under me completely. I was almost grateful that I could not write to Mama so that she could go on thinking that Miriam was alive, at least for the time being.

Every night, as I lay alone in my bed, I despaired of ever seeing Yakov again and tried unsuccessfully to put the thought that he might be dead from my mind. I often wept until I fell into blessed sleep. Then every morning when I woke, I hoped anew that he lived and I carried an image of him whole and well in my mind. I often thought that the Occupation would never end, that I should make an effort to escape from France because it would belong to the Nazis for the rest of my lifetime. But then I remembered my promise to Avram. And what if my Yakov survived and came looking for me and Shayna in Crevecoeur? I had to stay.

When summer arrived, the orchards and fields burst with flower and fruit, as if mocking our grief. Miriam's fruit trees ripened and became heavy with their luscious burden; Madame de la Reine sent a couple of men to gather some of the peaches and cherries, which she distributed to the villagers. I could not bite into even a single cherry without weeping. Only a fraction of Miriam's fruit was harvested and the rest was picked off by birds and animals or fell to the ground and rotted. I felt as if I had betrayed her by failing to ensure that all the fruit was eaten or preserved.

When Shayna turned four, we made her a cake. There was no pony cart, flowers, or bonfire. She had been a talkative toddler, but now she said little. I missed her constant questions and blamed myself for the change in the child. She was sensitive and had certainly absorbed some measure of my grief. I wished that I could muster more enthusiasm about life for her sake. I continued to make up stories for her and Isabel, although I struggled to keep the characters safe and free of worry. The one activity that lit up Shayna and Isabel was dancing. Catherine and I would sing and clap while our girls danced. Although our singing didn't have the verve of happier times, it sufficed for the children. Catherine declared that Shayna would become a professional dancer. Once, when she told Shayna, "I think you will be a dancer when you grow up," Shayna replied, "I'm a dancer now." Her reply brought a rare smile to my lips. If not for my little dancer, I do not think I would have survived the war. Her delight in the smallest wonders of our existence, her naïve and imaginative questions about the natural world, and her unconditional love for me, Catherine, and Isabel kept me going from one day to the next.

TWELVE

Ruth

I SUCCUMBED TO CHAOS. I would look around the house and see that things were not in order and nothing was done properly, but I did not have the time or energy to fix it. Papers piled up on the counter (where did they all come from?) and would have to be sifted through to ensure that nothing important was buried or discarded. A mound of footwear lay in the front entranceway. Dust gathered on the pictures hanging on the walls. The only one I dusted religiously week after week was the painting of the Chinese lady. Most of our coffee cups had broken and I had not replaced them, instead using glasses and jelly jars for coffee or tea. The carpets seemed to never be completely vacuumed, and they needed to be professionally cleaned, but we didn't have the money for it. The blinds should have been washed, the front door repainted, and the kitchen table sanded and refinished. The doorknob to the pantry was loose and usually fell off in my hand. Once when it happened I sat down in the breakfast nook and cried.

I left more and more things up to the refugees to figure out for themselves, and so the refugees either managed to do them without my help or these things didn't happen. Towels were washed or they weren't. People enrolled in night school or they didn't. Job interviews and trips to the doctor were the highest priority, but beyond that I no longer felt obligated to transport everyone wherever they needed to go. Instead I provided an endless supply of bus maps and train schedules, which I stacked on the sideboard. Fortunately the Hungarian brothers had moved out, which made for a less volatile dynamic in the household.

Nate assured me the war would end soon and then our lives would be easier. The Nazis were capitulating to the Americans on all fronts. I tried to imagine what my life would be like when the war ended, but it was an abstract concept. The war robbed me of the joy I should have experienced during my third pregnancy. Even Nate, usually so optimistic, was increasingly reserved and serious as the war dragged on. Much as I tried, I could not help myself from resenting him when he sat down in the evening to read the paper while I managed the tasks necessary to put dinner on the table, clean up afterward, and settle the house for the night. My resentment came between us and I felt distant toward him. I'm sure that the fact that we did not see that much of each other contributed to our decreased intimacy. He worked long hours and came home tired. I went to sleep as early as I could most nights because my days began early.

Four-year-old Sophie had become my constant and most reassuring companion. I caught myself speaking with her as I might with a friend my own age. She was an observant child and often asked me questions about my interactions with others that revealed her ability to perceive the real conversations underneath the spoken conversations. Once, leaving Ida's house, I found myself asking her, "Do you think Ida is angry with me about something?"

Sophie replied, "No, she's just worried because Gary's not feeling well." And I was reminded of what an intelligent soul had been delivered into my care.

I often consulted with Sophie about what to make for dinner. "Pea soup or cabbage soup today, Sophie?"

"Pea soup, Mama; it's fatter." And I smiled. Pea soup was a heartier soup, a good choice for a cold winter day. I often made soup for dinner. It was inexpensive and filling and stretched to serve our large household. Soup and baked potatoes. Soup and large chunks of homemade bread. Soup and rice. On the Sabbath, chicken soup.

Occasionally I would feel myself plummeting into a pit of exhaustion and then I would ask Ida or Ray, who was still living with us, to watch the children so that I could crawl into bed in the middle of the day and take a nap. Once, I bought a fashion magazine, sent Sophie off to the park with Ida and her boys, put Irina down for a nap, and locked myself in my bedroom for a whole hour and perused that magazine full of glossy photographs. While on the one hand I realized with regret how out of touch I had become with the latest styles, on the other I thoroughly enjoyed imagining what sorts of hats I would have made to go with the dresses I saw in the magazine. I felt decadent for indulging myself in this way when I shared my roof with so many others who had lost everything when they had been exiled to America.

In August, as my due date approached, it seemed to me as if our entire motley household held its breath waiting for our baby. Because Irina had been a Caesarian, I did not need to convince my doctor to perform another one. We scheduled the delivery and fortunately I did not go into labor before the day arrived. When I regained consciousness from the Caesarian, I did not see any baby in sight and had to ask the attending recovery room nurse where the baby was. She sent someone to find my missing "bundle of joy." The nurses soon discovered that Big Nate had taken possession of our baby and he was in the neonatal nursery where he was showing off his new offspring to everyone (whether he knew them or not) who appeared on the other side of the glass partition that ran the length of the wall. By the time he was located and steered in my direction, I was settled in a hospital room.

"She's a perfect girl. A ten!" he exclaimed as he bounded in the door with our newest daughter in his arms. We seemed to be practiced at the art of producing girls. It would have been nice to have a boy, but I was grateful for a healthy girl. I could see that Nate had fallen in love with our daughter already. His boyish excitement made me laugh. What a dear, devoted father. I felt a rush of affection and greeted it like a long-lost friend as I was reminded of why I had married this man in the first place. Nate wanted to name the baby Sarah, and I thought it was a beautiful name.

When Sarah and I came home from the hospital, Nate took a week off work to look after "his girls." In the greater scheme of things, a week didn't amount to much. But for Nate this was a grand gesture of his care and concern and I accepted his attention graciously. After the week, he went back to work and I was left with three children under the age of five, including a newborn, and the same house full of refugees.

Fortunately, Sarah was an easy baby. Fascinated by the constant stream of activity in our busy household, she especially loved to study the older children, following their every movement with her large, luminous eyes. Irina was surprisingly gentle with Sarah; surprising because Irina was a wild one and gentle was not ordinarily in her repertoire. She would do somersaults and other tricks for Sarah, who played her role as the captive audience magnificently. As Sophie and Irina vied for Sarah's attention, they began to fight with one another more and more frequently. This new level of sibling rivalry challenged me daily. I found myself screaming at my darling little girls and then feeling terrible remorse afterward.

I could not shake the sense of despair that descended on me whenever I thought about how long it had been since I had communicated with Rivka, Miriam, or Avram. At unexpected moments I would find myself overcome with a feeling of panic, so that I could barely breathe and my heart raced. What if I lost all of them in Europe the way the people in my house had lost their families, friends, and entire communities? I wrote to Mama and Papa with stories about my children and avoided discussing our family in France. I was sure that Mama was as worried as I, and I did not want to add to her worry. But I constantly wondered who was providing safe harbor for my family while I was harboring these people who slept in my home and ate at my table.

And then the most astonishing thing happened. The war ended. Just like that.

Everything changed.

The small flame of hope flared and roared to life.

THIRTEEN

Rivka

WHEN THE AMERICANS HAD entered the war, a surge of optimism had rippled through Crevecoeur. But then nothing tangible came of it for us. So when we began to receive news that the Allied forces were defeating the Nazis, we were afraid to believe it at first. Then, as if a gate had opened and we had shot through, we dared to hope that the war might end and that France would one day again belong to us. I both dreaded and longed for the definitive news about Yakov that an end to the war would bring.

On a dewy spring-green morning, I looked up from my work to see Madame de la Reine in her buggy at the end of the row of vines. She waved her arms like a flapping raven and shouted. We could not hear her words, but ignited by her excitement, we left our work and hurried to meet her. I limped on my bad leg as others ran ahead. Before I reached the buggy, I saw my co-workers dancing and hugging each other. "The war is over!" they called to me and to one another.

"How do you know?" I questioned Madame de la Reine. "Are you sure?"

"Absolutely," she answered. "Hitler is dead. The Americans have begun to liberate the prisoners from the concentration camps in Germany."

I remembered Miriam saying that she hoped that one day she would look up from her mending and tending and the war would be over. I would have to look up for both of us. I should have been more excited, but I felt only terribly weak.

The very next day, three men who had left the Resistance to return home traveled through Crevecoeur. They were followed by more wayfarers who wandered through the village on the way back to their homes and the lives that had been interrupted by the war. Every time someone straggled through, the villagers fed them, offered them a bed for the night, and questioned them about people who had left years ago to fight in the Resistance. It became increasingly difficult for me to concentrate on the work in the vineyards, to which I had committed myself for the duration of the war. I wanted to leave and look for Avram and Yakov, but that was not practical. They knew where to find me and I had no idea how to find them.

The dismal twilight that had fallen over the village lifted and a new spirit filled people. Everything mattered again. The village children were drunk with excitement. They ran through the streets singing and ringing bells. Many of them, like Shayna and Isabel, could not remember a time of peace. They had so much to try to understand.

I wanted to write to Ruth as well as the family in Palestine to let them know that I had survived, but I couldn't think of how to frame the words to tell them about Miriam; and I had no news to convey about Avram or Yakov yet. How could I possibly deliver the blow to Meir that his daughter and grandson had perished? My heart broke again whenever I imagined him, Mama, and Papa reading such a letter. The postal service was in a bit of a shambles anyway, so I had a brief reprieve. But after a week of agonizing about how to write to them about Miriam's death, I drafted letters to Mama and Ruth, included Catherine's address, and sent the dreadful words on their way. About Miriam, I wrote only that she and her son were killed and provided few of the gruesome details. I promised to write again the moment I knew about Yakov and Avram.

One evening I came home and opened the door to find a man standing by the fireplace. At first my heart leapt up with the hope that it was Yakov, but then I realized that I did not recognize him. Catherine introduced him as Babette's husband, Christian. He had survived and returned to discover the enormity of his loss. He was a handsome man, with straight, sandy-brown hair and wide-set green eyes. He had farmer's hands, his spatulate fingertips lined with callused creases. He had risked everything to join the Resistance, and he had lost it all. I remembered his children well, especially the baby whom Miriam had nursed at her breast. I recognized the children's features in Christian's face, an eerie glimpse of how they might have looked had they lived to adulthood.

By the time I arrived, Christian had already told Catherine that her husband had died early on in the Occupation. Catherine accepted the finality of it with grim resignation. She had already spent five years virtually widowed. "I have a lot of practice at being a widow," she told me, bitterly. "And to think that I spent all those years lighting candles in the church and praying for the safety of a dead man."

We fed Christian and invited him to sleep in our house so that he would not have to return alone just yet to the house he and Babette had shared with their children. After we put the girls to bed, we sat up late at the kitchen table telling Christian as many stories as we could remember about his children and how happy they had been during their years with Miriam and Robert on the farm. In the morning, Christian played with the girls while Catherine made breakfast. Watching him with our daughters was bittersweet; I was glad for his survival but could not turn my thoughts away from all that he had lost. He had brought us a pound of good coffee, which we had not had in a long time. The first sip was so delicious that it tasted like it had music in it.

As Catherine placed bowls of oatmeal in front of each of us around the table, Christian asked me, "What will you do now that the war is over?" I heard Catherine's sharp intake of breath as she anticipated my answer.

"I'll stay here with Catherine until they finish liberating the camps, or until I lose hope, whichever comes first," I said. "My husband was in Auschwitz. If he survived, he will look for me here. And there is my brother, Avram, who fought with the Resistance and who may still live."

It would be difficult to leave Crevecoeur with or without Yakov. But I was not a farmer. I longed to return to the city. Perhaps I would be able to enroll in college eventually. And I had to think of my daughter, who would have many more opportunities in her life in Paris than in a little rural village. I didn't mind if I never saw a vineyard again. Well, maybe once or twice, in the early morning mist, when the earth smelled as fresh as the first day of creation.

Christian returned to his caretaker's house on Robert's land. Since Robert's family line ended with the deaths of Robert and his son, Christian took over the land and began the work of bringing it back into service. No one protested. Christian had a reputation as a good farmer and would put the land to good use. He joined us for dinner most nights. Isabel had stubbornly decided that he was her father returned from the war. Catherine didn't have the heart to argue with her about it. If the fabrication eased the child's loss, then so be it, let her make up stories. Stories had helped us grope our way through the darkness of the war, and stories would carry us into the future.

One evening, a couple of weeks after Christian's return, as we sat at the table together, there was a knock at the door. When Catherine opened it, Avram stood in the doorway. Invincible Avram! I flung myself into his arms. And then, behind him, I saw another man, a man of skin and bones with enormous eyes and close-cropped hair. I recognized his hands first, and with a gasp, as if the life had left me and then returned in a fraction of a second, I flew to him. I clung to his bony frame and wept, rendered speechless in all six of the languages I spoke. Yakov had defied his persecutors, kept his promise, and returned to my arms. Hitler had failed and my Yakov had triumphed. He had come out of Auschwitz alive. I remembered that American magician, Houdini, who could escape from any entanglement, who had promised that if it were possible to return from the dead, then he would do so. Yakov was my Houdini.

Shayna tugged Catherine's skirt. "Is that my papa?" she asked shyly.

"Yes, sweet one, that's your papa."

"What happened to his eyes?" she asked.

Catherine kneeled down nearer to the child, puzzled. "What do you mean?"

"There is something wrong with my papa's eyes," Shayna insisted.

"He has seen terrible things and it will take time for the reflection of them to leave his eyes," Avram said. He understood completely what my four-year-old saw when she looked into the haunted eyes of her father.

I released my husband and went to Avram, embracing him, clinging to his neck and sobbing. How could I have been so blessed as to have both of them return to me alive when so many others had suffered such enormous losses?

Yakov sat in a chair and beckoned to Shayna to approach him. He took her hand in his.

"Did you really make my dolly for me when I was a baby and you were away in the war?" she asked.

"I did," Yakov answered brightly, "and I would have sent you more things if I wasn't so busy fighting."

"That's my papa," Isabel piped up, pointing to Christian. "He was fighting in the war too."

Catherine started to say something but Christian put a restraining hand on her arm. He scooped Isabel up and tickled her under the arms until she laughed. Yakov began to laugh at the sight of them and then broke off in a fit of coughing.

"He needs a doctor," Avram said.

"Are you hungry?" I asked. Other than softly repeating his name as I clung to Yakov, and then repeating Avram's name as I clung to him, these were the first words I was able to draw up out of the pool of my relief and gratitude.

"Starved," Yakov said.

As Catherine and I brought plates and utensils to the table for the men, Shayna and Isabel decided that they must sing a song for Shayna's papa and uncle. "On a wagon . . ." they began singing, in their squeaky voices.

"Music of the angels," Yakov told them as he applauded. After dinner, Catherine took the girls to get them ready for bed. Once the little ones had gone, I introduced Christian properly, as Babette's husband, father of the children Miriam had fostered.

Although weak, Yakov remained animated and in good spirits. Avram, on the other hand, appeared to have lost all mirth. He twice attempted to shift the conversation to the liberation of the death camps and each time Yakov swiftly changed the subject. Christian shared with us news about the new work of rebuilding France. Yakov warmed much more readily to this topic. Meanwhile, I thought back to the evenings Catherine and I had sat in this kitchen, drinking tea and imagining this moment, or rather imagining the return of our husbands. The absence of Catherine's husband made me feel all the more grateful for my good fortune.

When Catherine suggested that she prepare a bed for Avram on her couch (assuming of course that Yakov would share my bed), Yakov asked

Christian if they could sleep in his barn. "We are filthy," he explained. "We have traveled a long way without stopping. We need to bathe before we will be fit to sleep indoors."

I was surprised and a little hurt by this, yet somewhat relieved as well. Even though having him return was glorious, it was also a shock. I could not imagine what he had been through and I had some trepidation about hearing about it, discovering how it had scarred and changed him, and understanding what it would mean for us to ease back into our marriage. It was going to take time for Yakov and me to reacquaint ourselves and adjust to the people we had become over the more than four years that we had been apart.

"Don't be ridiculous," Catherine said, "I can change the sheets after you use them. Please stay." But Yakov would not be dissuaded from his plan, and so he and Avram left for the farm with Christian for the night. After the men departed, I lay awake for a long time enjoying the unaccustomed absence of dread.

The next morning, I went to take my leave and thank Madame de la Reine for giving me work and protection. I thought of the many good deeds that had originated at Madame de la Reine's generous hands. She embraced me and declared, "I'm overjoyed that your husband survived. And grateful that you stayed here with us in Crevecoeur. Thanks to you, my field hands know how to read. And our village can boast that we protected the family of Philippe."

Teaching my friends and co-workers to read had helped me survive the war. My motives were so selfish that I frequently forgot how much my students had gained from my work. Madame de la Reine's words made me feel as though I had given something of value back to this community that had sheltered me at such risk.

I returned home to find Catherine boiling the day's laundry on the stove. She informed me that Yakov was outside with the girls. I found him washed clean and wearing some of Christian's clothing (which drooped off his skeletal frame), sitting on a barrel behind the house and watching the girls, who were dancing for him while they sang a tune they seemed to have made up on the spot. I prepared lunch, after which Yakov and I went to Robert's farm. We walked through the house that Robert and Miriam had shared, now silent and shuttered. Then we walked through the orchards as I described what it had been like when Miriam had lived there with the children. Neither one of us spoke of Miriam's death. We talked instead about how she had lived. Yakov hung on every word that I could offer about Miriam's defiance of the grim life the Nazis attempted to impose on us during the Occupation.

We entered the empty barn. "She had so many animals," I told Yakov. "When you approached the house, the dogs would come out to greet you, and maybe a goat or a potbellied pig. You could always see her cats sleeping perched on the roof of the porch. Sometimes their tails hung down like bell pulls. Chickens sauntered through the yard, usually following a puffed-up rooster with its chest thrust out like a domineering general. There were horses, cows, and sheep. The children used to play up there in the hayloft."

I peered into the hayloft, half expecting Babette's daughters to poke their heads out of the hay, full of giggles. Then Yakov turned me gently to him and kissed me with a kiss that he had saved within him for years. My legs went weak underneath me and I kneeled down in the hay. Yakov knelt with me and, as if praying, we kissed and touched each other's faces. Tentatively, bashfully, we began to rediscover each other. Yakov was hesitant about removing his clothes, painfully embarrassed.

"What is it?" I asked gently.

He replied barely audibly, "I have many unattractive scars."

"So have I," I told him, "they just don't show up on my skin." And I undressed him and ran my fingers over the scars. He had a road map of welts on his thighs, which he told me were from where the bullets had lodged and then been removed when he had been shot. His back was peppered with the permanent marks of torture; some were round circles and others were in the shape of short, jagged lines. And there were other scars on his body. I did not ask. I ran my fingers across them and kissed them each. Then I took his wrist in my hand and turned his arm over to reveal the blue tattooed numbers on his forearm and I kissed the tattoo. "You are all the more valuable to me because you survived it," I told him. And Yakov finally broke down and wept in large, dry sobs. He lost his breath, and caught it again, lost it, and caught it. I wept with him and held him until the storm of our sorrow had passed.

Then he came to me in both body and spirit again and our lovemaking in the barn that day carried in it the power of the hope that had sustained us and the lives we had clung to and had ultimately wrested from the war. Afterward, bedded down in the hay, we discussed what to do next. We agreed that we wanted to reestablish our lives in Paris as soon as possible. In the late afternoon, we returned to Catherine's, where a letter from America awaited me. It had been addressed to me and Miriam at the farm.

I stared at the photo of Ruth and Nate with their three children. All girls, the youngest a baby in Ruth's arms. The oldest looked the same age as Shayna, and I wished that they could play together, although I realized that these cousins probably had little in common, not even a common language. Even if Ruth spoke to her children in Yiddish or Russian, I had not been able to speak these languages to Shayna for fear that they would give us away during the war. It angered me that my daughter had been robbed of this part of her heritage, and I resolved to teach her Russian in the coming years. Ruth had matured and she looked so much like Mama. Our letters to one another had crossed in the mail, and so she did not know yet about Miriam. I was sorry that she would have to worry about

Avram and Yakov until I could get another letter to her with the news that they had survived. Her letter closed with a plea for me to emigrate to America. Her husband could get us the papers we needed. We could live with her until we got settled. She had it all figured out except that I was not the woman she imagined. Ah, well, dear Ruth, I thought, if I had not gone to America to escape the war, I certainly would not go now. I had a country of my own.

Catherine prepared a dinner of baked potatoes and cabbage soup. She had managed to obtain some duck eggs, which she fried. I felt so light that I fairly danced around the house, singing to the children. Then Yakov hid a spool of thread for the girls and had them look for it, telling them if they were hot or cold, until they found it. He crawled on the floor with them and the girls jumped on his back, which precipitated a coughing fit, forcing us to put an end to that game. Christian and Avram joined us for the evening meal, bringing with them the season's first apricots from Miriam's orchard. We held hands around the table while Christian said grace. I felt fit to burst with thankfulness for my good fortune, until Catherine dissolved in tears. Wide-eyed, the girls looked from one adult to another for a clue as to what had gone wrong.

"I'm sorry," Catherine apologized, dabbing at her eyes with her sleeve. "I'm so silly. All these years I have prayed for the war to end with all my heart, not once considering that when it did I would lose my partner."

I put my arms around Catherine and held her. Caught up in my own happiness, I had been insensitive to my dear friend's plight. "I'm so thoughtless," I said with remorse. "I was not thinking of your loss."

"It's not my husband who is on my mind right now," Catherine explained. "It's you, dear sister. Am I to lose you? And Shayna, whom I have helped you raise from a baby? I can't imagine my life without you and soon you will be off to America and I will never see you again."

I had turned so quickly toward the future that I was forgetting about what I would leave behind. "First of all," I assured Catherine, "we are not going to America. France is our home. We can't imagine living anywhere but Paris. You know that I am a city mouse just as much as you are a country mouse. Paris is only a day away by train. We will see each other often. The children will visit and continue to grow up together. You have not seen the last of me."

Catherine smiled weakly with relief.

Shayna jumped up from the table and skipped around in a circle. "I'm going to Paris? I'm going to Paris! Oh, Maman, can I have ballet lessons? Can I wear a pink tutu and dance on a stage?"

My heart leapt with joy at the thought that I could offer my daughter a future, at last. Perhaps one day she really would have ballet lessons. A door out had opened back up for us in the narrow world in which we had hidden.

"Can I have a tutu also?" piped up Isabel, not to be outdone.

"We shall see," Catherine replied. "Now come eat your dinner."

Later that night, in the privacy of our bed, I asked Yakov if he wanted to talk about Auschwitz. He replied vehemently that he wasn't willing to give the Nazis that satisfaction.

"I don't understand," I said, puzzled by his logic.

"If I tell you about the horror, then you must suffer the pain of hearing and knowing, and then you must carry it with you as I do. In that way, the Nazis torture you as well as me. Then if you tell someone else, they too must suffer. I am not willing to spread the pain. I refuse to perpetuate their torture by telling about it."

I was relieved, because, in truth, I did not want to hear stories from Auschwitz, or any other stories about the horrors of the war. I would have listened only if Yakov needed to speak about it for his own healing. Yakov was trying to put it behind him. I hoped that Avram would reach a similar decision about telling the story of Miriam's death and that he would find a way to move beyond the war as well. "You don't need to talk about it? I mean, for yourself? For your own health and well-being?" I asked, just to be sure.

"You and Shayna are all the medicine I need," Yakov said, and I wondered if it could be that simple.

Avram decided to stay in Crevecoeur. He offered to help Christian manage Robert's farm. It seemed that working on the farm where Miriam had lived brought him closer to Miriam, brought her back to him in some small way. Avram had spoken little since his return from the war and had carefully avoided being alone with me. It was Avram who took us to the train station when we departed. As we rode the cart through the countryside, people from nearby farms lined the road. To my amazement, they raised their hands in a victory sign and called out *"Vive Philippe!"* to Yakov, who nodded his head to acknowledge his supporters and made a victory sign in response. I was astonished to see the evidence that my Yakov had become a folk hero.

When we arrived at the train station at last, we encountered about twenty people who had come to say good-bye to Yakov. Among them were men and women whose lives he had saved and who had fought with him or who had family members who had fought with him. We boarded the train amid a crowd of well-wishers, and I realized that I had not had an opportunity to say good-bye properly to Avram. He, alone, of those closest to me, did not seem to have recovered his passion for life. We parted with too much unsaid. I silently asked the spirit of Miriam to look after him in my absence.

As the train pulled out of the station, my thoughts flew ahead to Paris and the life that I would resume there. My daughter would receive a fine education. I would take her to the theater and the ballet. Yakov could write for a newspaper again and we would see if we could find any of our old circle of friends. It had been so long since I had considered the possibilities for constructing a just society, and the time was right to make fundamental changes that would have a lasting impact on the future of France and the future of the world.

FOURTEEN

Ruth

WITH THE WAR OVER, I could safely write to Rivka and Miriam without endangering them. The only address I had for them was in Crevecoeur at Miriam's farm. I made Nate and the children sit for a picture and then I wrote, praying my family had survived.

As we read about the liberation of the camps and the horror of what happened there came to light, Nate kept saying, "If only we could have gotten more of them out."

The wrenching images emerging from the belly of Germany stalked my spirit and frequently prevented me from sleeping. Although I fell asleep instantly when I crawled into bed at night, later, when the baby woke me for her feeding in the wee hours, I had difficulty going back to sleep. The images of those emaciated faces from the camps paraded through my mind until bluish dawn crept into the sky like a bruise.

At the time that the war ended, we still had four houseguests. There were two sisters, who hoped to return to Europe, but who needed to earn enough money for their passage, and a young couple, Chaim and Pessela. One afternoon, Ira telephoned to tell the sisters that he had received word that their father had died in the Bergen-Belsen concentration camp two weeks before the war ended. He had a telegram from their uncle, which he read aloud to them. When I learned what had happened, I called our rabbi, who immediately came to the house and sat with them, while I got on the phone and rounded up the ten adults (a *minyan*) required for formal communal Jewish prayer. That evening, many more than the needed ten arrived at our house so that the sisters could say the Mourner's Kaddish for their father. Nate came home from work early to participate. Sophie was old enough to understand what had transpired and she clung to Nate, who picked her up, despite the fact that at five years old she was too big to be carried, and held her on his hip as he stood in prayer.

I was unable to pray with them because I had to take Irina upstairs and read to her to calm her down after she had a fit of frantic crying. She did not understand what was going on; nevertheless, at the age of two and a half, she was a sensitive child and she absorbed the grief and pain in the house without comprehending why it was there. I stayed in her bed with her until she fell asleep.

That night, after settling Sarah back to sleep at two-thirty, I lay awake staring at the ceiling. Nate was awake too and he took my hand in the dark and held it, running his fingers across the wedding band on my finger.

"I can't stop myself from thinking about the camps and all those who were lost," I said. "All those souls. So many lives. The devastation in Poland is particularly hard to accept. Yakov, my brother-in-law, was from Poland, you know. Polish Jewish culture is functionally gone. The term *the lost tribes* has taken on a new meaning for me. Do you remember the book about that man Ishi in California who was the last of the native Yana people? It makes me wonder if there was some feature of the way of life of those Yana people, or some feature of Polish Jewish culture, that might have been essential to the survival of the human race and now it has vanished." I fell silent and he stroked the palm of my hand with his thumb.

"They are calling it the *Shoah*, the Holocaust," he told me.

"That is an appropriate name for it, if such a thing can be named at all." I had not heard that term before and I turned it over in my mind. "I'm grateful we brought out as many as we did."

"I'm glad to hear you say it. I know it has not been easy."

"No it hasn't. But when I think about what would have happened to them if they had stayed, well, I guess that's one of the things that keeps me awake at night. I think it will be a long time before I recover. If ever. I'm proud of what we did. I'm proud that we did not sit idly by, complicit by our inaction."

"Then you're not angry with me for taking them in?"

"Oh, Nathan." I sighed. "I was never angry at you for taking them in. It was just a lot of work helping these people to get settled in America."

"Some of them were more difficult than others. I'm thinking of Yossel, of course," Nate chuckled.

"Oy, Yossel," I said. "But I would certainly not wish him, or any of them, dead in those camps." I laid my head on Nate's chest, which rose and fell with his breathing. "It was just so hard, Nathan. I wish it wasn't so hard. I would have managed it better if I could have had even a small piece of time to myself every day, or even just a few times a week. Like the time you took for yourself in the den in the morning and sometimes in the evening. I feel as though I have not had time to myself for the entire length of the war. Sometimes I have thought I would lose my mind."

"But you haven't."

"Yes, well, that is a miracle right there."

He brought my hand to his lips and kissed the center of my palm. "I love you very much and I could not have done this without you."

In the ensuing weeks, Nate aggressively sought donations to buy passage for the sisters, in mourning for their father, to return to Europe. A master at fund-raising, Nate was able to put them on a ship to be reunited with their uncle. That left only Pessela and Chaim, who were trying their best to secure work and get situated in their own apartment. Pessela was earning money making lace for an Irish family, but it didn't bring in enough income for them to live independently yet.

On a crisp, clear afternoon, I found a blue airmail letter in the mailbox. I recognized the handwriting at once and held the letter to my cheek as though it were a caress. I sat down abruptly on the front steps, crying with relief that she was still alive. It took me a moment to collect myself before I gingerly opened the envelope, as if it might explode. Rivka wrote that she and Shayna were alive. Miriam and her son dead. Yakov in Auschwitz, perhaps alive and perhaps not. Avram also a question mark.

I put my head between my knees and fought to remain conscious. I took a deep breath and started the letter again from the beginning. As the news sank in, I wept. The shape of the world had altered irrevocably. I put the letter into my apron pocket and returned to the kitchen. Through my tears, I cast my eyes over my shiny toaster and my kitchen wallpaper with the cheerful yellow buttercups, and I tried to imagine working at dawn in a vineyard, my baby cared for by a washerwoman. I tried to imagine waking in the night to a house full of soldiers, being dragged from my home at gunpoint, watching my children die. Rivka sounded so wistful, so optimistic, so wise. I could no longer imagine my sister. I could no longer imagine the circumstances of her life. I closed my eyes, held the letter to my heart, and prayed for the lives of Avram and Yakov.

Pessela found me standing in the middle of my kitchen with my head bowed and she put her hand on my arm. I turned to her and, although we were not on such friendly terms, I embraced her. She could see that I was crying. In Yiddish I explained, "I have had a letter from my sister in France. She is alive, but our other sister and her children are dead. My brother remains missing. The last known whereabouts of my brother-in-law was Auschwitz. It is possible that they are alive, but . . ." I trailed off, choking on my words. Pessela comforted me, cried with me, held me for a long time until we both stopped trembling. I'm sure she was thinking of her own family, over sixty relatives, close to her, none of whom had escaped to America as she had, all of whom had perished.

When Nate came home, I handed him the letter. But the little girls jumped all over him, hanging from his arms and legs, ready to wrestle, so he put the letter on the counter for later. "She lives?" he asked, eyebrows raised.

"She lives." A wave of relief crossed Nate's face. "But Miriam perished," my voice broke, "and she does not know yet about her husband and my brother." Nate's shoulders fell and a look of exhaustion, or perhaps defeat, passed over his features before he turned his attention to the children.

Later, while I put the girls to bed, he read the letter. When I came down to the living room, he handed it back to me. I sat next to him on the sofa and read it again. Until that moment, I'm not sure I fully comprehended that the war had finally ended.

In a few weeks I would receive word in another letter from Rivka that Avram was alive and that Yakov had miraculously survived Auschwitz. Rivka promised to write again with an address in Paris. I somehow could not quite believe that I would never see Miriam again. I imagined that she was not dead but only far away from me, living on her farm, raising children and growing fruit.

When Chaim and Pessela finally moved out of our house and into their own apartment, I was able to find snatches of time for myself. I sewed outfits for the girls in the evening on my sewing machine, which, except for a brief time when I was pregnant with Irina, had slept untouched in a closet throughout the war years.

One night, as Nate played with the girls in the living room, I overheard Sophie tell him, "Papas don't wash the dishes. Mamas work and papas play." To my great surprise, the next evening Nate came into the kitchen after dinner and picked up a dishrag. I stopped and stared at him as if he had produced a goldfinch out of his vest pocket.

"Sophie," he shrugged. "She thinks I don't work."

Irina tugged at Nate's leg. "Be a bear. Growl."

"He's helping Mama," Sophie explained.

But Irina insisted on sitting on Nate's foot, so he dried the dishes, growling, with our persistent daughter wrapped around his leg.

A few days later, I came home at dusk from a late afternoon checkup at the pediatrician for the girls to find Nate in the kitchen, radio blaring swing music, his shirtsleeves rolled up, cooking spaghetti sauce! We sat at the long table in the dining room, in the middle of the week (not even Sabbath), and ate together. We'll see how long this lasts, I thought.

After I put the children to bed, I came back downstairs and curled up on the sofa next to Nate, who still had his shirtsleeves rolled up, revealing his muscular forearms. I turned his arm over and brushed my lips across the inside of it. We kissed on the sofa like courting teenagers.

"It makes such a big difference to you?" Nate asked.

"What?"

"That I cooked dinner?"

"Of course it does; it confirms that my needs matter," I said. I could see him processing this, his brow wrinkled. "Don't think about it *too* hard. You'll hurt yourself," I warned as I pulled him on top of me. We made love on the sofa, the daring of it heightening our excitement.

The next day, I felt an unaccustomed contentment while I cleaned up the breakfast dishes. Sophie and Irina had draped old sheets over the living room furniture and I heard them giggling inside their fort. The sun coming in the window over the sink cast an amber glow on the cabinets. I felt that I had rediscovered a level of intimacy with Nate that had escaped us in recent years; and I thought about how a marriage is a living organism unto itself.

Not long after the war ended, I received a brief note from Avram that said he was coming to America to look for a parcel of land to buy. He thought he would start a farm. I was pleased, although something about the tone of the letter made me wary. I wondered why he wanted to buy land in America. Why not France? Or Palestine? When he arrived, I was overjoyed to see him, but he responded with reserve and remained subdued. He had brought only a small suitcase with him.

He liked to watch the girls play, but did not play with them. He watched them with the same faint, removed smile with which he watched everything. Nate asked him about the war, and he remained fairly reticent on the subject, although after a good meal and a glass of wine, he could be coaxed into telling buddy stories about his exploits in the Resistance with Yakov, who had carved out a reputation for himself. I got the sense that Avram's activities in the Resistance were more conservative and cautious than Yakov's.

When I asked him why he wanted to settle in America, he said, "America is the safest place I can think of to live. I have spent enough of my life in extreme danger. I don't care to do it again."

"What about Palestine?" I asked. "Have you thought of returning to Palestine?"

"The British are imprisoning and deporting Holocaust survivors in Palestine by the dozens and the Jews there have begun to wage a guerilla war against the British. I don't wish to be a part of it. I have had enough war to last me a lifetime," Avram said.

I had been so caught up in following the situation in Europe in the aftermath of the Holocaust that I had not paid much attention to the events unfolding in Palestine. Avram's words reminded me that I had family there as well and gave me something new to worry about. I wrote to Mama and Papa and asked them if they were safe. I asked if Benjy would like to come to America if we provided him with a ticket to make the journey.

Avram stayed with us for only one week and then took the bus to Vermont to look for property. I wondered how on earth he would manage since he spoke such poor English. His visit left me melancholy. I missed the fiery boy I had last seen in Palestine.

I did not hear from him for some weeks, and then I received a crackly phone call. He told me that he had purchased a piece of land and he gave me a post office box address in a town I had never heard of, that required a magnifying glass and twenty minutes of searching for me to locate on a map. I wrote to him regularly, even though he rarely wrote back. It was as if he had dissolved. Sometimes I caught myself thinking of Avram as if he had died. I had to remind myself that a version of him still lived in a remote corner of Vermont.

With the war behind us, Nate became more involved in local community affairs. He joined the synagogue board of directors and chaired the fund-raising committee. He joined the city planning commission. His commitments usually required that he attend meetings at least three nights a week. He came home to have dinner with me and his girls and then he went out again, returning after I had gone to bed. I missed him. We had finally reclaimed our home and our life, and our relationship was better than it had ever been, but I resented the frequency of his absence. I wanted to get him away from his busy schedule, so I suggested that we take a family vacation. Nate agreed to spend a week at the Jersey Shore with me and the girls. We picked a weekend and I booked rooms at a hotel. I could hardly wait to have the maids and other hotel staff wait on me, and I looked forward eagerly to having time with Nate.

On the morning that we left for the beach, the car felt piled high with good spirits. The girls giggled and bounced in the backseat. I had dressed them in matching outfits and put bows in their hair. Even Irina had submitted to the bow, despite the fact that she hated dressing up (she said she looked like a cupcake). I imagined our family pulling up at the hotel, picture-perfect. Sometimes I perceived myself as the poor immigrant girl who had made good in America, a genuine success story. Well, I knew how much work I had put into that picture.

Nate reached over and patted my knee.

"I'm looking forward to getting you far away from meetings and committees," I told him.

"I'm looking forward to getting myself far away from them," Nate replied, with a smile that showed his irresistible dimple.

I dozed off and woke when Nate pointed out the ocean to the children. The vision of the sparkly waves rushing in to meet the sand took my breath away. The sun trumpeted out of a brass-blue sky. The day shimmered in the heat.

The hotel overlooked the water and stood on the edge of the beach itself. While Nate checked in at the counter, I stood in the lobby with the girls, who gazed out the window. They looked immaculate to me in the matching dresses I had made for them on my sewing machine; Sophie in pink, Irina in blue, and Sarah in lavender. But then they argued over who would press the button in the elevator and Nate wound up pressing the button himself as he yanked Irina roughly by the arm. Sarah started sniveling and Sophie stuck her lip out and expostulated "no fair."

"Life is no fair," Nate told Sophie. I sighed.

We had booked two adjoining rooms so that Nate and I could have some privacy. The girls jumped up and down on the bouncy beds in their room as I unpacked while Nate went downstairs to find a cup of coffee and a newspaper. Nate and I were keeping a close eye on the events unfolding in Palestine because it looked like the British were planning to leave and that the region would be partitioned into a Jewish state and an Arab state. I wondered what this might mean for Mama and Papa, Benjy, and Meir. I could depend on Nate to find a paper and inform me if there had been any change in the situation in the Middle East.

"Can we go swimming before dinner? Please?" Sophie pleaded. It was rather late in the afternoon, but I wanted to go to the beach as much as the children did, so I assented. I left Nate a note.

With Sarah's delicate hand in one of mine, and Irina's firm hand in my other, I ran across the sand. Sophie held Sarah's other hand. Like a wild chorus line, the four of us ran to the water's edge where the waves washed in over our feet. The girls hopped up and down, shrieking in delight, and then they shot off, away from me, running up and down the beach, flirting with the surf, those white-capped ripples decorated with bubbles, foam, and strands of seaweed.

I inhaled a deep breath of salt spray and gazed off to the horizon where I saw a ship passing far out on the ocean. Then I cast my eyes up the beach, where I caught sight of two familiar figures. A woman held the hand of a little boy who waved a lollipop. "It's good to see you again," I whispered, as I watched the two slowly wend their way toward me. But as they came closer I realized that they didn't really look like Mama and Benjy, and the child didn't have a lollipop at all but a stick, which he threw into the surf. I wondered what Benjy was like now that he was grown up and went by the name of Benjamin. I would have to ask Mama to send me a recent picture of him.

Sitting down on the beach, I hugged my knees to my chest and enjoyed my view of the sparkling waves, dancing with the late afternoon light. The sound and motion of the ocean filled me with a pervasive sense of peace and contentment. So this is why Mama always went to the sea, I thought; I should have done this a long time ago. I would probably have sat there until the sun went down, but Nate appeared to bring us back inside. I laughed when I saw him. He still wore his driving clothes and he squished out to me in his city shoes, which brimmed with sand. He sat next to me on the beach, in his good pants.

"You found us."

"Of course." He squinted at the ocean. We both looked across the water. Then he turned to me and said, "You're beautiful."

I blushed.

"Perhaps you thought I no longer noticed," he continued. "But I do."

"I don't see you often enough to know if you notice or not," I told him. "You're away from me so much of the time. I wish that you were home more."

"I know it," he said. The children had spotted him and were running up the beach toward us. Before they could engulf us with their chatter, Nate added quickly, "I'll see what I can do to free up more of my time. It has gotten a bit out of hand."

An instant later the girls surrounded us, hopping up and down, all talking at once about their discoveries. Sarah had found a chunk of dark-blue glass, polished smooth by the water, and everyone had to take a turn looking through it. Irina demonstrated cartwheels at the water's edge. Sophie wanted Nate to explain why the ocean made waves.

Back at the room, I made the girls shower and dress for dinner. ("Why do we have to take a shower? We're not dirty," Irina whined as she sat on the little balcony and picked sand from between her toes.) After dinner, when I had put the girls to bed, Nate and I retired to the balcony and shared a bottle of wine.

It was an excellent vacation and was over much too soon. On our final afternoon at the beach, we spent hours building an enormous sand castle and decorated it with shells, seaweed, seagull feathers, and rocks.

Irina hauled a mass of gloppy seaweed up the beach.

"Put that back in the water," Nate told her. "It's disgusting."

"It's for the dungeon," Irina declared dramatically.

"Yes, well it smells awful," Nate said.

"Dungeons are supposed to smell awful," Irina replied. Sometimes, I wondered what I would do with that one, who was more challenging than the other two.

As we pulled out of the hotel parking lot to return home, I looked out the car window and saw in my mind the sand castle and sculptures we had left on the beach. I wished that I could keep the previous afternoon at the beach in a glass jar on my bureau, to open now and again when I needed a whiff of joy.

A few weeks after our beach vacation, when the air had turned cold with fall coming on, I was in the kitchen fixing dinner. The girls were playing under the dining room table. As Nate came in from work and opened the front closet to hang up his coat, I could hear the girls quarreling. I didn't want him to come home to discord, so I wiped my hands on my apron and started out to see what the problem was. Before I reached them, I heard Irina shriek with rage and Sarah began crying hard, the way she cried when she was badly hurt. I ran into the dining room in alarm, but Nate had reached the girls first. After that, everything happened so quickly. I remember crawling under the table to scoop Sarah up and that the child was bleeding from the forehead where a big bump had already begun to bulge. Irina had overturned two chairs and Nate had her by the wrist as she writhed in anger.

Nate demanded to know what had happened. Terrified, Sophie stuttered that Irina had thrown a metal car at Sarah. I was so focused on

Sarah that I failed to realize at that critical moment how far over the edge the children had pushed Nate. Had I realized, I might have been able to intervene and defuse the situation. I will never know. I took Sarah into the kitchen, sat her up on the countertop, and put ice on her forehead. Through Sarah's fussing and crying, I slowly became aware that Irina was screaming in the other room.

I opened the dining room door and saw Sophie plastered against the wall, shivering, her eyes wide. Nate had removed his belt and was hitting Irina's legs with it.

"Nate," I shouted at him hoarsely. "Nate, she's a child, not an animal."

"Then she should learn not to act like an animal," he retorted. But I had broken the spell of his fury and he dropped Irina in a weeping heap on the floor and retreated to the den, slamming and locking the door behind him.

I was trembling. Nate had spanked the children before, but beating them? With a belt? Shakily, I stood Irina up and sent her upstairs to wash her bleeding legs.

Sophie followed me into the kitchen. "He's not fair," she told me quietly. "He has no right to whip her." I left Sarah with Sophie and went to see about Irina.

The girls and I ate dinner in stony silence. Nate did not emerge from the den, where he spent the night on the couch.

Alone in our bed, I had one of the most intense versions of the Chinese dream that I had ever had. I had been having them off and on over the years. They were particularly unsettling because I dreamed about a time and place that I had no way of knowing about. At first the dream had always been the same as it was in the hospital after Irina was born. The husband shouted while I hung my head and cried silently, the gardener appeared, the young woman collapsed on the floor, and I woke up with waves of grief washing over me. But over time, other detailed images of Chinese culture had appeared at random in the dreams, such as a tea set laid out on a table or a hand mirror lying on a bed. Just the year before, I had checked out a few books about Chinese art and culture from the library. From these books, I discovered that the clothing that I wore in the dreams, and that the young woman who usually appeared in them wore, suggested that the dreams took place during the Manchu Qing dynasty. It was the same culture and historical period depicted in the painting that I had bought all those years before and that hung over my fireplace. The dreams did not diminish my love for the painting, which continued to give me great pleasure whenever I looked at it.

The night after Nate whipped Irina, the dream ended, for the first time, with the young woman in the peach jacket being raped, and I woke from it in a cold sweat. I could not go back to sleep and I watched the gradual light of sunrise creep across the walls of the room. I could hear Nate in the kitchen and I chose not to go downstairs. He left for work without even coming upstairs for a change of clothing. I wondered if he felt any remorse.

I kept Irina home from school that day because she had huge welts on her legs and I was embarrassed to send her out like that, a walking advertisement of family failure. Irina spread her paper dolls on the dining room table while I did my housework. She had not spoken to me about what her father had done.

At ten o'clock, Ida came over for coffee, as she did every Wednesday. We sat together in the breakfast nook, out of Irina's earshot, and I told her what had transpired.

"You're blowing this out of proportion," Ida warned.

I was shocked. I thought Ida would be an ally.

"It's not a crime to discipline your children," she said.

"That wasn't discipline. It was abuse."

"Irina is a headstrong child. If you don't check her behavior now, then you won't be able to live with her as a teenager," Ida cautioned.

"Children can be reasoned with like anyone else," I asserted.

"Izzie spanks the boys when they don't behave and he took his belt to Gary once. It's unpleasant, but a necessary part of parenting. I'm grateful to Izzie for doing it because I wouldn't have the heart for it myself."

"My father never raised a hand to any of us, girls or boys," I said, with a waver in my voice. Papa had never seen my babies or held my children in his lap.

"It has a lot to do with temperament. Perhaps it was not necessary with the children in your family. Some children are wilder than others. And you know for a fact that Irina is a wild one. Don't worry about sending her to school. No one will think twice about it. They know you and Nate are not abusive parents. Nate and Izzie were both belted by their father when they were growing up. And me. Look, look right here." Ida leaned across the table and pointed to a scar above her eyebrow. "That's from my father's belt buckle. It swung around and smacked me once when he was giving me a whipping."

"He could have taken out your eye. I don't care who does it; it's not right, and it's not going to happen in my house."

The girls avoided their father for a few days, but gradually they seemed to forget about what had happened and things returned to normal. I made one attempt to speak to Nate about the incident, but he would not listen. "They aren't babies anymore. They need discipline and you are too lenient. I refuse to raise out-of-control, defiant children."

Who is out of control? I thought it, but did not say it. All I could do was try to remain vigilant and prevent such an explosion from occurring again.

In the middle of the night a persistent clanging drew me up out of deep sleep. Disoriented, I looked over at Nate, who sat straight up in bed turning the radio on and off, without realizing it was the phone ringing. Semiconscious, Nate put the radio down and turned the alarm on the bedside clock on and off. Then he turned the lamp on and off.

Even though I myself was still half asleep, I laughed. He looked so comical. "It's the phone," I told him. He looked at me blankly.

"The phone," I repeated. I got up and walked around the bed and picked up the phone. Nate promptly put the blankets over his head.

I was still chuckling about Nate, when it began to dawn on me that someone was calling us in the middle of the night, and that was not a good thing. I heard a distant voice say my name through veils of static. I couldn't understand the words. Then I realized it was Hebrew. It had been so long, I couldn't understand it. The voice switched over to Yiddish. Vaguely familiar. Suddenly I recognized it. Papa!

"Papa, Papa, please slow down," I responded in Yiddish. I had not spoken to him since they had called me on my birthday the previous year. And before that? I couldn't remember when. International phone calls were expensive and Papa and Mama did not have a phone in their own home on the kibbutz.

"Ruth," he repeated, "I'm sorry, I have bad news. Your brother Benjamin was killed in the war."

"The war?" I asked, wondering why a little boy would be fighting a war, before I remembered that he had grown up during the many years that we had been apart.

"The War of Independence. For Israel." As he said it, I remembered reading about it in the newspapers. After the British had left Palestine and it had been partitioned, the Jews and Arabs had begun fighting.

"Benjamin was killed?" I asked, although I had heard what he said quite clearly. Then my thoughts became jumbled and I wanted to speak to my mother. The only way I could process what Papa had just told me was to speak to Mama. "Mama," I said. "Let me talk to Mama."

"I'm sorry," Papa continued. His voice cracked. "When Mama received the news, she had a heart attack."

"No, no," I moaned. Silence. "Papa?"

I heard him sob and then I knew.

"We lost her," Papa told me in a choked voice. "We lost her too. It broke her heart."

It couldn't be. I had expected to take the girls to see her one day. Or to send her a ticket to come visit us again in America. I had still harbored a hope that I could convince Papa to move to America. Mama was the glue; even from over the ocean, she was the glue. Without her the family would fly apart completely and succumb to the geography of our separate lives.

"Papa, you are so far away."

"I am far away," Papa echoed. Papa had never written to me; it was always Mama who wrote, regularly, with all the news. Why hadn't she prepared me for this eventuality? Told me that Benjy was a soldier? I could not bear the thought of not receiving any more of her letters. I had written to her about my worries during the war and about my daughters. My letters to Mama were like a journal of my life. I could never write in the same way just to Papa. It would be entirely different. Papa. I could not imagine what he must be going through, to lose his wife and his son, one immediately after the other.

"Papa, why don't you come stay with me in America? Please, come for a visit."

"I will write to you," Papa promised. "Kiss the babies for me."

"Oh, Papa, they aren't babies anymore. They're all in school now. Even Sarah, who is in kindergarten."

"So then kiss them each twice for me; kiss them on both cheeks," Papa said.

"Wait, wait. Don't go. Will you be OK?"

"I have many friends here. I have Meir. I will make it through."

"Take care of yourself, Papa."

"I will write soon."

"Does Rivka know?" I asked.

"She has no phone," Papa answered. "I will write to her. To her and to Avram."

"Papa, Papa. You are so far away. I love you."

"I love you too. Shalom, my little bird," he said.

"Shalom, Papa," I said, but he was already gone. I put the receiver back in its cradle and sat for a long time and stared at the phone. I do not remember when Nate took me in his arms and held me while I wept. Was it while I was speaking to Papa or after he hung up? He was still holding me at dawn when the rising sun began to wash the room in light, and then he had called Ida, and she was there, and I heard the girls' voices as they awoke, but I did not go to them. The doctor came to the house and gave me something to help me sleep. When I woke up in the afternoon, my mind was clear, and I began to accept the dull ache of my loss, an ache that would descend on me whenever I woke from sleep for many weeks to come.

I sat *shiva* for Mama and Benjamin for a week in our house, which filled with friends in the evenings when the rabbi came to lead us in the Mourner's Kaddish. Romek sat in mourning with me. His stories from his childhood with Mama were a comfort, even though I had heard most of them already over the years. Netya and Ida organized the synagogue sisterhood to cook us meals every evening. My girls adored having food appear in abundance for dinner each night, and they crowed to each other with excitement over what had turned up on the dining room table. I had lost my appetite, so I was extremely grateful that I did not have to cook for others during that time.

Try as I might, I could not imagine Benjamin as a dead soldier. Instead I imagined a small coffin with a little boy inside, wearing shorts, hair tousled, one fat finger raised beside his bright face. I could hear him say, "Just one, just one more lollipop." I wondered exactly how he had died and if he would be honored as a hero in the new state of Israel if it survived. I wrote to Papa and asked him these questions. It was hard for me to write the words "*Dear Papa*" without also writing "*and Mama*." Our long newsy letters, Mama's and mine, had been our lifeline to one another.

I continued to talk to Mama in my head, as I had done for years. I could not sleep at night for thinking about her. I would try to relax by picturing myself in Mama's cousin's house at the beach on the Mediterranean, and I would imagine I could hear the distant murmuring of the voices of Mama and her cousin conversing after they had put us children to bed. I listened for the slap of the waves in the distance and tried to remember the exact fresh scent of the air so close to the water. I remembered a white china cup with bluebird patterns around the rim that belonged to Mama's cousin and how I loved to drink lemon tea with honey from it. I imagined sipping the tea while Mama wove my hair into a braid down my back.

I had an impulse to write to Miriam and fill her in on the news of the last few years and kept composing letters to her in my head. One day I actually wrote a long letter addressed to both Miriam and Mama together, as if they would sit across from one another at the kitchen table and take turns reading my words aloud. I told them the latest news about my daughters. I marveled at how quickly they were growing and that I wished I could slow it down to enjoy it more. I described an idea that I had for a dress I wanted to make if I could find the time. I told them about my neighbor's prolific plum tree and explained how many of us in the neighborhood made plum jam together every spring when the tree bore fruit. They would have especially enjoyed that part. I asked Miriam about her son and her farm, as if she would reply. I asked them how much honey Mama put in the jars when she preserved apricots. I was panicked that I couldn't remember the recipe and I doubted that Rivka would know. After I wrote the letter, I wrapped it in a purple swatch of fabric, buried it in a back corner of my yard, and marked the spot with a flat stone. Sometimes I went to that spot to pray or to speak to Mama and Miriam when I was sure no one was watching me.

If I had not been so preoccupied with my own grief after Mama's death, then I would not have let my guard down and allowed my resolve to act as a buffer between my high-spirited Irina and her father lapse. He was stubbornly determined to bend her spirit to his will. That is how I made the mistake of taking Sophie shopping with me one day and leaving the younger girls with Nate. I should have taken Irina as well.

The moment I entered the house, I could tell something was wrong. The girls were nowhere to be seen and Nate sat reading in his lounge chair in the den. He did not look up when we entered. A sullen silence hung over the house.

"Where are the girls?" I asked.

"Upstairs," Nate answered curtly.

I found Sarah first, curled up under the covers in my bed, trembling. As soon as she saw me, she leapt at me and threw her arms around my neck. "Oh Mama, Irina and Papa had a terrible fight. He hit her. I was so scared."

How could he put our children through this? Didn't he see what it did to the whole family? He was the adult. Irina was a child. I did not understand why he could not find a way to control himself.

"Well, I'm home now," I said, hugging my baby. "You stay here with Soph while I have a talk with Irina."

"She's in her room," Sarah informed me. "She didn't cry or scream. She was so quiet. It was awful. I hate him."

I found Irina lying stiff on her bed. Her legs had been torn open and blood stained the bedspread. Tears sprang to my eyes. For an instant I entertained the notion of taking the girls, leaving Nate, and going to live with Romek and Netya. It was an impossible scenario and I knew it. I had no way to support them financially. It would be like starting over again in America. Besides, though I was furious with him, Nate was my husband and I loved him. One day these girls, even my unruly middle daughter, would be grown and would leave me, but Nate would still be there. I had to deal with this situation somehow and I felt at a loss. If Mama were still alive, I would have confessed my troubles to her in a letter and asked for her advice, even though she was likely to worry about me and the children. But Mama was not alive and I had to find a way to handle both Nate and Irina.

"Irina," I said softly.

She turned and I saw in her eyes such defiance that I felt as if I had been slapped. I took a deep breath and brushed Irina's hair from her face as I sat on the edge of the bed next to her. "What happened?"

"See for yourself," she said as she pointed to her legs. "I didn't even do anything." She turned away from me. Nate would not have beaten the child over nothing and it angered me that whatever Irina had done, she would not admit to it.

"Go wash your legs and I'll put some antibiotic on them. I'm going to have a word with your father." The child was only ten years old, but she acted like an adolescent. Challenging her elders. Arrogant. Moody. She was temperamental and unfathomable and difficult. But that didn't give Nate the right to physically abuse her.

I went downstairs to confront Nate. I stood in the doorway. Nate ignored me and kept reading. "I would appreciate it if you would refrain from beating my children," I said coldly.

"And I would appreciate it if you would make an effort to discipline them so that I don't have to be the one who always does it," Nate retorted. "I don't like being the bad cop. But I will not have smart-mouthed, disrespectful children. My daughters *will not* talk back to me, or any other adult for that matter."

"So you intend to teach them good manners by visiting your bad manners on them?" I struggled to contain my fury.

"I intend to have well-brought-up children that I don't feel ashamed to take with me in public. I want to be proud of their behavior. That one walks all over you."

I left the room before I said something I would regret. I was angry at both of them. Why did I feel as if I had to choose between them?

A few days later, when Nate asked me what I thought about him running for city council, I encouraged him to do it because it would keep him away from home. That would make it easier for me to orchestrate keeping Nate and Irina apart except for times when I was able to be present.

Nate was at his best with his daughters when they were babies and toddlers. He was not doing so well with them as they grew up, especially with temperamental Irina. He had difficulty adjusting to their moods and messy emotions. Perhaps he would have done better with sons. In some ways, I reflected, Sarah was Nate's surrogate son. She was the most able to forgive Nate for his transgressions. Through thick and thin, she adored her father and retained an intuitive sense about his emotions and needs, often saying or doing just the right thing at just the right moment. As Nate ran for public office, Sarah suffered the most from his absence. I couldn't win. I had one daughter who couldn't live with Nate, and one daughter who couldn't live without him. Thank goodness for Sophie.

After Nate was elected to the city council, we rarely saw each other during the week except over the dinner hour when he came home to eat a family meal. I had to schedule his time for family outings or events. When we spent time together as a family, the girls were prepared for him and he for them, and things went more smoothly.

Over the years, as the girls became teenagers and then budding women, Irina and Nate grew more distant from each other. Irina was a force unto herself, it seemed. I tried my best to hold them apart. Nate appeared to have been influenced by my disapproval to some extent in that he spanked her with an open hand rather than using his belt on her on the few occasions that she drove him over the edge. I did not approve of spanking children either, but it was better than whipping them with a belt.

The last time Nate went after Irina was when she was twelve years old. The whole family had stayed up late listening to a radio show together that night and I had made popcorn. The girls had helped me prepare dinner and Nate came home in a rollicking good mood. While we cleaned up the kitchen after dinner, Nate brought in a magazine he had been reading and read a funny story aloud. He had me doubled over with laughter. Then he told the girls about a special radio show, a romantic comedy. So we gathered around the radio in the living room. If only I hadn't made the popcorn. But I did. I stood in the kitchen at the stove, with Nate kissing the back of my neck, and shook the kernels in the hot oil until they burst open. It made me crazy when he kissed the back of my neck like that and I couldn't wait to get him alone, in the privacy of our bedroom.

While listening to the radio show, Irina inadvertently dropped pieces of popcorn on the floor. After the show, Nate asked her to pick up her mess and she flatly refused.

"Why do I have to clean it up by myself? I'm not the only one who was eating popcorn. I'm not picking it up all by myself," Irina insisted, with an attitude that would infuriate even a Buddhist monk.

I could see that Irina didn't realize that she was the only one who had dropped the popcorn, so from her point of view it was a grave injustice that she had to pick it up. She refused to take another look at the situation. Nate was the adult and should have recognized what she perceived and dealt with her with more patience, but all he saw was the disrespect and the attitude.

"Please, just pick it up and be done with it," I begged our stubborn daughter. "Come, I'll help you," I offered in desperation.

"You'll *help* her?" Nate bellowed incredulously. Irina stamped her foot. Nate snapped. Sarah, Sophie, and I chased after them as Nate dragged Irina into her bedroom and locked the door. With me and Sophie banging on the door, he gave Irina a whipping. Sarah wound up picking up the popcorn, which made Nate even more furious. He withdrew to his den, fuming, with the Sunday newspaper.

I rocked a shivering Sarah to sleep and tucked her in next to Sophie. Irina was still locked in her room and she wouldn't respond to me when I knocked on the door. I slept alone in Sarah's bed that night, fully clothed, unable to bring myself to share the bed with Nate or to even enter the room he inhabited. I wept with self-pity and frustration. The day had shown such promise. I wished that he could have transcended the situation with Irina for my sake, for the sake of both of us, in order not to ruin the magic of the evening and the mounting desire, hidden from our daughters, that had been building between us. In fact, even as I lay in Sarah's bed, after all that had happened, I wished that he would come to me and take me in his arms and forget about everything except us for one brief burning moment.

I tried not to fall asleep that night because I was sure that I was so upset that I would have one of those Chinese dreams and that it would be a bad one, ending with that horrible rape of the young woman that was the worst part. But I finally couldn't keep my eyes open. The dream came as anticipated and in it everything appeared hyper-real and too familiar, and I knew before it happened exactly what would happen. That night, the dream was more vivid than it had ever been. I could smell the sweet scent of the flowers so strongly and I could distinctly feel the tears running down my cheeks. The husband who shouted at the young woman was, without a doubt, a Chinese version of Nate. It was quite clear in the dream that night that the young woman was in love with the gardener, who ran off through the garden. I remained submissive and silent, as usual. But that night, when I looked up briefly and my eyes met those of the young woman in the peach-colored jacket, I recognized her. She was Irina. I gasped, which prompted the husband to slap me across the cheek. I cradled my cheek in my hand as he led Irina roughly from the room. Then I was looking through a window into a bedroom where a man raped Irina (not some faceless woman as before). He was a stranger, much older than Irina. As she screamed and sobbed, the man seemed to become more sexually excited and he hammered into her with greater force. It was the worst nightmare I had ever had in my life and I woke from it sobbing.

After the popcorn incident, Nate never raised a hand to Irina again, thank goodness. The following year, as he was removing his belt to go after her over some other equally ridiculous infraction that escalated because of Irina's rebellious attitude, Irina locked herself in our bedroom where there was a phone and called the police while Nate went to find a screwdriver to spring the lock on the door. Before he could unlock the bedroom, the doorbell rang and a shocked Nate found two police officers on our porch questioning him on charges of assault from his daughter, which looked especially bad for a city council member.

Later that night, in our bedroom, Nate confessed to me that he could not continue to summon up fatherly affection for Irina. "She is self-absorbed, disrespectful, and rude," he said, "and I simply don't like her, as a person. I care about her theoretically, as my daughter. And theoretically I want her to be happy. But I don't like her." The anger in his face gave way to his compassion for me. "It is unfortunate that you have to live with this situation, that two people you love are so antagonistic toward one another. You don't deserve this. But she refuses to cooperate and I have lost my affection for her. I don't know how to deal with her other than to wash my hands of her."

"Perhaps it would be helpful if you talked to the rabbi about this," I suggested to Nate. "He has been counseling families for many years and he might provide some insight that would make a difference."

Nate shook his head slightly in disbelief as he said, "I don't need counsel from the rabbi. I know exactly how I feel about that child, and I don't want anything to do with her anymore. We have a major personality conflict and I am unable to raise her effectively."

I wondered how he could talk about such deep feelings so logically, how he could compartmentalize his relationship to his own child like that. But I was afraid to press him. Then the image of that Nate-like man in my Chinese dreams popped into my head, and I wondered if there was a connection between my dreams and the reality of our situation. Were my dreams trying to tell me something, and if so, what?

"I don't want that impossible child to drive any more of a wedge between you and me than she already has," Nate continued. "She could destroy our family if we let her."

"I hope you'll understand that I don't share your feelings and I'm not willing to write her off," I said firmly.

"Understood," he replied.

From that moment on, he seemed to let go of his attachment to her. I couldn't fathom how a parent could possibly make a conscious choice to do what he did. He withdrew from her emotionally. I would never forgive him for it, but I had no choice other than to find a way to live with it.

As for myself, I was, frankly, afraid of Irina. I was afraid that she would ruin my marriage and destroy the family. So I avoided confronting her. Sophie and Sarah sensed how volatile the situation was in our family and consequently they didn't question the things Irina got away with that they could not, like not bothering to tell me where she was going and then staying out late at night, choosing to remain in her room and not join the family for dinner, and wearing nothing but black to school for weeks on end. She kept the door to her room closed at all times, whether she was in there or not. When Irina was away from home, she left the door unlocked; nonetheless, I would never have gone snooping in her room. I didn't much want to even look inside because it was a chaotic mess. It would have been impossible for me to clean in there and I decided that when she moved out I would have it professionally cleaned and repainted. Until then, I let it be.

While Nate cultivated his detachment toward Irina, I was not willing to give up on maintaining a relationship with her, and I continued to ask her questions and to try to engage her in conversation. Once, I invited her to go with me and Sophie to have our hair done and to get a manicure.

"Are you saying my hair looks bad? And my nails?" she scoffed. She had failed to comb the back of her hair for several days and it resembled a wad of uncarded wool, but she couldn't see it since that part was in the back. Her nails were ragged and stained with dye from an art project. But her appearance truly had nothing to do with my offer. I wanted to include her in a mother-and-daughter ritual. I wanted to treat her to an afternoon at the beauty parlor, which was a splendid luxury for me and Sophie. Irina turned my offer into a criticism. I couldn't do anything right as far as she was concerned.

Our opinion, mine and Nate's, did not matter to Irina. She disappeared into her own show and refused to sell us tickets. By the age of fourteen, she was ready to leave home, and I have no doubt she would have done so if she had a way to support herself financially. She dismissed me and Nate; we were merely one of life's annoyances she had to deal with. She spent much of her time sequestered in her room (often listening to jazz on her record player), or else at the art studio at school; she drew constantly both at the studio and at home. She never offered to show me her work, but I often asked about it and sometimes, at my prompting, she would share selected pieces with me. I could not complain about her performance at school, since she got top grades in all her classes, which was surprising to me because she seemed to do it effortlessly, often not even studying as far as I could tell. She completed her homework on time, and her teachers described her as shy, studious, and extremely intelligent. She never brought friends around to the house, like her sisters, who provided a continuous stream of both girls and boys who came by to study with them or to listen to music or to get ready to go out for the evening. Sophie's and Sarah's friends stayed for dinner quite often or gobbled up all the cookies I had baked in the afternoon while they were at school. But no one ever came home with Irina. I worried about her being such a lone wolf. I wanted her to be happy and I couldn't imagine someone so isolated being happy. I never for a minute stopped loving her, even though I did not understand her, and I made an effort to tell her so from time to time, but wondered if she believed me. During her teen years, Irina became more and more absent from our lives, until our family was like a smile missing one of its front teeth.

Not long after Sarah turned thirteen, I experienced a hormone change that confused my calculations in my cycles and to my amazement I became pregnant. Still more amazing (to me) was the fact that I wanted this sunset baby. Just like Mama having Benjamin, the darling of her mature years. I wanted my own late-life baby. I was sure it was a boy. Once they recovered from the shock, Nate and the girls (including Irina) shared my excitement. I even imagined that perhaps this baby would bring the family closer together and help heal the rift between Nate and Irina. But at eighteen weeks I began to bleed and the doctor put me on strict bed rest. I lost the baby a week later. It was a messy miscarriage. The placenta did not disengage cleanly. The last thing I remember before losing consciousness was Nate's panicked face.

I woke later to see the shadowed hood of descending twilight folding over the sky outside the window of my hospital room. A machine monitored my heart, beeping mechanically in the antiseptic silence. Nate, his face ashen, sat next to the bed and held my hand.

"What happened?" I whispered.

"You hemorrhaged. They had to give you a transfusion. Your stubborn daughter, Irina, insisted that they use her blood because she claimed that the blood in the blood bank could be tainted. I don't know where she comes up with this kind of stuff. I was in no condition to argue. They ran the blood straight from her vein into yours." Nate paused, while I smiled with pleasure at the news that Irina had been so concerned about me.

"We nearly lost you." Nate's voice broke.

"And the baby. I'm so sorry."

"There was nothing you could do about it. You were right, though. It was a boy."

"I suppose we can try for another one," I said hopefully.

"Or not try, which is how we wound up with this pregnancy," Nate replied. Then he leaned over and kissed me gently on the lips, as if he might shatter them if he pressed too hard. "For a little while today it was touch and go. You scared me."

"I guess I made it through."

"I guess you did," Nate said, patting my hand. "While you were sleeping, I tried to remember as many of the times that we have made love as I could. I thought about when we made the girls."

"How do you know which times we made the girls?"

"Not the exact times, just when we were trying; I mean for Sophie and Irina, since Sarah was a surprise. Remember that night after Ida and Izzie's anniversary party?"

"Stop, you're embarrassing me." If I had had enough blood in me I would have blushed.

"Embarrassing you? You're my wife. I was thinking that every time we have made love it has been a little different. Do you know what I mean?"

"I do," I answered.

"You are such a beautiful woman. I wish that I could remember every single time that I have ever made love to you." Nate kissed the inside of my palm and tears sprung to my eyes.

"Nathan."

"I had forgotten how much I love you. But I remember now. I won't forget again."

We could have tried to have another baby, but we didn't. We had moved on to another time in our lives and our relationship. I recognized this and welcomed it. As the girls sailed out into womanhood and the pursuit of their own lives, I returned to my sewing with fervor, and I began a renewed love affair with hats. I started selling hats and dresses on commission out of a local boutique.

Sometimes, when I looked at the young women I had raised, I missed my baby girls. I found great comfort and companionship in the presence of my daughters, even my mysterious sphinx, Irina.

My girls.

Sophie had a rich social life packed with invitations. She raced from one event to another. During football season she had cheerleading practice every night and games on the weekends. She served as secretary for the synagogue youth group, and I couldn't keep track of all the clubs at school that she had joined. The phone rang constantly and it was always for Sophie. She and I went shopping for clothing together about once a month. She was always in the height of fashion. She told me about her activities, her friends, and her triumphs.

Irina, who was probably Sophie's diametrical opposite when it came to fashion, wore the same jeans and an oversized flannel shirt day in, day out. I could hardly wrest the jeans from her to launder them. Irina rarely told me about her life, despite my efforts to be interested and ask questions. She abandoned the school's art studio in her junior year in high school and, instead, spent long hours in the art studio at the local community college, where she took classes more advanced than what they offered at the high school. I made a point of appreciating her accomplishments as an artist. This was one of the few topics of conversation that drew her out and I sometimes had success engaging her in a meaningful conversation when I managed to get her to talk to me about her artwork. She made paper and then made things out of the paper, like lampshades, stationery, and earrings. I had put up a couple of her lampshades in the house, even though they did not match the décor, and I bought stationery from her and used it. She had a passion for Japanese art and studied Japanese flower arrangement. She painted in oils and drew pencil sketches and she used a technique called "batik" to print patterns on fabric. She must have been only fourteen when she first began to take the train into Manhattan on Sundays to sell her work at street fairs and open-air markets. The extent of her imagination astounded me. I was so proud of her and so shut out of her life, both at the same time.

Sarah was my homebody. She liked to bake, curl up in a chair with a thick book, and grow flowers and herbs in the yard. She was always eager to help me in the garden. She was extremely athletic, frequently going with friends on long bicycle rides or hikes, and she played tennis quite well. She was on the swim team at school. She socialized mostly with a close-knit group of friends who went to the movies, played cards, or listened to music together. She remained close to Nate throughout her teen years.

Thus my girls grew up and soon didn't need me anymore. It angered me that Nate had closed his heart to Irina, but there was so much more to him than that, and Irina was difficult. Perhaps Nate and I did not raise our girls as perfectly as I would have liked, but I think we did well enough. Whenever I remember those first years after the war ended, when the girls were still little, I picture Nate crawling around the floor in his shirt-sleeves with his daughters squealing and jumping on his back. In most ways he was a good daddy and always an excellent breadwinner. So on the whole, I would say that I did well for myself and I am satisfied.

FIFTEEN

Rivka

WE ARRIVED IN PARIS after the war with nowhere to stay and almost no money. We registered at a center for displaced persons and the three of us slept there on cots while Yakov and I searched for jobs. By the time we met with a caseworker, Yakov had found carpentry work and had seen a doctor who diagnosed him with bronchitis and malnutrition. The doctor gave Yakov a shot of penicillin and prescribed a strong vitamin supplement, which we could not afford to buy. Once Yakov began working, we started looking for an apartment. We hoped that our caseworker could help us find Tamar if she was still alive. The last time Yakov had seen her was just before the invasion of Paris. The caseworker was an overwhelmed Swiss woman, who peered at us kindly from eyes brimming with bad news. She took notes about Tamar and the following week she called us to her office. "How I wish that I could tell you that she escaped to safety," she began.

"I did not expect her to survive. She refused to leave Paris, and she and her husband were religious Jews who belonged to a synagogue. How did she die?" Yakov asked grimly.

"An observer reported that he saw Nazi soldiers throw her into the Seine during the invasion."

"She didn't know how to swim," Yakov said.

The ticking of the second hand on the wall clock seemed terribly loud in the silence that followed. The caseworker nodded wearily. "That's right," she confirmed at last.

"And her husband?" Yakov asked.

"Shot."

"Then they died at the beginning of the Occupation," Yakov said.

"During the invasion of Paris," the caseworker replied.

"At least she did not suffer deportation to the camps," Yakov noted, as he brushed his thumb over the blue tattooed numbers on the inside of his forearm. He had just learned that his sister was murdered by the Nazis and his reaction was gratitude that she had been spared from extermination in Auschwitz. It occurred to me that Yakov was wresting a positive aspect out of the sad circumstances of his sister's death. He reminded me of Miriam and her stubborn effort to do everything in her power to give those children a splendid childhood, in spite of the Nazis and the war. I was not so obstinately optimistic. Although I had expected to learn that Tamar was dead, at the caseworker's news a blind fury swelled inside me. I wished that those soldiers who had so carelessly tossed my sister-in-law into the river were suffering torturous remorse. We did not even have so much as one photograph of Tamar. Nothing of her life remained except our memories of her as a young woman untouched by the events that followed her death. She had introduced me to Yakov. Our marriage, it seemed, was to be her only legacy.

Shortly after we received the news about Tamar, I found a part-time job as a bookkeeper for an electrician's company and we moved into a small apartment around the corner from my place of employment. The apartment was close to a school Shayna would attend in the fall. Yakov took the bus to his various carpentry jobs. I had done what Miriam had wished to do; I had looked up one day from my work in the vineyard and discovered that the war was over and I could return to my life in Paris. It felt like coming home, like returning from exile. The places we had frequented, like the cafés, held such good memories. I loved the cultural stew of Paris, the vibrant and varied street life. Able to write letters to Ruth and Mama again, I shared with them the images of my daily life and the happiness that my return to Paris brought me.

Yakov had heard of a program for former Resistance fighters that would pay tuition for attendance at the Sorbonne. This had been his dream before the war and he applied to the program. We hoped that there would be a stipend attached to the tuition scholarship for Yakov, to help with our living expenses. I fantasized that I would have the opportunity to attend college too at some point in the near future.

Not long after we moved from the center for displaced persons, the Swiss caseworker turned up at the door of our apartment. It was in the evening and I was clearing the dinner dishes as Yakov prepared to retire to the tiny living room to read the newspaper. Shayna hummed to herself as she sipped chamomile tea and drew with crayons on discarded newspaper. Apologizing for dropping in unannounced, the woman seated herself next to Shayna and removed her hat, placing it neatly beside her handbag on the kitchen table. "I have news of your family," she told Yakov. "I had no way to reach you short of coming to your home like this."

"What family?" I asked, puzzled.

"Your husband," the woman said as she nodded in Yakov's direction, "had family in Poland before the war."

Yakov sucked in his breath. We had assumed that his family in Poland had been exterminated with the rest of Polish Jewry. Before the war, the majority of Europe's Jews (outside of Russia) lived in Poland, and there were more Jewish losses in Poland than in any other country. It didn't seem likely that anyone from his family would have survived.

"As it turns out, Yakov's brother sent his two sons to Switzerland before the war in an effort to save their lives. His effort was successful," she reported, as she sat back with a satisfied smile on her usually grim face, delighted to bring good news for a change.

"Where are these boys?" Yakov asked.

"Are they in good health?" I asked.

"Who cared for them during the war?" Yakov continued. "How old are they?"

The caseworker flashed another smile as she held up a hand to stop the overflow of questions. "Hold on, I can't answer everything at once. Micah is ten years old, smart as a whip. Isaac (but you must call him Zac, or he will correct you) is thirteen and very serious. They are in excellent health. We were contacted by an orphanage for Jewish children in Switzerland and the minute Zac learned he had an uncle living in Paris he packed his brother up and they got on the train. Can you take them?"

I did not know whether to rejoice at the news that the boys had survived the war or to hide under the bed at the prospect of supporting and raising two more children. It looked like I would be following in Miriam's footsteps by taking in orphans.

Yakov, as usual, accepted this extraordinary turn of events with amazing calm and practicality. "We have nowhere for them to sleep. And no clothing. Can you help us find some bedding?" he asked our caseworker.

"They are used to doing without," the woman assured us. "Zac gives every appearance of being an extremely resourceful young man and Micah is purported to be quite bright if we are to believe the report from his school that he brought with him. I expect that they will help you figure out how to care for them."

Yakov had registered at the center for displaced persons in order to find his sister and instead wound up finding the sons of his older brother. The boys arrived the following evening, each of them carrying a small, worn rucksack. When I opened the door, I discovered them standing on the landing, holding their caps in their hands.

Zac was tall and appeared older than his years. He had a peach-fuzz mustache, clear blue eyes, and sandy brown hair. Micah had a child's mouth and the same delicate bone structure as his brother. His eyes were a deeper blue than Zac's. When I looked down at their hands, I caught my breath. Their hands were exact replicas of Yakov's hands, only smaller. They also had the little peak in the middle of their eyebrows that Yakov and Shayna had.

Yakov came up behind me in the doorway. "Let the boys in, Rivka," he boomed.

I knew him well enough to realize that Yakov's bluster was designed to conceal how moved he was to see his nephews. He wrapped them each in turn in a welcoming embrace. The boys put their bags down in the living room and came to stand awkwardly in the kitchen. Shayna hid behind my skirt.

"Are you hungry?" I asked them.

"No, thank you," Zac answered for both of them.

"I would like something to drink, please," Micah spoke up timidly. Zac shot him a piercing glance, so quick one might have missed it, but I saw it.

"You live here now. If you are too polite to accept anything to eat or drink, then you'll starve," I told Zac. "Besides, the water is free." It would take some doing to make these children feel comfortable. And how would we feed such big boys?

Shayna started kindergarten the week after Zac and Micah arrived. Conveniently, Micah took Shayna to the school every morning so that I could go straight to work. Zac had no interest in attending school. He wanted to apprentice as a carpenter and Yakov easily found him an apprenticeship through the guild. I thought the boy should be in school, but Yakov won that argument.

"If he wants to learn a trade, then so be it. We are fortunate that he knows what he wants to do and that it will provide a good living," Yakov pointed out.

"I suppose it's the teacher in me. I think that one so young should have the opportunity to learn more about the world before having to work."

"He has already learned more about the world than any child his age should ever know," Yakov replied.

"I rest my case," I said. But I did not interfere with Zac's plan for himself.

We made beds on the floor in the living room for the boys and immediately started to look for a larger apartment, although it would be some time before we would find anything we could afford. The boys needed shoes; neither of them had a pair that fit. Zac needed work clothes, and Micah needed something decent to wear to school. I thought it would be a good idea for them to go to the doctor to be checked out, but that would have to wait. They were so serious that it worried me; it seemed unhealthy.

The week that we bought Micah glasses, we had little money for food. One evening during that week, it rained hard and the roof began to leak right over the stove. I put a pot on the burner to catch the drips. For dinner that night I made giant baked potatoes and boiled carrots in chicken broth for dinner. As we ate our meal and watched the rain drip into the pot, I burst out laughing.

"What is it?" Yakov asked. He probably wondered if I had finally come unhinged.

"Rain soup for dinner tomorrow," I giggled.

Yakov laughed. "Ladies and gentlemen, for this evening's entertainment we will watch it rain in our kitchen," he announced.

Micah began to giggle, and then he began to laugh, and then Zac caught the laughter from Micah. Shayna jumped up from the table and danced around the little kitchen until her dress caught on the oven door handle. Yakov, in mock horror, cried, "Oh no, the soup has Shayna." This sent the boys into peals of laughter. Shayna dangled from the stove like a merry marionette. When Yakov released the tension on her dress, she fell over on the floor. She popped up instantly and danced to the beat of the raindrops. After that merriment, the boys relaxed more, laughed more, talked more. Something long forgotten, something about belonging to a family and having a home, was gradually coming back to them.

Micah did well in school and Zac enjoyed his apprenticeship. Zac made no effort to conceal his ambitions for his brother. He wanted Micah to become a doctor. I wondered if this was what Micah wanted for himself. He seemed as if he had the compassion and dedication necessary to be a good doctor. He certainly had the aptitude for science.

In the spring, opportunity entered our lives. Yakov was accepted to attend the Sorbonne starting in the fall through the program to provide a college education to former Resistance fighters. He was awarded a full scholarship as well as a stipend for living expenses. He hoped to one day teach political theory. Shortly before we received Yakov's acceptance, Zac started earning a living wage for his work in the carpenter's guild. And then Micah received a scholarship to attend a science academy for the summer. After the misfortune that we had experienced, it felt as though our lives were turning around. We were able to move into a three-bedroom apartment on the Left Bank, not far from the Sorbonne.

I was jealous of Yakov, since I would have given anything to attend university, but grateful that at least one of us would have the opportunity. He had earned the privilege with his blood during the war. When I wrote to Mama about it, I told her that I hoped I would have my turn to attend college one day too. In the meantime, I once again had the playground for my mind that Paris offered and that I had enjoyed before the war: the museums, the library, the free concerts in the parks, and the inexpensive upper-balcony seats at the ballet and theater.

Shayna made friends easily and I was always meeting other mothers through Shayna and her little pals. Morgan, the mother of one of Shayna's friends, came from England. Morgan was willing to help me improve my English, which had atrophied since my youth in Palestine. She also helped immensely by looking after Shayna while I worked part-time (in the mornings) throughout the summer. I wished I could take the children on a vacation somewhere, like to the beach, as Mama had taken us. But I could not afford to take the time away from work. I wrote to Catherine that I would try to save some money for a visit the following year.

When the brisk hand of autumn snatched the bright summer's warmth out of Paris, I went to work full-time. After school, Shayna walked the two blocks to my office and sat in the back room doing her homework, drawing pictures, or reading. Micah had landed a scholarship to stay on at the science academy and Zac started calling him "Little Doc."

In the sleet-gray days of winter, Avram came to Paris. On the afternoon of his arrival, Yakov skipped class so he could meet the train, and I left work an hour early, stopped at the bakery, and then hurried home.

When I came in the door, I ran straight to Avram and embraced him. "You are all bones," I scolded him. "Doesn't Christian feed you on that farm?"

He muttered something awkwardly, like someone unaccustomed to conversation.

"Avram has some news," Yakov encouraged.

"Yes, yes. I have good news," he said. "Christian and Catherine are getting married. They plan to reopen the big house on the farm."

"Robert and Miriam's house?" I asked, and Avram nodded. "Well, we could see that coming from her letters. I'm glad *they* finally figured it out. That's wonderful news," I said, thinking that the spirit of Miriam would rejoice at the fact of her house being a home again.

"And tell her the rest," Yakov prodded Avram.

"The rest, yes. The rest is that I'm moving off the farm. I'm going to America."

"America? But why? When?" I could not conceal my dismay.

"I'm a fifth wheel on the farm with Christian and Catherine getting married. Besides, I'm ready to leave France. This country holds too many bad memories for me. I can't breathe here." For a moment Avram appeared quite desperate.

"So will you stay with Ruth?" I asked, trying to control the rising panic I felt. I had already lost Ruth to America, and now, it seemed I was about to lose Avram to America as well. Or had I already lost him to the war? He was so changed. He was thin and angular; his hands seemed too large and his cheeks were sunken. He looked ten years older than he really was. His deep brown eyes, which had always been so expressive, were veiled and inaccessible.

"I'll stay with Ruth at first. But I want to buy some land, my own farm." For one brief moment a spark flickered in Avram's eyes. "Far away. A farm far away by itself." The spark extinguished.

"You have money to buy land?" I asked.

"From my father." He didn't explain further. I thought about our family in Palestine. It felt like a century since I had boarded that train to Athens. I resolved to write to Meir, a special letter just for him. He had lost so much in the Holocaust.

"I had better get supper started. Yakov has probably told you about our adopted sons. They will come home hungry." In the kitchen, I put the kettle on and nearly burst into tears. This husk in my house was not the boy with whom I had grown up. I remembered that Avram quite clearly. The war had killed that Avram.

Shayna, who had been in her bedroom, heard me in the kitchen and wandered in with her dollies. She sat under the table and played while I fixed our evening meal. She followed me into the living room when I returned. The men automatically switched from French to Hebrew when Shayna entered. I had started to teach her Russian, speaking it with her frequently, but she had never heard Hebrew before. She listened for a couple of minutes and then asked, "What are you talking?"

"We're talking Hebrew," Yakov told her. "A long time ago we lived in a country together where people speak Hebrew."

"Like Mama used to speak Russian?" she asked.

"Exactly," Yakov answered.

"I'm talking Zegrewla with Jennie," Shayna explained as she seated her doll in her lap. Her father's story sounded so far-fetched that she felt obliged to outdo him. "We used to sing Zegrewla together on an island in the ocean where we lived a long, long time ago in a different life. We say 'talking Zegrewla' but we mean 'singing' because you have to sing Zegrewla or nobody will understand you."

"I see," Yakov said, leaning toward Shayna, "it's a very musical language."

"Completely musical." Shayna gave a firm and serious nod.

Avram's face softened slightly. He said to Shayna, "I have heard that those island languages sound like singing, but I have never had the pleasure of hearing it for myself."

She grew thoughtful, perhaps wondering if Avram was joking with her. But he maintained a fairly straight face. "I think it's true," she said finally.

At that moment Zac and Micah arrived. Zac had stopped at the library on his way home from work, had met Micah there, and they had walked home together. Zac greeted Avram with a steady look and a firm hand-shake. I could see that Avram was impressed with our Zac. The men opened a bottle of red wine with the meal and, while we ate, the boys questioned Avram about his years in the Resistance with Yakov. Although Avram spoke little about himself, it didn't take much coaxing to get him to share hair-raising stories about Yakov's heroism. Embarrassed, Yakov modestly attempted to steer Avram around to buddy stories that did not feature the famous "Philippe."

Before going to bed, Shayna climbed up into Avram's lap and patted his cheek. As she looked into his eyes, recognition crossed her face. "I remember you," she said. "You brought Papa home to me." A ripple of emotion passed over Avram's face, a thin pinch to his forehead just between the eyes. It came and went in an instant before Shayna kissed him good night.

The boys stayed up late that night listening to the men's war stories. I left our bedroom door open so I could drift off to sleep to the murmur of the familiar voices floating in from the kitchen, like summer rain tapping on the roof. It reminded me of those nights in our cousins' house on the Mediterranean when I fell asleep to the soft voices and subdued laughter of Mama and her cousin talking in the kitchen down the hall from our bedroom.

On the morning of Avram's departure, I rose early with him to prepare his breakfast. He had to be at the pier by seven o'clock. I made him a strong cup of coffee, toasted him a thick slice of bread, and spread it with butter and raspberry jam. I sat across from him at the table. We were alone. "I'll write to you when you send me an address," I promised.

"I'm not a good correspondent," he warned.

"I know. But I'll write to you anyway."

I watched him eat as we sat in awkward silence.

"Stop staring at me," he requested.

"I'm waiting for word of the true Avram," I said.

"The true Avram," he repeated, with a dry, choked laugh.

"Why are you really going to America?"

"I told you. I'm sick of Europe," he nearly hissed, with a vengeance and a hatred of shocking intensity. "And I'm sick of standing at the window looking in at the things I will never have." He spoke this last almost inaudibly.

"What things?" I asked.

"Family."

"Yakov and I are family. Stay in Paris." Avram snorted by way of response.

We left many things unsaid that day. We had been so close when we were children, and now he felt so far away from me. I heard the words he said, but I thought perhaps he was trying to tell me something beneath the words that was too oblique for me to grasp.

"In Europe, family grows from history," Avram said that morning, before he left. "It evolves over time with roots shot down deep into the past. I have lost those roots. Americans create family out of thin air."

"I disagree. Family is carried within you. It has nothing to do with place. Every day of my life I speak to Mama and Ruth." More quietly I added, "and Miriam."

Avram winced. He reached across the table and took my hands. He turned them palms up and gazed into them as if peering down a long tunnel. Then he looked at me and smiled, a real smile, just for a moment. I hoped that the damage done to him by the war would heal one day. When he let go of my hands, I stood and fetched a couple of magazines down off the shelf.

"Here," I told him, "these are for Ruth. Paris fashion magazines with lots of pictures of women's clothing. And I have this photograph of Shayna and the boys for her. I was going to mail these to her but you can take them with you."

"I brought something for you from Crevecoeur, but I wasn't sure how to give it to you," he told me. He produced a small jar of jam from his pocket and handed it to me. "When Catherine reopened the big house, she found jars and jars of Miriam's preserves in the root cellar."

I looked at the lid on the jar where Catherine had written in her rounded hand MIRIAM'S LAST. The label on the front of the jar read CHERRY JAM in Yiddish. A message in a bottle.

By the time Avram's cab arrived to take him to the pier, Yakov had gotten out of bed to say good-bye. Yakov and I stood in the doorway together and waved. But Avram departed without looking back.

"He was my guardian angel throughout the war," Yakov said as the cab disappeared. "I would never have survived if not for him." I knew why Avram had protected Yakov so fiercely, but Avram and I had not spoken of this at all.

I loved learning English and practicing it with Morgan. It was one of those few things I did just for myself, the way another woman might treat herself to a manicure. I worked so hard in those years that I did not have much free time. I got up early to prepare breakfast and pack lunches for the family. I worked all day and came home to make supper, do household chores, help Shayna with homework. I wished the laundry would just stay done. Zac's clothing always needed mending. He would have done his own mending, but he worked so hard already that I insisted on doing it for him. I had a habit of talking to Miriam in my head while I was doing the mending and it became a sort of meditation for me. Every evening on my way home from work, I stopped at the corner grocer's for fresh fruit and vegetables. He became a good friend, asking me how my day had gone, his green eyes twinkling.

One evening, I opened the mail box at the bottom of the stairs and pulled out a thick, pale-blue air letter. "Auntie Ruth, Auntie Ruth," Shayna sang, knowing how I loved my letters from Ruth. When we entered the apartment, I put the letter up on a shelf in the kitchen, saving it to read to myself later as a treat before I went to sleep.

Zac had begun setting the table as best he could around Micah who, with outspread schoolbooks, attempted to continue his studies while his brother clattered about like a crazed busboy. Zac had prepared boiled noodles with fried cabbage and onions, what Mama called *chalushka*. I shooed Micah off the table, promising him he could have it back after dinner. He slunk into the living room with a book to join Yakov, who already sat in there reading.

Shayna helped Zac finish setting out the dinner things, and then she called the family to come eat. Yakov and Zac launched back into a discussion about economics that had begun before they came to the table, which had really begun months ago and would probably never conclude as long as the two of them drew breath. I asked Shayna about her day at school and she told me Morgan's daughters were going to start ballet lessons and she wanted to do it too. Micah told me about his day at the academy.

After dinner I cleaned up the kitchen and washed out a few pairs of socks in the sink, then hung them up to dry. By then Shayna was ready for bed and I took down the thick book of fairy stories that we had checked out of the library. After she fell asleep, I returned the book to its shelf and quietly closed the bedroom door behind me.

Then, finally, I took down the pale-blue air letter from America. I slit the top with a butter knife and unfolded the thin paper. The letter began: "Dearest Rivka, Papa is unable to call you because you don't have a telephone. Perhaps he sent a telegram? If not, I am sorry to be the one to bring you the sad news. Our mother and brother have died." Mama. Benjamin. Although we had arrived at peace in France, there was still a war raging elsewhere in the world, and it had devoured my mother and my baby brother.

I had not imagined when I left Palestine that I would never see Mama or Benjy again. I remembered that spring day when the British soldiers arrested me. The memory tasted of apricots. Benjy was still a little boy with a round face then. I had never known him as a man. I had an image in my mind of Mama standing over him protectively while he played at the water's edge on the beach. No wonder Mama's heart had burst with the news.

Yakov poked his head in. "Everything all right?"

I said nothing, just handed the letter to Yakov, who read, shaking his head slowly from side to side. When he finished he looked up at me. "I'm so sorry."

I took the letter from him and put it in my pocket. "It's time for bed," I said.

Yakov threw me a look of disbelief.

"What?" I demanded. "I'm tired and I have to get up early tomorrow morning and do it all over again. You know, go to work, care for the children, keep up the house. I don't have the luxury of being able to set aside time to mourn for my mother."

Yakov heard in my voice a deep exhaustion, uncharacteristic bitterness, and self-pity. For a moment my persistent optimism collapsed under the weight of my grief, which was compounded by our continued worries over finances and the ever-present toll that the war had taken on me. An ongoing gratitude for having survived permeated our lives and so we usually did not permit the challenges presented by our finances to get us down. Yet these challenges did get me down sometimes. Our limited income meant lack of time and lack of freedom. Yakov always appreciated the hard work that I did to make it possible for him to pursue his studies. Hearing that note of despair in my voice, he took me in his arms. I dissolved in his sheltering embrace and wept for my loss. Nevertheless, in the morning, I got up as usual and went to work. And the next day. And the next. Because I was still living and breathing despite the fact that others were not.

I began a letter to Papa and Meir several times, but each time I gave up after the first few sentences and threw out my attempt. Before I had the chance to write to him, Papa wrote to me. I could not remember ever receiving a letter from him before. It was always Mama who had written. The letter was short and to the point. He didn't know that Ruth had already delivered the tragic news to me. What his letter lacked in content, he made up for by enclosing a photograph of Mama with Benjamin. I stared at it for a long time and finally propped it against a teacup on the table while I wrote that letter to Papa and Meir at last. I resolved to travel to Israel to visit them when I had enough money to do so. It felt like such a time was far in the future.

Although we were cash poor, our lives were rich in all the most important ways. Our children thrived. Shayna loved her school, where she was surrounded by friends who frequently visited our home, just as Shayna frequently visited theirs. Zac and Micah shared Yakov's infectious optimism about life. I tried to be attentive to the boys and to support their interests and value their ideas. When they saw me doing without new boots in order to purchase books for Micah, they understood the message. They always helped with chores, especially Zac. He made me little things out of wood, like candlestick holders and a step stool so I could reach the top cupboards in the kitchen. Yakov often brought fellow students home to eat supper with us and I felt that the children benefited from the variety of opinions about politics, society, history, and economics that filled the conversation at those shared dinners. I relished talking with Yakov's friends, who shared their many thought-provoking ideas.

In my heart I knew that I was a linguist and a teacher and that I had talents lying fallow. But the most important task in front of me was raising these children who had nearly lost their future during the war. When I was weary from the work of caring for them, I would hear Miriam's voice in my head cheering me on, and it encouraged me. It was a good thing I could not have any more children of my own, because I would have done it. I would have liked Yakov to experience fathering a small child, but during the war my cycles had stopped and they never started again. It was just as well. I had my hands full with the three I already had and there would have been less of everything for them had I been able to have another baby.

The years following the war were an exciting time in Europe, even for a hardworking mother. Yakov and I had many politically active friends and we hoped we could help build a new society. We remained active in the Communist Party, which was accepted as part of the fabric of the French political scene. Yakov wrote regularly for a Communist newspaper and also published articles in other journals and magazines.

Of course it was Shayna who set things spinning in a new direction, just when I had settled into the predictable measure of my days. Her friends, Morgan's daughters, had been taking ballet lessons two evenings a week for several months already when Shayna started tagging along with the girls to watch their lessons. Apparently she would stand in the anteroom, with the door open to the studio, and silently imitate the moves the teacher taught. She chatted with the teacher, Annika, and brought her little gifts, like an apple, a pencil, or a piece of fudge. Annika seemed to have a lot of tolerance for my chipper daughter. Then one day Shayna announced that she had won a scholarship to ballet school.

"Annika wants to teach me," Shayna told us. "She likes me."

Yakov was of the opinion that if Shayna had talent, then we should pursue the opportunity for her to receive professional training. "She has taken the initiative and found herself a teacher," he said. I was more wary of the offer.

When I went to the studio to thank Annika, she told me, graciously, that any child so desperate to study dance should be given the opportunity. Shayna started attending lessons twice a week. But before long, she spent all her time at the ballet studio. I missed my daughter, but it made my life easier because I didn't have Shayna underfoot at the office at the end of the day when I was trying to finish work.

Then one evening, Shayna brought a note home from Annika, who wanted to meet with me. Oh no, here it comes, I thought; now that the child has become attached to dance lessons, the teacher is going to ask for payment. I could barely feed and clothe these children, how would I pay for dance lessons? After dinner I put on my threadbare coat, left the family in the warmth of our kitchen, and walked over to the dance studio. When I entered, Annika was eating a sandwich on the piano bench. She hopped up and found me a chair. The mirrors along the wall unnerved me. I turned the chair so that I couldn't see myself.

"I'm so glad you could come," Annika greeted me.

"Of course," I said. "Shayna seems to have a passion for ballet."

"It's more than a passion," Annika informed me. She had an intensity that was disquieting. "I don't suppose you realize how talented she is."

"Every mother believes her children are special."

"Yours is more than special," Annika continued. "I have taught dance for seventeen years and I can assure you that she is remarkable. I would like to have her come for a private lesson on Saturday afternoons. I have only one spot left right now, late in the day. Can she do it?"

"How much will this cost?"

"Nothing," she said, with a wave of her hand that seemed more like a fragment of escaped dance than a gesture with which to punctuate her offer. "I believe that with proper training your daughter has the potential to become a professional ballerina. My payment will be the pleasure of teaching a brilliant young talent. If you agree, I will prepare her to audition for the National Ballet School. I think she will be ready to try an audition in about three years."

"Three years! She's only eight years old," I reminded her. Annika's assessment of my daughter's supposed remarkable talent seemed a bit far-fetched and slightly melodramatic.

"With ballet you must start young," Annika explained. "For this reason, the National Ballet School has a children's program. Don't worry; it is a well-rounded education with academic studies as well as dance."

"But you must realize that we can't pay for private schooling."

"All the students at the National are scholarship students. They are the future of classical French dance. One cannot buy one's way into the National; one earns it."

I liked that idea and it reminded me of why I wanted to remain in France, a country that did not persecute its Communists but instead embraced our ideas as promising and progressive. If the country did not lean toward full-blown Communism, at least it tended toward Socialism. The fact that one could not "buy one's way," as Annika phrased it, into the National Ballet School, for instance, was a good example. "Please don't raise her hopes. I would hate to have her disappointed," I said.

"Believe in her." The intensity of Annika's gaze made me uncomfortable. "She has a gift. I can't imagine that she will be disappointed. I will tell you a secret about myself, but don't let it leave this room." Annika leaned close to me, her eyes twinkling with amusement. "I do not think of myself as a dancer; I am a teacher. It would give me such pleasure to take on your daughter as my student."

Her words reminded me of my experience teaching Nicole, my first literacy student, and a pang of envy shot through me. How I had enjoyed teaching during my time in Crevecoeur! Nothing compared to the pleasure of seeing one of my literacy students crack the code, as it were, and understand in a brilliant flash exactly how printed words corresponded to spoken language. I wondered if I could find a way to fit some small opportunity to teach adults how to read back into my life.

I thanked Annika for the free lessons and walked home lost in my thoughts. I would have to write Catherine and let her know about Shayna's ballet lessons. She had maintained that Shayna would grow up to be a dancer. It seemed so unattainable during the war years and I had not allowed myself to dare to hope for a future as rich as this for my daughter. By the time I arrived at our apartment, Shayna had gone to bed. I told Yakov what Annika had said about our daughter's talent. And about the National Ballet being free. I knew he would be as pleased as I to hear about that. With his usual enthusiasm, Yakov embraced the whole fantasy: his daughter, a prima ballerina.

"Don't look so worried about it." Yakov danced around the kitchen on his toes.

"Looks like the talent runs in the family, Aunt Rivka," Zac laughed. I could almost imagine my husband in a pink tutu. I had to laugh too.

"What? What?" Yakov tried to look innocent. He was such a boy sometimes. After all that he had been through, it was a gift to see that he had retained some of the lightness of his youth.

Before going to bed, I crept into Shayna's tiny room and peeked at my daughter as she slept. I remembered how Shayna and Isabel had danced together. Tears filled my eyes. It was dance and music that had carried Shayna through those difficult war years, and it was beginning to look as if dance and music would carry her through the rest of her life as well, whatever else it might bring. I imagined my little Shayna, all grown up, on a great stage. Was I really raising a gifted dancer? For a brief exultant moment, I pictured Shayna surrounded with flowers and admirers. Then I tucked the covers up around her slight shoulders.

After Yakov completed his baccalaureate degree in political theory, he decided to continue on for his doctorate. He was beginning to make a name for himself by publishing scholarly articles about erudite topics, such as the relationship between economic systems and democratic principles applied to government, and the faculty in his department placed a lot of weight on publication. He was offered and accepted a fellowship as an instructor at the Sorbonne. When Yakov began teaching, Zac, who was earning a good living as a journeyman carpenter, moved out into his own apartment. He still gave us part of his paycheck, however. At first I did not trust our improved financial situation, and in any case my longstanding habit of frugality would have been impossible to break. But eventually I allowed myself to believe that we were financially secure, and so I woke up one morning to the realization that the family no longer needed my paycheck. I promptly quit my job and enrolled in college.

Meanwhile, true to her word, Annika worked Shayna hard. The harder Shayna worked, the harder she wanted to work. I often worried if Shayna's obsession with dance was healthy. Yakov maintained that it was more than healthy; it was essential. "Unless she lives and breathes dance, then she won't work hard enough to become successful at it," he said.

Everyone else could admire her talent and dedication, but I was her mother, so I was the one person with the job of thinking about her happiness, and I worried that if she focused on dance to the exclusion of everything else in her life, then she would be in danger of being an unhappy person. I didn't think it necessary for her to have to choose between brilliance and happiness. She could have both.

She auditioned for the National Ballet two years in a row. The first year she did not get in and she was deeply disappointed though not as devastated as I had feared she would be with that result. I remembered our conversation in which Annika had assured me that my daughter would never be disappointed. She had been wrong about that. Fortunately, Shayna had inherited her father's persistent optimism and she began preparing to audition again within weeks of receiving her rejection. The second time, she was accepted and invited to complete her schooling at the National. If our life had revolved around ballet before, once she was accepted to the National it was consumed by it. During the same month that Shayna began attending school at the National, Micah started medical school.

My personal goals were more humble than those of the other members of our illustrious family. After completing my own college degree, I settled into a job teaching adult literacy as well as French as a second language at a community college. It was a far cry from my husband's eventual professorship at the Sorbonne, but I would not have wished to trade places with him for a minute. I loved my work and counted my blessings every day. I spoke frequently to Miriam and Mama in my head, which comforted me and helped me to sort out my thoughts. Ruth and I wrote long letters to each other. I wrote to Papa too, but my messages were shorter, and when he wrote back he always said the same things, telling me about the weather and his health.

Not long after the war ended, I had read in the newspaper that a warehouse filled with Jewish ritual objects was discovered in Berlin. It housed over three hundred Torahs as well as prayer shawls, prayer books, silver Torah ornaments, and many, many other items used by Jews who observed the holidays and laws of Judaism. The Nazis had stored these artifacts with the plan of opening a museum about Judaism that would depict the life and religious practices of an extinct race of people. The Torahs and other objects in the warehouse were in the process of being catalogued by the English and they were to be distributed to Jewish communities around the world as soon as possible. I wrote to Ruth about it and Nate was able to arrange for one of the Torahs to be sent to their synagogue.

When I look back on my personal experience of the war and the years I spent in Crevecoeur, as I do less and less often, it seems sort of unreal, as if it happened to another woman. I can barely remember how I managed to spend so much time in the vineyards performing manual labor. If I were required to do a job like that now, I would go crazy in a couple of days. At times I remember Miriam and her children so vividly and feel the loss of them so powerfully that I ache for the life we could have led and that the war shattered. At other times, I can hardly believe that Miriam is actually dead and I keep thinking I might see her again one day. Yakov never speaks about Auschwitz. Instead he passionately relates stories about his underground years with the Resistance, and certain friends persist in calling him "Philippe."

I write to Avram diligently every couple of months and tell him about our lives. He occasionally sends a postcard with a brief note. Once he sent a photograph of several handsome black-and-white goats in front of tall sunflowers. I fear that Miriam's suffering continues to live in Avram's anguished soul and I wonder how he is able to reconcile himself with being so cut off from our family who shares in his loss. I have gathered from my correspondence with Ruth and with Papa that Avram writes to Meir at the kibbutz on the Galilee where he and Papa still live, but Avram doesn't say much of import. He sends his father news about his small community and his farm. If someone were to ask me how Avram is doing, I wouldn't know what to say.

Even as the distance increases between that time and this, the war clings to the edges of our lives, always in the background, like faint music drifting over the surface of water. Whenever I attend a special family event, such as Micah's graduation from medical school, Shayna's first performance with the adult company of the National Ballet, or Zac's wedding, I say a silent *Shehecheyanu*, the prayer of gratitude for living to experience this moment in time. In my heart, I believe that my family's survival, however much we were decimated, and the survival of others like us, utterly thwarted the evil intent of the Nazis to annihilate us. By our survival, and the ability of our family to flourish once again, we defeated Hitler more completely than he could have imagined possible. We are not an extinct race. Our confiscated Torahs have been redistributed and are read from in our communities rather than being confined to glass cases in museums. Our children will thrive and we will multiply and grow again in numbers. I have sat in the darkened theater at the National, triumphantly watching my Shayna defy gravity with her graceful flight across the grandest stage in France, and at such moments I think, despite the exceptionally high price we paid: *WE WON THE WAR.*

SIXTEEN

Rivka

I HAD NOT SEEN my sister in over thirty years when she wrote to tell me that she was planning a trip to France to visit me. She explained that Nate refused to fly and didn't care for travel, which was one of the biggest reasons she had not come to see me sooner, but she had finally decided to make the trip without him. Yakov and I had applied for visas to travel to America many years before but had been denied entry because we were former card-carrying Communists. That whole experience soured us on ever wanting to pay a visit to America, which remained in the grips of Cold War hysteria.

When Ruth arrived at Orly Airport, she took the train from there into Paris. Under a cloudless blue sky, Yakov and I drove over to the train station to meet her. Waiting on the platform, I trembled with excitement, so that my teeth actually chattered against each other, as my eyes darted among the travelers, scanning each face. Then suddenly Mama's face jumped out of the crowd to meet me. Our eyes locked as Ruth hurried into my waiting arms. It was uncanny how much she resembled our mother. We clung to each other and turned slowly in a circle of reunion, both of us crying openly, oblivious to the curious stares of the strangers who surrounded us.

When she released me, Ruth took Yakov's arm by the wrist and turned it. She ran her left index finger over the military blue numbers tattooed on the inside of his forearm, the numbers she knew would be there but had never seen. Her eyes brimmed with tears as she lifted his arm to her face and brushed the numbers against her damp cheek. Yakov enfolded her in a hug.

"It's all right," he whispered in Yiddish, "it's the past. And this is the present. In spite of all of it, here we are."

"But at what price, dear brother, at what price?" Ruth said, as she brushed away the tears on her cheeks with her hand.

"Girls, girls," Yakov chuckled, for he had not seen us together since we were girls. "Enough tears. I brought only one handkerchief. Let's part the sea and step out on dry land already."

I laughed as I wiped my eyes on Yakov's one handkerchief. "I am a sentimental fool," I apologized. But even as I said it, I knew that I was understating my emotions. I had often wondered if I would ever see any member of my family again as long as I lived, and here was my sister standing in front of me. It was more wonderful than could fit into words; all I could do was cry and laugh and cry again.

"Let me see how heavy this bag is." Yakov lifted Ruth's suitcase. "Ah, you must be a more practical traveler than my Rivka, who takes the andirons from the hearth when she travels."

"Oh, for goodness' sake," I protested. "Once. Only once, I took andirons, and he won't let me forget it," I told my sister.

"I had to carry them," Yakov defended himself.

"You packed andirons?" Ruth asked incredulously.

"Catherine needed a new set so I brought them to her as a gift," I explained.

"Catherine?" Ruth raised her eyebrows in a characteristic gesture that nearly made me laugh out loud with joyful recognition. I squeezed her around the waist affectionately. She was still so slender and elegant and I had grown fat with middle age. I looked like I was the older sister. We began to walk down the platform, arm in arm.

"Catherine in Crevecoeur. The woman I lived with when we went into hiding during the war. I owe her my life. The least I can do is ensure that she stays warm in the winter."

Ruth stopped walking. "The last time I saw you was in prison. I never had a chance to thank you properly for getting yourself arrested."

"What do you mean?"

"Your arrest bought my passage to America."

"Then you owe me a ticket."

"A one-way ticket," she pointed out.

At the apartment we prepared one of Mama's favorites, a sweet noodle dish called *luxshen kugel*. I opened my recipe box and showed Ruth my copy of the recipe, written out in Yiddish in Mama's lopsided handwriting. Mama had sent it to me in one of her letters.

Ruth ran her fingers over the words with longing and affection. "It always catches me up short when something as simple as this, a recipe, calls a loved one back from the dead."

I turned the flame down under the egg noodles. As we prepared Mama's recipe we shared our news about our children. Ruth had written to me that Sophie had completed her law degree and married a doctor named Max. Such a wonderful husband, and the wedding was lovely, with every detail in place. Ruth said that Sophie was studying to take the bar exam. "She wants to practice immigration law," Ruth said, as she measured out raisins.

"That must come as no surprise, after spending so many years of her early life in a house filled with immigrants," I pointed out.

Ruth glanced at me thoughtfully. "No, I suppose not," she agreed.

"And Sarah?" I asked.

"She has declared her major in elementary education," Ruth told me with an unmistakable note of pride in her voice. "I guess she inherited your teaching gene."

I drained the cooked noodles and melted butter into them.

Ruth had planned her visit to coincide with ballet season in Paris so she could see Shayna dance the principal role in *Giselle*. I mentioned that Shayna had gotten us tickets for the following night.

"What of Irina? The artist?" I asked as I opened a container of sour cream and passed it over to Ruth.

She sighed and brushed an imaginary stray hair from her forehead with a gesture of habit. "I have to work at our relationship. I hope that one day she will marry and have children of her own and that then she will better understand the nature of my love for her. For the time being, she seems happy in her life, for which I am grateful because she is one of those people who is so smart that they are a bit socially flat-footed and I have often worried how functional she would be in the real world. She was quite the lone wolf as a teenager, but she seems to have a group of friends now at college. Although I can't get her to talk with me about her life much. She has her own apartment and is in her last year of art school. Where is your cinnamon?"

I reached over to the spice rack and handed Ruth the cinnamon. As she took it from me, she asked, "How are your boys? Yakov's nephews?"

I told her about Micah, a doctor, with a thriving practice in Paris, where he served mostly immigrants, primarily African émigrés. He worked with families uprooted from their homelands and communities when they fled from torture, violence, and other trauma. His wife was a midwife and they both devoted themselves to healing. They had two lively, talkative little girls with pigtails and a skip in their walk. I promised Ruth she would have a chance to meet the girls.

As I poured honey into a measuring cup, I gave her the update on Zac, who had built a well-respected construction business of his own. "He is a big-hearted, jovial fellow, quite the opposite of the sad-eyed, serious youth who stood on our doorstep after the war," I told Ruth. "He smokes fat cigars and drinks brandy after dinner. He married a Hungarian Jew, also a refugee. When he announced that he was engaged to her, Yakov's response was, 'A Hungarian wife will be a handful.' Handful or not, Zac is quite content with her. They have five exhaustingly athletic children, whom they are raising in blissful chaos in a rambling, disheveled older house on the outskirts of Paris. I am constantly amazed at the number of toys with wheels that cover Zac's front yard and walkway when I visit. Zac claims the bicycles, roller skates, and toy cars keep the weeds down. I suspect that half the youngsters in the neighborhood park their gear at Zac's."

I put a hand on my hip and wagged a finger at Ruth. "And what about your Nate? You should have insisted he come with you."

A twinkle of amusement and affection sparked in Ruth's eyes, which then seemed to turn inward to a place only she could see. "He won't travel. How did I wind up with such an unadventurous husband? You will have to come to America if you want to meet him."

"Well that won't happen until your paranoid country changes its opinion of Communists," I reminded her with disgust.

Ruth ignored my jab at America and asked, "And Yakov enjoys teaching?" I had written to her that Yakov had carved out a fine position for himself as a professor at the Sorbonne.

"Loves it. He was born to do it," I answered. "He has published a book and he writes a regular column in a widely circulated Socialist newspaper. He has an entourage of ever-changing serious young men who follow him around, recording his wisdom in their pocket journals. In my opinion, it's excessive. I'm sure it has to do with his reputation as a former Resistance fighter."

"And you, too, are a teacher," Ruth interjected.

"Not at the Sorbonne like my scholarly husband," I noted. "I teach older students. My favorite class is my adult literacy class. I also teach French as a second language and beginning Russian. I need to feel as though I am doing something worthwhile. Teaching was always close to my heart and now I am finally able to do it. I also make a bit of a ruckus with my political work, such as helping to organize demonstrations and other political events. I was even arrested once for protesting the French involvement in Vietnam."

"Isn't that dangerous?" Ruth asked in alarm.

I shrugged. "Perhaps."

"Those daffodils are delightful," Ruth observed. I had filled a blue vase with daffodils and placed it in the center of the table where the flowers radiated good cheer like a miniature sun.

After we ate dinner, and had enjoyed the *kugel* we had made for dessert, Ruth and I sat at the table in the rays of the daffodils and looked through the photographs Ruth had brought. We came across a picture of all of us at the beach when we were children. Mama had paid a photographer to take that picture. She bought Benjy a lollipop to keep him occupied so he would stand still. "We had many good years in Palestine, didn't we? Mama was happy then," I said.

"She was. So were we all. We deserved it, though, after Russia. Growing up with Avram and Miriam in our house made it feel like a big family."

"Mama loved raising us. We broke her heart when we scattered to the four corners like we did," I said wistfully.

Ruth stared hard at the picture of our childhood faces. "Miriam and Benjamin broke her heart. Avram would have too if she had known what the war did to him." She looked up from the page. "What really happened to Miriam? Why do you and Avram refuse to tell me the whole story?"

"Please believe me when I say that it is better this way," I replied.

"I've often wondered exactly how she died."

"How she lived was an inspiration and I would love to talk about that. Knowing how she died serves no constructive purpose." I was determined to shut the door on Ruth's question.

"It serves a constructive purpose for me. It might be better for you to not have to tell what happened, but I think it would be better for me to know, no matter how horrible the truth may be, and I think that I have the greater ability to judge what is better for me than you do. Without knowing, it is as if I cannot entirely define the shape of my grief."

"Leave your grief shapeless. I wish I didn't know exactly what happened to Miriam. I begged Avram not to tell me. But at the time, he had to tell for the sake of his own sanity."

"Well, it didn't work."

"How is that?" I asked, although I knew the answer.

"Is it sane to live alone in a remote corner of Vermont and to have no attachment to any community? To believe that the world is going to hell in a handbasket so it's better to stay uninvolved? Is that sane?"

"I think it's sane to find peace among trees and animals when humans have caused someone as much pain as they have caused Avram."

The shadows of the evening deepened and a cool darkness crept into the corners of the room. I turned on the lamp and poured more tea.

"I will tell you this much," I conceded. Ruth leaned forward eagerly, as if preparing to unwrap a special gift. "She lived well and was happy. She was an example to others. She refused to let the war touch her, even though it caught up with her in the end. She took care of sixteen wonderful children, including her own son, Akiva, and those children were her life. The Nazis murdered her and those precious children. Avram found her husband living as a crazy beggar afterward. He asked Avram to shoot him, to end his agony. Even at the last, Robert had such reverence for life that he could not take his own. Avram did as Robert requested of him."

"He shot him?"

"I would have done the same," I told her evenly. She was bewildered. So I reminded her, "You have not lived through a war, at home, in your own country."

"I have lived through a war at home in my own house," Ruth replied hotly. "Wondering about you, Miriam, and Avram, while rescuing people who had lost their entire family to the death camps."

I was taken aback and realized that I had misjudged. "I'm sorry. I have no right to belittle your experience of the war. I should not have implied that you did not suffer."

"Apology accepted," Ruth said.

I paused to gather my thoughts. "As for Robert, I think that there are times when the peace of death is preferable to the despair of a painful and hopeless life." I wondered if Ruth would be receptive to my ideas on reincarnation. I trusted her and so I rushed headlong into it. "But then, I believe that death is a doorway to the next level in the journey of the spirit."

"You believe in life after death?"

"I believe that the spirit continues through many lives."

Ruth said nothing, but she did not dismiss me out of hand, so I continued.

"I am convinced that I remember fragments from past lives that I have lived and that occasionally I recognize the spirit of someone whom I once knew in a previous life. I never speak about it because most people would think I'm crazy and also because I find that it usually makes people uncomfortable." I caught myself lowering my voice, as if someone listening outside the door might rush in to arrest me if they heard my words.

"There are a lot of people who believe in reincarnation," Ruth said noncommittally, without revealing one way or another her own belief. "How do you know that you are recognizing someone or remembering a previous life?"

"I just know. In my heart." I tapped my chest with two fingers. "It's hard to describe. It's a recognition beyond ordinary recognition. It's a deep certainty."

"I have a recurring dream that seems more like a memory than a dream at times. Perhaps I am remembering a past life," Ruth told me, haltingly.

"What do you dream?" I asked.

Ruth hesitated.

"Don't worry, I'm taking you seriously," I said. I was amazed that we were having this conversation. I rarely felt comfortable discussing this topic. It was a relief to speak about these things openly.

"When you say a recognition beyond ordinary recognition, that describes the feeling I have in these dreams. They're not ordinary dreams. Everything appears hyper-real and too familiar and I know what will happen before it does. It's hard to explain the difference between these dreams and everyday dreams. I think of them as my Chinese dreams, because everyone in them is Chinese, including me, and they seem to take place in China."

"That's interesting," I said. I wondered why her dreams were set in China since it was a setting far from anything familiar to her.

"Pretty strange, isn't it?" Ruth replied. "I dream about details of Chinese culture that I have no way of knowing about. I have no idea how this stuff got into my brain. The things I find in my unconscious astonish me."

"So what happens in the Chinese dreams?" I had never had a memory or recognition that I associated with reincarnation in the context of a dream.

"It's not pleasant," Ruth said.

"Then I'm duly forewarned. What happens?"

"Well, here is the usual sequence. I am standing in a room with my husband and my daughter. The husband is a version of Nate, and the daughter . . ." Ruth trailed off. "I have never told anyone about this before."

"I'm not judging. I'm just listening. It's a dream," I said. "It's not real."

She nodded and swallowed. "It seems real, though. The daughter is a version of Irina. The dream takes place on a hot, humid night. I am inside with the doors and windows open. A breeze passes through the room. A strong scent of flowers drifts in from the gardens. Did you know that scent in dreams is uncommon? I only smell things in the Chinese dreams, not in ordinary dreams. I am submissive and silent. I stare at my feet. My husband is shouting at my daughter, who is weeping. A young gardener is outside and he looks in the window at my daughter before he runs away. I think she is in love with him. I think my husband forces her to marry someone else instead. I remain silent because I am afraid of my husband. Occasionally I dream that he hits me across the face. The dream usually ends with . . ." Ruth stopped and I waited for her to continue, without speaking, without moving a finger.

"At the end of the dream, I am looking in a window at my daughter who is being raped by a man much older than she, and she is screaming, and I am helpless. I am unable to intervene to protect her." Ruth's hands were shaking.

"What do you think about this dream?" I asked.

"For many years, I simply dreaded it and had no idea why I dreamed it. But after I began to recognize the husband in it as a distorted Chinese version of Nate and the daughter as a similarly distorted version of Irina, I began to wonder if I was remembering something from a different life. My Nate is nothing like that Nate, I assure you. My Nate has never raised a hand to me. He is a loving father for Sophie and Sarah. He doesn't get along with Irina and they had some difficult moments when she was growing up, as I shared with you a little in my letters during that time. But I believe in my heart that there is still love there between them. Perhaps one day they will forgive each other for their failings and rebuild their relationship. That's my hope. So tell me what you think."

"Your dream," I paused, searching for the right words, "is not the sort of past-life recognition with which I'm familiar. But, in my opinion, you're probably right about remembering a past life in which these events happened. I would be inclined to say that the three of you have an opportunity to work through the errors of that life in this one. Maybe this is Nate's chance to resolve a past mistake, and if he doesn't do it this time around, it will come back again the next time around, and the next, until he deals with it."

"Then he will have to deal with it in the next life, because he would never hear this explanation. It would be so much silly nonsense to him. And you have to admit that it does sound a lot like nonsense," Ruth said.

"Not to me. It sounds quite sensible to me. And I hope that you are resolving it with Irina so that your spirit can move on to the next level from here, whatever that may be," I advised.

Ruth took my hands in hers across the table and held them for a long moment. She closed her eyes, nodded her head, and then met my gaze. The discord in her family obviously disturbed her deeply. I said nothing so that she could take the time she needed to pull herself together. "I am not willing to lose my daughter and I am being persistent in maintaining my relationship with her. If the Chinese dreams are about a previous life in which I failed her, then I am determined not to repeat that mistake. I love her very much, even though I will never understand how on earth her mind works." Ruth released my hands. "Enough," she said. "I am tired."

"I'm sorry; I should have realized. Of course you are worn out from your journey. Let me get you settled." I fetched Ruth a set of towels and showed her to the guest room.

Later, in my own bed, sleep eluded me. Long after Yakov began snoring gently, I sat at the window wrapped in my bathrobe and gazed at the sky. The clouds moved rapidly, first obscuring, then revealing a nearly full moon. A storm rolled in, crackling with electricity. It reminded me of the warm thunderstorms that appeared without warning during our summers at the beach when we were children and how we would stand outside with our heads thrown back catching the raindrops on our tongues. The thunder stepped out slowly, a heavy beast shaking itself awake. Then rain pelted down, a comforting patter on the roof. I asked myself what I had accomplished in my life. It was Miriam's old question that continued to follow me throughout my days. I was still trying to answer it. I raised three children. I taught people to read and to speak new languages. I survived the war, and that was surely a significant accomplishment right there. I made a good marriage. I glanced at Yakov's sleeping form and smiled. I asked myself if this was enough, and if I were to die in this moment, if I would go peacefully, feeling that I had made my contribution, if I had made a difference in the world, and if I was prepared for death.

I thought about the perspective on life that was possible for an old soul that has experienced many lives. Such a fully evolved soul would have the ability to see existence from a broader perspective, the ability to see that cultural context, race, and gender only last as far as one lifetime. Therefore, ultimately there is no "other" but only "us." I liked to think that I possessed such an old soul. I wondered how long the fully evolved souls must wait for all the other souls to catch up. How much human suffering and environmental damage must occur before enough souls have gone around enough times to figure it out? And how do I act differently in the world if I believe that the life of the spirit transcends death? I felt old and tired and overwhelmed by the failings of humans. The rain brushed over the house in waves, hammering hard, tapping softly, then hammering again. A bluish-gray tint washed over the damp streets and buildings. The lines of objects blurred, disappearing into shadows and altering the view from my window in ways that made it lose its familiarity. I nodded off to sleep in my chair.

I woke about an hour later, stiff and cold. My bad leg buckled when I stood up and I caught the back of the chair for support. Whenever my leg buckled, I thought of Miriam and the day that Avram came to tell me she was gone. I crawled into bed beside Yakov's warmth and rested my hand on his shoulder. Touching him soothed me and quieted the voices of the ghosts and reveries that clattered inside my head. Listening to the lullaby of his steady breathing, I drifted back to sleep.

For the two weeks of Ruth's visit, I felt suspended outside time.

When I took her to the ballet to see Shayna dance in *Giselle*, we ran into Annika and I introduced her to Ruth. "If it weren't for this woman, Shayna would never have joined the National," I told Ruth.

"Not true!" Annika disagreed. "That child would have danced no matter what happened. I just got lucky. She came in through my door."

We met Shayna for lunch at an outdoor café one afternoon. As she explored her bowl of bouillabaisse with her spoon, Ruth asked Shayna, "What is your first childhood memory? The oldest one."

"My oldest memory," Shayna began thoughtfully, as she swirled a dry white wine in her glass, then took a delicate sip, "is one of my birthday parties. Miriam decorated a pony cart with flowers. I will never forget the thrill of that pony cart. We sang and danced. I received a huge bouquet of fragrant lavender and bright-orange nasturtiums, a little wooden giraffe, and a dress with cherries printed on it that I wore constantly afterward."

Shayna's memory brought tears to my eyes.

"That was the party that Miriam made for you, wasn't it?" Ruth asked Shayna, as she patted my hand comfortingly. I had written to Ruth about that party on more than one occasion and she was well aware of how much that effort from Miriam had meant to me. It was also the last time I saw our sister alive.

"That's right," Shayna answered.

"For years I worried that your memories of your early years would be dismal because of the war and our poverty afterward, so I'm relieved that you seem to have come through unscathed," I said.

"I never felt deprived," Shayna told us. "I was surrounded by people whom I loved and who loved me and we had a lot of fun. I could see that there were things we could not afford, but the things that mattered, we had. I even spent part of the summer holidays in Crevecoeur each year for ten or more years while I was growing up. Micah went with me a few times when I was very young. Maman sent us on the train to stay with Aunt Catherine. Isabel and I would chase butterflies, pick peaches and almonds, and ride horses; and I returned to Paris browned by the sun and full of stories about the goats and dogs and the fields of sunflowers. That is the childhood I remember, not the war."

"Shayna's trademark as a ballerina," I explained to Ruth, "is her ability to seemingly defy the laws of gravity. Photographers thrive on capturing her in midair, as if in flight. They have nicknamed her the Oiseau."

"That means 'bird,' doesn't it?" Ruth asked.

"Yes, that's it," I confirmed. "I have often speculated that the terrible state of the world during Shayna's early years left her with an unconscious desire to flee the planet, and so she propels herself airborne as frequently as possible."

"Not true, Maman. You exaggerate. I have no desire to flee. What I have is quite simply a passion for the dance."

"To the general exclusion of everything else much of the time," I said.

"And why not?" Shayna raised an eyebrow in mild irritation. "Papa would be the first to say that my commitment is essential, and he is right."

"I agree with him about that. I am not faulting you for your hard work and commitment. You know how proud I am of your accomplishments. But I am not one of your fans, I'm your mother, and I'm not talking about success or greatness. I'm talking about your happiness. Dance depends on the agility of the body," I pointed out, "and that is finite. I worry about what will happen when your body begins to age and refuses to obey commands. What kind of life will you have then?"

"I'm still seeing Pierre, if that's what's bothering you. But I will never change my mind about children. If Pierre can accept that, then I will never leave him. That is his choice."

"You're asking him to make quite a sacrifice," I said. "Even if you don't wish to carry a baby in your own body, I don't see why you're so opposed to adoption." Was it for Pierre or for myself that I argued? Shayna's choice not to have children would end my family line with a hard stop. I loved Zac and Micah, but they had come to me half grown already and they were not blood of my blood. Suggesting adoption was a mere grasp at straws. Pierre was not the only one who was making a sacrifice to bow to Shayna's wishes.

"I have quite a few friends who have adopted children," Ruth said in an effort to help solve the problem. "And your parents adopted Zac and Micah. There is nothing wrong with adoption."

"I do not intend to live the sort of life that is conducive to raising children," Shayna explained to Ruth. "It would not be fair to them. Maman and I have discussed this and she is aware of my thoughts on this subject."

"Are you sure that you won't regret that decision?" I asked anxiously. "Even when you're older and the agility of your body fades?"

"Dance is my life. Dance is my children. I intend to enjoy the few years I have left as a principal dancer and when I become too old to be a prima ballerina, I will choreograph. Furthermore, there is no rule that says I can't perform in modern dance or jazz dance pieces. Modern dancers perform for many years longer than ballet dancers. I have plenty of options in my future."

"Your mother wants more for you than the adoration of fans," Ruth suggested quietly. "She wants for you the circle of family."

"I have plenty of family," Shayna replied. "I have my parents, Micah and Zac and their families. Isabel and her tribe in Crevecoeur. Lord knows she has enough children for us all. And the National Ballet is my family. I grew up there. I have known where my heart lies for as long as I can remember. I am never as completely alive as when I am inside the dance. Don't you see? In that moment, I am pure spirit, burning brightly. There is nothing that compares. I am nothing more than a servant to the dance."

I patted Shayna's arm as I turned to speak to Ruth. "How did someone as down-to-earth as myself manage to raise the Oiseau, I ask you? We are so different from one another. Shayna believes art defines life, whereas I believe that life defines art."

Shayna placed her empty wineglass on the table. She leaned forward to emphasize her words. "For me, creating art is imperative, inescapable, and personal. Of course art defines life."

"Art is one of many tools for change," I said.

"Spoken as a true political activist," Shayna observed. "If we are to continue this conversation, then you must buy me another glass of wine."

"You should have been an attorney," I observed in exasperation, as Ruth laughed at the vigor of our discussion.

The day after our luncheon with Shayna, Ruth and I made a pilgrimage to Crevecoeur and stayed in Miriam's house. Catherine and Christian had produced a matched set of twin boys to keep Isabel company and they all lived in the farmhouse that had once belonged to Robert. The twins were large, strapping fellows with broad shoulders and clear eyes and were cheerful, soft-spoken, and as devoted to farming as their father. Isabel had married a farmer when she was yet a teenager. She already had three children, the youngest a fat, round-faced toddler who chattered nonsense words constantly, and she was expecting another baby already. She seemed determined to repopulate that farmhouse as swiftly as possible with her brood. It pleased me to know that Miriam's cherry trees would fill with children when the cherries ripened in season and the shouts of little voices were once again echoing across the fields, through the barn, and in the spacious country kitchen.

Ruth and I walked into the orchards together. "Do you remember how Miriam named that tree Elijah when we were children?" Ruth asked me.

"Of course," I replied, "she really could be ridiculous sometimes."

"I wonder what she would have looked like in her fifties," Ruth said. "I wonder if she would have resembled her mother."

"Do you think we would recognize each other if she appeared right there by that apple tree at this very moment?" I asked as I pointed.

We gazed at the tree for a minute in silence.

"I could almost see her where you pointed," Ruth said. "I could almost see how she must have been when she lived here." Ruth brushed tears back from her cheekbones with the palms of her hands and said, "Wait for me here. I'll be right back." As I watched, she walked through the orchard picking yellow and violet wildflowers until she had a substantial bouquet. Then she proceeded to the apple tree and laid the flowers at the base of it. When she returned to me, her eyes were dry. She looped her arm through mine and we returned through the tall grass to the farmhouse in silence.

Back in Paris we toured dress shops for hours. Ruth could not walk past a shoe sale or a handbag in a store window without pausing for a look. She shipped two cartons of dresses and a carton each of hats and shoes back home. We sipped tea in the outdoor cafés and visited the Louvre. I took Ruth to Versailles and told her the story of how Miriam met Robert by the lavender. I felt Miriam there with us, and the past and present merged briefly as I stood beyond the grasp of the headlong rush of time.

On Ruth's last day in Paris, we went for a stroll through the Tuileries Garden, arms linked, fitting as many words as possible into the day. We talked about the years we had spent raising babies, children, adolescents. Years of worry and pride woven with the dreams of mothers. Years heaped with endless sandwiches packed in paper bags, laundry, dishwashing, and mending; the piles of papers migrating home from school; birthday parties and scraped elbows. The small tragedies and daily celebrations. The years of letting go, hoping for our children's success in the world. Turning our thoughts toward grandchildren. Realizing that once the children are grown, then their happiness is dependent on factors outside a mother's control, happiness that can't be provided by baking cookies or an outing to the beach.

We talked about our husbands, those early years in the first glow, the years of sacrifice to allow the husbands to pursue their dreams, the exhaustion and despair of the war, the refugees Nate took in, the years of service that took the famous Philippe away from his family, the limitless love that we women feel for the father of our children. Desire, partnership, putting up with the incorrigible maleness of men. The way that love ducks its head and then resurfaces ever more powerfully again and again over the course of a marriage.

Our women friends, how we couldn't get by without their comfort, support, reaffirmation; the sheer delight of female companionship. The practical, well-ordered world of women, and the great pleasure of women working together, those meal preparation rituals that afforded hours for conversation in the kitchen. Sharing life cycle events and late-night conversations over a glass of wine or a cup of tea. Celebrating small successes, sharing our convictions.

We talked of Ruth's love of harmony and visual beauty and how that translated into her designs for dresses and hats, my love of teaching languages and literacy, my faith in the power and the purpose of words. We talked about dreams deferred and the effort to not begrudge children, husbands, and friends the time and energy we gave to them. Not begrudging, but remembering with vivid clarity the frustration of having an avalanche of commitments preventing us from pursuing the work for which we had a true passion, our spiritual nourishment. Oh, that life of the spirit. What we see here before us, as terrible or splendid as it may be, is no more than a drop in the vast ocean of spirit.

Together at last, the two of us brought back to each other, piece by precious piece, the glorious days and hours spent in Mama's house with the family in Palestine that grew from the kernel of Miriam's idea to combine our families. When the far edge of evening cast a purple shadow on the hedges and the flowers folded for the night, we headed for home.

"Despite our losses, we have been fortunate," Ruth said.

As I agreed, I realized that I had heeded Miriam's words throughout the years and taken care to remain grateful. "My dear sister," I said to Ruth as well as to the one who was no longer with us, "I have perfected the art of counting my blessings."

PART TWO

Rina

One

I WILL ALWAYS REMEMBER the exhilaration I felt on the day I moved out of my father's house to attend art school. The trunk of Nate's car yawned open on the street in front of my dormitory, revealing its contents like jewels in a treasure chest. I unloaded my few belongings, hand carrying the many delicate items, such as a spray of peacock feathers rolled in newspaper and my jars of seashells, stones, and marbles. I liked to put my jar of marbles in the window where they would catch the light. Nate remained silent while Mother fussed and chattered about the most inane things, such as the menu for the evening that was posted on the cafeteria door and the small size of the closet in my room. I restrained myself from interjecting any of the sarcastic retorts that popped into my head in a concerted effort not to hurt her feelings, reminding myself that soon she would be gone.

Once we unloaded my possessions, my parents offered to take me for a bite to eat, but I declined, so they had no excuse to stick around. I submitted to an engulfing hug from Mother, who kissed me on both cheeks. Nate gave me an awkward pat on the arm. Then they mercifully melted into the flurry of activity in front of the dorm. I closed the door to my room and leaned back against it with an internal whoop of joy as I grabbed my freedom in handfuls and pulled it toward me.

I was used to having a lot of time alone and had worried about how I would live with a roommate, but I lucked out. My roommate's family lived only a few blocks from the campus. Her father had paid for her to have a dorm room to give her the full college freshman experience, but she never stayed there. She barely moved anything into the dorm from her parents' house. After she arrived, and we introduced ourselves to each other, she made up her bed and then left. I didn't see her again for a week after that.

Once my roommate came and went, I ventured out into the hallway, which buzzed with activity. Other young women on my floor nodded and smiled at me in passing and I nodded and smiled back. I wondered which of them would become my friends. I managed to find the dorm supervisor and asked her if I could remove my mattress from the bed frame; I preferred to put my mattress right on the floor. An hour later, a baffled and bemused janitor disappeared down the hall bearing my bed frame off to the basement. I took down the curtains and replaced them with bright green and black batiks of African drums. I hung my pictures, posters, and photographs on my side of the room. I set out my collection of pottery, wood carvings, shells, dried flowers, feathers, and stones. I surrounded myself with the beauty that was my shield and my inspiration.

Dinner at the cafeteria was beyond dreadful for me, a vegetarian and proponent of natural foods. The white rolls, mystery stew, mashed potatoes, frozen peas, and yellow Jell-O turned my stomach. I walked down the street where I found a neighborhood market and bought Swiss cheese, whole-wheat crackers, mustard, and fruit. I bought a bar of sandalwood soap and held it under my nose all the way back to my room. I felt so light I thought I might float into the sky like a shred of silk.

The next day I registered for my classes, most of which were prerequisites. I did manage to sneak in a class entitled Art of Primitive Peoples. In the evening I went with a couple of women who lived on my hall to a coffeehouse called the Jackrabbit. They had heard that the Jackrabbit had good jazz. Practically everyone in the place wore black and smoked cigarettes. The performance for the evening was a man reading poetry while another man played jazz music on a saxophone. I couldn't make sense out of the poetry, but I kind of liked the counterpoint rhythm between the saxophone and the poet's voice.

I didn't have much to say to the women who had introduced me to the place, but I talked with them a little between the musical numbers. I had never been good at chitchat. Except for the cigarette smoke, which burned my eyes, I liked the Jackrabbit. Our waitress was about my age and had long blond hair that thinned at the ends around her waist. Her eyes were ringed with heavy black eyeliner. A silver serpent arm-bracelet with glowing green eyes coiled around her upper arm. She wore gold hoop earrings and a large orange cloth flower in her hair. Her name was Norma and I thought she looked pretty interesting.

The next day, when Norma turned up in my Introduction to Design class, we recognized each other immediately. All the students studying graphics, like me, had to take a full year of Introduction to Design. I was much more curious about my fellow design students than I was about the women who lived in my dorm. I was pleased that Norma was in the class, since I had liked the looks of her from the moment we saw each other at the Jackrabbit. And I was grateful to have Norma to talk to before our class began. I had not had any real friends in high school. The people who went to my high school had not seemed capable of doing anything constructive with their time, in my opinion. But now I was certain I would meet people who would contribute interesting ideas to a conversation, who had ambition, who felt passionate about art and were willing to work hard to create it, and I was determined to make some friends.

When the professor arrived, she introduced herself as Margaret, and then she divided the class into three work groups. Norma and I were assigned to the same group. In retrospect, I have wondered if fate had a hand in that first day (assuming there is such a thing as fate). Margaret could not have guessed how well the students in our work group would get along and how important we would become in one another's lives.

Our group, which assembled around a cluster of worktables, included me and Norma; Dale, a wispy, light-skinned Negro man; high-spirited and hilarious TJ, who used a wheelchair to get around; Skip, a country boy fresh from the farm; and Arthur, who was a reticent, mysterious Negro man, as dark chocolate brown as deep Harlem from which he came. When the first class ended, TJ suggested we go out for lunch together to get better acquainted. After passing up a pizza parlor and two delis with stairs at the front entrance because TJ couldn't get inside in the chair, we went to the campus student union for sandwiches. The student union was wheelchair accessible with an accessible bathroom. I had never before considered the challenges presented by trying to go places with someone not put together to go up stairs.

The student union was located on one side of the quadrangle in an older building. It had long narrow windows and comfy furniture. This was the first time I had been inside and I liked the cozy, well-worn feel. We sat at a large, round, wooden table.

TJ seemed to think it was his sworn duty to take on the role of the emcee. "OK, time for the encounter group," he announced. Norma and Arthur groaned and rolled their eyes. "Everyone has to play," TJ warned. "I want to get to know you." His genuine, straightforward, and upbeat manner defied resistance.

"Cut to the chase, TJ," I teased.

"You bet," TJ replied. "You go first." He pointed at me. "Irina."

My mind went blank. I said nothing.

After an awkward moment of silence, TJ said, "OK, I'll go first," pointing to himself instead. "I'm from Scarsdale. I have two older sisters. My parents are divorced. Dad lives in Malibu, and even though he's good at paying the bills, we never see him. Can't blame him too much; I mean think of the choice: Malibu or Scarsdale? Tough one." TJ grinned irresistibly. "Because I'm in a wheelchair, it makes it extra hard for me to get a date on Saturday night, so I spend most of my time thinking about women with large breasts." Skip registered surprise at this comment. Norma and I cracked up. Arthur's "Mr. Cool" facade crumbled as he guffawed loudly. TJ continued, "Women are deep, you know. Anyway, I'm passionate about art and I consider myself lucky to have the opportunity to study it. And, I might add, I'm good at it. I intend to be highly successful so I can snag some of those aforementioned women."

TJ's exuberance broke the ice and each of us in turn shared information about ourselves. Norma, who was sitting next to TJ, went next. She told us she came from a working-class family in a steel town in Pennsylvania and she said her parents had thrown her out of the house because she wanted to go to college instead of going to work. "They probably figured that if they threw me out I'd have to go to work anyway, but then I got a scholarship and I landed a job at that club called the Jackrabbit, so I can manage to take care of myself. My ace in the hole is that I don't need a whole lot of sleep."

I was sitting next to Norma, so it seemed like I was next. Unaccustomed as I was to talking about myself much, I felt uncomfortable when everyone around the table turned their eyes to me. I liked these people more than I had liked anyone in a long time. I was determined to push myself to open up more and to take some risks that would help me connect with other artists at college. I swallowed my fear and told them that I had been a loner in high school. I asked them to be patient with me because I was a little timid, and I shared that I was beyond elated to move away from home and be in college at last. "I'm on a creative achievement scholarship," I concluded, hoping I didn't sound too boastful. "I'm proud of that."

"Absolutely," TJ said, clapping. "Congratulations."

"Where did your name come from?" Arthur asked. "Irina sounds kind of old-fashioned to me."

"My mother chose it. She's Russian. I'm not sure where she got it. Maybe I'm named after a Chekhov character."

"It seems sort of formal," Dale observed.

"I've never really liked it," I admitted.

"What would you like to be called instead?" Norma asked. "No one around here knows you yet. Make up a new name and we'll call you that."

It had never occurred to me to go by a name other than Irina, but I absolutely loved the idea. I tried to imagine telling my sisters that I was using a new name. Sarah would probably like the idea and Soph would probably tell me I was being silly. Thinking about them made me smile. I would probably have gone crazy growing up in that house without them, even though they could be so annoying with their trivial interests. Soph was preoccupied with clothes and parties and she had been a cheerleader for years. I did not get how anyone in their right mind could waste so much time and energy cheering for boys playing football. Sarah at least took school more seriously than Soph did, but she was way too athletic, going on bike rides for hours, playing tennis, swimming. How could anyone be so enthralled with sports? My mind had wandered. Meanwhile, no one at the table had said anything. They were giving me room to think, and I appreciated it. I looked around at their expectant faces, and I felt such gratitude for the possibility of having real friends at last that I got an actual lump in my throat.

"What about just Rina?" I asked. "What do you guys think?"

"I think that sounds more contemporary than Irina," Arthur said.

"Absolutely," Norma agreed, "I think Rina suits you."

"I like it," I told them. "It feels right." I had chosen a new name to go with my new life.

TJ asked, "Anyone else want a new name? Alrighty then. Moving right along, Skip, what's your story?"

Skip laughed. "You just don't quit," he told TJ. He looked down into his lap for a moment and then lifted his head and told us, "The honest truth is that my dad mortgaged the farm to send me to college."

"Are you serious?" I asked.

"I wish I wasn't, but I am. I grew up in a tiny rural community. We are talking dirt road, out in the boonies with the foxes, snakes, coyotes, possums, and an occasional bear, also in Pennsylvania, it so happens," he nodded in Norma's direction, "where I was a big fish in a little pond. My whole life, everyone at church said I was so talented and that I'd make something of myself someday. So now I'm supposed to become a successful graphic designer and then help buy back the farm. I'm the oldest of nine kids. We're Christians; Methodists to be more precise. My mom makes the best peach pie in five counties. What else do you want to know?"

"You're a Methodist?" Norma remarked, "and your dad sent you to college to hang out with *art students*? What was he thinking? You'll be straying from the path of righteousness in a heartbeat."

"It's not like that," Skip responded, self-consciously.

"Technically, I'm pretty sure I'm Christian too," TJ said.

"I was raised Jewish, but I don't do any of that stuff anymore," I told the others. I had stopped going to synagogue with my parents a long time ago, and I didn't think of myself as Jewish. I didn't think of myself as any category other than an artist. But when it came down to it, I couldn't quite say that I had no religion. I still genuinely enjoyed going to Uncle Romek and Aunt Netya's for Passover, which was a freedom holiday with meaningful rituals. And at the back of my mind tugged the memory that my mother had lost an adopted sister in the Holocaust.

"I'm an atheist," Norma stated flatly.

"What about you?" TJ asked Arthur.

"Raised Baptist. I still go to church sometimes," Arthur answered. Although it was hard to get Arthur to lighten up, he seemed to be warming to us. He was handsome, with clear skin, large hands, and broad shoulders. "I was raised in Harlem. I still live there with my family. My passions in life are art and the civil rights movement."

"I can get behind that," TJ replied. "What about your social life? Any women?"

"That's none of your business, Mr. Big Breasts," Arthur rebuffed him, but with obvious good humor.

"My turn," Dale said. "I'm from Virginia," he drawled dramatically with an attractive southern accent. "Dad's a retired colonel." Dale grimaced. "I have enough older brothers in the military to successfully stage a family invasion of Lithuania. I'm the youngest, and my grandmother talked Dad into letting me go to art school for a few years. When I graduate, I'm supposed to go out to West Point to have my edges sharpened. I'm not sure how I'll get out of that one. Maybe I can change my name too and I'll disappear."

TJ, who I was starting to think viewed humor as the appropriate response to every situation, told Dale, "That's not necessary. If you turn sideways you'll vanish and dear old Dad won't be able to find you. Just don't put on any weight."

"Sorry to break up this Kodak moment," Norma said, "but I have to go to my next class." Our lunch gathering ended abruptly. When I left that table on that first day of class, I was ecstatic. I had found the kind of kindred spirits I had wished for all my life. I hoped I would be able to shake my old standoffish habits enough to get to know them and become friends. I resolved to work at it. After all, I was in the process of reinventing myself as Rina, wasn't I?

When Mother called to see how I was doing after my first week at school, I told her I had changed my name. I expected a melodramatic response from her when she heard that news and was surprised that she seemed to take it in stride. Maybe she would get on my nerves less now that I didn't live with her.

Two

AS I BECAME BETTER acquainted with my work group, as well as other students in the art program, I began to feel, for the first time in my life, like I had colleagues, like I had found other members of my species. Our class with Margaret met each morning. We learned in the first week that Margaret was a successful graphic artist who owned her own business. When Norma asked her why she was teaching Introduction to Design, she replied that she enjoyed helping young artists just starting out. She said it kept her on her toes.

One afternoon, a few weeks into the semester, Margaret opened the design studio for our work group to finish up a project. As we cleaned up after ourselves in the early evening, we discussed whether art mirrors reality or vice versa. Margaret invited us back to her live-in studio in the West Village to continue our discussion. TJ had to be carried up a long flight of stairs, but we were growing accustomed to the challenges we faced in going places with TJ and we all pitched in to airlift him and his wheelchair into the studio.

I loved everything about Margaret's studio from the moment I laid eyes on it: the posters on the walls, the sound of the traffic in the street below, the smell of the paint on the easel. Margaret boiled water in a big green kettle and made Earl Grey tea for us. As she poured the hot water into each of the earth-toned mugs, which she told us she had made herself on a potter's wheel, Norma admired them one by one. Margaret asked if any of us read poetry. We greeted her question with an embarrassed silence.

"I'm hearing crickets," Margaret said with a slight smile.

"Why do you ask?" Norma asked.

"Because I'd like to introduce you to some poetry." Margaret hooked her hair behind her ears and studied her bookshelf. "There was a poetry movement that emerged right after World War II called imagism. I think that as artists you would benefit from reading some of the imagists."

"I dunno," TJ responded skeptically. "I'm of the opinion that poets have the ability to take the simplest observations and convert them into incomprehensible equations by explaining them in language that only someone with a PhD in English can decipher."

"Hey, give it a chance," Dale said, poking TJ.

"What's an example of an imagist poem?" Norma asked.

"I'll read you one." Margaret thumbed through a book and found a page. "Here's a famous poem by William Carlos Williams. 'So much depends upon a red wheel barrow glazed with rain water beside the white chickens.'"

I remembered studying that poem in high school. Williams had written another one about cold plums that I vaguely remembered too.

Skip offered a polite observation. "I like it. We have a red wheelbarrow on the farm. It reminds me of home."

"Skip wants an A in Introduction to Design," TJ said with a grin.

"What does it mean?" Arthur asked Margaret.

"You don't get it?" TJ asked Arthur, rolling his eyes. "Some guys just robbed a bank, they have to make it to the getaway vehicle, which is a red Corvette (the wheelbarrow), but the car is surrounded by cops, referred to as chickens, and everything depends on their ability to make it to the Corvette and get out of there before it starts raining again."

"Shut up," Norma admonished TJ.

"You're being ridiculous," I added, but TJ seemed unfazed.

Arthur was not distracted. "Forget TJ; what does it mean and why did you tell us that poem?"

"Well, it's a poem about observation, about really looking at things, really seeing the wheelbarrow and the chickens. Williams is saying that everything depends on our ability to truly see what we're looking at," Margaret explained. "It has to do with your earlier conversation about art and reality. It is incumbent upon us as artists to see and to reflect what we see authentically in our work because we have the technical skill and the talent to do so. Our communities depend on us to do so."

"You extracted all that out of a poem about a wheelbarrow and chickens?" TJ asked incredulously.

"I looked at it carefully." Margaret drove home her point. "I am of the opinion that reading good poetry can improve one's art." She proceeded to distribute poetry books to us on loan. "Just take these home with you and browse through them at your leisure; see if anything in them speaks to you," she instructed.

TJ declined the thin volume that she offered him. "I'm sorry," he told her, "I'm just not a poetic kind of guy."

In the kitchen, later, I savored the ritual of washing out the mugs and standing them up in the wooden dish rack to dry. As I washed them, I reviewed the evening's conversation in my mind, picking up the ideas and reexamining them like souvenirs from a lovely vacation.

It did not take Margaret long to introduce us to W. B. Yeats, Ezra Pound, and T. S. Eliot. "These are the forefathers of modern poetry," she proclaimed. Margaret's favorite was Wallace Stevens, but none of us could make hide nor hair out of him. TJ told Margaret that he would need an English/Stevens dictionary to read that stuff. He didn't go up to Margaret's as frequently as the rest of us because of those daunting stairs.

Margaret introduced me to the poetry of Adrienne Rich, and I soon became infatuated. Rich practically reinvented the English language with her startlingly original metaphors. I felt as though some of the frustratingly abstract thoughts that had been drifting at the back of my mind were pinned down by Rich and given a shape so that I could make sense of them. I liked her idea that language did not go far enough for us to express our ideas, but it was all we had and we needed to use it the best we could, even if it was sexist and racist and charged with meanings that undermined the uses to which we wished to put it in order to communicate.

Arthur got hooked on poetry too. Apart from having memorized the words to "Lift Ev'ry Voice and Sing," his previous experience with poetry was limited. Margaret encouraged Arthur to read the classic Negro poets, like Paul Laurence Dunbar, Langston Hughes, James Weldon Johnson, and Claude McKay. Arthur declared that poetry was one of the most powerful political tools he had yet encountered. One evening, at Margaret's, he started talking about the use of poetry to advance social change. I had never become involved in political activism, and his references to his activities, such as attending demonstrations and rallies and going to hear a leader named A. Philip Randolph speak, intimidated me a bit. He said that it was the duty of the poet, as well as the artist, to transform society.

Margaret disagreed. "The role of the artist is to hold a mirror up to life," she said, "to make sense and meaning out of the seemingly chaotic and pointless unfolding of events. The artist defines the human condition, and politics is simply one aspect of that. Can you name any great work of art, that endured, that was created with a solely political intent?" She didn't give him time to think before she continued. "Politics is rooted in the moment, and great art transcends the moment. Any art that has political change as its primary purpose is fleeting by its very nature because the politics of the moment is fleeting. Great art is timeless because it speaks to the human condition, not politics. Politics is ancillary."

"Politics *is* the human condition," Arthur countered. "Look at Shakespeare. He inspires political change. Look at *The Tempest*. It's an allegory for transforming the rigid class structure of Elizabethan society."

"*The Tempest* was not written to cause social change, and its primary design has nothing to do with mere politics," Margaret insisted.

The Tempest was one of my favorite Shakespearean plays, and I loved it for the musicality of the language, the fascinating characters, and the fantastical elements. I had never once thought of it as a tool for social change.

"I think you two define politics differently," Norma interjected. "I don't think you can talk about politics until you have agreed on a definition of the concept." I could see that Norma was right and I wondered if Arthur and Margaret could see it too.

"Everything is political," Arthur asserted. "Politics is constantly in my face because of my skin color. The dominant culture has control over when I do and do not have to deal with the fact of racism. I wish I had the power to decide when I want to fight my battles, but I don't. My battles jump out at me arbitrarily, often when I am least in the mood to deal with them," Arthur flashed. "Don't take this the wrong way, but you, being white, can't understand exactly what I'm talking about. And I'm not implying that you're racist when I say that."

"I don't have to be a Negro to understand it," Margaret replied. "I hope you'll believe me when I say that I do understand. Negroes don't have an exclusive franchise on oppression." A cloud had passed over her face, and I wondered about it, convinced that something important about her had just eluded me.

"My aunt was killed in the Holocaust," I said softly, unsure of why I felt compelled to share that information at that moment. "Not all white people are part of the dominant culture," I added, fearing that Arthur would disagree, but he didn't.

"I understand," he said. "Sorry if I was a bit overbearing. I get worked up."

"What's the use in comparing suffering?" Skip asked. "Negroes, Jews, women, heck, think of how the Catholics and Protestants have gone at it. When you scratch below the surface, we've all suffered. Arguing about who has suffered more only divides us."

"OK, I can agree with that," Arthur said. "All I'm trying to say is that my every action, every piece of my work, is automatically political in this country because of my color. I don't have the luxury of art for art's sake."

"Art as politics. Art for art's sake. Art for social change. Can't it just be art for the purpose of bringing more beauty into the world? Just to make people feel good, for Pete's sake?" TJ asked, with a note of uncharacteristic exasperation in his voice.

"Who's Pete?" Dale asked, batting his lashes coquettishly and then, putting on his best southern accent, "You never tole me 'bout no Pete." Arthur smiled indulgently at TJ and Dale and did not pursue the conversation.

In the future, after the concept of "Black Power" entered the collective consciousness of the country, the terminology swiftly changed from *Negro* to *Black* (and much later to *African American*), but when I was in college the preferred term, the term that Arthur and Dale used to identify themselves, was *Negro*. When the terminology changed, so did my memory of my college years, and I couldn't imagine ever having referred to Black people as *Negroes*. But we did back then.

During my first weeks and months in college, every day was a new adventure. My thoughts tumbled head over heels. Even in sleep, my mind continued to process ideas, so that I had vivid dreams, often heavily laden with images of freedom, such as birds escaping from cages. I often drew my dream images. When Margaret commented on the theme of freedom recurring in my work, I told her about my dreams and she suggested that I keep a dream journal. She loaned me a book by Carl Jung as well as *The Poetics of Reverie* by Gaston Bachelard.

"Do any of you guys get your ideas for some of your work from your dreams?" I asked the others one day at lunch in the student union.

"Of course," Norma answered, as if it were obvious. "But where are you going with that question?" She took a bite of her chicken salad sandwich.

"I have generally assumed that other artists get ideas from dreams, and then lately I started to wonder if that was a fair assumption or if it was based on my own experience. And that made me wonder if my experience is normal," I said.

"Normal is relative," TJ pointed out.

I had plucked up the courage to share my thoughts about my creative process and I was determined to continue before I lost my nerve. "For years I've drawn images of patterns that come to me in both sleeping and waking dreams; by 'waking dreams' I mean daydreams or meditative states. I think these images and patterns don't all spring from my imagination. I think some of them come from a deep memory of other times and places, such as former lives or Jung's well of cultural memory. Certainly not all my work comes from my memory, but I sometimes wonder if my most genuine work does," I said carefully.

Norma recited from Adrienne Rich, "The bones of the mammoths are still in the earth."

"Do I sound crazy?" I asked. I liked Norma's allusion to the mammoths.

"Not at all," Dale touched my arm in reassurance.

Arthur said, "It sounds like it happens of its own accord, but can you ever call up these memories at will?"

"Can you control them at all?" Norma asked

"Do you play with the memories or do they play with you?" Skip added.

"Wait," I said. "Too many questions. I need to think about it."

While I was thinking, TJ said, "The operative word is *play*, you guys. Creative process is play. Thinking has a tendency to get in the way of creative process."

"I believe," Skip said tentatively, "and I know you all don't share this belief, but I believe that the playful, creative ideas come from God."

"And I respect your belief, Skip," I said. "But I'm not so convinced about God, and I think that, for me, many of my creative ideas come from memory, and I think that the human mind holds far more, I mean hugely more, information than any of us can grasp, including memories from past lives and past cultures. It's Adrienne Rich's mammoths lurking. We just need to figure out how to summon them and how to understand what they're trying to tell us."

Three

ONE EVENING, I WENT with Dale and TJ to Arthur's house in Harlem. He was still living with his parents and took the subway to school. Arthur wanted us to hear a record by a terrific new all-girl singing group. He had a friend in Detroit who had sent him one of their records, otherwise he wouldn't have known about them because they weren't being played on the radio in New York. They had recently changed their name from the Primettes to the Supremes. He was right about them. They were phenomenal. "Have you ever heard anything like this?" Dale kept exclaiming as he snapped his fingers to the beat. We couldn't sit still and listen, we had to dance. Arthur played the record three times. Even TJ danced, pushing his chair back and forth with his right hand while he held my hand in his left. He tried to spin me under his arm and backed over Dale's foot in the process. Dale wasn't hurt and we had a good laugh.

"Check this one out," Arthur said, and he put on a mood piece, a song about slavery that started out with the sounds of a ship's hull creaking, the ocean, and slaves moaning under the swell of the music. As I listened, powerful and frightening emotions rushed through me. The hair on the back of my neck stood on end. The recording made me feel terrified, grief-stricken, and deeply disoriented. I became dizzy and I had to sit down with my head on my lap.

Arthur realized right away that it was the song and he lifted the needle from the record abruptly. Dale and TJ didn't seem to make the connection between the music and my dizzy spell. TJ rubbed the back of my neck with concern.

"I'm OK," I assured them. "I'm just a little faint. I'll be fine in a minute." I had felt much better as soon as Arthur stopped the music. Dale insisted that I needed to get a brain scan, which made me laugh. He sounded like my mother. Arthur put away the record that had set me off, and he played some music by The Miracles instead. Smokey Robinson's velvety smooth voice worked its magic on me. I relaxed and once again enjoyed the tunes Arthur wanted to share with us.

Later, as Dale helped TJ down Arthur's three front steps, Arthur wrapped his long fingers around my upper arm and leaned close, "The slave ship song did it, didn't it?" I nodded. "That song sometimes does it to me too," Arthur confided. "History has a habit of not going away." For me, it was more than history; but I could not yet explain exactly what had happened.

Four

BECAUSE NORMA WORKED AT the Jackrabbit and it was wheelchair accessible, we hung out there a lot in the evenings. I met my first boyfriend at the Jackrabbit. He played the clarinet with a jazz band. I noticed him noticing me from the stage while he performed, which made me feel like a celebrity. After the first set, he edged over to my table. "May I join you while I'm on my break?" he asked. He grabbed a chair from a neighboring table, turned it around, slid it in next to me, and sat on it backward.

"What did you say your name is?" Arthur asked, sizing him up.

"I didn't. My name is Michael." He held his hand out to shake Arthur's. It seemed like more of a challenge than an introduction.

"And yours?" he asked, turning to me even before releasing Arthur's hand.

Arthur refused to be brushed off. "How long have you been playing?" he asked Michael.

"Clarinet, only a few years. I've played the sax all my life."

"Why'd you switch?" Arthur asked rather aggressively.

"I didn't. I play both," Michael said, with a slight note of irritation in his voice.

Dale put his hand on Arthur's arm. "Check this out," Dale said. "Dante just came in. Come with me. I want to have a word with the brother." Dale gently but firmly guided Arthur out of his seat and across the room, leaving me to get acquainted with Michael without further interference.

"I don't think your friend likes me," Michael grinned.

"He's a little overprotective," I replied. "He's a good friend. We're in the same program at college."

"I sort of figured that he's not your brother," Michael joked.

"He's as close as I'll ever get to having one," I said. "I have two sisters."

"And what are you and your friend studying in college?" Michael asked.

"Art," I told him, "we're in art school together."

"Really? What is your medium?" Michael warmed to the subject.

"I'm studying graphic design, but I use a lot of different media. Sort of experimenting."

"That's exactly what jazz is about," Michael said approvingly. "Experimenting."

"Maybe that's why I like to listen to it."

"I think it's time for me to go play some more of it." Michael smiled as he stood to return to the stage. "Wait for me after the show?" he asked, as a pink flush crept into his cheeks.

"I think I will," I replied, with a half smile.

By the time Michael's group finished their last set, my friends had left. Michael and I drank a beer together, lingering until closing. He had pale skin and practically transparent hair, so blond he looked almost albino. He must have spent all his time indoors. He told me that he had grown up in the suburbs in a small town Upstate, where his mother had, over the years, become the hub of cultural activity. She had insisted that he take music lessons. After fifteen years of classical training, he had fallen in love with jazz and that was all he played these days. Michael walked me back to the dorm and before we parted he invited me out to dinner.

On Monday, when I walked into design class, TJ chanted, "Rina and Michael sittin' in a tree." I smacked TJ with a book.

"Please, TJ, I like him, so don't tease me."

That evening, Michael took me to an Italian restaurant with red and white checkered tablecloths and candles glowing on every table. We ate spaghetti, salad, and excellent garlic bread. I felt as if I were in a movie. I could even hear the soundtrack in my head with the music swelling to crescendo as I wound my pasta around the tines of my fork.

Michael seemed to want to talk about his mother, and I began to suspect that he had a complicated relationship with her. "Do you know what her favorite song is?" he asked. "It's 'Surrey with a Fringe on Top' from that musical *Oklahoma*. If you can believe it. How could a woman who loves musicals produce a son who plays jazz? Sometimes I wonder if I was a changeling."

"I've actually wondered the same thing myself. I'm so different from the rest of my family."

"How so?" he asked.

"Well, for one thing, I think we have different values. I just don't get the relevance of some of the things that they think are important."

"Interesting. I think I share my parents' basic values, but their tastes, no way," Michael said.

"My mother is preoccupied with the most mundane things, like keeping the house tidy and wearing a pair of shoes that matches her dress," I said. "I don't have the patience for it. I feel guilty when I lose my patience with my mother, but not with my father. My father and I flat-out don't like each other. But my mother and sisters mean well. My older sister, Soph, well, she's a sweetheart and I love her, even though she's like a younger version of my mother. Sometimes I just can't take another insipid remark of hers or my mother's. I have to steel myself not to be downright cruel." I took a big mouthful of spaghetti with marinara sauce. It was delicious and I chewed appreciatively.

Michael told me, "When my family gets intolerable then I figure they deserve what they get and I have no qualms about speaking my mind. But enough about my impossible family. Let's talk about something more interesting."

"OK, so tell me about your music," I prompted. "What is it that you love about jazz?"

Michael smiled broadly. "Everything, I think. It's the most amazing art form. When I play, I feel like I'm having this conversation with the other musicians and also with the audience, in this language that has the ability to capture what I feel so much more accurately than words. I love to improvise. When I improvise, I feel incredibly free. To improvise I have to go on faith that something wonderful will come to me, to us, as we play together. Sometimes it does and sometimes it doesn't. I just have to hope the chemistry is there. When it is, it's magic."

"My friends and I talk a lot about where inspiration comes from."

"Inspiration is a pretty slippery character," Michael conceded.

I stirred my coffee and recited quietly, almost to myself, "I have measured out my life with coffee spoons."

"What?" Michael asked.

"It's a line from a T. S. Eliot poem called 'The Love Song of J. Alfred Prufrock.'"

"So you like to read poetry?" he asked.

"I'm starting to get into it. My professor, Margaret, thinks that a well-rounded art education should include studying poetry. She says art and poetry intersect."

He leaned forward, so I could feel his breath on my cheek, and said, "I think we're the intersection of art and music." My blood rushed with the thrill of Michael.

When we left the restaurant, he walked me to my dorm and kissed me outside the front door. After our date, I couldn't keep Michael out of my thoughts. One minute I would be trying to concentrate in a class, and the next I would be remembering something Michael had said or the way he looked when he was onstage playing his clarinet with the blue spotlight in his hair.

The change in my artwork was embarrassing, but I couldn't help myself. Open flowers and salacious fruit suddenly appeared everywhere in my patterns. My lines became visibly more fluid. I had sex on my mind and my desires could not be contained or compartmentalized. There was no way around it so I had to go through it, with my art revealing my awakening as I went.

Of course, it didn't require psychic ability for Margaret to figure out what was going on. She took me aside one evening and had a talk with me about birth control. I promised to make an appointment at a women's clinic she suggested.

Everyone teased me about Michael. Unfortunately, none of my friends actually seemed to like him. Norma said he was pretentious. TJ said he was too old for me. Dale said Michael wasn't smart enough for me and nicknamed him "the Rat" because of his light skin and transparent hair. Arthur called Michael a fake. I ignored them. I thought Michael was sexy, creative, and romantic.

When Michael gave me a hardbound copy of poetry by e. e. cummings, he broke the book in by reading aloud from it to me:

since feeling is first
who pays any attention
to the syntax of things
will never wholly kiss you

Michael especially liked cummings because of the rhythms in his poetry, and the way he read cummings out loud sounded like jazz. I loved how the poems shouted about love and rejoiced in the sensuality of the physical world.

Through Michael, who had already graduated from college a few years before, I met new people who weren't connected with my art school. It broadened my world. Although, as I started to get to know Michael better, and the initial luster wore off, I began to wonder, in the privacy of my own thoughts, if TJ and Arthur had Michael pegged from the start. He was a bit pretentious and sometimes arrogant, and I would characterize him as someone too stuck in his own head. But, so what? I still admired his freedom of thought and expression.

Michael brought me flowers, dedicated songs to me when he was onstage, and complimented me on how I looked. He often wore a beret, and glasses that were just like Dizzy Gillespie's even though his eyesight was practically perfect without them. Sometimes he wore a plum-colored scarf, which appeared to be thrown casually over his shoulder (although I caught him arranging it when he thought no one was looking). Michael had a talent for artifice that at first I confused for the genuine article. But not to entirely disparage Michael; he thought that artifice *was* the genuine article. I discovered that I could appreciate well-wrought artifice.

At least I had the good sense not to drop my friends and spend all my time with Michael. My sister Sarah had a high school sweetheart who consumed her life and I viewed her relationship with him as a cautionary tale. She seemed happy and I guess it worked for her, but as for me, I couldn't allow myself to pin my own happiness in life on a relationship with only one person. I saw a little less of my gang, but I remained loyal and passed up numerous opportunities to see Michael in order to hang out with my own friends. Anyway, I was of the opinion that the fact that I had a life of my own made me more attractive to Michael. I was not exactly "playing hard to get," but more sending him a signal that I did not depend on him to fill the bulk of my emotional needs.

Five

I DIDN'T CARE FOR dorm living. For one thing, the dorm cafeteria food was inedible and I had a quarrel with my mother when I suggested that she and Nate should quit paying for the meal plan. She was worried I wouldn't eat nutritional meals. I convinced her that the cafeteria food was far from nutritional by describing the meal choices in lurid detail. But I disliked the dorm mostly because I felt more comfortable when I could spend substantial time alone, and I simply couldn't get used to communal living. Even though my roommate was rarely in our dorm room, I hated having so many people around in general. It was hard for me to feel centered.

When I broached the subject of moving out of the dorm with my anxious mother, she became so distraught that she put Nate on the phone, which for her was a desperate move since she knew how badly Nate communicated with me. He proceeded to deliver a lecture about the cost of living, which made me wonder if I was anything more than a line item in his budget.

Summer was fast approaching and I couldn't imagine ever living with my parents again. Fortunately, dear Margaret came to my rescue. She got me a gig helping maintain the gardens on the grounds of a college administrator's home in Manhattan in exchange for a small apartment in a converted carriage house on the property. I called Mother and tried to explain to her why I had to stay in New York for my artistic development. I think she started crying, but couldn't tell for sure on the phone, and she begged me to come home for the summer. It was ludicrous.

"Mother, you know how we get on each other's nerves when we live together. We'll get along better if I have my own place and I just come to visit," I argued.

She knew exactly what I meant, but my parents had still not agreed to let me stay in the city for the summer when I landed a job at the Jackrabbit. That decided the issue because I had become financially independent. I had my scholarship to cover my tuition; my living situation was a trade, so I didn't have to pay rent; and the Jackrabbit job would pay for the cost of my food and school supplies. I suspected that as a businessman, Nate felt some measure of pride that his most headstrong daughter had taken the initiative. Anyway, to my amusement, he made a point of giving me his permission to stay in the city for the summer.

In the nearly four months since I had met Michael, and as I thought more and more about the prospect of making love to him, I had been drawing flowers like crazy. They flowed from my hand in a steady stream. Arthur encouraged me to try to sell the patterns for wrapping paper. When I talked to Margaret about Arthur's suggestion, she loved it and she took the reins, turning the wrapping-paper idea into a business venture. She invited me, as well as a number of her other students, on board to provide the patterns. That's how I found myself designing wrapping-paper patterns for Margaret's cottage industry, which she named Call It a Wrap. This became another source of steady income for me.

Three weeks before school ended for the summer, Arthur, Skip, and Norma helped me pack up my stuff and haul it over to my new place. I then proceeded to have a fabulous time decorating. I covered the walls with fabric swatches and my favorite art prints. I filled the windowsills with pottery, ceramics, and colored bottles that glowed amber, iridescent blue, and deep sea green in the late afternoon sunlight. I put out my curled shells and my shapely rocks and all the things I had collected and loved to look at. I burned sandalwood incense in the evenings. My apartment was a work of art, a wonderland, a shrine.

With my first paycheck from the Jackrabbit, I bought myself a kimono. It had a periwinkle background and large peach flowers with black detail. The kimono felt like a magic coat. I put on my kimono and worked late into the night at my drawing board, producing flower patterns. I was so busy getting my new place set up and drawing flowers half the night that I didn't call Michael for several days after I moved into the carriage house. When I telephoned to give him my new number, he complained, "How could you move into a new place and not even invite me over for dinner?"

"I was totally swamped with the move. And dinner is not in my repertoire. You know that I don't cook," I said in my defense. He knew this was true. I ate cheese and crackers, salad, and fruit most of the time. Cooking held no interest for me.

"OK, don't cook. We can order out," Michael relented.

I agreed to get Chinese take-out with him that evening. We opened the cartons on my new used coffee table and sat on the floor. It was a warm evening, on the cusp of summer. We ate slowly and drank sparkling water, enjoying the lovely view of the gardens from my windows.

"You need a TV," Michael said.

"What for?" I asked.

"News. Sports. Saturday Night at the Movies. Maybe a sitcom now and then. Documentaries about Louis Armstrong or how whales communicate."

"Do you watch all that stuff?" I asked.

"No, but I might if you got a TV."

"I can't afford a TV. I just bought a bike."

"Who wants to come home from a hard day in the dog-eat-dog world and watch a bike?"

"Well, I can't ride a TV to the grocery store."

Michael grinned. Then the grin transformed into a serious expression. Michael leaned over and kissed me, and as we kissed, the desire to touch him raced through my blood. When he released me, Michael asked softly, "Do you know how much I want to make love to you?"

"Show me how much."

"You've never done it before, have you?"

"No. But you have, haven't you?"

"Yes," Michael confessed, "I have. Does that bother you?"

"I don't think so."

"I can wait if you're not ready," he said, but I could tell his heart was not in that offer.

"You don't have to wait."

Michael felt my nipples through my thin tank top. "You're sure?"

"I'm sure," I whispered.

He turned out to be a sensitive and thoughtful lover. He planted a trail of kisses all the way down my body, even kissing my toes, and every once in a while he came back up to kiss me on the mouth and check to see how I was doing. He entered me so gently, with such restraint, despite the fact that he was obviously extremely aroused, that I wanted him even more, and it was all over quickly for both of us. Afterward, I ran my fingers lightly across his chest as I savored our new intimacy, my access to a male body and the pleasure it could give me. I jumped up and took down a volume of Dylan Thomas that Michael had given me a few weeks earlier and read aloud the poem entitled "On the Marriage of a Virgin." When I finished reading, Michael grinned and said, "I take that to mean that it was good for you."

I climbed on top of him, laughing, and entangled my legs in his while Michael played with my thick hair, which tumbled down my back, as he started expounding on Dylan Thomas and then, somehow, on the subject of European drama and then about drama in America and soon the ritual of drama. We were lying naked in bed together and he was delivering a lecture on the purpose of drama. Sometimes he could get so trapped in his head. But soon he got hard and so we made love again, this time both of us managing to last a little longer when he was inside me. After that we finished eating the Chinese food, went for a walk in the garden, then made love again, and, finally, slept late into the next day.

A few days after my big night with Michael, Margaret met me for lunch and we hadn't even finished looking at our menus when Margaret leaned across the table to ask, "You slept with him, didn't you?"

"Does it show? Did he leave some kind of mark on me?"

"You seem self-satisfied and a bit overly delighted."

"Well, I'm not in love with him," I assured her. "But he's a dear man and we had a good time."

"I'm not so sure that I would describe Michael as *dear*, but I'm glad you're enjoying yourself. He better be good to you because if he's not, then TJ and Arthur will have him knee-capped."

"It's none of their business," I replied curtly.

Margaret's eyebrows shot up and she said, "I guess it isn't."

We ordered sandwiches and talked about summer plans, Call It a Wrap, and a photography show we were looking forward to that would be opening in the fall at the college art museum. I felt comfortable enough to finally ask the question I had been burning to ask for months.

"Margaret, why aren't you seeing anyone? You seem like the type of person who would be in a relationship by your age, you know, like with a big, warm, bear of a man who wears thick cuddly sweaters and paints in oils or something."

Margaret sidestepped the question. "What's 'by your age' supposed to mean?"

I had asked and been soundly rebuffed.

Six

WORKING AT THE JACKRABBIT with Norma, I had a glorious summer filled with poetry and music, laughs and late night parties, and plenty of intellectual conversation. My landlord had a gardener and I worked under his direction in the gardens around the carriage house, pulling weeds, deadheading finished flowers, wrapping the fruit trees in netting to keep the birds off, and doing many other chores. There was never a shortage of work in the garden.

Dale, Skip, and TJ had gone to their respective homes for the summer and Arthur worked ten-hour days on a construction crew when he wasn't sleeping off his exhaustion in his bedroom at his parents' house in Harlem. He quit his job a couple of weeks before school started again and went to register voters in the South with the Freedom Riders, which sounded pretty dangerous to me, but he came back in one piece. Margaret vanished to Guatemala for six weeks on a research grant. That basically left me with Norma for the summer. And Michael.

Michael performed at the Jackrabbit a few times that summer and he often hung out there during my shift. He and I spent long hours in my carriage house apartment drinking beer, listening to jazz and the new hits coming out of Motown, making love, and getting into heated conversations about art, music, poetry, theater, and whatever books we happened to be reading at the time.

Michael sometimes left poems pinned to my door while I was out. The first one he left was "i like my body when it is with your body" by cummings, typed on a chartreuse piece of paper.

I checked the *Kama Sutra* out of the library and insisted on attempting a variety of acrobatic positions, which Michael found entertaining. I bought sexy black underwear, much to Michael's delight. We did it in a hammock, on a chair, in the shower, and standing up between the coats in the front closet at a party. One night Michael brought over some cocaine, which we snorted, and it made my whole body feel way more sensitive to Michael's touch. After that, I sought out more cocaine, and in its absence, Michael and I smoked pot. The pot didn't do much for me sexually, although it made Michael relax and get out of his head, so that he had a better time and consequently I had a better time. But drawing was my preferred activity when I got high. So I started buying small amounts of pot for myself.

I didn't visit my parents once during the entire summer. Finally, in August, I spent one weekend with the family. Mother baked my favorite kind of cookies and made a fuss over me. It was embarrassing. I didn't mention Michael to her, but I told my sisters about him on Saturday night when we sat in the backyard talking, after our parents went to bed. I made them promise not to say anything about him to Mother or Nate. It was kind of nice to hang out with them, and the subject of boyfriends was something that we could discuss together. Sarah was growing up and I felt like I had more in common with her than I did before I had left home. I returned from the weekend with my family to find Michael fuming, offended that I had failed to invite him to go with me to meet the folks. I agreed to take him in the near future, though I had no such intention.

Hanging out with Michael and his circle, I became good friends with his buddy Lee, who played the piano, guitar, saxophone, and drums. She was studying composition at the Brooklyn Music School. I introduced Lee to Norma, and the three of us went to the movies together a few times. Every Friday night in August we went out to eat at a Moroccan restaurant that I had recently discovered. When TJ, Arthur, Dale, and Skip returned to school in the fall, I brought Lee around to meet them, which infuriated Michael, who cross-examined me about my reluctance to invite him to do things with my art school friends. I couldn't very well tell him that my friends called him "the Rat" and found him pretentious. Once school started, I spent more time with them and less with Michael. He was jealous of Lee for fitting in with my gang and he found foolish reasons to get angry with me. He would pick fights over petty things so ridiculous that I didn't know how to respond. I just hoped we would manage to weather the difficulties that had entered our relationship.

Seven

MICHAEL INVITED ME TO spend Thanksgiving with his
family and I accepted, mainly because I wanted an excuse to stay away
from my own family. I had to consciously exercise restraint to prevent
myself from being rude to Mother when she initiated one of her frequent inane conversations, such as a discussion about the merits of using
shoe polish to touch up a worn leather handbag. She actually sent me a
recipe for a tuna-noodle casserole that contained canned green beans and
cream-of-mushroom soup. She completely forgot that I hadn't eaten fish
in two years and that I was into natural foods, not vegetables from a can.

When I informed Mother that I had a boyfriend and that he had
invited me Upstate for Thanksgiving with his family, she immediately
asked if he was Jewish. I answered that he wasn't and could tell that she
therefore assumed it was not a serious relationship. Later, in retrospect,
I wondered if I would have been better off spending Thanksgiving with
my own dysfunctional family instead of spending it with Michael's dysfunctional family.

Michael had been "an accident" in his parents' later years. He had
three older sisters with heaps of noisy and demanding children. His much
older brother had no children and a bellyful of anger at their father for
reasons I never figured out. His mother doted on Michael, who made
sarcastic comments about everything from the frozen peas to the pilgrim
centerpiece (which really was horrid). When I couldn't stand it anymore,
I snuck out to the garage to smoke some pot and after that the whole
charade became hilariously funny. Especially the pilgrim centerpiece. I
giggled my way through the entire dinner. We fled after breakfast the following morning, with Michael driving back to the city in the first snow-
storm of the year in stony silence.

When we pulled up in front of my carriage house, I invited Michael in. "I don't think so," he grumbled.

I stared at the side of his head. "Maybe we should call it quits," I said, though I didn't mean it. I wanted to see what he would say.

"OK," he replied, refusing to look at me.

I was shocked by his response. I had not expected him to agree to splitting up. I grabbed my backpack and bailed from the car. The snow blanketed the gardens that I had worked on during the summer. The branches of the bare trees appeared unfamiliar beneath their winter white. As I ran into the carriage house, I half expected Michael to follow, grab me from behind, apologize, whisper a poem in my ear. But instead he drove off into the swirling snow.

On the Friday and Saturday of Thanksgiving weekend, I smoked pot and drew. I thought Michael would call, wanting to talk, to work things out. But the phone rang only once. It was Mother calling to ask about my Thanksgiving and to tell me about theirs. I told her I split up with my boyfriend and I didn't want to talk about it. She was surprisingly sympathetic and even remembered to call me "Rina" without a hint of amusement in her voice. I found myself describing to her one of the flower patterns I was working on and then she suggested that I treat myself to some mu shu vegetables for dinner, knowing how much I liked mu shu. She told me about a new Chinese restaurant that Aunt Ida had discovered in Manhattan that made spicy eggplant. I actually felt a little better after I talked to her and I called the restaurant and ordered both the mu shu and the spicy eggplant and had them delivered to my door. They were delicious.

I hadn't slept much the night before and by the time I finished eating my take-out I was exhausted. I fell asleep on the couch and had a terrifying dream. I stood in front of my parents, only they weren't Mother and Nate, they were Chinese and they didn't look like my parents, but there was something about them that seemed sort of like my real parents. My dream-mother wore a modest, baggy, deep-blue silk dress with gold embroidery that went from her neck to the tips of her toes, and her head was bowed so that I couldn't see her face. My dream-father was angry and he shouted at me. It was a humid evening and I smelled the scent of flowers, strong as ripe melons, coming from a lush garden somewhere nearby. Through the open window, I saw a handsome man with a smooth, hairless, muscular chest and gentle, work-worn fingers. He was a gardener, but I didn't know how I knew this. He had deep eyes that wrinkled at the corners from past laughter. He opened his mouth to speak, but then he closed it again and turned away. I was overcome with grief. Then suddenly the scene dissolved and I was in a dim room, lying naked on a bed where a man pinned me down roughly beneath his body as he forced my legs apart with his knee and then he raped me. But I did not struggle. I had a feeling of complete helplessness and submission. His mouth was open as he panted with each painful thrust inside of me, and his breath smelled so badly of rotten meat that I gagged and screamed, and then I woke up shaking and crying.

I couldn't remember ever having had such a vivid, realistic dream in my life. After I woke up, it seemed as if the events in the dream had actually taken place. I wished I could forget it or shake it out of my head, but it wouldn't go away. I felt so unclean that I had to take a shower. Then I bundled up and went walking to relieve my anxiety. By midnight my feet had taken me to Margaret's studio in the Village. From where I stood on the sidewalk, I could see a dim light burning in the back bedroom, and, feeling miserable, I went up and knocked on her door. I heard Margaret's voice in the distance calling "Hold on, I'm coming." She answered the door in a maroon, floor-length chenille bathrobe. I had never seen her in anything but blue jeans. Her hair fell loosely around her shoulders and her face glowed in the soft amber light. She was beautiful.

"Did I wake you?" I asked.

"No, come in. Is something wrong?" Margaret seemed hesitant and uncertain. It occurred to me that she didn't actually want me to come in. But I needed to, so, selfishly, I stepped inside anyway.

A woman's voice called from the bedroom, "Who is it? Is everything OK?"

"Everything's fine. It's one of my former students," Margaret called back.

A tall, slender, Latina woman appeared in the doorway. She wore a large T-shirt with a picture of Daffy Duck on the front. She had straight, shiny, blue-black hair that fell almost to her waist. Giant silver hoop earrings tickled her neck.

"This is Gloria," Margaret introduced her. "Gloria, this is Rina."

"Michael and I split up and I just had the most terrifying nightmare," I blurted out tearfully.

"Ay, muchacha, you need chocolate," Gloria said, and went straight to the refrigerator. While Gloria made steamy mugs of Mexican-style spiced hot cocoa, I told Margaret about my nightmare and about what had happened with Michael over Thanksgiving.

"Maybe he'll come around next week," Margaret said encouragingly, while she patted my hand.

But Gloria's voice piped up from the kitchen, "Forget him. There's a lotta fish in the sea."

As I sipped the excellent cocoa, I did forget Michael because the scene in front of me was far more interesting than my own troubles.

"So how do you know Gloria?" I asked Margaret.

"We met in Guatemala over the summer," she answered curtly.

"I was on a work crew building houses in a village, and Margaret was painting up on a hill. I stayed and built an extra house just so I could have enough time to woo her," Gloria chattered. Margaret blushed.

I practically slapped my forehead and blurted out "Aha!" What an idiot I was for not figuring it out before. I wondered why Margaret seemed so anxious about my discovering her secret. Perhaps she was afraid that I would judge her harshly or think less of her because she was a lesbian. That was absurd.

"How romantic," I said, before rounding on Margaret. "Why didn't you tell me you were seeing someone?" I asked.

"Listen. This," Margaret gestured back and forth between herself and Gloria, "this relationship is potentially dangerous for me. Teachers are regularly fired for being gay. They have been fired on mere suspicion of it. Many people assume that if a teacher is a lesbian, then she is perverted and will force that perversion on her students. I love my job. So I have to be discreet. I trust you will be discreet for my sake as well, otherwise I would not have opened the door to you."

I took a sip of my cocoa. "Is it OK if I tell the others?" I asked.

"What others?" Margaret replied, even though I was certain she knew what I meant.

"You know; TJ, Norma, Skip, Dale, and Arthur," I answered, thinking back to the evening when Arthur had accused Margaret of not understanding what it felt like to experience persecution.

"I would rather have them find out like you did and not as a result of gossip."

"They'll be happy for you," I reassured her.

"Don't be so sure. Skip comes from a traditional Christian family. Homosexuality and that good old-time religion have never mixed well."

I slept on Margaret's sofa that night. I had no more bad dreams, and by the morning Michael seemed much less important.

Eight

TJ, DALE, AND ARTHUR actually took me out for a beer to celebrate that I had dumped "the Rat." It hadn't gone down that way, but I didn't protest when they described it like that.

It bothered me that I had spent my summer making love to Michael and now we had absolutely nothing to do with each other. It was especially difficult when he came into the Jackrabbit and barely acknowledged my existence. We had gone from intimacy to vague acquaintance in a blink. Once, when I waited on his table, I almost screamed at him, "We made love in the gardens under a full moon and now you act like you barely know me?" But I didn't. I kept my cool.

I was angry at Michael for the way he had ended the relationship, but I was curiously relieved that it was over. By the end, I had fallen out of love with him, if I ever even had been in love in the first place. I would be wary of getting too involved again too quickly in the future. Having lost my virginity as well as my boyfriend, I started viewing men from a different perspective.

Thinking I needed a new image, I got my ears pierced, cut my hair shorter, and started wearing sandalwood essential oil. I bought a dozen thin silver bracelets from an Indian import shop and wore them on my left wrist where they tinkled against each other whenever I moved. I wanted men to desire me. I didn't want one boyfriend anymore; I wanted variety.

The best part of my relationship with Michael in the end was Lee. Loyal to me, she quit hanging out with Michael as soon as we split up. Lee, Norma, and I often went out dancing together. Lee had taken a gig as a back-up singer for a rock band called Chicken and the Biscuits. She was one of the biscuits. Norma and I went to hear her sing with them as often as we could. Our nightlife was a fun diversion; however, one of the biggest reasons that Norma, Lee, and I got along so well was because all three of us took our studies so seriously. We only found time to go out on the town once or twice a month, but when we went, look out. After a couple of beers, I became a shameless flirt and a competent seductress. I was not particularly subtle. I had a habit of flat-out propositioning guys I found attractive. I didn't pick up strange guys in bars because that seemed risky. I felt more comfortable with the guys I met at parties thrown by people I knew from college or guys I met when Lee's band had an after party at someone's house on the nights when they performed. We kept our occasional ladies' nights out completely separate from our friendship with TJ, Dale, Arthur, and Skip.

Our art gang met for lunch most days at the student union and we went over to Margaret's some evenings, but less often since Margaret had become protective of her personal time with Gloria. Arthur wasn't around as much because he was seeing a woman named Bea. Bea came from a down-to-earth family of preachers. She had a strong commitment to community service and she ran a soup kitchen for the homeless in Harlem with her sisters. Arthur had met her when he volunteered at the soup kitchen. I felt trivial next to Bea because she made a difference in the lives of people in the real world. What I did with my time seemed to me like play by comparison.

Arthur didn't often bring Bea to hang out with the rest of us, although one memorable night, Skip and Bea had a blast quoting scripture to each other at the Jackrabbit. Bea didn't have a lot of leisure time, and she generally had bigger fish to fry. She rarely afforded herself the luxury of tramping down to Arthur's college campus for fun. I wondered if Arthur ever wearied of going out with a woman who took life so seriously.

In my sophomore year, I developed an obsession with the artwork of indigenous peoples and I sought out exhibitions and images of African tribal art, Native American art, and Maori designs. The art of indigenous peoples struck me as infinitely complex, insightful, and not at all as simplistic as the art historians painted it in their critical discussions in my textbooks. My professors referred to it as "primitive art," but I found that term offensive because I thought the works (and the cultures from which they sprung) were highly civilized. I found more than inspiration in the work of indigenous peoples; I found recognition. The art as well as simple objects of everyday use conjured powerful feelings in me, touching me deeply, and sometimes triggering a bundle of emotions that I began to think of, for lack of a more precise term, as sense-memories. On the one hand, I experienced pleasurable sense-memories of a rich life that was connected in a spiritual way to the natural world. When I looked at photographs of blankets, baskets, or tools made by Natives, I could practically feel these objects in my hands and I swore I could smell wood smoke. I could picture myself protected and hidden by a dense grove of ancient trees. On the other hand, I also experienced unpleasant sense-memories that filled me with an undefined anguish, such as that time I listened to the sounds of the slave ship on that record at Arthur's. Once I stopped to talk to a man at the flea market who was selling wooden carvings of animals from the Ivory Coast. I picked up one of the elephants from the table in front of him and an overwhelming feeling of loss swept through me. I quickly put the elephant back because handling it made me want to weep. I was convinced that I had a deep cultural memory, imprinted in my DNA, that was connected to Africa and the Native tribes of North America.

I persuaded Skip to take an anthropology course on preliterate cultures with me. I had this idea that the structure that written language imposed on the brain limited abstract thought and I was curious to learn more about art produced by human imagination free of that structure.

"I think that art, music, and dance operate on the highest levels of abstract communication between people," I told Skip.

He answered, "They're also the highest levels of communication between humans and the divine. Art can be a form of prayer."

"I have a bad habit of thinking of Christians as religious fanatics," I confessed, rather sheepishly. "I need you around to remind me that Christians are not, by definition, out to convert everyone else, and that people who believe in God aren't necessarily tied down to religious dogma."

"That's a bit of a backhanded compliment," Skip said, with a good-natured grin, "but I'll take it."

Nine

IN THE AUTUMN, Call It a Wrap began to take off. There were half a dozen of us former students of Margaret's who supplied her with wrapping-paper patterns on a regular basis and she was selling the designs as rapidly as we produced them. I was one of her more prolific designers, producing patterns based on Navajo weaving motifs, Maori tribal identifications, and flowers. Despite my success designing wrapping paper for Call It a Wrap, my passion lay elsewhere. Throughout the long, dark days of winter, as the snow erased the road marks of the world outside, I retreated to my carriage house, got stoned, and built masks. My preoccupation with mask making carried me into the spring and the semester was almost over before I knew it.

That semester, Lee, Norma, and I often smoked pot together and wandered in the gardens surrounding my carriage house apartment or listened to music. Every once in a while, Lee scored some mescaline or psilocybin mushrooms and then she and I would hole up in the carriage house for a couple of days on a hallucinogenic trip. When I was tripping, every single object in the world moved and breathed with a life of its own. I could see and hear plants growing, the spirits of rocks spoke, and a window into the world of indigenous peoples opened up for me. It was a world in which all of life, every entity in nature, had something to teach, a message for humans if we only could figure out how to listen. I felt that I was translating my hallucinogenic experiences into my masks, so that they came alive in ways that inanimate objects seemed to come alive when I was tripping. I experimented with a wider variety of media, particularly textiles, and incorporated found objects, such as feathers, shells, leaves, pressed flowers, stones, and pieces of wood, into the masks.

A couple of weeks before the school term ended, on a warm, flower-scented spring evening, my friends came over for dinner. We sat on the lawn outside the carriage house on Indian bedspreads and ate pizza. Dale contributed several rolls of uncooked cookie dough, his favorite treat, for dessert. Skip and TJ tossed a baseball back and forth.

Dale had come out of the closet to everyone but his parents the previous year (he lived in fear that his father would find out). He had brought his new flame, Richard, to my picnic and they were giggling beneath the honeysuckle with Lee. Norma, Arthur, and I sat on my kitchen chairs, which had migrated onto the lawn. Norma and I started talking about how much Dale's art had changed and flourished since he had publicly embraced his sexual identity. He was particularly good at pen-and-ink sketches and previously produced tiny drawings with great attention to detail. Lately he was doing larger pen-and-ink drawings with heavy lines and broader strokes. He had also begun to paint in watercolors, a new medium for him. I had become accustomed to seeing his art in black and white for so long that the bright colors of his watercolors were almost shocking.

"Every time I see a new one, I'm taken by surprise," I said.

"We've all evolved as artists. Look at Skip," Arthur said. "His drawing has become so much more fluid and relaxed."

"Look at you, for that matter," Norma said to Arthur. "Remember those intricate, itsy-bitsy Chinese paper cuts you used to make? And now you're painting large-scale pictures on the sides of buildings with that mural project."

"That's different," he pointed out, "because I'm not actually doing much of that painting. The kids do most of it. I'm more like a counselor."

"A conductor," I said, picking up a twig and pretending to conduct a symphony. "I thought I'd be a graphic designer and now I'm making masks."

"You're a terrific graphic artist. Marketable and good. But you're getting sidetracked," Arthur said.

"What do you mean?" I asked, hurt by his criticism.

"Never mind; I shouldn't have said anything," he replied.

"No, what do you mean?" I persisted.

Arthur sighed. Then he looked up and caught my gaze. "You spaced out. You got into drugs with Michael and you spaced out. Your graphics are getting fuzzy. They lack the precision that you had before. The technical proficiency. Your graphics work was inspired and high quality. These masks you've been doing," Arthur shrugged. "Well, face it; they're folksy and sort of sloppy."

"Arthur," Norma cautioned.

"I can't believe that you, of all people, would fail to appreciate the beauty of masks. You're like those condescending academics who don't consider crafts in the same league with fine arts," I snapped.

"The problem is not the medium," Arthur responded, a little more gently. "The masks are OK. But your work used to take my breath away. Maybe your masks could too, but they don't. I'm not saying this to hurt your feelings. I'm telling you because you're a good friend, and I care about you. I think you're doing too many drugs."

I stalked inside. Norma followed and started to help me clean up the kitchen. A few minutes later, Arthur's form filled the doorway.

"I didn't mean to ruin things," he said. "I'm going to take off. I'll see ya later." But his absence ruined the party even more than his biting words.

"It's that moralistic, Bible-thumping girlfriend of his. I just don't get what he sees in her anyway. She's so humorless," I complained to Norma, who said nothing in reply.

In June, Lee and I invited TJ to do mushrooms with us and we ventured on a hilarious escapade in the gardens where I lived. Giant sunflowers from another planet pursued us. We collected sparkling precious gems off the garden pathways and filled our pockets with them, only to discover later when the drugs wore off that we had collected ordinary, damp gravel. We watched the roses grow, had visions, and communed with trees and insects on an excursion around the duck pond.

It was a summer completely different from the previous one, when I had devoted all my attention to one boyfriend. I avoided any possibility of entanglement in a romantic relationship and instead picked up a different guy every few weeks for a one-night stand, usually a musician passing through at the Jackrabbit. There were so many attractive men to be reeled in on a flirtatious glance. And I was enjoying my independence too much to compromise myself in exchange for a lasting relationship. I expected a lot out of my one-night stands, though. I required more than sex. I wanted to touch a man's soul, if only briefly. I made my lovers tell their stories, their childhood, their history, their passions, their dreams. I kept a man up all night making love and speaking his deepest self. I had no desire to possess my lovers, only to know them. As for the young men, they relished the beauty and romance of the carriage house filled with my art, music, books, and me, with my fervent questioning, a woman who made love to a man's story of himself. When my lovers left in the morning, they left with a certain clarity of purpose. They never returned, and I did not wish for them to do so.

Ten

ONE BLUSTERY DAY IN October, while I sat at the big round table in the student union with my friends and ate lunch, I started thinking about the prospect of spending Thanksgiving with my family. Even though lately I had been enjoying the company of my sisters more, I didn't relish the idea of going home for the holiday. I had just spent a weekend with the family right before the start of the semester. Soph had graduated from college in the spring and was continuing on to law school while Sarah was packing to leave home to start her freshman year. The three of us killed a bottle of wine together after Mother and Nate went to bed on Saturday night, and Sarah, who was pretty tipsy, took us to the basement and gave us a tour of the bomb shelter that Nate had built, complete with a showcase of the canned food and a demonstration of how to work the kerosene lantern and assemble the cots. I sat down on one of said cots and laughed until I cried. Nate and I avoided each other for the duration of the visit because we were so uncomfortable in each other's presence, and I could only take so much of my mother's agonizing over what to cook for me for dinner. She persisted in asking me from time to time, "Are you still vegetarian?" It had been almost five years. Did she actually think it was a phase I would outgrow? I couldn't face the discussion about my health and proper nutrition that I anticipated would occur as a result of my refusal to eat turkey.

"Hey, you guys, what is everyone doing for Thanksgiving?" I asked. "I don't want to go to my parents' house. I'm thinking of staying home by myself and eating a cheese sandwich."

"You don't even eat turkey, so don't go fishing for pity with that cheese sandwich stuff," TJ said, refusing to bite the bait. But Lee bit.

"You can't spend Thanksgiving by yourself. I'll come over and we'll make some mashed potatoes and salad or something," she offered. "I wasn't planning to go home anyway."

"My Thanksgiving last year was a bust," I told Lee.

"Ah, yes," Arthur crossed his arms over his chest and grinned impishly. "If I recall correctly, you had rat for dinner last year."

"Norma, pinch him for me; I can't reach," I said.

"No way I'm going home for Thanksgiving," Dale told us. "I'm spending it with Richard. We could do something with you two," he offered.

"If you guys are doing Thanksgiving, then count me in," said TJ. "I wouldn't miss it."

"Me too," Norma added. "In fact, we can do it over at my house. Everyone else will probably be gone and we have a big dining room table."

Even Skip agreed to stay in town. "I'm going home for Christmas, so I'll see my folks then. It'll save Dad the cost of my train fare if I stick around here for Thanksgiving."

"I promised Bea I would go to her family for the holiday. I didn't know you guys were going to do something." Arthur bowed out with noticeable reluctance.

"You can't get out of it?" TJ asked.

"It would hurt Bea's feelings," he said.

"That's OK; more delicious food for us," Lee teased Arthur.

"Do any of you know how to cook a turkey?" Dale asked.

"Good question," TJ said. "Do any of us know how to cook a turkey?"

"Let Rina do it. She'll stuff it with cheese and crackers," Arthur suggested.

"Yeah, and what would you stuff it with? Grits?" I countered.

"That's low," Dale said, "real low."

Unfazed, Arthur boasted, "My mama does a dressing that's so good, the turkeys line up at her kitchen door begging to be her bird. They say, 'Please, ma'am, please let me lay down on your platter.'"

TJ laughed. "Hey, man, I'm going to miss you at the table."

"I'll miss you too," Arthur replied.

I called Mother to tell her that I was going to spend Thanksgiving with my friends and she laid the Jewish mother guilt trip on me. "Listen," I said firmly, "last year I had a dreadful Thanksgiving and I'm determined to enjoy myself this year. None of my friends are going home. We're doing the holiday together. You won't miss me. You have Soph and Sarah."

"I will too miss you," she insisted. "Sophie and Sarah do not equal Rina. But Rina is a stubborn young woman and I know I can't change her mind."

I had to smile at her persistence. She drove me crazy, but there was no denying that she loved me. I softened and invited her to meet me for lunch on the Saturday after the holiday. That seemed to make her happy and she said she'd bring Sophie and Sarah. I could handle that.

On the Friday before Thanksgiving week, I was in my comparative literature class, when an instructor I didn't know knocked on the door, entered,
and talked quietly with our professor, who began to cry. Our professor
leaned on her desk to steady herself and announced, "The president has
been shot."

At first, I didn't understand and thought she meant the president of the
college, but it quickly became clear that it was President Kennedy who had
been shot. The class was immediately dismissed. As I hurried to the student
union, where there was a TV, and where I thought I might find some of my
friends, I was struck by the extent to which I was living in an ivory tower,
consumed by my own art projects and oblivious to current events.

At the student union, I found Norma and we stood with our arms
around each other, eyes glued to the TV, surrounded by disbelieving students, some weeping as they watched Walter Cronkite break down and
cry while reporting on the events unfolding in Dallas. Arthur edged his
way through the crowd and stood at my elbow.

He said softly, "A country built on violence is doomed to produce
more violence."

"How do you stop it?" I asked, not really expecting him to be able to answer.

But he did. "Dr. King," Arthur said. "Dr. King knows how to stop it."
Arthur's church had rented a bus only a few months earlier and he had traveled with them to DC to participate in what had been called the Poor People's
March on Washington. When Arthur returned from the march, he printed
up copies of a speech that Dr. King had delivered there and he distributed
it to everyone he knew. I had read the speech and it made me inclined to
believe that Dr. King really could inspire people to change for the better.

Everywhere I went during the days after Kennedy was assassinated,
people were serious and subdued. I had never experienced anything like
it. The whole country grieved. I called my mother one evening and talked
to her about it. She said the mood of the country reminded her of what
it felt like during the war. By the time Thanksgiving rolled around, my
friends and I desperately needed to shake off the pervasive sense of gloom.
A day of good cheer and, literally, thanksgiving was in order.

Norma lived in a large, cooperative household (the residents affectionately called it "the coop"). She said the coop reminded her of her big,
nutty family, from which she had been exiled by her tyrannical father. On
Thanksgiving the coop emptied out and Norma filled it with us.

Norma and TJ took responsibility for the turkey, and they took their
responsibility seriously. TJ actually bought *Joy of Cooking* and they read
up on cooking turkeys. TJ slept at the coop on Wednesday night and
they stayed up late making a blue-ribbon turkey dressing, arguing about
whether or not to put the turkey gizzard into the dressing and how much
sage and how much celery to use. Norma wanted to make a cornbread
dressing and TJ was horrified at the thought. Finally, Norma agreed to
allow TJ to pulverize the gizzard and liver and put them into the dressing

and TJ agreed to the cornbread and, in the end, they made peace, made dressing, and made it to sleep by midnight.

In the morning, they stuffed the bird and put him in the oven. The rest of us arrived for a late bagel breakfast and to prepare "all the trimmings." Dale and Richard insisted that they would make Dale's grandmother's recipe for "light rolls," which had to rise several times. The two of them fussed over those rolls on and off for hours as they prepared their dough and watched it rise and prepared it and watched it rise and cut it and watched it rise and always at the exact right temperature and placed in the exact right spot in the kitchen. Every time TJ found them in the kitchen, he rolled his eyes and quipped, "Laurel and Hardy make light rolls."

I chopped vegetables for a salad. Meanwhile, Lee worked on a sauerkraut casserole she wanted to try. It had sour cream, shiitake mushrooms, and adzuki beans in it. Lee was vegetarian like me, but unlike me, she loved to cook. She made cranberry sauce from scratch with whole fresh cranberries and orange juice. Norma and TJ would make gravy from the turkey scraps and Skip was in charge of the mashed potatoes. Richard had bought two pumpkin cheesecakes for dessert. We were drooling with anticipation.

At around two o'clock, Lee and I went out to the front porch in our ski jackets to smoke a joint. We had just sat down when Arthur stormed down the street and up the walk. I could tell something was wrong the minute I saw him in the distance by the way he walked, head down, swift steps. I watched him approach, my hand poised in midair, holding the unlit joint. Lee and I looked up at him with concern from where we sat on the step.

"What?" he challenged us by way of a greeting.

"What happened?" I asked.

His fists stuffed into his pockets, he kicked at the bottom step with his boot. He looked up at the sky. "I had a fight with Bea. We split up."

"Gosh, that's what I did for Thanksgiving last year," I said, as I fired up my cigarette lighter and put the joint to my lips.

Arthur grabbed the joint out of my hand and flung it into the shrubbery. "Stop smoking that crap!" He glared at me.

Stunned, Lee and I simply stared at him for a moment. I could not recall ever seeing Arthur so out of control. He smoldered like a volcano. Because I couldn't think of anything else to do, I stood up, leaned forward, and wrapped him in my arms. "If you don't want me to, I won't," I said gently, as if we were the only two people in the whole world. "We're going to have a great Thanksgiving. Just our family. Thank goodness you're here."

Arthur put his arms around me. His shoulders rose and fell as he took several deep breaths. With each breath, he seemed to relax one notch and gain control. As I withdrew from the embrace, I gave him a peck on the lips.

"Me too," Lee sang out. "I want a kiss from Mr. Right too." She

jumped in on Arthur and gave him a kiss also. Arthur managed a weak
smile. Then Lee and I bolstered him up on either side, as if he couldn't
walk on his own, and pretended to assist him into the house. We led him
into the kitchen, where Lee called to TJ from the doorway, "Look, Pa,
Beetle Bailey made it home from the war for the holidays."

"Only minor injuries," I chimed in. "He lost his liver."

"We can fix that," TJ replied, "we got lotsa liver in the fridge."

TJ, wearing a Daniel Boone beaver hat and two pink oven mitts, had
the oven door open and was squirting the turkey in a vaguely obscene
manner with a turkey baster.

As Arthur laughed his deep, rumbling laugh, I climbed out from under
his arm. "What's with the beaver, TJ?" Arthur asked.

"My niece gave it to me for Halloween. You like it? I feel like a hunter
in it. You know, good turkey-roasting hat."

"The beaver's in the gravy," Norma added, pointing to the pan on the
stove. "Yum, yum." It was so hot in the kitchen that Norma had stripped
down to a tank top and shorts.

"Where are Dale and Richard?" Arthur asked.

"Watching football," Skip answered. He stood at the sink and peeled potatoes. He was wearing a backward yellow rain slicker to protect his clothes.

"Home at the insane asylum for the holidays," Arthur muttered.
"What the heck are two gay guys doing watching football?"

"Are you kidding?" Norma exclaimed. "All those tight buns in uni-
forms? They're in heaven."

"C'mon TJ," Arthur said, "we better get in there and model some real
male bonding for them before it's too late."

"Yeah, right," TJ rejoined. "Male bonding. Jockstrap. Urinal. Six-pack."

"Hey, speaking of six-pack," Arthur hinted. Norma opened the refrigerator, pulled out a beer, and handed it to Arthur.

"Me too," TJ said. "Norma, how would you like to take charge of this
turkey baster?" he asked. Norma took it from him and the two men beat a
hasty retreat into the living room to watch football with Dale and Richard.

After they left, Lee turned to me and asked, "Did you still want to
smoke a number?"

I shook my head. "I guess not. Not right now."

By six o'clock we had set the long wooden table in the dining room.
We lit tall orange candles. Dale and I had crafted a flower-themed centerpiece from cardboard, construction paper cutouts, and dried leaves.
We placed fluted wine glasses and cloth napkins at every place setting. TJ
carved up the turkey and, after much bustling in and out of the kitchen,
the table was weighted down with the products of our labors in the
kitchen. There was nothing left to do but sit down and eat.

"We should say grace," Skip insisted.

"Let's go around the table and each give our own thanks," Lee suggested.
So we took hands around the table and each said our own blessing in turn.

TJ spoke last. "I'm so grateful to have all of you as my friends and I give thanks to be here with you for this exceptional meal. Finding a group of friends that feels like a family is a rare blessing. I give thanks that this rare blessing came to me in my life." The unusual seriousness of TJ's tone made my eyes fill with tears.

"You're right, TJ," I said, as I wiped my eyes with my napkin, "we are a family. And in this family I am loved for exactly who I am."

"Rina's crying because she can't eat turkey," TJ teased.

We ate and ate and ate and ate. Dale and Richard complained that the light rolls were not light enough and they would have to make them lighter next year, but I ate about four of them slathered in butter and couldn't imagine them tasting any better. We all said that Lee's sauerkraut casserole went extraordinarily well with the rest of the dinner, all of us except TJ, who wouldn't touch a shred of cabbage if his life depended on it. My carnivorous buddies claimed that the turkey was tender and delicious. And we agreed that nothing would ever taste as good again as that meal tasted if we all lived to be a hundred and four.

After we ate, we left the dining room as it was with the remains of the feast sprawled across the table like a plundered village and retired to the living room where Skip lit a fire in the stone fireplace and Norma served Irish coffee. We lay draped over couches and chairs and the thick rug, rubbing each other's feet, heads in each other's laps, like a heap of contented cats before the hearth. TJ kept nodding off to sleep and snoring loudly, then jerking back to wakefulness.

"Do you think I should get my makeup kit and do his face?" Norma asked us.

"Don't even think about it," TJ snorted, his eyes opening to slits and then sliding shut again.

"He's faking it," Richard hissed in a stage whisper.

"Hey, TJ, if you're faking it, then ixnay on the oringsnay," Dale called.

"This was the best Thanksgiving ever," Lee said, sighing with satisfaction. Lee's feet were in my lap and I was giving her a foot massage while my feet were in Arthur's lap and he was giving me a foot massage. Norma took Arthur's foot into her lap and started massaging it.

"You know how when we said grace, and TJ said that about being a family?" I asked. "Well, I think this is what a family is supposed to feel like and I don't think I ever felt that before. Growing up, I felt as though I couldn't do anything right and that my parents were constantly critical of me. The things that were important to me didn't matter to them and it seemed to me that they wasted their time on such trivial stuff. But with you guys, my life matters. What I do matters. I feel valued."

"I'm sorry you had such a hard time when you were growing up. I'm lucky to have such a close-knit family. I can't imagine what it would be like to not get along with my dad," Skip observed.

"I wish I was born into a Native American family, like in the Black Hills of South Dakota or something. Or into a tribe in Africa somewhere," I said fervently. "I used to imagine that I had been left on my parents' doorstep in a basket."

"Maybe you're a Martian," TJ suggested.

"Shut up; Rina is serious." Norma reached behind her back and smacked TJ.

"You can smack me there anytime," TJ told her, "no feeling in that knee."

"Ignore him," Norma told me, "and he'll go away."

"No, I won't," TJ contradicted her.

"Continue," Lee commanded.

"Sometimes I really do kind of feel like a Martian," I said. "I have seriously wondered if I'm maybe psychic without the training to control it. This strange thing happens to me from time to time."

"Can you bend spoons with your mind?" Dale asked.

"Oh, stop!" Lee said, though we all laughed. "Let Rina talk. What is the strange thing?"

"I have these flashes. I call them 'sense-memories,' and they're triggered by seeing or handling art or objects of everyday use made by indigenous people, like Native Americans, or Aborigines, for instance. Objects like baskets or blankets can do it. I get this feeling that I used these objects once upon a time. Like I know something about them, about how they came into existence in a hut or a tipi. It feels like my memory began centuries ago. Sometimes the memories are peaceful and sort of spiritually rejuvenating and at other times they're terrifying. It makes me a bit cautious about opening the door into my creative process since I'm a little scared of what might surface. Arthur, remember that day when you played that slave ship song?"

Arthur nodded. He remembered all right.

"What's that about?" Richard asked, looking from one to the other of us for an explanation.

"I played a song about slavery," Arthur explained. "TJ was there, and Dale."

"I remember," TJ said.

Arthur continued. "It starts out with the sounds of the ocean and a ship groaning and slaves moaning in the hold of the ship. I played it for Rina once and she flipped out."

"Because it brought up these intense feelings of loss and terror for me. The same kind of thing happens a lot of times when I see certain artwork, or hear certain music, or look at ordinary objects connected with certain cultures. And here's the kicker: I identify with arts and crafts of indigenous cultures, as well as the emotions and recognition that these arts and crafts trigger in me, far more than I identify with the objects and rituals of the Jewish culture in which I was raised. I felt so," I paused, searching for the word I wanted, "so misplaced while I was growing up. So restless.

I've never felt at home anywhere. But lately, when I'm with you guys, I feel more like I might be coming home."

"Me too," Dale said. "There are not many places where I feel like I'm accepted and loved for just who I am. Like it's OK that I'm gay, that I'm a bit eccentric, that I'm Negro, that I'm not butch, all those things. I don't feel like a freak around you guys."

"That's exactly it," TJ agreed. "When I'm with you guys, I don't feel like a freak. I'm just a guy who happens to need a wheelchair to get around."

I thought, as I rarely did, about his deformed legs and how hard it must be for him to have strangers stare at him.

"What a relief to have a place where we can sit down together as human beings, and not be stuffed into a preconceived notion or a stereotype or a label," Arthur said. "A place where we can let down our guard and regroup, before going back out there into the insanity of a racist society where everyone sees my skin color first and can hardly get past that to the person I am inside."

"I hear you, brother," Dale said.

"This is the way it should be," Lee pointed out. "I know some people would say we live in a fantasy world, that our lives are not reality. But as far as I'm concerned, this is the reality and what other people want to foist on us as 'the real world' is the distortion. I don't want to accept a world in which some maniac shoots and kills the president. If that's the world, then it needs to change. It needs to transform into a world that resembles ours, the one we have right here."

Norma leapt to her feet. "OK, I want us to make a pact. Right now. Promise that we will make every effort to spend every Thanksgiving from now on together. Forever. Even when some of us have a passel of snot-nosed obnoxious children or a partner who gets on everyone else's nerves."

"What if the partner is someone like the Rat?" Dale asked.

"It won't be," I assured him.

"How obnoxious will the children be?" TJ asked. "And how much snot?"

"TJ, you have to agree, no matter how annoying the partners are or how obnoxious the children are," Norma demanded.

We stacked our hands together and recited after Norma, "We solemnly swear to spend Thanksgiving together whenever possible."

"And I want Lee to take a special oath to always make that sauerkraut stuff again," Arthur added.

Even after we cleaned up the dining room and the kitchen, and even after we ate the pumpkin cheesecakes, we lounged in the living room late into the night, talking and dozing and listening to music, snug in the warmth of friendship, just being who we were.

Eleven

ALTHOUGH I WAS PARTICULARLY inspired by artwork produced by indigenous cultures, I was not foolish enough to think that I had nothing to learn from the great artists of the Western canon. I diligently studied the "Amazing Dead White Guys," as Margaret affectionately called the European masters. I learned to look closely at the play of light on objects from the impressionists and the quality of light from Turner. I learned the uses of vivid color from Renoir and Toulouse-Lautrec. I loved Michelangelo; I mean, who doesn't? I was less excited about modern art and could do without paintings of three yellow brushstrokes in the middle of an otherwise empty canvas or realistic renderings of dead rats on the coffee table. As far as I was concerned, modern painting wasn't in the same league with the rich, detailed tapestries and gold-threaded fabrics of the *Lady of Shalott* (either Meteyard's or Waterhouse's). I had a weakness for Pre-Raphaelite images of beautiful, despondent ladies pining away for lack of a lover, such as Isabella and her gruesome pot of basil or William Morris's Mariana, who waited eternally. In spite of myself, I felt a connection with these sensual women who yearned for a man to make their lives complete.

By my senior year, I had given up doing drugs. I realized that Arthur's opposition to my drug use came from a sincere love for me and the desire to see me do my best work. He was right about the fact that I worked better when I stayed away from drugs, which clouded my mind and muddied my art. I would always believe in the value of the mind-expanding experience that hallucinogens provided, but I had experienced it, learned from it, and moved on.

Margaret, who had bought a house with Gloria and converted her West Village loft into a studio, still employed me to design wrapping paper. I worked in a variety of media. I drew flowers with colored pens and water-colors. I embroidered fabric, mostly for pillows. I painted small simulated tapestries in oils. I used traditional African and Maori ceremonial styles and materials to build my masks, which had evolved over time and were quite different from the folksy early versions that Arthur had criticized. I produced my various and vivid visual interpretations of the world. I was prolific. I didn't worry about how I would support myself after I completed school because I had plenty of prospects and leads for work. I dreaded completing school for other reasons. I had read *Sentimental Education* by Flaubert in a comparative literature class in my junior year and ever after the title stuck with me as the definition of my education. I had loved every moment of art school and I didn't want it to end. Things would change for me and my circle of friends after we graduated and went in our separate directions. We would never be together in the same way again.

It was during those twilight months at the end of my college career that I met Tegema. His band played their Jamaican music at the Jackrabbit while I was waiting tables. The band's drummer, Tegema had short dreadlocks, smooth clear brown skin, and an alluring dimpled smile. The muscles in his arms moved in liquid rhythm with the beat, easy and sure. I wanted him.

I brought him a cold beer between sets. He declined the beer, flashed me those dimples, and asked what time I got off work. When my shift ended, he beckoned to me, and I slipped into the seat next to him in a dark corner of the club.

"I think I'm falling in love with Jamaican music," I said.

"I'm glad you liked it," he said. I watched him put a bottle of sparkling water to his broad, sensuous lips.

"Do you come from Jamaica?" I asked.

"Haiti," he answered. "We have reggae too."

I nodded and looked down at the label on my beer bottle. I really wanted him. "Would you like to come home with me tonight?" I asked. He studied me carefully, as if to confirm I had said what he thought I had said. A slow smile spread across his face and I knew I had him. I put our unfinished drinks up on the bar and we left.

Outside, he crammed his two large conga drums into the back of a Volkswagen Beetle. I sat in the front with the seat pulled forward against the dashboard.

"How did you start playing drums?" I asked.

"I have always played drums."

"How did you wind up in New York?" I asked.

"I came with my family from Haiti when I was a little boy. My parents returned to the island after ten years. They took the younger children with them, but us older children were too Americanized and didn't want to leave." His talking sounded like singing.

"You must have a big family," I said. Just open your mouth again, and speak, I thought.

"Eleven brothers and sisters."

"Counting you?"

"Counting me."

"Do you ever go back to Haiti?"

"Not often."

"What is it like there?"

During his telling we arrived at the carriage house. The string of chili pepper lights that I had hung in the front window twinkled gaily.

He didn't want to leave his drums in the car so we brought them inside, each of us carrying one. As he set his drum down in my apartment, he turned slowly around in the middle of the floor, gazing at the visual feast I had created in my home. "Marvelous. Beautiful. Magic," he pronounced.

I kissed his luscious, ripe lips and he kissed back. I lifted his shirt over his head so my fingertips could drift across his smooth, muscular chest. I ran my hands down the curve of his back. I touched the front of his pants, where I could feel him pressing against the fabric, a trapped bird beating against the drapes. He pulled me to him.

Tegema was not the first Negro I had slept with, but I found myself inexplicably moved by his color. I made love to his dark beauty, the rich brown essence of who he was. In the morning, I asked Tegema if he would come back again. And he did. Once or twice a week, Tegema turned up either at my carriage house apartment or at the Jackrabbit and I brushed aside my busy life to make room for him. Sometimes, in his absence, my yearning for him became unbearable.

When we lay entwined together, I asked him questions and he answered with the history of his life. I especially liked to hear about his childhood in Haiti, which prompted him to draw up long-forgotten memories. It had nearly killed him when his parents ripped him away from his homeland and brought him to New York. When he grew more comfortable with me, he told me that as a teenager he had become addicted to heroin. He had been in and out of prison and in and out of rehabilitation programs for six years.

"If you'd seen me on the subway back then, you would've moved to another car to get away from me," he said. "I was a mess."

He had damaged his health, lost his teeth, lost his direction. He finally began taking drumming seriously during his last stint in prison and when he got out he joined a band. The band gave him focus. He started attending a Haitian church. Between his spiritual connection with the church and his drumming, he managed to stay clean and sober for the first time in years.

Then came his lucky break. He landed a role, as a drummer, in a movie to be filmed in Haiti. His contract included the replacement of his teeth so that he would look right for the part. His new set of dentures provided him with an irresistible smile, which he took to Haiti for the film shoot. In Haiti, he told me, he put some of his personal ghosts to rest. He was proud of the fact that he had landed the film job on the strength of his drumming. The confirmation that he had talent changed his self-image, changed his life. Now he had enough work to support himself. He still attended his Haitian spiritualist church, where they believed that the body was a temple and therefore focused on both spiritual and physical health. I told him I could tell that he paid attention to his health because his skin glowed the way it does with people who eat a lot of fruit and vegetables and drink plenty of water. After the hard times he had survived, Tegema savored that image of health and spiritual well-being. He was the most handsome man I had ever had in my bed.

But I had honed the technique of the one-night stand and I didn't know how to sustain an ongoing relationship. Tegema turned up when he wanted to see me. I never asked for his phone number and didn't know how to reach him. I was rather partial to the romance of the mystery in our relationship. On the other hand, I would have liked to have him as a more reliable and regular fixture in my life. I lost my appetite for other men.

Then, one night, several months after we had met, Tegema appeared at my house, made love to me especially slowly and sensually, and afterward, as we lay entangled in each other's arms, he said, "I won't be coming here again."

"What do you mean?"

"I'm getting married."

"Married?" I tried not to sound as shocked as I felt.

"To my homegirl. We go back a long way. She knew me when I was messed up. We have a son together."

"Does she know about me?" I asked.

"Yes. Like I said, we go back a long way. She was there when I was a mess and she helped me straighten out."

I was angry that this other woman knew about me while I had just learned about her. It meant that her relationship with Tegema was so much stronger than my inconsequential, fleeting affair with him.

"And what possessed you to want to marry her now?" I asked. I wondered if there was anything I could say or do to make him change his mind.

"You," he said. Tegema turned on his side to face me and swept my hair off my neck, leaving his fingers enmeshed in the thick of it behind my head. "I'm getting married because of you. Your questions led me to myself. You and your carriage house and your beautiful artwork, like a temple. I made a pilgrimage to the temple and I found my path. My path is away from the temple. Don't be sad. I cherish every minute I've spent with you."

"I helped you realize that you should marry someone else," I replied, unable to keep the bitter irony out of my voice.

"Don't be angry. She is my destiny."

"And what am I?" I asked.

"One man's last taste of adventure before going home, but, one day, another man's homegirl, another man's temple," Tegema answered.

"Tell me what you loved the most about me," I commanded, selfishly.

"Your questions," Tegema said.

I made love to him carefully and deliberately one last time before he left. I wanted him to remember the sweetness of my touch with longing for the rest of his life.

I never saw him again.

When I told Norma and Lee about our final conversation, Norma's response was, "You inspired a man to marry someone else. Now that's an interesting talent that must be useful for something, though I can't think what."

"You drove him into the arms of another woman," Lee teased.

"No, I *was* the other woman," I reminded her. "I drove him into the arms of his wife."

I tried to joke with my friends about the split with Tegema, but I was unsuccessful. The loss hurt and I couldn't quite summon up the ability to laugh it off as I would have liked. Twice after he left I had that frightening, vivid dream in which I was that Chinese girl whose father shouted at her, who watched with anguish as that handsome gardener departed, and who was then raped by the man with the rotten breath. That horrible dream had a habit of turning up whenever I was seriously upset about something.

The first Saturday night after Tegema had left, I went to the Jackrabbit and got roaring drunk on gin and tonic. At first my friends didn't realize what was going on. But when I fell off my chair and sat on the floor in a heap, crying, Arthur picked me up and carried me out. He had borrowed his cousin's car for the night and he piled me into the backseat. He drove me home and carried me into my house, where he sat me on the couch. I probably looked as if I was starting to sober up, although my limbs still flopped around like dying fish.

"Tell me something," I said, while making an effort to focus my eyes on Arthur's face. "If I was a Negro girl, you would spend the night, wouldn't you?"

"Rina, you're drunk," he replied.

"I know I'm drunk. You don't have to tell me I'm drunk. I'm not stupid. I'm just drunk."

"So you don't know what you're talking about," Arthur said.

"I know what I'm talking about," I insisted. With my limp arm, I tried to gesture back and forth between myself, seated on the couch, and Arthur, towering above me hesitantly, halfway between the couch and the front door. "If I was a Negro girl, you and me, we would've been something a long time ago, wouldn't we?"

"I'm not going to have this conversation." Arthur scowled.

"If I was a Negro girl, you would probably spend the night right now."

"But you're not a Negro girl, you're drunk, and it's time to say good night." He turned sharply and left, shutting the door hard behind him.

The next day, I phoned Arthur to thank him for taking me home. I pretended I couldn't remember what I'd said and I simply apologized for being rude. Arthur graciously said he had already forgotten about it.

Twelve

AFTER TEGEMA, I LOST interest in one-night stands. I wondered if I should give up on men altogether. Margaret seemed so happy with Gloria. I was curious about relationships between women. When I tried to imagine how they made love, it excited me. I wanted to experiment with making love to a woman, to at least see what it felt like. I asked Margaret and Gloria to take me along with them to one of the lesbian bars they frequented.

"Are you kidding? I could lose my job. You're a student, for heaven's sake," Margaret declared in alarm.

"So what am I going to do, report you? Besides, I'm not in your class anymore. I'm one of your *former* students."

"There are a lot of people out there who would love to expose a scandal like that. Imagine: a college professor foisting her perversion on a young protégé. I don't think so, Rina. You're going to have to make your own path of discovery, just like I did."

"And if you run into us in a lesbian bar, you don't know us," Gloria said with that impish grin of hers.

I shared with Lee that I was curious about lesbian sex. I asked her if she ever thought about it.

"Absolutely," she said. "But it seems hard enough to meet a guy. I have no idea how I would meet a woman to sleep with, especially since I'm not sure how serious I could ever get with a woman."

I told her about my failed attempt to talk Margaret into taking me to a lesbian bar.

"I'd go with you to a lesbian bar," Lee offered.

"Do you know one?" I asked.

"No. But I know who to ask. Dale and Richard," Lee said.

"They sure know all the gay guy hangouts; do you think they know anything about lesbians?" I wondered, skeptically.

Dale and Richard sent us to a bar that was not what I had in mind at all. I had imagined a mellow, slow-dance, private, all-women club. Instead, Lee and I wound up in a wild dance club with a flock of exotic creatures dressed in outlandish costumes that relied heavily on the use of a feather boa. It was fun, but in a Halloweenish way, not in a self-discovery way. And I couldn't tell which women were really women and which ones were men parading as women. It was kind of unsettling.

Lee and I left well before midnight and went back to my carriage house, where we popped popcorn, drank beer, and listened to music.

"I don't know what I expected," I told Lee.

"Well, I was up for maybe picking someone up, you know, but not a woman who might turn out to be a man in the process of becoming a woman," Lee said.

"I heard that," I replied. I studied Lee. "Why don't we experiment with each other?" I suggested.

Lee giggled. "Are you serious?"

"Sure, why not?" I answered. "We have the equipment."

"I don't want to ruin our friendship." Lee's face crinkled with worry.

"Well, let's promise that it won't," I said.

"You make it sound so easy," Lee told me.

"It will be. It will be just fine."

So after a great deal of nervous laughter and joking, we discarded our clothes and explored each other's bodies. We were hungry for the experience and it did not take long for us to surrender to the moment and give and receive the pleasure of one another's touch. Over the next few weeks, we spent the night together several times. Usually Lee would initiate an encounter. But pretty soon, Lee met a woman whom she seriously began to court. Our relationship would have potentially compromised that one, so we stopped having sex together. I didn't mind because I had discovered that for me being with a woman was nowhere near as satisfying or intense as being with a man. Making love to a woman was fun and pleasurable, while making love to a man was transformative. I learned from the experience that I definitely preferred men and that I was not inclined to be a lesbian. However, as the academic year began to come to a close, I didn't have the time to pursue either women or men. I focused on completing my courses and my degree. I considered applying to graduate school, but in the end I decided that it was time for me to go out into the world for a while. Maybe graduate school would be the right thing for me in the future, but I needed a break from school before I could think about tackling that.

Skip had accepted a teaching job at Pennsylvania State. Right after graduation, Skip and his family would take the train back to the farm, where Skip would help out during the summer, and then he would begin teaching in the fall so he could start helping to pay off his parents' mortgage. He would not have many occasions to return to New York.

Norma was preparing to move to Paris to do a fashion design program at the Sorbonne for a year. She talked of nothing else and we listened to her indulgently because she was so excited about it. She had received a scholarship to the program and planned to stay in New York for the summer, but in the fall she would leave for France.

TJ had taken a job with an advertising firm in California. He would return to his mother's home in Scarsdale immediately after the graduation ceremony to pack for his move to Berkeley. He had a plum of a job waiting for him and he couldn't wait to go. He heard it would be easier for him to get around in California since Berkeley was supposedly much more wheelchair accessible than New York. And no snow!

Arthur had recently completed overseeing the painting of another large, public mural by teenagers in Harlem. He was considering going on for a master's degree in architecture, but he also kind of liked the idea of going to California with TJ for a year or so before going back to school.

Dale's father still expected him to go to the military academy once he graduated, to toughen him up, sort of a finishing school for guys. But Dale was trying to pluck up the courage to tell his parents about Richard and to inform his father that, unlike his brothers before him, he had no plans for a military career. He couldn't stand to continue living a duplicitous life.

"The sooner I tell him, the sooner he'll get over the shock," Dale said. "I think if I do it in the right way, it will turn out OK in the end. It seems like I've spent my whole life hiding from my father's disapproval. I can't do it anymore. I swear I'd rather be dead."

"Don't say that," Richard responded in alarm.

"You know what I mean," Dale said.

Richard patted Dale's arm. "Nothing a little trip to the Riviera won't cure." Dale and Richard had some money saved and they planned to travel together in Europe for a few weeks before looking for work.

I was going to be the one left behind. I was still making wrapping paper for Call It a Wrap, I had my job at the Jackrabbit, and I was preparing for a show of my masks at the college gallery over the summer. I had no plans to leave New York, where I had felt like I belonged ever since I was a teenager selling my work at craft shows and flea markets. New York was my natural habitat. I was not looking forward to graduation, and in truth, I dreaded leaving school. Even TJ couldn't cheer me up with his goofy sense of humor.

Our gang had agreed that we would escape from our families and meet at the Jackrabbit at ten o'clock on the night before graduation. I arrived at the café with my heart pounding in my ears, worried that one or another of my friends wouldn't show. But slowly we assembled at our usual table. Even Lee, who would not graduate from her music program until the following year, joined us.

I kept thinking, When will we meet again like this? I didn't want us to splinter off in all directions. How had the time gone by so quickly? I put my head down on my arms on the table and cried; I couldn't help myself. My whole life, I had searched for a place where I belonged. Here, with these friends, and for these few years, I had found a place where I finally fit in. But now it was over; that feeling of belonging was dissolving like a mirage. And the more they tried to comfort me, the more I cried. "I'm sorry," I apologized, dabbing my eyes with a paper napkin, "I don't want everyone to go away."

"We'll keep turning up, like a bad penny," Skip promised, "and we'll always have Thanksgivings."

"Isn't the line 'We'll always have Paris'?" Norma asked. "How about Thanksgiving in Paris?"

"You could all come down to the farm for Thanksgiving," Skip suggested.

"Look out," TJ warned, "pretty soon he'll be inviting us to slop the hogs with him and his dad."

"Oh, for once be serious," Dale chided.

"I'm always serious," TJ replied. "I don't know how to lighten up; that's my problem."

"And what's wrong with slopping hogs?" Skip demanded.

"It's OK," I assured them, "I think I'm all right now." But when we parted, Norma offered to spend the night at my place so I wouldn't be alone and I accepted. It would be comforting to wake up in the morning with her there to share breakfast with me.

In later years, I would remember hardly anything about my graduation ceremony because of what happened afterward. Mother, Nate, Sarah, Soph, and Soph's husband, Max, came into the city to see me "walk" for my diploma during the afternoon ceremony and they took me out for dinner afterward. I was touched at how happy Mother was for me. Nate gave me a substantial check as a graduation gift, which was good of him. They took the train home after dinner. The next morning, TJ left for his mother's house in Scarsdale, Skip headed to his family's farm, and Dale went back to Virginia to come out of the closet to his parents.

Thirteen

 ON THE SECOND EVENING after graduation, I put on my periwinkle kimono with the large peach-colored flowers sprawled across it and sat down at my drawing board. I opened the window so I could hear the rain beating on the roof and on the canopy of trees that ringed the pond. I had barely started working when a sharp knock at the door interrupted me.

I peered through the peephole. Arthur stood in the entranceway, his hair wet, his shirtsleeves rolled up, and looking altogether more disheveled than I had ever seen him look. Norma stood behind him, chewing on a cuticle. I quickly opened the door.

"What is it? What happened?" I asked urgently.

"Dale . . ."

"Come in," I interrupted. I didn't want to hear bad news in the entranceway. I wanted it confined to my apartment where I could contain it.

Before I had entirely closed the door behind him, Arthur blurted out, "He's in jail in Virginia."

"What the hell happened?" How dare anyone arrest our sensitive friend?

Arthur sunk into my saggy couch. "He called Margaret," he explained. "He was not in good shape. Margaret says they arrested him for assaulting his father with an antique sword. He and his father got into an argument and Dale grabbed the sword off a display rack on the wall and attacked his father with it. His mother had already called the police, who arrived in time for Dale's father to have him arrested."

"His father had him arrested?" I asked, incredulously, while at the back of my mind I recalled that I had once called the police on my own father.

Arthur stared at his hands. "He was the only other brother in our grad-uating class."

"He's not dead, Arthur; he had a fight with his father, is all," Norma reminded him.

"Sometimes it all overwhelms me." Arthur looked up at us. "We can't afford to lose Dale. I can't afford to lose him. We've got to do something."

I squatted in front of him and took his hands in mine. "He's not in danger. He's just in jail."

"Every brother in jail is in danger. And he's gay to boot," Arthur reminded me.

"We have to go to Virginia," Norma said.

"Do you think his own father would press charges?" Arthur asked. We looked at each other miserably, guessing that Dale's own father would.

"Where's Richard?" I asked.

"With Margaret and Gloria."

"Norma's right; we have to go to Virginia," I agreed. "I'm going to make some tea while we figure this out." I went into the kitchen and put the kettle on, took three cups out of the cupboard, and found some tea bags. I opened the drawer, took out spoons. Arthur came into the kitchen and sat at the table. Norma remained in the living room where she called the train station to find out the schedule for trains from New York to Virginia. Arthur folded his hands and dumbly followed my movement with his eyes. I stood at the stove staring at the kettle, waiting for it to boil.

"That's a beautiful kimono," Arthur said.

"Thanks. It's my artist uniform."

Arthur smiled fleetingly. He looked down at his folded hands. "My father had a friend he grew up with, name of Charles, who set himself on fire. He didn't make it. What kind of pain would someone have to be in to set himself on fire? If every action has an opposite and equal reaction, then it will take centuries to complete the reaction to slavery before my people can begin to recover from the damage done. Centuries to do the damage, centuries to undo the damage."

I didn't know what to say to that.

When the kettle whistled, I turned off the gas. Arthur stood behind me. He took my shoulders in his hands and squeezed them slightly, then he ran his fingers down my arms to my hands, where his fingertips drifted away from my body. I froze, electric, afraid to turn around. I could feel the warmth of Arthur's breath on my neck. He stepped back away from me and sat down.

What had just happened?

"After we get Dale out, I'm going away," Arthur said. "Out of New York."

I steadied my voice with great effort as I turned to face Arthur. "Where will you go?"

"Berkeley. With TJ."

"You won't like it," I said.

"What makes you say that?"

"I can't imagine you staying away from the heartbeat of Harlem for long."

"Perhaps you're right. But I can always come back. Anytime."

"I'll still be here when you do." Our eyes locked.

Norma entered. "I called the train station for the schedules. Then I called Margaret and she said she would rent a car and drive us down tomorrow morning. She has Richard with her and he's not good. D'you think I should call TJ and Skip?"

I poured tea. "We should let them know what's up, but I don't see why they need to come. There're enough of us going."

"Are you two OK?" Norma looked back and forth at us. "You're acting weird."

"Just upset about Dale," I mumbled.

"Me too," Arthur said, staring into his tea.

The following day, we left early to make the trek down to Virginia. When Margaret picked us up, she had Richard in the car and he looked like hell. Thank goodness she had decided to drive us. When we got down there we went straight to the jail, but we were informed that Dale had been moved. The officials at the prison refused to tell us where he had been taken. Margaret drove to Dale's parents' house. She told us to wait in the car.

From the car, we could see her talking to Dale's parents on the front porch. It did not look like an amicable exchange. We could hear Margaret shouting at them. Arthur opened the door of the car just as Margaret turned and walked briskly from the house. When she got back to the car, she was trembling with rage and instead of getting in she stood on the roadside embankment and threw stones into a meadow for a few minutes. By then it was starting to get dark.

While Margaret was throwing stones, a furtive-looking, frail, elderly woman appeared beside the car. She rapped at the window. Norma and I got out of the car and Margaret came over to us.

"Yes?" Norma asked the woman.

"I'm Dale's grandmother," she said. "This is awful, just awful. I can't stand it."

"What's going on?" I asked, as Arthur and Richard joined us, forming a protective circle around Dale's grandmother and shielding her from view.

"He dropped the assault charge," she said quietly, "and had him committed to the psychiatric hospital. I wrote down the address." She passed a piece of paper to Norma. "I have to go." She began to cry. "If you find him, tell him Nana loves him very much," she said, choking on the words, before she hurried away.

It was nearly ten o'clock by the time we arrived at the psychiatric hospital, which was closed for the night behind a locked gate. Richard stood outside the gate staring at the windows until we coaxed him back into the car. We found a motel and checked in, then went to an all-night diner to get something to eat. The whole situation felt surreal. Back at the hotel, none of us could sleep, so we stayed up watching *Some Like It Hot* on the TV, then the guys went to their room and we women finally dozed off.

I shared a bed with Norma, and Margaret slept in the bed next to us. Just before sunrise, I had that horrible dream that ended with that man raping me. I woke in a sweat, but fortunately I had not soaked Norma's side of the bed. I got up, showered, and dressed. The others were beginning to stir by then. I went in search of breakfast and came back with muffins and coffee for everyone. After we ate, we returned to the psychiatric hospital where we sat in Margaret's car outside the gate until it opened. At the front desk we asked to see Dale. The receptionist informed us that only immediate family could visit him.

"We *are* his immediate family," I told the receptionist.

"How are you related?" she asked, curtly.

Margaret demanded to speak to Dale's doctor, who turned out to be a condescending twit with a plastic jack-o-lantern smile who tried to brush us off.

"On what grounds has he been committed?" Arthur challenged, refusing to back down.

"That is confidential information," the twit replied.

Arthur grabbed the little man by the lapels. "You can't commit someone for homosexuality. He's being detained against his will." Instantly, a dozen burly orderlies appeared and ejected us from the building. Richard sat on the front steps and wept. Arthur and I circled the building, shouting Dale's name at the windows, which brought the orderlies out. They escorted us to our car and told us to leave the premises before they called the police. For lack of a better plan, we remained in the car, parked outside the grounds of the institution. It seemed to make Richard feel better to be near Dale even though he couldn't see him. Eventually we went to a diner for lunch and then returned to our parking spot outside the institution. Margaret and Arthur had just about decided that we should go back to Dale's parents' house when we saw his parents drive out through the gate. Dale's father parked their car and walked over to us, his movements mechanical and controlled. He wore a suit. Margaret rolled down the window. Richard took one look at the man's face and began to whimper. Dale's father's face was a mask of grief.

"It's over," Dale's father informed us. "He's dead. You are free to return to your depraved lives." He turned crisply on his heel, went back to his car, and drove away.

Margaret got out and walked to the guard's booth at the gate. She was allowed to use the phone in the booth. When she returned to the car, she confirmed that it was true. Dale had hanged himself with a bed sheet.

Fourteen

AFTER DALE'S DEATH, HIS parents refused any communication with his friends. But Dale's Nana wrote a letter to the design department, which wound up in Margaret's hands. She passed it along to Richard. Dale's Nana begged for a few of Dale's drawings and provided the address of a friend of hers where the drawings could be safely mailed. Richard sent a sheaf of drawings to her and included a nude sketch of himself that Dale had done. He wrote on the bottom of it "I loved your grandson" and signed his own name.

Norma and I organized a memorial service for Dale at Margaret's place. There was to be a reception afterward, with all of Dale's favorite foods, including uncooked chocolate chip cookie dough. We lined the walls with his artwork and put up a board of drawings and photos of him. At the time of his death, Dale had been working on a series of pieces featuring the Casablanca lily, a huge white flower with petals that furled like giant ruffles around a rigid pistil and large stamen covered in orange pollen that stained everything at touch. You couldn't walk away from a Casablanca lily unchanged. The lilies grew four or five at a time, prolific, fecund, from a thick stalk. Norma insisted that we buy Casablanca lilies for the memorial reception. The challenge with these flowers was their size and fragility, which made them difficult to wrap. So Gloria, Norma, Lee, and I went to the florist shop and purchased bunches of the lilies, which we hand carried to Margaret's studio. I thought with satisfaction of how much Dale would have cherished the image of the four of us, dressed in black, solemnly carrying large white lilies through the streets of the West Village.

The sight of the lilies was hard on Richard. I suggested that we step out together onto the metal fire escape that crisscrossed down the side of the building like an erector set gone haywire. We sat together on the top step.

"I still have trouble wrapping my head around the fact that he actually did it," Richard said, staring off into the distance. "I realize he had years of rage built up and that suicide is partially anger turned inward. I get that. But how could he do this to me? I thought we were happy together."

"He loved you," I said. "I don't know how he managed to lose sight of that."

"I keep thinking that I should have been able to prevent him from doing it," Richard said. "I go over and over it in my head."

"All of us are asking ourselves that question, what we could have done differently. I wonder if maybe he was afraid that the psychiatrist had the power to cure him and he didn't want to be cured," I said.

"Yesterday," Richard continued, "when I was looking through his drawings to choose which ones to display for this, it occurred to me that perhaps he had a moment of doubt, a moment when he believed that being gay is a perversion, a disease. I wonder if, deep down, he thought there was something wrong with him."

"*You* don't think you're diseased, do you?" I asked Richard. He studied his shoes. "You don't think there's something wrong with you, right?"

Silence.

I took Richard by the shoulders and said, "You're normal. You just happen to like boys." I felt an urge to apologize to him for dabbling in lesbianism, for treating it as a game, not taking it seriously. I had flirted with it, but Richard and Margaret lived it. I felt ignorant of the reality of their lives. "I can't imagine what you're going through," I said.

Richard held his hand out for me to take and I did. "It helps to be with people who loved him and who knew how extraordinary he was," he said. His words brought me back to him, to Dale, and to the reason we were coming together, which was to celebrate Dale's life.

"Come on," I said. "Let's go back inside. Let's love the dickens out of those gorgeous lilies."

After Dale's memorial service, Arthur drove me home. He had a train ticket to California in his pocket. I had asked him to have a farewell dinner with me. Just us. But when we returned to the carriage house in the early evening, we weren't hungry.

The two of us had not often been alone together. In my kitchen, Arthur sat in a chair and loosened his "church clothes," unbuttoning a few buttons on his white dress shirt and rolling up his sleeves. His suspenders hung down off his hips. His undershirt dipped low on his chest. I studied him, noticing, as I often had, how handsome he was, not just because he was my dear friend, but from an objective, aesthetic point of view. His skin was taut and smooth over the ridge of his collarbone.

His beautiful long fingers, which I had frequently admired, rested on the table. His thumbs curved backward gracefully like the arch of a swan's neck. His face was a deep brown, with red tints that revealed his pint of Native American blood; his eyes, nose, and lips were large and sensual. I would have liked to try to sculpt his face in clay.

Arthur shifted restlessly in his chair. "What?" he asked. "You're staring at me; it's unnerving."

I had seen him almost every day for the past four years, and tomorrow he was leaving. How much time would pass before we saw each other again?

"I was thinking that I would like to do a bust of you in red clay," I said.

"My brain certainly feels like it's full of red clay at the moment," Arthur replied.

We struggled to make conversation, but our words floated like a thin film of oil over what became deeper and deeper water by the minute.

Arthur looked increasingly uncomfortable. Finally, he stood abruptly and put his jacket over his arm. "I have to go," he blurted. "After the . . ." His voice trailed off. "I can't do this prolonged good-bye. I'll be back. I'll be in touch." He gave me an awkward, partial hug and grazed my cheek with his, then bolted out of the door, leaving behind only his musky scent of coconut oil hair dressing, soap, and sweat.

I remained seated in the kitchen for a couple of minutes. When I finally stood up, I panicked. I ran to the front door and flung it open only to find myself face-to-face with Arthur, who stood as if carved in stone. We stared at each other in shock.

How long had we loved each other?

I wondered if I had the strength of character necessary to enter into a relationship with Arthur.

I wondered if he would take the risk of entering into a relationship with me.

As if reaching across a vast divide, Arthur gently took my hands in his. Ever so lightly, he ran his thumbs across my palms. Then he ran his fingertips up my arms, barely touching, up the inside of my sleeves, to my shoulders. He leaned forward and brushed my lips tentatively with his. Still he paused. We had restrained ourselves for years, for years held back. I knew him well enough to know that he had never imagined he would fall in love with a white woman. He had never intended to fall in love with a white woman. He didn't want to love a white woman. But I was not any white woman. This was me. His own Rina, who had grown with him and become his best friend over the past four years.

I held my breath.

With all my heart I hoped that he had the courage to come to me. I believed that I had the courage to go to him.

A veil lifted from Arthur's face and he kissed me hungrily on the lips, the neck, the throat, the collarbone, the lips again, pulling me tight against him with both of his large, capable hands. We were forming a new religion and we were the only two members, entering the temple together.

We stepped back inside the carriage house, closing the door behind us, and I leaned against it, for I was weak with wanting him. Arthur ran his fingers around the curve of my breasts, tracing their shape through the thin fabric of my dress. He drew me to him, revealing without inhibition the evidence of his arousal in the rhythmic pulse that throbbed in his trousers, which I opened. I reached in and held him between my palms. He moaned like the wind far out over the ocean, then he took my hand, urgently, and led me to the bedroom.

I had thoroughly enjoyed the many lovers of my college years. I had no regrets. But nothing in my past experience had prepared me for the sacred intensity of my desire for Arthur. I had never before looked a man in the eye when he entered me, but Arthur required it. The depth of our feeling required it. I lost myself and became every woman who had ever loved a man.

That night, we redefined the geography of our lives. We spent three days in the carriage house making love. The sun went down and the sun came up. The earth spun around the still point of ecstasy where we remained untouched by the events of the world, oblivious, wrapped in the truth of each other. In those first days, I began my lifelong devotion to Arthur's splendid anatomy while Arthur delighted in my body with the reverence of an artist appreciating beauty.

Arthur missed his train.

I came home in the world.

Fifteen

THE SUMMER AFTER GRADUATION, Arthur and I moved into a charming old brownstone in Harlem, not far from Arthur's parents, whose warmth and acceptance of me never failed to replenish my spirit and remind me of all that was good in the world. Our friends were annoyingly unsurprised about the evolution of our relationship. Norma said, "It's about time." After TJ pretended to chew me out for stealing his roommate, he said, "I wondered when you two would figure it out." Lee just laughed her head off. Skip remarked that we would have the most beautiful children. I would have liked to have been able to tell Dale and to see the slow smile that would have spread across his face.

My parents had met Arthur at our graduation, so they knew who he was when I announced that he and I were moving in together. I was not surprised when Nate used my relationship with Arthur as an excuse to definitively cut me out of his life. At least he didn't do anything melodramatic, like say the Mourner's Kaddish for me. He simply told me he didn't want to see me or talk to me anymore and that I was not welcome in his house. He said I failed to respect or appreciate my Jewish heritage and that thousands of years of tradition and culture were dying with me, or something to that effect. If we had previously had a real relationship, then I might have been upset. But we hadn't cared for each other since I was a little girl. Mother's reaction to my relationship with Arthur was entirely different from Nate's, and I wondered what words passed between them before they reconciled themselves to the arrangement they agreed upon. I was barred from the house by Nate, but Mother remained adamant about continuing her relationship with me.

The week after Arthur and I moved into our new place, Mother insisted that she wanted to take us out to dinner. I was hesitant, but Arthur was eager to get to know her better. Mother arrived at our door on the evening of our dinner date weighed down with bags and in a cheerful mood. She produced a blender from one of her bags and presented it to us as a gift. I suppressed a groan.

"Mother," I said, "this was not necessary and it's extravagant. I don't even cook. I'll never use this."

She wagged a finger at me and cut me off mid-complaint. "If you don't use it, then I will when I come over to cook for you. It is not at all extravagant and it's good for making soup and for fruit smoothies," she said. I realized then that she would probably never be able to have me over for dinner in her own house again because of Nate's decree, and I relented, but before I could thank her, Arthur stepped in and did it for me.

"Thank you. It's a lovely gift and I apologize for my ungrateful roommate," he said as he poked me in the arm with his index finger. He reached for the blender. "I'll just put this in the kitchen."

"Wait, there's more," Mother said, foraging in her bags. "I have a couple of other things here." She proceeded to lift a magnificent blanket out of a large paper bag. "I want you to have this quilt. Your grandmother and my friend Chaya made it around the time Sophie was born. I have had it stored away for safekeeping, but it deserves to be used by someone who will appreciate the handiwork."

I took the quilt from her and stroked it like a silky cat. This was a one-of-a-kind magnificent gift that I would cherish and I was amazed that she had thought to give it to me. I unfolded it and spread it across the sofa so I could see more of the pattern.

"This is gorgeous," I said. I put my arm around Mother's waist while I admired the beauty of the quilt and gave her an affectionate squeeze. "Thank you so much." I stepped forward and patted a section of turquoise, orange, green, and purple squares. "Why have I never seen it before?"

"I didn't use it because I didn't want it to become worn. But now I ask myself, what am I saving it for?" Mother said. "It was made to keep a loved one warm. I want the two of you to have it. I want you to put it on your bed and to sleep under it. Consider it my blessing, my way of tucking you in at night. I'm delighted to see my daughter in love with a good man. I would be lying if I said that I'm not disappointed that you're not Jewish, Arthur, but at the end of the day, all I want for my children is for them to be happy and healthy, to have fulfilling work, a loving marriage, and a comfortable home. Frankly, you had me worried for a while, Rina, but I'm no longer worried. I'm happy for you."

What could I say to that? I hugged her and then we kissed each other on both cheeks, the old-fashioned way, and I didn't feel awkward at all. I felt genuine love for her.

As we drew apart, Mother said, "Your father and I will just have to disagree on this subject. I have made it quite clear to him that I refuse to lose my daughter as a result of his obstinacy. He doesn't want you at the house. Fine. I'll just have to come here. So." She reached into a smaller bag and produced a round loaf of bread. "Russian Jewish tradition," she explained. "When someone moves into a new home, it's traditional to bring a round sweet loaf of bread, so that your life in your new home may be filled with sweetness. And," she said, taking a salt shaker from the bag, "salt. Because Jews are hopelessly cognizant of the unhappiness that may befall us at any moment. Some salt to remind you that there will be tears in your new home as well. But let's hope they are more often tears of joy than of sorrow, right?"

"I'm a bit overwhelmed," I admitted. Even though we were so different from each other, Mother had consistently made an effort to remain in my life. I doubted I would ever know how much that effort cost her in the context of her relationship with her husband.

"I wish you and your father could get along with each other. But," she shrugged, "I will tell you what I told him. I refuse to choose between you. I will love both of you." Her voice quavered. "That is my final word and the two of you will have to deal with that."

I liked it. I liked that she was defying him. I resolved to make a stronger effort to be more patient with her when her concerns seemed trivial to me, and to show her more kindness, more tolerance, even when she was completely off the mark. I felt more inclined to try to explain to her what went on inside my head instead of just ignoring her and letting things pass. Arthur looked so smug standing there holding the round loaf under his arm, the salt shaker in one hand and the blender in the other. I was not looking forward to the "I told you so" he would lay on me later.

"You never cease to surprise me, Mother," I said. "Just when I think I have you figured out you throw me a curve ball."

"It shouldn't surprise you that I'm not willing to lose you just because your father is so foolish."

"It's not that. It's that you set your boundaries with him and that you gave me this incredible quilt, which I will treasure," I explained.

"Good. That's settled. Now let's go eat. I'm hungry," Mother said with a tone of finality.

"Would you care for some sweet bread and salt?" Arthur offered with a grin.

"Actually, I *could* go for a slice of bread with butter to tide me over to dinner," Mother answered. The two of them headed to the kitchen together like conspirators. Alone, I examined the quilt more closely. My grandmother, whom I had never known, had sewn these stitches, chosen these pieces of fabric, left this reflection of herself with my mother when my mother was around the age I was now. For one brief second I felt sad that I had chosen to bankrupt a rich cultural inheritance that extended back centuries in time. Then the second passed and I felt wealthy beyond measure.

Sixteen

NOT LONG AFTER ARTHUR and I celebrated our second anniversary in our apartment in Harlem, Sarah moved back in with Mother and Nate. When Mother called to tell me, she said that Sarah was muddling through a difficult time and she asked me to offer her a shoulder if she needed one. Sarah and I had not seen each other much in the past year and we had grown apart simply because we were busy with our own lives. I wanted to make more time for her and I wanted us to get reacquainted. Even though I was not pleased to hear that she was having problems, I was glad that she had moved home and would be nearby. After she called to make a date to come see us, I told Arthur we should try to find out what was going on with her and to help if we could.

I was in the studio when she arrived and, as usual, I had trouble tearing myself away from the drawing board. I heard Arthur holler from the front door, "Sarah's here." He ushered her into the house and I met them in the doorway to the studio, pen in hand. I offered my sister a warm hug and kisses on both cheeks. Sarah wore peach-colored linen pants and a simple button-down white blouse. She was so well put-together that I felt self-conscious in my paint-spattered T-shirt and faded plaid shorts. But she immediately set me at ease when she said, "I love the purple toenail polish."

"Arthur says it looks like I slammed my foot in the car door," I told her, abandoning my pen on the drawing table and clicking off the high-intensity lamp. "Can I get you anything to eat or drink?"

"A glass of cold water, please," she replied.

We went into the kitchen. The windows stood open and the scent of marigolds, geraniums, mint, and sage drifted in from the backyard. I sat across from Sarah at the kitchen table while Arthur took a turquoise pitcher out of the refrigerator and poured water into a Mason jar for her.

"Have you talked to Soph lately?" Sarah asked.

"I've been trying to remember to call her every week to check in on her ever since she got the final word from the fertility specialist," I replied.

"I saw her last night," Sarah informed me. "She's so sad about it. It's like she's grieving for a dead person."

"She is, in a way. Just because they can't have children of their own, though, doesn't mean they can't adopt. I don't get why Max refuses to consider that. It's exasperating," I said.

"He's adamantly against it and she has decided not to argue the point," Sarah told me. "Max says adoption is a gamble and he doesn't want to be saddled with problems someone else created with poor prenatal care."

"Spoken as a true obstetrician," I noted.

"Children are always a gamble," Arthur said.

"But I think she'll be OK," Sarah continued. "She says that if she can't have children, then she wants an enviably full adult life, with travel, her career, lots of evenings out at jazz clubs and the theater. She bought season tickets to the ballet. They're planning to go to Vancouver for their anniversary and to Aruba in the spring. They might move into Manhattan. A doctor and lawyer, with no children to drain the bank account. They can afford a nice place."

"And what about you? You look tired. What's going on with you?" I asked.

"Ah, me, my least favorite subject. Do I look that tired?" Sarah responded.

"No, not at all," Arthur said, throwing me a reproving glance. "You look terrific."

Sarah took a drink of water from the Mason jar. "Hey, I brought you something." She opened her handbag and pulled out several cassette tapes, which she passed across the table. "Some music. These are some of my favorites. Have you ever listened to these musicians?"

I glanced through the tapes as I muttered "thanks." I noticed right away that they were all by lesbian artists. Margaret listened to this kind of music and had turned me on to some of it. It was sort of folksy, often political, and usually toe-tappingly percussive. In the music store it was labeled "women's music." Sarah had handed me some of the best-known music by the best-known women's music artists. And in a flash I understood what I was actually seeing. "This is women's music. What's the deal, Sarah? Are you into women now?"

She nearly choked on her water. She turned crimson and then she laughed so hard that she couldn't talk. Tears ran down her face and she wiped them away with the backs of her hands. Her laughter had a slightly hysterical edge to it. I glanced at Arthur, who looked as mystified as I, as we waited for Sarah to tell us what was so funny. "I'm sorry," she gasped. We waited for her to catch her breath and when she finally did, she said, "I have successfully hidden the truth about myself from so many people for so long because those people didn't want to see the truth. And it took so little for you to figure it out. It's too funny, and a relief, you know, to have someone in the family see me for who I am. I can't tell Mama and Papa. Papa would hit the roof. And Soph is so conservative."

Arthur sat down next to me at the table, reached across to Sarah, taking her hand in both of his, and demanded sternly, in a mock preacher's voice, "All right, Ms. Sarah, what the heck is going on with you?"

She spilled the beans after that. She had been in love with a woman named Peggy for the past three years. She and Peggy were in the same elementary education program together. "I wish you could have seen Peggy in action with children," Sarah said wistfully. "She was incredible. When we went to the park, she would have a group of children rounded up to play with her in the time it took for me to walk to the drinking fountain and back." Sarah had lived for the past year and a half at a children's home, where she worked as a "house parent." She told us that she and Peggy had landed the job together. They had been living in a converted attic on the top floor of one of the houses. But three weeks after graduation, Peggy left her for another woman. Sarah had not seen the signs of the split coming and was completely blindsided. Peggy quit the children's home and disappeared. Sarah didn't even know how to get in touch with her. She was a wreck after that and it was instantly obvious to the manager of the children's home that she and Peggy had been a couple. The manager freaked out and fired Sarah. It was the kind of story that would have made Margaret run out and hire a lawyer.

"Mother mentioned that you were recovering from a failed romance," I told her.

"Yeah, well," Sarah replied grimly, "she assumed it was with a guy and I chose not to enlighten her. I can't possibly come out to them. Look what Papa did when he found out about the two of you."

"We're different. Nate and I have never gotten along. My relationship is just an excuse . . . Never mind, this is not about me. I'm worried about you. So you moved back in with them. Now what?" I asked.

"I don't know what I want to do with my life," Sarah said mournfully.

"But you're a teacher, right?" Arthur asked.

"I don't have my credential yet, so I can't teach in the public schools, but I can teach in a private school," she explained.

"So you can basically go anywhere and get a job," Arthur said.

"I suppose," Sarah responded halfheartedly. "All I ever wanted to do is teach, but right now I'm feeling kind of beaten up and pretty lost. I'm not sure if I should be a teacher." Her voice had risen and she seemed as if she was fighting back tears.

Arthur flashed his gorgeous smile at me and said one word: "Margaret." I nodded in agreement.

"Yes," I told Sarah, "let us introduce you to our friend Margaret, who is a terrific teacher, and her girlfriend, Gloria. One chat with her and you will never consider giving up teaching again."

"I think you need a change," Arthur suggested.

"I agree," I added.

"A change? Like what?" she asked.

"A big change," Arthur continued, and I could practically see the wheels turning in his head. "There are lots of private schools that need teachers."

"That's true," Sarah said cautiously.

"So this is what I suggest," Arthur told her. "Maybe you could go to California and find a teaching job there and start fresh, far away from your old life."

"I don't know anyone in California," Sarah replied, wide-eyed.

"That's the whole point," I told her. "I think it's a great idea."

"We just happen to have friends in Berkeley," Arthur added.

"That you could stay with until you get settled. Pass me the phone," I said, and Arthur picked it up off the counter and handed it to me.

"Wait, I don't know," Sarah protested. "What you're proposing would be a pretty big change."

"You have nothing to lose," Arthur pointed out, while I dialed TJ's number. He and Lee were renting a house together in Berkeley.

"I bet you can line up a job for the fall if you go right out and start looking," Arthur suggested encouragingly.

"Maybe." She was beginning to warm to Arthur's idea. My parents would probably have a fit when they heard that their beloved baby was moving to the other side of the country, but so be it. I was concerned about Sarah and I agreed with Arthur that this would be good for her. I was pretty sure I could convince Mother that this was a sensible move. She had met TJ and knew what an upbeat person he was. He would be a good influence on Sarah and would help her pull herself back together.

When TJ answered, I explained why I was calling, then I put Sarah on to talk to him directly. I was thinking that Berkeley was a liberal college town, where she was bound to meet other lesbians. Before she got off the phone, it was settled. Sarah would fly out to California and look for work. One of the most appealing things about this plan was that Sarah would get to know TJ and Lee, whom I dearly loved.

Seventeen

"YOUR MOTHER CALLED," ARTHUR greeted me as I came in from the store and put a loaf of whole-wheat bread, still warm from the bakery, on the countertop.

"What'd she want?" I asked.

"She's your mother, Rina; she doesn't need a reason to call. But as it happens, this time she was on a mission."

"A mission?" I asked warily.

"She wanted to invite you to go with her to the Chinese Exhibition of Arts and Crafts. She offered to buy the tickets."

I sighed. "The Chinese Exhibition?"

Arthur peered at me over his glasses. He looked professorial. He was terribly attractive in his glasses.

"What does that look mean?" I asked, with a sly smile.

"How long have we been together? You know what that look means."

I shrugged.

"Just go. Is it so hard for you to spend a few hours with your mother at an art museum?"

"OK, OK, I'll go."

"And tell her about the baby," Arthur added. "She should have been the first to know; soon she'll be the last." He put his arms around my waist and clasped his hands behind my back, pulling me close so he could kiss me.

"But I'm only about fifteen minutes pregnant," I reminded him.

"All the better. Give her more time to enjoy the anticipation."

"I'm not telling her about the baby on the phone," I said.

"Then tell her at the museum."

"So I should go to the museum with her and tell her about the baby."

"Yes."

"Any other instructions?"

"That will do for now." He flashed me his most alluring smile, his eyes twinkling behind those sexy glasses. "Call her back so she can buy the tickets. You'll make her happy with the museum outing, and then happier with your news."

I set out to make her happy two weeks later when I accompanied her to the Asian Art Museum. But as we strolled through the exhibit, I experienced a growing sense of anxiety. I had heard the term *panic attack* before and I wondered if that was what I was having. It was more than just the anxiety of knowing I was about to tell my mother that I was pregnant. It was similar to the unpleasant versions of those sense-memories that I had, but the sense-memories were brief, and this kept going on and on, increasing in intensity. After half an hour of studying cases of women's personal-care possessions, such as jade and wooden hair sticks, hand mirrors painted with tiny flowers, and combs carved with birds, I was possessed by a surge of fear. My throat constricted and I became short of breath. I had never had asthma before, but it felt like what I imagined an asthma attack would feel like.

"Sit here," Mother commanded, putting her arm around me and guiding me toward a bench.

Then the strangest thing happened. I physically recoiled from her. I could not bear to have her touch me. Her voice, her very proximity made me feel sick to my stomach. I desperately needed to get out of the exhibit. I reached for the wall to steady myself as I stumbled out of the room and collapsed on a bench near the exhibit entrance. I put my head down on my lap. Mother hovered at my elbow and put a hand on my back. I wanted her to take her hand off of me.

"Maybe we should go outside," Mother suggested.

"No, no, I'll be OK in a minute," I managed to say as I sat back up and shrugged her hand off. "Can I just sit here by myself for a little while?"

"Are you dizzy?" she asked.

I was starting to feel a little better now that I was outside the exhibition. "No. I was for a minute, but I'm better." I could breathe again.

"What happened?"

"Can I explain later?" I begged. "I just need to sit here for a few minutes. Why don't you go back inside. I'll wait for you here." Whatever it was, a sense-memory or a panic attack, I wasn't comfortable talking with her about it, and I figured that when I told her that I was pregnant, that would be an adequate explanation.

"Are you sure?" Mother hesitated. "I don't want to leave you if you're not OK."

"I'm fine now. Really. Please go."

Mother paused and turned in the arched entranceway to the show to glance back at me. She was framed by two gigantic porcelain vases encased in glass that stood sentry at the yawning mouth of the exhibit. The delicate burnt orange and black painting of tree branches on the vases threaded out into a confusing map to nowhere. The image of Mother in that entranceway brought on a new wave of anxiety as dizzying pinpoints of light filled my vision. I put my head back down in my lap and then I passed out.

According to Mother, I was only unconscious for a minute, but during that brief blackout, I was dragged into that room of sweet scent and sorrow in that Chinese dream scenario and the loss of the gardener broke my heart. I snapped myself back to consciousness before the rape part happened, thank goodness. I don't think I could have endured that part of the dream at that particular moment, with Mother hovering over me and strangers and museum guards running to our aid. Whatever the nature of the episode I had been experiencing, it really did begin to dissipate after I blacked out and then came back to consciousness. I was no longer dizzy at all.

I tried to reassure the concerned people who had surrounded us that I was fine and able to stand. I stood up quite steadily to prove it. "I think I need to eat something," I said.

"I'll take her to the cafeteria; where is it?" Mother asked the two museum guards who had remained at my side. They directed her to the ground floor and we went immediately.

I sat at a table by a tall window and Mother bought us sandwiches and juice. I didn't want to explain to her about the recurring dream or my sense-memories. I was feeling closer to her than I ever had in my life, but I did not feel close enough to share these aspects of my inner life with her. Maybe I would be able to talk to her about these things one day, but this was not the day.

She fussed unnecessarily in her concern for my well-being, taking the paper off my straw for me, placing an unneeded fork on a napkin next to the plate with my sandwich. Finally, to my relief, she sat down across from me and studied my face. She left her sandwich untouched. She was visibly shaken.

"I'm fine now, Mother," I reassured her.

"No, you're not. You're not fine and I'm not fine and it's not fine. It never has been fine. I'm not talking about that dizzy spell upstairs, I'm talking about . . ." she trailed off. "Please forgive me," she said.

"For what?" She was making me self-conscious and embarrassed.

"Forgive me for so often choosing your father over you."

"He has no right putting you in that position."

"I wasn't talking about him banning you from the house," my mother clarified. "I was talking about the beatings when you were a child."

I was taken aback. "I never blamed you for those. I'm not sure you could have done anything about those."

"I could have left him."

"If you had left him," I said, "then how would we have survived?"

"To this day, I'm not sure."

"You thought about it?" I asked with incredulity.

"I would be lying if I said it had never crossed my mind. You nearly destroyed our marriage, the two of you. You with your horrid stubbornness and him with his dreadful intolerance. I never understood why you were so defiant or why it made him lose his temper so completely. Sometimes I was incomprehensibly angry at the both of you. I can't understand how two people whom I love so dearly could hurt each other so much. I would guess that you are pretty angry about the way he treated you."

I sighed. For me, this was such old material and I didn't care to rehash it, but it didn't seem as if I had any choice. "I was angry at him a long time ago. I've let go of it. Anger, holding grudges, all that negativity is a waste. The object of that kind of anger never warrants the energy invested in it."

"You can honestly say that?" she asked dubiously.

I drank some orange juice, which made me feel much better. Maybe my blood sugar had been low or something like that related to my pregnancy. I began to eat my sandwich and spoke between bites. "Yes. I can. He's not a part of my life anymore; I've moved on. Actually, I don't think about my childhood much. It seems irrelevant now. My childhood would have been easier if you and I had similar interests or similar lifestyles or if we even made sense to each other. But, let's face it, we don't make sense to each other. I honestly don't get what the big deal is about having a house so clean it never looks like anyone lives in it. And I know that you think my house is repulsive because of the clutter and mess. I use my house. You admire yours. That's just one example. But it's the way we are about everything. The things that I value are not important to you and the things that give you pleasure and peace of mind are inconsequential to me. I'm not saying that to hurt your feelings. I'm just saying it because it's true."

"Irina," she said as she shook her head from side to side. She picked up her sandwich and took a small bite out of it. "How on earth did I produce a child so absolutely unlike me? I hope you know that no matter how little I understand you, I'm proud of what you have made of yourself and I have never loved you any less than your sisters just because you and I have so little in common. And, although you will find it hard to believe, there was a time when your father loved you more than he loved me. He lost his way when his adorable babies grew into headstrong, moody, independent-thinking women. When you were small, though, he was the finest father any child could have. I wish you would remember that childhood and remember him like that, and not the way he was with you later."

I recalled sitting on Nate's foot, my arms wrapped around his leg, while he walked across the living room growling. I supposed that if I tried, I could remember how he was when I was very young. But what was the point? I said, "It must have been hard for you to reconcile what you knew as a woman about the young women who were your daughters and what you knew as a wife about the man who was your husband."

"You are a wise young woman," she said. "A marriage is hard work at the best of times. It begins with the 'I do' and then it's a choice we make again and again every single day. When you add children into the dynamic, it becomes exponentially more complicated."

"Well, I'm going to find out about that complication firsthand pretty soon," I told her. She looked puzzled. "I'm expecting."

"You're expecting?"

"A baby, Mom; I'm expecting a baby. That's probably why I had that dizzy spell."

As comprehension spread over her face, my mother put down her sandwich and wiped away tears of joy with her napkin.

Eighteen

THE NIGHT AFTER I went to the Chinese Exhibition of Arts and Crafts with my mother and told her I was pregnant, I had a different version of my recurring dream. It started out the same, with me standing in front of the usual Chinese parents, but unlike any other time before, my dream-mother lifted her head and I saw in her face a calmness and resolution as she stepped between my dream-father and me. The dream-parents seemed more like my real parents than they ever had previously. I smelled the familiar ripe-melon scent of the flowers. My dream-father shouted angrily and my dream-mother put her hand on his arm. He bowed his head and wept, his shoulders heaving. My dream-mother nodded to me. Through the open window, I saw the handsome gardener, who, instead of walking away this time, came to me and took my hand and we left together, threading our way through the gardens where shell-pink flower blossoms hung huge and luminous on their delicate stems, and I rejoiced. When I woke in the morning sunlight, the memory of the sweet fragrance of those glorious blossoms lingered. Arthur turned to me and rested his hand on my stomach. Our baby was in there, mysteriously growing every day. We had no evidence of its presence yet because it was too tiny, but like so many parents before us, we went on faith that at the appointed time our child would join us, fully formed, infinitely complex, awaiting our discovery.

After that night, I never had any version, good or bad, of that Chinese dream again.

Nineteen

 NATE ANSWERED THE PHONE. He never answered the phone. Why this time?

"I've had a baby," I announced. Then, quickly, before his interference could dampen my excitement by even a fraction of a decibel, I said, "Please put Mom on the phone."

"She's upstairs sewing. I'll get her." Pause. "I hope you are happy." I supposed that was the closest to a blessing that I would ever receive from him.

"I am. I'm very happy," I told him, wondering if my words were a slap to him or if a place in his heart that he refused to recognize filled with joy at my news.

I savored my euphoria as he left to find my mother. My house looked like Mardi Gras. Our baby was passing from hand to hand as she was circulated among our jubilant family and friends, and I wondered where she had gone. I had showered off and dressed in one of my favorite tent-like purple maternity dresses. I was settled comfortably on the living room couch with my feet up, surrounded by mauve, burgundy, and violet quilted pillows, with a glass of Champagne in my hand. Despite the speed with which I had delivered, many of our closest friends had arrived in time to see our baby girl's entry into the world. Music blasted. Arthur's father was leading a line dance. The dining room table was laden with food. Paper storks hung from the lighting fixtures. I caught a glimpse of Margaret and Gloria in the kitchen exchanging a kiss.

Mom picked up the phone and asked, breathless with excitement, "We have a baby?"

"She's here," I said.

"A girl? And she's healthy?"

"She couldn't be better. You have to come over right away. I talked to Soph and she'll pick you up at the station if you want to take the train. Call her. Mom, you should have warned me about labor."

"You can't really warn someone sufficiently; it's something you have to experience yourself," Mom replied. "It sounds like a party over there. Where are you?"

"At home. A lot of people are here."

"What are you doing at home?"

"She was born at home," I replied.

"You had her at home?" Mom asked, with a note of alarm in her voice. I had not told her we were planning a home birth because I didn't have the patience to listen to her fuss and also because I didn't want her to worry. Now I was feeling too happy to get annoyed with her. This was her baby too and I couldn't wait to show her our beautiful daughter, her granddaughter. I refused to spoil my elation with a discussion about the merits of home birth. "It's OK, we planned to have her at home. We had three midwives here and a lot of friends. We're fine, absolutely fine."

She seemed to relax at this news. "What is her name?" she asked.

"Miriam. I have always loved the story about your half sister and her bravery during the war." I heard a small sob escape from my mother. "I wish I could say that we had picked that name before she was born, but we didn't. We had talked about a few African names ahead of time. But we agreed that we wanted to see our baby before we chose the name. Kind of an African tradition. Then the minute I saw her, I thought, this is Miriam. Arthur loves it. He's up on his Bible stories and says Miriam danced by the waters with her tambourine when the Israelites crossed to freedom during the Exodus from Egypt. How soon can you get over here?"

"Let me call Sophie. I should be able to get there in a couple of hours," Mom said. "I love the name. Your aunt Rivka will also be so pleased."

"OK. Hey, I have to go. I have a house full of people. And I have to find my new daughter. She's here somewhere," I said with a laugh.

"Should I bring anything?"

For a brief moment I imagined answering that she should bring my father. "Yes, please. Cream cheese. We're running out and we have a lot of bagels. And I have a craving for *rugelach*, can you pick some up at the deli?"

"You've got it, honey. I'll see you soon."

When Mom and Soph arrived a couple of hours later, the throng of our friends parted to let them through as Arthur's mother, wearing her flowery apron, ushered them into the living room where I held court. I passed Miriam to my mother and she peered into the tiny nut-brown face ringed with an abundance of softly curled hair.

"Such a beauty," Soph cooed as she leaned over Mom's shoulder to see. Then she told me, "Max was horrid about the home birth. I don't know what I expected from an obstetrician. He says you're irresponsible and put the baby in danger. I told him you had three midwives and he claimed that three midwives don't equal a doctor. We had a huge argument. Too bad. I'm glad you didn't let the doctors bully you into a hospital birth. This," she waved her hand at the abundance surrounding us, "is much better."

I was touched by her support. "Thanks for defending me. I hope that Max doesn't keep arguing with you about it."

"It's fine," Soph assured me. "I'll just make him a *kugel* the way he likes for dinner and he'll forget all about it," she laughed. "He's fickle. And a Hedonist!"

I patted the couch next to me and said, "Mom, please sit." She sat on the edge of the couch. Soph opened a paper bag and handed me a few *rugelach*, then headed for the kitchen.

TJ and Lee had both flown in from California so that they could be in town for Miriam's birth. At that moment, Lee appeared with her saxophone hanging from her neck. "I wrote a piece for the baby and I wanted to play it for her," Lee announced.

"Arthur," I called, "come over here." Arthur threaded through the crowd and stood by my head with a hand on my shoulder as we turned to Lee to accept her tribute. She launched into an exquisite jazz riff on her sax. I could feel Mom's back stiffen against my leg as she clutched Miriam to her ferociously. I imagined that she was resisting an impulse to cover the baby's ears. I sipped my Champagne and enjoyed the jazz sax. Miriam was mine, to raise in a house bursting with loud music. My mother would have to get used to it.

After Lee's performance, which was met with cheers and appreciative applause, Mom handed the baby back to me. For a moment, I viewed the celebration through my mother's eyes: our gay friends, Richard so swishy in his little white ruffled apron and Margaret and Gloria so lovey-dovey; the three godmothers, Norma, Lee, and Margaret, wearing the godmother tiaras that Arthur had made; TJ blowing bubbles and tossing confetti at the guests; and Arthur's family dancing to loud R&B music wherever they could find floor space. It was a rowdy scene for a birth celebration.

"I realize that you're probably a bit uncomfortable with this, but it's the way I live," I told Mom firmly.

"I know," Mom answered quietly. "It's true that my fingers are itching to clean up this house. Those stacks of magazines. The coffee cups leaving rings on your tables and windowsills. The heaps of papers and clutter. I don't understand how you can live in such disarray. But as you say, this is the way you live. I would be lying if I said it's not a struggle for me, but I will continue to work at keeping my thoughts to myself and accepting your lifestyle." She touched my cheek gently with her hand. "Because I love you. And I want you to be happy. Nothing will ever change that. Now that you are a mother, you will learn what it means to love a child."

My eyes filled with tears. "Miriam and I are blessed to have you in our lives," I said.

"I'm sorry your father isn't here. It's his loss. But I can't change him any more than I can change you. I can only love you both."

"You do an admirable job at that."

"It's good to hear you say so. Listen, would you at least let me sew you some curtains for the front windows?" Mom pleaded. "Any passerby can peer right in. Now, with the baby, you should have some privacy."

"OK, curtains," I assented. She had caught me in a moment of weakness. I could do this much for her. "But I have to like the material."

"Agreed," she said with satisfaction.

I held my hand out to her. "Agreed," I echoed, and we shook on it.

PART THREE

Miriam

One

I COULD NOT POSSIBLY remember the welcome into the world given to me by my parents and their eclectic circle of friends, but I heard the story so many times while growing up that I thought I remembered it. I imagined with vivid clarity the balloons, flowers, jazz saxophone, paper storks, and abundant food. I have often thought that the extravagant celebration marking my arrival contributed to my belief that, despite the tragedies of the world, it is still a wondrous place filled with beauty awaiting our notice.

I was named after my grandmother's sister, a woman hidden in the shadows of family history, who rescued orphaned children and then perished in the Holocaust. Mama told me I looked like a Miriam, so she had to give me that name. Daddy loved the name because he had an image in his mind of the Old Testament Miriam standing on a promontory by the waters of the Red Sea during the Exodus from Egypt, her colorful garments whipped by the wind, her tambourine raised above her head, celebrating freedom.

Mama says that from the moment of my birth, I was delighted by even the smallest details of life and I had a smile for everyone. She claims that I was so happy to be here that everything pleased me. I was an only child. Every time someone asked my father about when he and Mama were going to have another child, he would say they were done having children and that they had gotten it right the first time.

My parents' many childless friends seemed to think I was a collective child, to be shared and played with by all. I grew up showered with affection by these doting aunties and uncles who were artists, musicians, and performers. So, of course, I was given many opportunities to use my own creativity. The walls of our house were covered with my drawings and paintings. I started piano lessons at the age of four. Dance lessons at the age of five. Gymnastics. Drama. Ceramics classes. Mama and Daddy enrolled me in everything they had ever wanted to do as children and hadn't had the chance to try.

Despite the fact that my mother lived in jeans and T-shirts, she dressed me in the most stylish outfits, with matching accessories. I think I was simply another canvas for her prolific creativity. I didn't notice what I wore until I started school, at which point I rebelled and insisted on wearing overalls most days. Nothing beat the comfort of a good pair of Osh Kosh B'gosh. But by that time Daddy had already filled half a dozen photo albums with a record of my fashion-plate years.

Apparently my schooling was a source of disagreement between my parents, though I didn't realize this at the time. Mama thought that her parents had misunderstood her as a child, that they had not recognized her identity as an artist or attempted to nurture and support her creativity. She wanted me to go to a private school that focused on the arts. Daddy insisted that a Black child needed to attend public school. He felt that I should be exposed to many different kinds of people and that it was imperative that I have an authentic experience of growing up Black, not the sheltered experience of a private school education that few Black children were privileged to receive. He believed that learning to deal with people who were very different from me was a lesson in itself. He won that argument and I went to public school, although I heard my parents discuss the merits of private school versus those of public school on many occasions over the years. "The public school system and the public library are the bedrock of a democratic society," Daddy insisted. And sometimes, when they had a disagreement about something else, Mama would say, "You got your way with the public school, so don't tell me I'm intractable." Whatever arts education I missed out on by not going to a private school, I'm sure I received through the after-school activities in which my mother enrolled me.

Those extracurricular activities were hardly necessary, because our chaotic and creative household burst with artistry. Mama was a one-woman private art school education unto herself. More than once, my parents moved the furniture out of the living room so that friends could choreograph a dance. I remember Aunt Lee playing a song on her saxophone that sounded as if the saxophone was talking in a language of its own, while I sat in my bunny jammies and ate cornflakes for dinner at the kitchen table. One afternoon Uncle TJ and Daddy stretched a white canvas across an entire wall of the studio, and by the time I woke up the next morning every inch of the canvas glittered with images of a jungle scene painted in acrylics.

So many people came through our house that I never quite sorted out the difference between friends and family. My parents' friends *were* our family, and I called some of them "uncle" and "aunt" even though we were not actually related. To add to the confusion, Daddy had so many brothers, sisters, cousins, nieces, and nephews that I couldn't keep track of all of them. I spent a lot of time at Big Momma's house, playing with my cousins. Two of my aunties disapproved of Daddy's relationship with Mama because Mama was a white woman and they humphed and crossed their arms across their bosoms when Mama came around. But Daddy said not to bother about them. He called them "The Busy Sisters." Everyone else seemed to like Mama well enough, including Daddy's little sister Jo, who came to our house often and drank rich, fragrant coffee with Mama.

Big Momma went to a Baptist church every Sunday with Granddaddy Pete, and she took with her any grandchildren who could sit still and behave during the service. Mama never went to church because she was Jewish, and Daddy never went to church because he said he had God in his heart and he didn't have to go to church to hear God's voice. Fortunately, they let me go to church with Big Momma and Granddaddy Pete. I learned to sit still because I loved church, mostly for the singing, but also because at church I got to see my cousins. Sometimes, us cousins giggled when the preacher puffed up and popped his eyes during the sermon. He was large and wore loud paisley-printed suits, so that he resembled an animated sofa. Granddaddy Pete would frown at us down the pew, but he had a little twinkle in his eye, so we knew he wasn't really mad; he just wanted us to hush up so the grown-ups could concentrate on the word of God. The best part, the part we waited for patiently, came after the service when we went downstairs to the social hall for lunch. Fried chicken, biscuits, black-eyed peas, collard greens, sweet potato pie, macaroni and cheese, mashed potatoes, angel food cake. I could close my eyes and taste that church food anytime, night or day.

Before, during, and after the food, the grown-ups told stories about what they saw happening around them in the community and discussed their ideas about politics and social change, the civil rights movement, and the Vietnam War. These were the kinds of things that I also heard my father talk about with his friends at home. And the elders at church told stories from way back in oldie times. The church talk taught me about the world. We children heard some of the stories of the elders more than once, mainly because old people have a hard time remembering if they told you something already or not. Mr. White told about the time he got the flat tire in Brooklyn. Mr. Joe told about when his brother came to visit from Alabama; he had a lot of stories about that visit. Miz Dee would describe her wedding day down in North Carolina. She remembered every satin detail, just like it happened yesterday. Brother Dru's daddy was born a slave in Mississippi and he told stories about his daddy's slave days, the Civil War, and coming north. Some of his stories made the short hairs on my neck stand on end. I sometimes wondered if Brother Dru made up those stories, because they seemed so unbelievable.

Young people told stories about things we didn't understand, like the block association, something called affirmative action that could help you go to college, and the Black Panthers. I wondered about the Black Panthers. I imagined large agile cats with intelligent faces; jet black, sleek and shiny, crouched unseen in the subways where they waited for someone to attempt to harm a Black brother or sister. Then the Black Panthers would spring to their defense, claws razor-sharp, teeth bared. When I woke at night with a fear of the dark, I found comfort in the fantasy that the protective panthers watched over me.

If Daddy's family was a big Sunday dinner, then Mama's family was a little bowl of berries. I had no cousins on Mama's side. Aunt Soph and Uncle Max couldn't have children, so they borrowed me as often as possible. They had a special corner just for me in their guest room. It was filled with books and wooden toys, including a whole train set. Aunt Soph would get down on the floor with me and build a train track clear around the living room. Uncle Max did magic tricks. My favorite was when he made a quarter come out of my ear because I could keep the quarter afterward. Aunt Soph always looked beautiful with her hair up in a fashionable style and she baked raisin bread that smelled like a cozy inside day in winter. Aunt Sarah lived in California when I was in elementary school, so I didn't see her that often. She later moved to the East Coast, but by then I was older. When I did see her during the years when I was little, she gave me the best toys, like a truck that I could take apart and put back together, a play tool belt with plastic tools, or a set of Tinker Toys. I liked the way she talked to me, as if I was grown up and I had something important to say.

I never met Mama's father. He didn't get along with Mama. Occasionally, when I called Grandma Ruth, he would answer the phone. When he heard it was me, he just said "hang on" and went to get Grandma Ruth. I imagined asking him a question, but I never had the courage to do it. When I thought about him, I usually thought about those two words he always said. *Hang on.* I couldn't figure out why Grandma Ruth was married to my grandfather, because she was lovely and warm, full of hugs and cookies. I didn't usually ask Grandma Ruth about him because I could tell that it made her sad to discuss him with me. Even though I knew it would make her sad, when I was in first grade I pestered her for weeks to tell me what he looked like until she finally brought me a photograph of him dressed up in a gray suit and standing in front of an old-fashioned car. She helped me put it in the drawer beside my bed and cover it with a book so that my mother wouldn't see. "Let this be our secret," she cautioned. I took his photograph out and studied it from time to time, imagining conversations with him and wondering what he would say if he ever did talk to me.

Grandma Ruth came to our house every Thursday and cooked us a big dinner, with leftovers for days. Mama didn't like to cook, so we ate out or got take-out and brought it home or had it delivered. But Grandma

Ruth loved to cook. One of my favorite things that she made was matzo ball soup. She always brought us a big bag of cookies that would last almost until the next Thursday. Oatmeal raisin, chocolate chip with walnuts, peanut butter, lemon bars, or *rugelach*. At a holiday called Purim she made triangle cookies with poppy seeds in them. After Mama and Daddy, the person I loved the most when I was small was Grandma Ruth. She called me her "one and only."

I must have been at least seven or eight years old before I realized that not everyone had parents who got along as well as mine. I rarely saw them exchange words in anger. One of the few times I remember them raising their voices to one another was when I was five years old and Daddy decided he was going to take me to the Emergency March on Washington to protest the mining of harbors and escalation of bombing in Vietnam. At the time, I was much too young to understand what it was about, of course. My father demonstrated against the war on a number of occasions, but I was too young to remember any of that. The one time I remember was when he took me on the train to Washington for the Emergency March. There was a huge scene between him and Mama before we left. She had cried and yelled at him. He had packed my bag and she had tried to unpack it. He picked me up and carried me out of the house without the bag. I was scared and he told me that sometimes I had to be brave and that he wouldn't let anything bad happen to me in Washington.

Years later, as a teenager, I talked about the incident with Mama. I could see from the emotion in her face that it still bothered her. She explained that the Democratic National Convention had erupted in violence only a few years earlier and that she was afraid for my safety, and for my father's. Mama said she thought that Daddy, who had been active in the civil rights movement, would grieve for the death of Dr. King for the rest of his life, and that right before he died, Dr. King had turned his attention to ending the War in Vietnam.

"When your father went to that march with you," Mama told me, "he believed he was walking in Dr. King's footsteps. I didn't have any quarrel with that. I just didn't think you were old enough to go with him. I never could forgive him for taking you against my wishes. He insisted that you were old enough to see that people had to stand up for what they believed in if we ever wanted to see things change. I told him there would be plenty of time for you to stand up for what you believed in when you were a little older. He disagreed."

"How did you two sort it out afterward?" I asked her.

"While the two of you were gone," she said, "I went to stay with Big Momma and Granddaddy Pete. Big Momma made me a cup of coffee and sat down with me at her kitchen table and I just cried for a long time. Then, after a while, I stopped crying, and Big Momma said to me, 'Baby, you got to understand that this is what you signed on for when you fell in love with a Black man. He's not a tame Black man. He won't just step aside. He's going to speak up when he sees injustice. And he's going to teach your daughter to speak up too.' I reminded her that speaking out against injustice is as much a Jewish tradition as a Black one. That wasn't why I was mad at him, and she knew it. I was mad because I thought you were too young and he was putting you in danger. Big Momma told me, 'Black girls younger than Miriam have had to face much worse than a war protest.' By the time you and your father returned, I had my anger under control. He apologized for scaring me. He apologized for losing his temper. But he never apologized for taking you to the march against my wishes."

"Going on that march is one of my clearest early memories," I told my mother. "I forgot to be scared when we got on the train. It became an adventure. The people with us on the train sang songs and ate food together. I had some delicious chocolate cake. At the march, Daddy put me up on his shoulders so I could see above the crowd. I remember the Washington Monument and how huge the statue of Abraham Lincoln was at the Lincoln Memorial. We marched, sang, and chanted. There was lots of drumming, and everyone had signs. I was with Daddy and I felt completely safe, even though some of the signs had terrifying pictures of dead people on them that gave me bad dreams afterward."

"You talked about it for weeks," Mama said. "It was funny because you would tell people about what happened when you and Daddy went to the war." She smiled then as she remembered my words with amusement. "That's how you referred to it. When you went to the war. Even though I understood, even though I heard what Big Momma told me, even though you came back unharmed, I still have not forgiven your father for taking you when we had not agreed to it together."

Two

WHEN I WAS EIGHT years old, we moved to Kenya so that Daddy could accept a two-year teaching position at the University of Nairobi. My parents agreed that it was an opportunity they could not pass up, and they were excited for our family to experience life in Africa. While we were in Kenya, Mama continued to work for Aunt Margaret's wrapping-paper company and illustrated children's books for an American publisher. I liked it when she did a children's book because I could watch the pictures grow on her drawing board and wonder what the story was about until the book was finished. She shipped her drawings back to America in wooden boxes. She also had a job embroidering on one-of-a-kind jackets made by a company in Boston. The company made children's jackets and I had a green one that my mother had embroidered with butterflies. It was one of my favorite pieces of clothing.

In Kenya, the faces I passed in the streets were predominantly brown faces, just like in Harlem back home. But in Kenya, unlike in America, all the professionals had brown faces too. My doctor, the policemen, judges, and businessmen were brown, as were the musicians, artists, and journalists. When I watched Jomo Kenyatta and government officials on TV, I saw brown faces. While living in Nairobi, I soon spoke English with an African-style British accent that I never completely lost, and I became fluent in Swahili.

After we had lived in Nairobi for a few months, Mama took me to a hair braider named Kila, who tamed my thick hair into intricate patterns. We became regulars, returning every couple of months for Kila to rebraid my hair. Daddy said she braided twice as fast as his sisters back home. When we marveled over her miraculous braiding speed, Kila just laughed, and her laugh sounded like water tumbling over stones. Kila had moved to Nairobi from her home village of Baranja. While I sat under Kila's racing fingers, I asked her questions about Baranja and she told me stories about the people of her village and her life growing up there. Mama frequently remained with me while I had my hair braided, sitting in the corner on a wooden stool and embroidering jackets while she too listened to Kila's stories about Baranja. One afternoon, I told Kila that I wished I could go to Baranja and meet the people she talked about in her stories.

Mama looked up from her embroidery and asked Kila, "Would it be possible for us to visit Baranja?" And that's how Kila wound up arranging for us to rent a cottage in Baranja during the summer after Daddy's first year at the University of Nairobi ended and before his second year began.

We arrived in Baranja by jeep on a brilliantly sunny day filled with the chatter of monkeys playing in the nearby trees. Although no one in my family spoke the local language, many of the villagers spoke English and almost all spoke Swahili, so I could talk with the village children and make friends. Our cottage had a thatched roof and beaten-dirt floor. When we first arrived, the villagers greeted us warmly. But then, to our bewilderment, after a couple of days the villagers seemed to avoid us and closed up tight like hard-shell crabs. Mama had agreed to swap embroidery techniques with the village women while we were there, and although they had discussed this initially, no one seemed willing to meet with her. I overheard Mama ask Daddy if he thought the villagers had a problem with her color. He said he didn't think so, but he could only speculate. We wondered what had brought about the change. By the middle of our second week there, no one spoke to my parents, who only received curt nods from the villagers.

I fared better in my relationship with the village children. Every morning, I left our cottage with a small metal bucket and a shovel, humming to myself, and I spent the day wading through plump juicy melons and ruffled green leafy vegetables as I worked and played with my new friends in the communal garden. Different villagers turned up on different days to tend the garden, which supplied the village with all its food. The garden included barns, goat pens, chicken coops, and a small mill. To me, it was a fairyland.

We had been in Baranja two weeks, and still had not figured out where our visit had gone wrong, when Mama received a telegram from Aunt Soph saying that Mama's father, Nate, had died of a heart attack. When Mama read the telegram out loud, I started to cry.

"We need to go see Grandma Ruth," I said through my tears. "She needs us. She must be so sad." Mama put two chairs together side by side and sat me in one of them before sitting down next to me. She put her arms around me and held me against her. Mama and I had written a letter to Grandma Ruth every week since we moved to Africa, and Grandma Ruth had sent us a few boxes of cookies that had been a bit stale by the time they arrived but were delicious nonetheless. I kept a framed picture of me and Grandma Ruth by my bedside to remind me of what she looked like.

Mama held me, without saying anything, until my tears had subsided, and then she said, gently, "Miriam, we can't go to America right now. It's too far away and we can't afford a trip like that. By the time we would get there, the funeral would be over anyway. Your grandmother has Aunt Soph, Uncle Max, and Aunt Sarah to look after her, and she has a lot of friends. She's going to be sad, but she'll be OK, I promise you."

Daddy knelt down in front of me. "We can write her a letter, right now, and you can tell her how much you love her. I'm sure she'll understand why we can't go to America to see her."

In my head I could hear my grandfather's voice saying "hang on" when he answered the phone at Grandma Ruth's house.

The next day, Mama and Daddy got up before sunrise to travel to the nearest city to attempt to place a phone call to America, and while they were gone, I stayed with the family of a boy whose name meant "Loud Mouth" in the village language. Loud Mouth had earned this name because he indiscriminately said whatever popped into his head. Loud Mouth and I dug in the garden together. We pretended we were gophers on an American prairie as we squatted and turned a new bed for the grown-ups to plant sweet potatoes.

"Are all Americans rich?" Loud Mouth asked.

"We're not rich," I answered.

"Then how come all Americans have cars?" Loud Mouth asked.

"We don't have a car," I answered.

"Are all Americans wasteful like your family?" Loud Mouth asked.

"What do you mean?"

"Your family wastes the food. It's disrespectful to the spirits."

"What are you talking about?" I demanded.

"Your family takes more than you need from the garden and it rots in your house. Then you don't bother to return the spoiled food to the soil to feed new plants. We call your family the Wasteful Ones," Loud Mouth informed me.

"We try to figure out how much food we need, but sometimes we don't figure it out right," I said.

"What do you have to figure out? Come to the garden every day and just take what you need to eat," Loud Mouth instructed, looking puzzled.

"We don't want to have to shop every day," I said, realizing even as the words left my mouth that they made no sense in the context of the village life. "Until we came here, we shopped for food at the store in Nairobi," I explained, although my explanation sounded lame even to me.

"A garden isn't a store," Loud Mouth pointed out. "You can come to a garden whenever you're hungry."

"I'll tell my parents what you said," I promised my friend.

I had fallen sleep by the time Mama and Daddy returned to Baranja from the city that night, but the next day, I told my cosmopolitan parents, who never cooked meals, about my conversation with Loud Mouth. The three of us immediately went to speak with Kila's sister about it. Kila's sister looked embarrassed as she explained to us how the garden and the compost system worked. They did not waste what had required so much effort to produce. Kitchen scraps, such as rinds, eggshells, and even the little bit a person left on the plate when he got full, went into the compost system at the communal garden. As she spoke, it became clear that our family had failed to comprehend something so basic about living on the earth that the villagers did not know where to begin to enlighten us.

"We couldn't figure out how to explain to you how to behave without insulting you," Kila's sister said anxiously. "I hope I have not offended you."

Once that misunderstanding was cleared up, our stay in Baranja improved. I regretted that our time there was so short because I liked living in the village even better than I liked living in Nairobi. Before we left Baranja, Mama made a mask with a wide, smiling mouth and gave it to Loud Mouth to express our gratitude to him for tipping us off about the problem. Loud Mouth loved his gift from Mama, and he was wearing it when he waved good-bye to us at the end of the summer when we departed to return to Nairobi.

After our two years in Africa, I didn't want to leave. In child's years, I had lived there forever and it was my home. I had wept when we left New York and I had said good-bye to Grandma Ruth, and I wept when we said good-bye to our African friends and boarded the plane to leave Kenya. The biggest thing I had to look forward to upon our return to New York was seeing Grandma Ruth again and I wondered how she would be now that her husband had died. I was especially interested in seeing her house, since I had never been allowed to go there before we went to Kenya. But we didn't immediately return to New York. Mama and Daddy's college friend Norma (who always smelled like a wonderful perfume she called Muguet) had an apartment in Paris where she stayed for part of the year. We flew from Nairobi to Paris to see Auntie Norma and to "poke our noses in a few European museums," as Daddy said.

Three

IN PARIS, AUNTIE NORMA took us to two private fashion shows; she had even designed some of the dresses in one of them. Since we had just come from Africa, she seemed to think that she needed to take us to all the best African restaurants. My favorite was an Ethiopian restaurant where we sat on the floor on cushions. One evening, we went out to eat at an Algerian restaurant. Auntie Norma wore a bright dress with pink, purple, and turquoise flowers printed on it, and a straw hat with a thin purple ribbon tied around the brim. When she laughed, her hat bopped up and down. While waiting for the meal to arrive, Norma laced her turquoise fingernails into each other in front of her chin.

"I took the liberty of buying us tickets to the ballet for Friday night. They're dancing Prokofiev's *Cinderella* and it's purported to be an extraordinary production. A friend of mine, who has been writing dance critiques for thirty years, told me he has seen seven different versions of it, including one performed by the Russian ballet, and that this one is the best ever. The costumes and scenery are supposed to be terrific."

"*Cinderella* will be perfect for Miriam," Daddy said. "We love that story, don't we, baby?"

I agreed enthusiastically.

Mama asked, "Who choreographed it?"

Norma tapped her chin with one turquoise nail. "I can't remember. But we can look it up when we go home."

"Because I have a cousin who was a ballerina with the French National Ballet for many years and, according to my mother, now that my cousin is too old to dance in a principal role, she has started choreographing," Mama said.

I wondered why I had never heard about this cousin and how I was related to her.

"Aren't you full of surprises?" Norma exclaimed.

Mama pierced several pieces of lettuce with the tines of her fork and put them in her mouth.

"Who is she?" I asked curiously.

"Grandma Ruth's niece," Mama answered.

"Your aunt Rivka's daughter?" Daddy asked.

"That's right," Mama said, and then told Norma, "My mother's sister, Rivka, lives in Paris. She's the one who survived the war. We named Miriam after their adopted sister, who was killed by the Nazis."

My ears perked up at this information. "You mean the brave Miriam who rescued the children?" I asked, for Grandma Ruth had told me the story about my namesake who grew up with her in Palestine.

"That's the one," Mama confirmed. "Rivka has one daughter, Shayna, and she choreographs for the National Ballet in Paris."

Norma clapped her hands in delight. "The Oiseau is your cousin? This is too much!"

"What is the 'wahzoo'?" I asked, imagining a person capable of contorting her body into the shape of a horned musical instrument.

"*Oiseau*," Daddy corrected, "it's French for *bird*, baby. It must be a nickname, right?"

"It is a nickname. They call her that because when she danced as a prima ballerina, she flew," Norma said.

"For real? Did she really fly? Not like with wings, right? Can we visit her? Can she still fly?" My words tumbled out like rubber balls bouncing down a flight of stairs.

Daddy looked at Mama and put his chin on his hand and batted his eyes, acting silly, "Yes, can we? Can we meet this mysterious ballerina cousin?"

"Oh, stop," Mama smiled indulgently, and, with a wave of her hand, said, "Of course. I was planning to look up Aunt Rivka. I just hadn't gotten around to it yet. I was too busy eating really good African food."

"Really good African food can be pretty distracting," Norma said, with amusement. When we returned to Norma's apartment, we looked up the *Cinderella* ballet in the newspaper and discovered that my cousin Shayna was, indeed, the choreographer. That evening, because we insisted, Mama telephoned Aunt Rivka. I listened with interest to Mama's side of the conversation. When she hung up, Mama informed us that Aunt Rivka spoke surprisingly excellent English, had scolded her roundly for not giving fair warning of our arrival in Paris, and had invited us for dinner the very next day, Norma too.

So the following afternoon found us on the second floor of a tidy, old-style apartment building on the rue de Rosny as Mama rang the doorbell. A plump old lady with puffy legs and thick, wire-rimmed glasses opened the door to greet us. She gave Mama a hug and kisses on both cheeks and then held her at arm's length for a good look, wiping her eyes, clucking her tongue, and exclaiming in monosyllabic French. After she finished with Mama, she turned to me.

Her eyes locked with mine as she sunk to her knees to face me at eye level. I don't know what possessed me then. I felt as if another person deep inside of me controlled me like a marionette as I placed both hands on top of my aunt's curly graying hair and gently ran my palms down the sides of her head and down her neck to her shoulders, as if this series of gestures was a ritual I was expected to perform. I squeezed Aunt Rivka's shoulders before moving my hands down her arms to her hands, which I held firmly. "We are blessed," I said, without the faintest idea why. I wasn't exactly sure what that meant, but I felt compelled to say it.

Aunt Rivka's lips trembled and she whispered in my ear, like a prayer, so that only I could hear, "We truly are blessed." She wrapped me in her arms, murmuring "Miriam, Miriam, Miriam."

I didn't mind. I felt like everything that might be wrong in the world was precisely right.

"I am so glad to see you," she said, as she released me.

Aunt Rivka stood up and welcomed Daddy and Norma warmly, and then she ushered us into the house where Yakov and Shayna eagerly awaited us. Shayna wore a white dress with red-purple cherries patterned all over it. The instant I saw her, I knew that I had seen Shayna in a cherry dress before, or imagined her in it. Or dreamed it.

"I knew you would wear the cherry dress," I told her as she embraced me.

"You did?" Shayna asked, laughing. "And how did you know I would have a cherry dress?"

"I don't know." I was bewildered. "I just knew you would."

"Of course you did," Aunt Rivka reassured me, as if it were the most ordinary thing for me to have had a premonition of Shayna's dress.

"And how old are you?" Shayna asked me in English, with a pronounced French accent.

"I'm ten," I replied.

Daddy and Yakov retired to the living room, where they pored over Yakov's books and papers and his memorabilia from his days in the Resistance. Daddy's college French served him well enough to communicate. Mama didn't know any French, but fortunately Aunt Rivka spoke English. Shayna, Mama, and Auntie Norma remained in the kitchen where Auntie Norma talked about the upcoming fall fashions, Cousin Shayna talked about the latest wave of modern dance that was coming over to Europe from America, and Mama talked about an art exhibition that Auntie Norma had taken us to the previous afternoon.

Aunt Rivka wanted to bake an apple pie to honor the "American relatives," as she put it. She enlisted my aid and we proceeded to cover the countertop in flour as she showed me how to make a pie crust from scratch. She put a mound of flour onto a large cutting board and had me use a pastry cutter to cut butter into the flour.

"Mama never bakes. She doesn't like to cook," I informed Aunt Rivka.

"Does your papa cook?" she asked.

"Not much. He's a good cook, though. I wish he cooked more."

"So what do you eat?"

"We eat out."

"That sounds like fun."

"It is."

"What about you? Do you like to cook?" Aunt Rivka asked, as we rolled out the dough with a wooden rolling pin.

"I'm not sure. I haven't done it much. Before we went to Africa, I used to help Grandma Ruth cook dinner."

"Your Grandma Ruth is my sister, you know, and she is an excellent cook. I'm willing to bet that you baked cookies with her."

"Sometimes, but usually she baked cookies before she came to my house and brought them with her," I explained. I remembered how much Grandma Ruth enjoyed cooking. It was not surprising that Aunt Rivka also liked to cook, since they were sisters. Talking to Aunt Rivka made me miss Grandma Ruth and feel like she was nearby, both at the same time. "Once at school we made peanut butter," I said.

"Did you like making peanut butter?" Aunt Rivka asked, as she lifted the circle of dough gently by the edges and placed it neatly into a tin pie plate.

"I did!"

"So maybe you do like to cook," Aunt Rivka suggested.

"There are a lot of things I don't know about myself yet," I told my aunt.

She studied me for a long minute. "You possess an old and wise spirit, did you already know that?"

I shrugged and began peeling pie dough out from under my fingernails. Aunt Rivka patted my hand. "Let's put these apples into the crust and get this pie in the oven."

At the end of the evening, when we stood in the doorway, Aunt Rivka gave Mama two big hugs. "The first one was for you," she explained, "and the second one was for my sister. Please give it to her when you see her. I know she is going through a difficult transition."

"What kind of difficult transition?" I asked in alarm.

"She's still getting used to her life without your grandfather," Aunt Rivka replied.

"My grandfather didn't like us," I told Aunt Rivka. "Because Daddy and I are brown. I never met him."

Aunt Rivka gave my hand a squeeze. "How sad for him to miss out on such a lovely granddaughter. Your grandmother loved him very much. I'm sure it broke her heart that he died without having met you. But now that he is gone, things are different for her, and they will be different for all of you."

"I think that we can go to Grandma Ruth's house now," I said. "We couldn't go before."

"That's true," Mama said. "I hadn't given that much thought. She has a beautiful house and now you'll be able to see it, Miriam." She glanced over my head at Auntie Norma, who put her arm around Mama's waist and squeezed. I wondered how long it had been since Mama had seen the inside of the house in which she grew up.

During our last week in Paris, we took Aunt Rivka and Uncle Yakov to the Ethiopian restaurant that we liked so much. They both needed help getting up off the cushions on the floor after we ate, but Uncle Yakov said that he wouldn't have minded staying stuck on the floor of that restaurant for a few days because the food was delicious. We did see our cousin's production of *Cinderella*. None of the dancers flew, but I loved it anyway. Cinderella's stepsisters were funny, and the costumes and scenery were as beautiful as Norma said they would be. We went together on a day trip to Versailles, where I walked hand in hand with Aunt Rivka through the gardens brimming with the blooms of summer. We had a picnic lunch that Aunt Rivka had packed in a basket lined with a blue tablecloth. We ate fresh baguettes, soft creamy Brie, spring onions, and sardines. The grown-ups shared a bottle of red wine and I drank cherry-flavored fizzy water. For dessert we had fresh raspberries that stained my fingers pink.

After our trip to Paris, we went on to Amsterdam and then to London before we returned to New York. By the time I emerged from customs at JFK International Airport and raced into the waiting arms of Grandma Ruth, I could remember almost nothing to tell her about the great museums of Paris, London, and Amsterdam, but I filled her in on every detail of the time I spent with Aunt Rivka. I gave her two hugs, one from me, and one from her sister. And whenever I tasted raspberries I thought of Aunt Rivka and our walk through the gardens at Versailles.

Four

BEFORE WE LEFT FOR Africa, Mama and Daddy had sold our brownstone in Harlem. Upon our return, we stayed with Big Momma and Granddaddy Pete while my parents looked for an apartment. I overheard Daddy and Granddaddy Pete talking about how Harlem had changed.

"It's them drugs," Granddaddy Pete said, as he shook his head sadly. "The folks selling them drugs have ruined the old neighborhoods."

Daddy agreed. "That's why we're looking over in the Village," he said.

"I don't blame you," Granddaddy Pete replied. "Don't want to raise a daughter out here in Harlem these days."

We moved into an apartment in an old Victorian in Greenwich Village. It had high ceilings and dark wood, and I could hear the rain on the roof of my bedroom. Grandma Ruth declared our new home "a marked improvement over the Harlem place," a comment that I could tell annoyed Mama.

Grandma Ruth was so happy to see me upon my return from Kenya that she baked me a three-layer chocolate cake to welcome me back. She seemed older and thinner than I remembered her, and much shorter. She marveled over how tall I had grown and how magnificent my hair looked in braids. I told her about baking pie with Aunt Rivka and asked her if she would teach me how to bake cookies. But the most exciting part about my return to America was that I finally got to see the inside of Grandma Ruth's house, which my grandfather had built before he married her. During our first week back, we slept over at Grandma Ruth's. I got to sleep in Mama's old bedroom, the one she grew up in. I thought it was the most beautiful house I had ever been in. From the painting of the mysterious Chinese lady over the mantelpiece to the rose-scented soap in the bathroom, I loved it. Grandma Ruth gave me a tour and she showed me some of her special things, like her tortoiseshell hand mirror on her dresser and the hats she was making in her sewing room, which was filled with fabric of every color imaginable.

"I'm sorry Grandpa Nate died," I told her, "but I'm glad that I can come to your house now." I didn't mean to make her cry. I told her that her sewing room was my favorite room in her whole house because it was the happiest room. That made her smile again. I helped her cook dinner. We made eggplant parmesan, which had been one of my favorite dishes from before I went to Africa. No one made it like Grandma Ruth, so cheesy and crispy on top.

Our first Thanksgiving back in America was a big deal because we hadn't celebrated Thanksgiving in Kenya and it was a special holiday to my parents. I understood that for my parents and their friends, Thanksgiving had nothing to do with pilgrims or the genocide of indigenous people. They had remade the holiday into an occasion when good friends come together to enjoy the warmth of each other's company and to give thanks for their friendship.

In early November, I overheard Mama on the phone with Aunt Soph. "You know I always do Thanksgiving with my friends," Mama said firmly. And then, "You're welcome to come, Soph, and I already invited Mom." Mama sighed impatiently. "Sarah is a grown woman with a P-H-D for god's sake; she can decide for herself where to go for Thanksgiving." Aunt Soph said something and then Mama replied, "Yes, it's a lot of people. When you decide, just let me know." Long silence. Mama glanced at me and rolled her eyes, looked at the clock. "OK. Love you too. Bye."

As soon as Mama hung up, I said, "Thanksgiving is my favorite holiday."

"I know you missed it when we lived in Kenya, baby. But, we'll make up for missing it in Kenya with a special Thanksgiving this year," Mama promised as she poured herself a cup of coffee. "I have insisted that our old gang from art school must come. I've got all of them rounded up except Skip. But I'm still working on him."

Grandma Ruth got the flu right before Thanksgiving, and Aunt Soph and Uncle Max, who did not wish to attend a big gathering anyway, were content to have a quiet holiday just with Grandma. They didn't want her to be alone. But Aunt Sarah chose to come to our house with the crowd. She had lived with TJ and Lee in Berkeley back before I was born and she said she wanted to see them.

All the old friends came. Lee had moved back to New York with her husband while our family was in Africa and she had a baby named Ezekiel whom they called "Zeke." TJ still lived in Berkeley, but he came to New York frequently on business. He flew out for Thanksgiving and brought his new girlfriend with him. Norma closed her apartment in Paris and opened the one in Manhattan for the winter. Margaret and Gloria agreed to come. Richard and his companion of many years, Mike, would be there, as they had always been before we went to Africa. Mama was successful at convincing Skip to come in the end too. He and his wife, Emma, planned to drive up from Pennsylvania in their station wagon full of towheaded children.

Most of our guests descended on our house early in the day. Baby Zeke and I sat on the dining room floor where he explored Mama's basket of old tops and lids to jars and containers that Mama saved for visiting babies. Zeke banged two metal pickle jar lids together like cymbals, sucked on them, and then dropped them to examine a mayonnaise jar lid, cooing at me the whole time.

TJ's girlfriend, Tasha, plopped down cross-legged next to us. She wore a Minnie Mouse sweatshirt and Tweety-Bird sneakers and she smacked on a juicy wad of blue bubblegum with which she blew giant bubbles. She offered me a piece of gum and the two of us tried to impress Zeke by blowing the biggest bubbles we could. Tasha got bubblegum on her eyebrows. I got bubblegum on my chin. Zeke clapped and chuckled.

In the middle of the afternoon, Skip's family arrived, which made the whole house feel full to bursting with the goodness of the holiday. Our kitchen smelled like turkey, yeasty bread, sage, and cinnamon. Auntie Norma had brought some French bread and Brie as an appetizer and I ate it greedily because the delicious smells were making me hungry.

Soon after Skip's arrival, I answered the door to let Aunt Sarah in. She had brought a friend named Jade. Jade was a slender Japanese woman with straight black hair that flowed to her waist. She was graceful and had a smile that lit up her face. Mama seemed particularly delighted to meet Jade and she gave her a warm welcome while Aunt Sarah looked on, blushing. Jade brushed Sarah's back lightly with the tips of her fingers and Sarah slowly stopped blushing. My eyes went from my quiet, gentle aunt Sarah to Jade and back again as it dawned on me that they were a couple, which explained why Mama was so pleased to meet Jade. It annoyed me that no one had bothered to tell me that Aunt Sarah was seeing someone. I would have to find out more about Jade on my own.

Skip took his children out to the backyard to play. He said they needed to burn off some energy before sitting at a dinner table. I went out back too and watched them throw several footballs in varying sizes that matched the sizes of Skip's children. Jade opened the kitchen door and the mouth-watering smell of roasting turkey wafted out. She closed the door and sat on the top step next to me.

"Where did you meet Aunt Sarah?" I asked her after a moment.

"At one of my jobs. I'm a landscape gardener and I do the garden for one of your aunt's friends from school," Jade answered. Her hair shone with a metallic bluish cast in the autumn sun as she tossed it over her shoulder. I played with the silver bracelets on her wrist. I removed a delicate bracelet shaped like a snake swallowing its tail and examined it. Jade didn't say something like "be careful with that" the way most grown-ups would. Instead she said, "But I'm going to give up gardening. I've gone back to school to study to be a therapist. I want to counsel children."

I kept playing with her bracelet and didn't look at her while I asked, because I had to know, "Are you Aunt Sarah's girlfriend?"

"Now you're getting nosy," Jade tapped my knee with a callused fingertip. The silver bracelets tinkled as they slid down her graceful, muscular arm. "Do you want me to be her girlfriend?"

I nodded as I replaced Jade's delicate silver bracelet on her wrist.

"I take that as a compliment. So I'll tell you a secret," she leaned close to me and I caught the scent of lilac soap coming off her clear skin. "Your aunt Sarah and I belong together."

At that moment Aunt Lee came out of the house with Zeke, who wore a snowsuit that made him look like a miniature Abominable Snowman. Jade and I laughed.

"That baby can barely move in that thing," Jade told Lee.

"I don't want him to be cold," Lee replied.

I left Jade and Lee to work out what baby Zeke should wear and went back into the kitchen, where Emma was helping TJ and Tasha make biscuits. There was flour everywhere, including on TJ's nose.

"This is worse than trying to bake with the children," Emma drawled. "TJ, that dough will rise in your stomach and make you sick if you don't watch out." TJ looked sheepish.

"You know who could never keep out of the dough," Mama said, as she chopped lettuce. "Dale." I had heard Mama and Daddy talk about Dale many times. He had killed himself. He used to be Richard's boyfriend, before Mike. I couldn't imagine Richard with anyone but Mike.

Daddy chuckled. "I remember that time Margaret made chocolate-chip cookies and Dale ate so much of that dough that Margaret didn't even have enough left to fill one cookie sheet."

"And then," Mama continued, "Dale stretched out on the couch. He was so skinny. His stomach inflated before our eyes when those cookies rose inside."

TJ cocked his head and squinted his eyes, remembering. "Now there was a man who surely could hold his dough," he said.

Gloria took my hand and told me, "Norma and Margaret are making table decorations in the studio. We thought you might want to help." I sure did. Tasha washed her hands and face and went with us. She still had flour in her hair. When we arrived in the studio, we found Mama's drawing table covered with construction paper, leaves, pinecones, and turkey feathers. There were two large vases of flowers on the floor.

"Ah, reinforcements," Margaret remarked.

"I have just the thing," Tasha told them, and she produced two little plastic turkeys from her back pocket. We made three different centerpieces and arranged the flowers into several small vases.

I had already filled my plate in my mind by the time we finally sat down at the table, laden to overflowing with the bounty that was the product of everyone's hard work. I didn't think that Loud Mouth's village would have approved of us cooking so much more than we could eat. Or maybe they would have after they saw us join hands and go around the table giving thanks for family, friendship, and shared food.

As my turn to speak approached, my throat tightened. I told myself that I didn't have to say anything if I didn't want to. But I wanted to, and I remembered what Aunt Rivka had said about me having a wise spirit. What good was a wise spirit without courage? So I spoke.

"I wish that all the children in the world could grow up with this many people to love them."

Mama's eyes filled with tears and Daddy squeezed her hand.

Five

ONE NIGHT AT THE dinner table, when I was in the eighth grade, Daddy turned to me and said, "Mama and I want to talk with you about high school."

I put my fork down on my plate. This sounded serious.

"There is a special high school that focuses on the visual and performing arts," Mama explained. "It has an excellent reputation. It's called Visual and Performing Arts High. I thought perhaps we would see if we could get you into it. Your father thinks differently."

I looked back and forth between the two of them.

"And we feel," Daddy continued, "that you are old enough to decide for yourself what you want to do. I would like you to continue on to Elisabeth Irwin High as we had originally planned. It's a progressive public high school right here in our backyard and I think we should take advantage of it."

I didn't think it was the right moment to tell my mother that I was not so sure I wanted to be an artist. It was something she had assumed about me and so I had assumed it about myself; but lately I had been thinking that I might want to go in a different direction. Whenever I spent the weekend with Aunt Sarah and Jade, as I did from time to time, they talked about their work helping troubled children and they made it sound so interesting and worthwhile. Aunt Sarah was a school principal and Jade counseled teenagers. Aunt Sarah gave me a novel called *Adam Misunderstood* to read and it was about a psychologist who helped a boy who had been orphaned. It was one of my favorite books. The one thing I knew for sure was that I wasn't ready to decide what I wanted to do with my life.

"So what kinds of classes would I take at Arts High?" I asked.

"You would take all the same academic classes," Mama answered, "but you would also have the chance to sign up for art classes not offered at Irwin. And in your senior year, you would work on a portfolio to help you get into college."

"Do you know if any of my friends are planning to go to Arts High?" I asked.

"I think maybe Cindy," Mama said. "Some of your friends might be interested if you told them about it and then you could apply together."

"What about band?" I asked. I had played the flute for three years and I wanted to continue.

"They do have a jazz band," Mama assured me.

"But," Daddy said, with a glance at Mama, "you have to audition to get into it and there's no guarantee you would make the band."

"You'll make it," Mama said. "You're very good."

But I realized that she couldn't know that for certain.

"We want to be sure that you understand that Daddy and I agree that this is your decision," Mama continued. "We just want you to have all the information before you decide."

I picked up my fork again and began to eat. I thought that maybe I would ask Grandma Ruth what she thought about this. And maybe I would even write to Aunt Rivka about it. Ever since I had visited her in France, I had been writing letters to her every month or two. Sometimes Grandma Ruth and I wrote to her together. I would get all the facts about the two schools and share them with Grandma Ruth and Aunt Rivka.

We didn't talk more about high schools that evening. But over the next few weeks, Mama and Daddy brought up the subject fairly often. Mama and I went on a tour of Arts High. Mama was excited about everything at that school. She loved the paintings on the walls in the administration building, the studios, the swimming pool, and the dark room. She even loved the antique mirrors hanging in the women's restroom. She was about ready to move into Arts High.

Finally, I confided in Grandma Ruth that I was starting to feel like I was being asked to choose between my parents and not two different schools. "That does it," Grandma Ruth said. "I'm going to ask your parents if it's OK with them if I take you to meet with a guidance counselor at your school. I think we should find out what she has to say about what these two different schools have to offer." So Grandma Ruth got permission from Mama and Daddy and she went with me to the meeting herself.

The guidance counselor was familiar with both Irwin High and Arts High. She asked me if I had any idea yet about what career I wanted to pursue. It was the first time in these discussions that anyone had asked me that question.

"I enjoy art," I told her. "It's one of my favorite subjects in school, and that's why my mother thinks I would like Arts High."

"That's what your mother thinks. What do you think?" the guidance counselor asked.

I glanced at Grandma Ruth, who gave me an encouraging nod. "I'm not ready to make a decision about what I want to be yet. But," I hesitated because I had never said it out loud before, "I might be interested in psychology."

"Well, perhaps a more broad-based high school experience than what Arts High offers would be more suited to your needs," the guidance counselor suggested. "Irwin High offers some excellent art classes and I believe they also have an articulation agreement with City College that would allow you to take a psychology course there in your junior or senior year."

I was grateful to the guidance counselor for helping me make a decision. I was sure I wanted to go to Irwin, but I felt apprehensive about telling my mother. I didn't want to hurt her feelings.

"It's your life, honey," Grandma Ruth said as she drove me home. "Your mother just wants you to be happy. She'll understand. I promise you."

When we returned to the house that evening, my parents were waiting for us expectantly. I related my conversation with the guidance counselor and told my parents that even though I loved art, I wasn't sure I wanted to become a professional artist like them, and that if I went to Irwin I could explore more options. "I'm sorry to disappoint you, Mama," I finished.

"I am disappointed," Mama said, "but I'm not disappointed in you, baby. I'm disappointed for myself, if you can understand that."

"I do understand," I told her. "And I think that if you are so in love with that school that maybe you should go there. You could teach a class there or do some workshops there or be a guest lecturer," I suggested.

"I would have given anything to go to Arts High when I was your age," Mama said wistfully.

"It didn't exist back then," Grandma Ruth reminded her, a bit reproachfully.

"That's true. I realize that," Mama said. "I suppose this is a bit of payback for me after what I put you through when I was a teenager."

I glanced back and forth between my mother and my grandmother as I tried to imagine what Mama might have put Grandma Ruth through, and then I thought about my grandfather and the fact that there were things he was not willing to forgive my mother for, and things she would never forgive him for either. Perhaps the fact that Daddy was Black was not the whole reason why Grandpa Nate had stopped speaking to my mother.

"Not payback at all," Grandma Ruth said. "It's just what happens. Parents and children have their differences and they have to pursue their own lives."

"Well, Elisabeth Irwin High it is," Mama said. "And it's a good school, nothing wrong with it."

In my sophomore year at Irwin, Mama bought us tickets to Arizona for a weeklong vacation right after Christmas. We fled the wet, snowbound

Northeast to spend a glorious week in the dry and dusty Southwest. The spare landscape was uncomplicated, clear, and inviolate. Mama fell in love with the iconic images of that landscape: a wagon wheel leaning in retirement against a worn barn; the desert stretching open and spacious to the horizon at gold sunset under a conflagration of orange and rose-pink clouds; the graceful, dramatic agave cactus reaching its clustered hands upward as if in prayer. So two years later, when I decided to go to college in Tucson, I told Mama that she had no one to blame but herself for introducing me to the wonder of the Southwest. Although Mama adored the Arizona scenery, she didn't want me to move out of the Big Apple. She said that sending me to Tucson was like sending me to Mars.

I said, "You're being melodramatic."

"As I recall, you made a dramatic break from your parents at Miriam's age," Daddy reminded Mama.

"Totally different," Mama corrected him. "We did not get along. Miriam and I get along just fine. Arizona is far, far away."

"Not by airplane, it isn't. You'll get used to it," Daddy said as he winked at me behind Mama's back.

"We should have had more children," Mama pouted.

"I can fix that," Daddy suggested.

Mama gave him "the look," which made me laugh.

"Or not," he grinned.

I boarded an airplane for Tucson with two suitcases, my sketch pad, Mama's teary-eyed blessing, and a bag of Grandma Ruth's best homemade *rugelach*. Once I got settled, I would have them ship me a few boxes that I had packed up.

Living in a girls' dorm was tame for me compared to living with Mama and Daddy and the comings and goings through our house of our friends in Greenwich Village. My roommate, Diane, was studying graphic design, and she had seen some of my parents' work in children's books. In recent years, Mama and Daddy had secured a considerable amount of work illustrating ethnic legends and folktales for a big New York publisher. Diane and I were compatible roommates, although she spent much less time in the room than I did. She had a boyfriend she hung out with a lot, plus she went to the art studio to work on class assignments in the evenings. Even so, Diane and I frequently met up at dinnertime to eat together at the dorm dining hall. I liked eating meals at the dining hall because it was convenient and reminded me of home, where we ate out all the time. I missed Grandma Ruth's delicious Thursday dinners, but she sent me a care package of cookies every few weeks and I shared it with some of the other women on my floor of the dorm. When those cookies arrived in the mail, I could hear them up and down the hall shouting, "Package from Grandma Ruth!" Then everyone would descend on my dorm room and the cookies would be gone in a matter of minutes.

One of the reasons I had chosen to attend Tucson was because they had both a good art department and a good psychology department. Even though I was leaning toward psychology for my career, I was not prepared to give up my affection for art entirely. That first semester, I took an English class, a math class, a class in art history (despite the fact that I grew up eating art history three meals a day), a child psychology class, and beginning Spanish. I had intended to find a band with which to continue playing my flute, but I was just too busy to fit anything else into my schedule.

At first, I was a bit uncomfortable at school because I had never lived anywhere where there were so few Black folks. I remembered what it was like when I returned to America from Africa and I felt conspicuous in my brown skin. There were few Black students on campus and even fewer in my classes. There was a handsome brother, named Mark, in my art history class. I tried talking to him outside class a couple of times, but he wasn't into it. He would cut me short, pinching his eyebrows together and setting his mouth in a firm line.

One day in class, the professor, a skinny and bespectacled white man with thinning hair, posed the question, "What characteristics do you think distinguish African art from other art?"

He elicited a few anemic responses. I thought the question bordered on racism and so kept quiet. How could you lump all of African art together like that, as if when you've seen one piece of art from the entire continent then you've seen them all? My classmates shifted uncomfortably in their seats.

"Mark," the professor called out, "tell me what characteristics you think distinguish African art."

"Why are you asking me? Just because I'm Black doesn't mean I know anything about Africa," Mark snapped. "I've never been to Africa."

"Surely you've seen African art. I'm not asking you because you're Black," the professor continued in a tone that sounded rather condescending to me. "I like to think of myself as being color-blind."

"Back in the 'hood, we'd call that just plain blind," Mark said with a terrifying ferocity.

The professor struggled to conceal his discomfort while Mark leaned back in his chair, crossed his arms, and glared at him. Our classmates stared into their textbooks with mock concentration while the professor proceeded to answer his question about African art himself. I was no longer listening to him, though; I was thinking about how rude Mark had been.

Outside the building, on the sidewalk, I ran after Mark and stopped him. "Why did you do that?" I asked angrily. "He messed up, but you didn't have to be so insulting. He still doesn't get what he did wrong. You had the chance to help him to understand the problem with the question and instead you just shut him down."

Mark gave me the up-and-down sweep with his eyes. "I don't need no high yaller girl telling me how to talk to Whitey. For all I know, your Daddy *is* Whitey."

His hatred chilled me. He made me feel like I had grown up in a sheltered Pollyanna-land, which I hadn't. All I could think of to say was, "For your information, my Daddy ain't white." The moment the words tumbled from my mouth, I wanted to bite my tongue. *Ain't?* I never used the word *ain't*. Was I trying to impress Mark with the authenticity of my Blackness by talking some kind of imagined ghetto lingo? Had he succeeded in making me feel so deficient as a Black woman that I had to prove my legitimacy by speaking in street slang?

A wry smile twisted Mark's face. "Then," he spat in reply, "you' Momma."

He turned on his heel and walked away, clearly self-satisfied about having played me by delivering the ultimate Black culture insult under the guise of ordinary conversation.

After that encounter, I felt uncomfortable whenever I saw Mark, who conscientiously ignored me. He was mean, he had a chip on his shoulder, and he intimidated me. The way he called out my mixed-race background made me cautious about approaching the few other Black students on campus. I wondered what Daddy would have said to Mark. I was relieved when we finished the class we had together and I never saw him on campus after that.

When I registered for the spring semester, I was determined to enroll in a more advanced psychology course. My academic adviser recommended a class being taught by a guest lecturer, a specialist in the psychology of persecution, who had published a highly acclaimed book on the topic of torture. "Granted, it's not the most pleasant subject," my counselor admitted, "but I read his book and the material is fascinating, insightful about both victims and perpetrators. Since he's a guest lecturer, you would miss the opportunity to study with him if you don't jump on it this semester." I was intrigued, and signed up for it. That class changed my life.

It seemed impossible to me that a person who had been tortured could recover from that kind of trauma. Yet it happened. There was always irreparable damage, but often people recovered, became functional, and many even went on to do great things. I was fascinated by the process of healing from trauma, from extreme psychological illness, despair, and depression. I certainly admired people who pieced their lives back together, but even greater than my admiration for the healed was my admiration for the healers, who assisted survivors on their journey back from the underworld of their suffering. What exactly could a healer do to help a torture victim return to life, return to feeling grateful to be alive, or at the very least be able to love again? For torture was ultimately the antithesis of love. How did a torture victim regain the ability to experience joy, I wondered. Not just in an extravagantly joyous moment, such as the birth of a child, but also in an ordinary joyous moment, such as coming upon a spectacular magenta flower in a walk across a meadow.

Even as I planned to continue to take classes in drawing and painting, I decided I would declare my major in psychology. My parents had raised me not to turn away from the knowledge of injustice; they had raised me to act upon that knowledge whenever possible and to make a difference when I could, to work to change things for the better. I began to see a career for myself as a therapist and I thought that I would like to help people find their way out of the narrow places of the damaged soul. I began to understand what people meant when they said they "had a calling." This work was calling me.

One night, during the last week of my freshman year, I took a break from studying for my final exams and went for a walk on the quad, where I sat on a bench and looked up at the sky. I had recently read an article that said that astronomers have verified that many of the stars we see at night died billions of years ago and their light has taken so long to reach our eyes that we gaze on the radiance of a long-dead celestial body. Two shooting stars arced overhead, one right after the other. I felt awed by the vastness of the universe in comparison to my own small self.

When I stood up to leave, I discovered that I was sitting on a newspaper left behind by a previous occupant of the bench. Busy with my schoolwork, I rarely read the paper, but I picked up this one and took it with me. Back in my room, I browsed through the latest updates on life in the wide world, the newsprint rubbing off on my fingers and making my hands feel dry, until a caption caught my eye. It read CHURCHES BLOCK DEPORTATION OF TORTURED REFUGEES. The article described efforts by a coalition of churches and synagogues to prevent the Immigration and Naturalization Service ("INS" they called it) from returning a handful of Salvadoran refugees to their homeland. Advocates for the refugees claimed that the Salvadorans faced torture and execution if returned to El Salvador. The INS would not grant the refugees asylum, since they said they had no substantial evidence to corroborate the refugees' assertion that they would be in danger if they went home. The article quoted Reverend John West as saying, "Last month a young Salvadoran man, on the eve of his return to El Salvador, hanged himself in his INS cell. His terror was so great at the thought of returning to the hands of the death squads in El Salvador that he chose to put an end to his life, to have control over his own death. These people need our protection. They need our help." The INS claimed that the young man suffered from depression and blamed prison officials for failing to remove the man's belt from the cell. I carefully tore out the article and slipped it into the back of my book about the psychology of torture for safekeeping.

Six

WHEN I RETURNED TO Tucson for my sophomore year, while I was unpacking my books, I came across the article about the Salvadoran refugees and scanned it for the name of the group working on their behalf. It was called the Sanctuary Movement. I picked up a current newspaper and thumbed through it, looking for more information about the refugees and the activities of the Sanctuary Movement. In the community calendar section I found what I was looking for. A Sanctuary Movement meeting was to be held on the upcoming Thursday evening at a local church.

I took a bus to the church for the meeting at the appointed time. A nun named Sister Marianne hurried over to introduce herself and welcome me when I entered. A diminutive woman, Sister Marianne had thin blond hair cropped short to her jawline. Her skin was almost papery in its translucence. She had piercing green eyes and wore a navy-blue skirt and V-neck sweater with a white blouse and, of all things, a narrow, navy-blue necktie. The sister's attire resembled a parochial school uniform.

"What brings you to our meeting?" Sister Marianne asked me.

"I read about Sanctuary in the newspaper and I wanted to find out more," I told her. "What do you do exactly?"

"The Covenant of Sanctuary Congregations is a group of faith communities working together to provide services and protection for Central American, mostly Salvadoran, refugees," Sister Marianne explained. "Today's meeting is a planning meeting, and we're about to start, so I can't discuss this further with you. But next Thursday we are doing a presentation for the Buddhists at the Zen Center. Seven o'clock. That meeting will be more of an introduction to the Sanctuary Movement and more appropriate for a newcomer such as yourself. I can give you a flyer with the information. Will you come to that?"

"I will. I want to find out more about the refugees," I told the nun. "I want to find out how I can help."

"Absolutely come to the presentation at the Zen Center. In the meantime, take some literature to read." She pointed to a table loaded with pamphlets and handouts.

I picked up a few photocopied newspaper articles about the activities of the Sanctuary congregations. The articles described court cases against Sanctuary workers who had risked arrest for harboring undocumented refugees, and they cited biblical sources as well as the Geneva Conventions as support for the unlawful activity of aiding illegal aliens. I was intrigued and a little frightened. Then I came across a poorly copied brochure that said at the top LISTEN TO THE STORIES. The brochure contained four short autobiographical paragraphs that were horrific personal accounts. The first began "I am a Salvadoran schoolteacher. I participated in the Salvadoran teachers' union. For this I was arrested and tortured with acid." I read the brochure, mesmerized, and felt as though a layer of protection surrounding my heart had split, peeled back, and fallen away.

History was being made at that very moment, even as I was reading the brochure, and perhaps I had the power to change it. Of course I knew that torture happened in the world, but I suddenly felt as though I had just stumbled upon it in my own community. I wondered what I could do to help the people who had told their stories in the brochure.

That night images of the torture I had read about in the brochure lingered in my mind and prevented me from sleeping. Maybe I didn't have the stomach for this involvement. My imagination magnified the things I had read about the torture victims so that I could see them happening in my mind's eye. I had difficulty sleeping all week, but each night passed a little easier than the last. I was determined to attend the meeting to which Sister Marianne had invited me, and so on Thursday I took the bus to the Zen Center.

I chose a seat at the back of the meeting room, in case I needed to hastily step outside if one of the stories affected me too deeply. The event was in a small room furnished with folding metal chairs, all facing forward, and full of Buddhists in brown robes, heads shaved. I had assumed the Buddhists would be Asian, but not all of them were. I had also thought they would be men, but I saw many women among them. Nevertheless, I felt conspicuous as a non-Buddhist and because I was the only Black person there.

Sister Marianne hastened to welcome me. She took my hand and said, "I'm so glad you came. You'll learn much more about Sanctuary tonight. May I ask your denomination?"

At first I didn't understand. Then I realized that she was asking about my religion. "My mother is Jewish, my father is Baptist. But neither one of them is observant. They're artists. They worship at the theater."

Sister Marianne laughed.

"I went to a Baptist church with my grandmother while I was growing up," I added.

"I myself am Episcopalian. I was just curious about you; I hope you don't mind that I asked. Well, we're about to start now," Sister Marianne nodded toward the microphone and patted my shoulder, then she turned briskly and went to take a seat at the front.

A minister spoke first and explained the structure of the Sanctuary Movement, which was a group of faith communities working together. He told us how the movement started after Reverend John West had stumbled upon a group of Salvadoran refugees stranded in the desert after being abandoned by the guide who had brought them across the border illegally. Reverend West's church took on the task of offering these refugees, and others, sanctuary in their homes and in the church itself. As the group of Sanctuary congregations grew, they began to provide medical care, legal aid, food, shelter, clothing, and, most of all, an avenue for the refugees to speak the truth about their experiences and the state-sponsored terror in their homeland, which was largely a result of U.S. politics and interference to promote and protect corporate economic interests.

The minister introduced two Salvadorans who had come to give testimony to what they had witnessed in their country. Lupe spoke first, telling about her husband's involvement in a labor union, for which he was killed. A friend came to Lupe and warned her to flee. Before she ran away, she insisted on seeing her husband's body. She described the condition of his body to the audience. The Spanish interpreter choked on her words and had to stop Lupe for a moment to regain her composure. Lupe waited. The interpreter wept as she translated. Lupe had left her toddler behind with her mother and escaped over the border. Sister Marianne found Lupe, seven months pregnant, behind the Safeway in Tucson, picking spoiled vegetables out of a dumpster. She brought Lupe to Reverend West's church. Lupe concluded her testimony by saying that she hoped to bring her mother and young daughter to Tucson one day.

Lupe sat down and the audience rustled. Many of the Buddhists wiped their eyes with the billowed sleeves of their dull brown robes. I also had to brush away tears, and I felt some trepidation about hearing another difficult testimony. But this was why I had come and I remained steadfastly in my seat.

The next speaker took the microphone. "I am Gilberto," he said in musically accented English. The translator approached but Gilberto waved her aside. "I can speak English. You can hear me?"

People nodded.

"You can understand me?"

"We are listening," a man called to him.

"I am twenty-four years old. I come from Pico, a small farming town. Before the death squads came, my family lived on the same land since the time of the gods." Gilberto paused.

He inspected the audience, casting his gaze around the room. When his eyes came to rest on me, I held my breath. I had this crazy momentary fear that if I breathed out, my spirit would float from my mouth into the room. It seemed to me that he held me in his gaze for a terribly long time. Then his eyes moved on. The Buddhists waited patiently for Gilberto to continue.

"I come from Pico but my family does not live there anymore. When the death squads came, they killed members of our community. They killed people in the church who believed the liberation theology. They killed people who had family members who worked against the government or who had joined labor unions. Usually we did not even know what their family members had done, since they had left our town long before the death squads arrived.

"When they killed people, they left them on top of the ground for the vultures. My brothers and I buried these people. At first the soldiers did not bother us for doing this. But soon they told us it was against the law to bury these bodies. We buried them anyway. So they took the men in my family to a prison. They gave us no food. Only water. My father had a weak heart. This was very bad for him and made us worried. They took us to a room where a girl was tied to stakes on the floor. She was about fifteen years old. She was not a person we knew. She was naked." Gilberto stopped and wiped his forehead absently with his hand, as if to dispel the visual images his words brought to him. He cleared his throat.

I had an impulse to run out of the room before he said what happened to the girl. But then Gilberto looked directly at me. It seemed to me as if he was giving testimony to me personally, though of course I knew that was not the case.

"The officers told us to rape the girl. My father said, 'She is a child.' In the room was a Norte Americano. He wore a uniform of the United States Army. He gave the officers directions about what to do. He told them, 'Say you will shoot them if they don't rape the girl.' An officer turned to us and said, 'We will shoot you if you do not rape the girl.' My youngest brother fell to his knees and began to cry. They shot him dead. They took us to her at gunpoint. My brothers wept. I could not weep. I left my body behind in that room and I floated up to the ceiling from where I looked down. That is why I saw the Norte Americano continue to tell instructions to the officers. He said, 'Tell them you will cut off her breast if they do not rape her.' An officer repeated the threat to us in Spanish. The girl began to scream. My father moved toward the girl and tried to take off his belt but his hands were shaking too much. 'You are too slow,' they told him, and they cut off the girl's breast. The girl fainted."

A moan of pain passed through the Buddhists gathered in the room. My heart beat loudly in my chest. I covered it with my hand and breathed deeply.

"My brothers dropped to their knees, weeping, begging for mercy. I alone could not cry. I had left my body standing down in that room and

I floated up above. They rubbed the child's breast in our faces. We tasted her blood. They shot my brothers. They released me and my father. I do not know why they spared me. Who knows why they do anything they do?" Gilberto paused. "After we returned to our home, my father starved himself to death within a few weeks." Gilberto shook his head. "My mother was frantic when she could not get him to eat. All my father would tell her was 'I could not take my belt off quickly enough.' And she asked me over and over again what he meant. But I refused to tell her. After my father's death, our family left Pico. My mother lives now in Mexico in an abandoned railroad car with the wives and sisters and children. They wash clothes to earn money. I am a gardener. I send most of the money I earn to them. I earn good money in the U.S., much more than I could ever earn in Mexico. The women and children are safe in Mexico. But I may be sent back to El Salvador because I am illegal." Fear leapt from Gilberto's eyes. "If I am sent back, they will not release me a second time."

No one spoke. Gilberto waited for the Buddhists to absorb his words.

Eventually a man in the front row asked Gilberto, "What can we do?"

Gilberto responded proudly, with a defiant note in his voice. "Father Oscar Romero, a leader of my people, was asked that question by a Norte Americano once, and he answered, 'Tell the truth.' That is what you can do for us. Tell the truth. Listen to the truth. Remember the truth. Don't let them make you forget it." Gilberto sat down. The microphone stood like the silhouette of a lone heron.

Sister Marianne stepped up and outlined the services Sanctuary provided and listed upcoming events. She took care to point out which activities were legal and which were illegal. She noted some upcoming nonviolent civil disobedience trainings for people interested in participating in blockades at the airport or INS building when deportations were scheduled to take place. She pointed to a table of literature and then invited us to have tea and cookies.

I could not yet make the transition back into the tea-and-cookies everyday world. I discovered that I had been gripping my chair so hard that I had vivid red imprints across my palms. I rubbed my hands to bring the blood back into them.

Sister Marianne sat down next to me. "Are you OK?"

"You must listen to them give testimony all the time," I said. "How do you do it?"

"I cry a lot," Sister Marianne answered matter-of-factly. "And I talk to Him about it," she pointed upward.

"If they catch him and send him back, he will be killed, or worse. How can he be protected?"

"Who? Gil?" she asked.

"Yes. Gilberto, the man who spoke. How can he remain safely in this country?"

"He could be granted asylum by the government, but that's tricky. We must prove he would be killed if he returned. And of course the Big Boys over at the Pentagon and in the CIA would not like to hear him describe the Norte Americano who directed the torture when he was in prison, because of the implications. They would prefer that people like Gil would shut up. But we're looking into getting him asylum," Sister Marianne assured me. "It's a bit risky, and a long, slow process, like everything else. If I wasn't a nun, I'd marry him," she said, with a quick laugh.

"What do you mean?" I asked.

"It was a joke," Sister Marianne replied. "If he marries an American, he can stay."

"He could marry me," I blurted, without thinking. Sister Marianne scrutinized me as a bird would eye a bit of straw, assessing its potential for building a nest. Perhaps she was trying to decide whether or not to take me seriously. I was trying to decide that myself.

"I was kidding. Marriage is not to be taken lightly. It requires vows before God. And there are hundreds of Gilbertos. If you become involved in this work, you will meet new ones every day, and you can't marry them all. Imagine marrying the first Salvadoran refugee you meet. Oh my!" Sister Marianne clucked her tongue as she rose to leave. She handed me a piece of paper. "Here's my number. Call me and we'll figure out something you can do that is a little less dramatic than marrying our refugees."

I stood on wobbly legs and studied Gilberto, who had stationed himself by a window where he sipped a cup of tea. Then I walked swiftly across the room to him, held out my hand, and we shook. I fell into his eyes. Without letting go of his hand or flinching from his gaze, I said, in my best Spanish, "I am Miriam, I am pleased to make your acquaintance, and I would like to marry you. I am an American citizen."

Gilberto's face opened in a gentle smile. "A generous offer, Miriam-an-American-citizen," he said. "I am an American citizen too, but of the other America."

"If you marry me, you will be legal," I pointed out.

"That is why you wish to marry me?" Gilberto grinned impishly. "I had hoped it was my striking good looks."

I shrugged as I smiled shyly, suddenly tongue-tied.

"My friends call me Gil. Since a marriage proposal is now on the table, I assume I can count you as a friend?" The tension of having told his testimony and the absurdity of the situation he found himself in got the better of him and Gil burst into throaty and genuine laughter. I joined him as the startled Buddhists turned from their tea inquiringly.

Gil and I left the meeting together and took a bus to the college campus where we walked around for an hour. We sat on a bench on the quadrangle and talked, at first in English, and then in Spanish so I could practice. We talked until the hands of dawn drew aside the fabric of night and since, by morning, Gil had not come up with a viable argument against marriage, we went to city hall and picked up the paperwork necessary to get married. After that, Gil walked me back to my dormitory and then took the bus home to his room in a rabbi's house where he lived rent-free. I took a long, hot shower and went to sleep, skipping my classes. Less than a week after we had met, we officially became husband and wife.

I did not tell anyone what I had done, not my classmates or friends at school, not my roommate, not my parents. After I married Gil, I was filled with a tremendous sense of satisfaction and peace. I felt as though I had opened a door and found myself inside a room where I sat down in front of the amber glow of a fire that warmed me through to my bones.

Seven

ALTHOUGH I MARRIED GIL to protect him, we both knew from the moment we first spoke that we might remain married. But we needed to take the time to get to know one another and to decide where we wanted to go with our unusual relationship. The intensity of our initial encounter, and the bold leap we had taken, made us self-conscious in the beginning whenever we met again. We had to work at relaxing and speaking about ordinary things.

In the evenings, particularly on weekends, when I could take a break from my studies and Gil didn't have to rise early for work the following day, we frequently met at Pedro's, a little café, where we drank coffee together. We swapped stories from our childhoods. I described the circuslike environment of my parents' house and how I had grown up seeing my parents' friends on TV, performing on Broadway, playing music at smoky clubs in Greenwich Village, and having exhibits of their artwork in the museums and galleries. Nothing could have been further from my childhood in New York than Gil's childhood in the Salvadoran coffee fields. He grew up hunting birds and making scarecrows. The farmers in Pico could predict the weather by sniffing the air, and by the time Gil left home he could do the same. He described a childhood dominated by the land, with the sun as their clock and entire weeks spent in the fields with his father and uncles and brothers, planting, harvesting, treating soil, tending crops. He knew everything there was to know about growing coffee. His concept of a social gathering was church, which he no longer attended since he had his own maverick beliefs, a sort of home-baked version of liberation theology with a good measure of Thoreauvian individualized ethics thrown into the mix.

When I discovered that Gil had never been to the theater to see a play, I took him to a college production of *A Midsummer Night's Dream*. He loved it, despite the fact that he couldn't understand a word of Shakespearean English. He said he could see why it was called a "dream."

Gil referred to himself as a gardener, but in fact he possessed a genius for agriculture and had a particular talent for growing flowers and herbs. Through the rabbi with whom he lived rent-free, he had been introduced to people in need of his services and he had built up a clientele that kept him busy enough to support himself and to send money to his mother in Mexico. He designed, planted, and nurtured an amazing volume and variety of stunning landscapes. After his arrival in Tucson, he taught himself, virtually overnight, about an entire range of plants and soils that had been previously unfamiliar to him. Because he spoke English, he was hired to oversee several large gardens and he, in turn, hired other Salvadorans to work with him.

I insisted that Gil take me to tour each of the gardens he worked on, including some he no longer tended but had set up initially. We walked hand in hand through each one, while he explained what he had tried to do and what he was working on in them. I took my sketch pad and watercolors or pastels with me and often attempted to capture on paper the beauty of Gil's artistry as it bloomed on terraces and decks, thrived in raised beds, and clustered at the base of shrubs and trees. I sent a few of my drawings to Jade. Even though she had closed her gardening business when she became a therapist, she still did a lot of gardening at the house she shared with Aunt Sarah in Brooklyn and I knew she would appreciate Gil's handiwork.

The beauty that Gil's gardens brought to my life contrasted sharply with the horror of learning the details of Duarte's brutality in El Salvador. Gil and his émigré friends described life in El Salvador before Duarte as a lost Eden, though of course it was not that perfect. And they tried to describe to me what it meant to live in a country ruled by state-sponsored terror. Their stories horrified me and inspired me at the same time. My anger at what had happened to Gil's people fueled my growing fierce determination to find a way to undo the wrongs.

Through Gil, I began to discover the thriving community of illegal immigrants who had fled not only El Salvador, but Guatemala as well. Torn from their home communities, they created a new one in Tucson and gathered for life cycle events, holidays, birthdays, and, quite often, just for the pleasure of one another's company. As I became more involved in Gil's world, I spent hardly any time on campus outside of my classes and also did not spend much time with other students. I was more intent on getting to know the Central Americans and on improving my Spanish.

With Sister Marianne as my mentor, I organized an in-home maternal-care service so that the women who feared they would be deported if they went for medical visits could establish a relationship with doctors and midwives during their pregnancy and consequently have someone they trusted to deliver their babies by the time the babies were born. Before long, word spread in the community, and refugee women began to frequent certain clinics and doctors' offices where they felt safe. Thinking that a lot of these women would benefit from mental health services, I began working to form a network of local therapists familiar with post-traumatic stress disorder who would offer free counseling to refugees who had suffered torture.

Gil and I had been married for nearly two months before I plucked up the courage to tell my parents what I had done. They were so irreverent themselves (and hadn't even married each other) that I didn't think that they would mind. But I couldn't be sure how they would take it. When I told them that I had gotten married, Mama laughed her head off. She didn't hold the institution of marriage in high regard, and the whole thing made a great story for her to share with her Bohemian friends. She said she trusted my judgment and that she couldn't wait to meet her son-in-law. Daddy, on the other hand, grumbled considerably. I was his little girl and he admitted that he had a fantasy about giving me away in traditional style, a blushing bride swathed in layers of white satin and lace walking down the aisle on his arm while tears stood in everyone's eyes. Yet even while he complained, he assured me he'd get over it. I asked Mama if she would break the news to Grandma Ruth. I didn't think that my grandmother would take my marriage in stride as easily as my parents had.

"You should give her the news yourself," Daddy suggested, with a tone that implied that I needed to take responsibility for my actions.

"No, it's fine; I'd like to tell her," Mama swiftly countered.

"I'll bet you would," Daddy said, but he didn't argue.

Soon after learning about Gil, Mama and Daddy offered to fly him to New York with me for the Christmas holiday. They wanted to invite "the family" over on New Year's Eve to introduce Gil to everyone. I explained to Gil that by "the family," they meant their close circle of friends. He said that sounded a lot like village life in Pico and that he couldn't wait to see New York.

"You'll hate it," I warned him. "It's about as different from a Salvadoran coffee field as a lizard is from an ostrich."

"I don't want to live there," Gil scoffed, "I just want to see it. All those different people packed into one place. Central Park. The Empire State Building. The Statue of Liberty. I have dreamed about Lady Liberty. And I want to meet your father. A man can find out a lot about a woman by talking to her father, you know," he teased, his dark eyes twinkling beneath the fringes of his long eyelashes.

"What does that mean?" I countered, suspiciously.

"I'd like to meet your mother too," Gil added immediately.

"You slithered out of that one neatly, didn't you?" I noted.

He shrugged and flashed me a grin. For a moment I thought he might kiss me, and I wanted him to, but he didn't. I was determined to remain patient and give him the space to kiss me in his own good time, but I hoped it would be soon. Meanwhile, I looked forward to introducing Gil to my parents and their friends. I was proud of him and I liked being his wife. In fact, I was falling in love with him. I wondered if he felt the same way about me.

Two days before Christmas we boarded a plane bound for JFK. Gil had never flown before and he didn't like it. Gripped in a cold sweat, he clung to my hand for nearly an hour after takeoff. I sighed with relief when the plane circled over the diamond glitter of New York.

Daddy and Mama met us at the gate with a warm welcome that touched Gil. They presented me with a huge bouquet of peach-colored roses. We collected our bags at the baggage claim. I fished out an unusual dried desert weed, carefully wrapped in tissue paper, that I had brought for Mama. Then Daddy got the car and picked us up in front of the terminal. He pointed out the sights to Gil as we wound our way through the traffic, across the web of the city, and into the friendly embrace of the Village. The radiant lights of the city dazzled Gil. Daddy parked the car in the garage and asked, "What do you think, so far?"

"When a person like me is living in the developing world and sees his family suffer under the thumb of a brutal dictatorship, and when that person sees his country struggling with poor resources, disease, these kinds of things, well, that person sometimes imagines coming to New York. I think everyone in my country imagines what it would be like to come to New York. It's the city of opportunity and prosperity, the city with everything. A man can make something of himself in New York with so many possibilities. When I was in prison with my brothers, I closed my eyes and pretended I was in New York, walking on the street, wearing good clothes, money in my pocket, my family safe at home in a white house with green shutters and flowers at the windows. I imagined that my nephew would play the saxophone. Now, finally, here I am in New York."

I studied Gil's striking Aztecan profile as he spoke. He had never shared his fantasy of New York with me. How long would it take for me to know him?

"New York certainly holds prosperity," Daddy said, "for a few people. But most of the people you see on the streets don't have much money in their pockets. They scramble to survive in the most expensive city in the world. You're lucky to live in Tucson."

Daddy carried my suitcase into the house and up the stairs, as Gil, who carried his own suitcase, followed. I trailed behind them. Daddy oriented Gil to his surroundings as we went.

"The bathroom is there. Those are the back stairs leading to the kitchen. Fresh towels in the linen closet," he said, motioning with his hand. Daddy plopped my bag down in my bedroom while Gil stood in the middle of the room, shifting awkwardly from one foot to the other.

"Is everything OK?" Daddy asked.

"Yes. Everything is fine," Gil replied. He glanced around, taking in the queen-size bed, blanketed with an elaborate handmade quilt, and the colorful framed prints on the walls that depicted Black children playing, Black musicians performing, and Black women engaged in a spirited game of bid whist.

When Daddy left, Gil sat gingerly on the edge of the bed and said, "They expect us to share a room."

"Well, we *are* married, aren't we?" I replied. "They don't know that we haven't slept together."

Gil nodded and came to stand in front of me. He put his hands around my waist, pulled me toward him, and he kissed me. Finally!

"I'm old-fashioned," he said.

"I know you are," I answered.

Gil released me and went to wash up, while I headed downstairs to the studio to see what my parents had on the drawing board. They were working on a children's book, set in Tibet, a folk legend. Library books open to images of intricate Tibetan woven fabrics spilled over from the worktable and littered the floor. On the drawing board there was a partially completed picture of a little boy talking to a bird, the boy's elaborate slippers a tribute to Mama's careful research.

True to form, Mama hadn't cooked anything for dinner. Instead she had scouted out a Salvadoran restaurant. We ate *pupusas* and *yuca frita* that were just as good as the ones that Gil's friends cooked in Tucson. Gil was pleased that my parents took him for traditional food from his homeland.

Back at the house, as we shrugged out of our coats and unwrapped our scarves from our necks in the entranceway, Mama asked Gil, "Does caffeine keep you awake?"

"I was raised in the coffee fields," he answered with a laugh.

"Match made in heaven," Mama remarked. "Our family loves a good cup of java. And *that* I know how to make. I have a Kenyan blend you have got to try."

It was cozy coming into the warm living room from the cold street. "I love this house," Gil said quietly to me in Spanish. "Everywhere I look I see something beautiful. Like that pitcher," he said, as he pointed to a pewter pitcher brimming with peacock feathers and pussy willows that stood on the corner of a desk. "The way it's just underneath that print of peacock feathers with the pewter frame that matches the pitcher. Even the pillows," he said, gesturing toward the assortment of handmade pillows on the couches, each one with a unique pattern but all in the same range of aqua, turquoise, and periwinkle blues.

I told Gil, "It was a good house to grow up in." I tried to imagine how the familiar beauty of my parents' home appeared to an outsider. At first glance it looked cluttered, but the contents of that clutter were carefully selected by my parents. I left Gil in the living room and followed Mama into the kitchen to make coffee. When we returned with the coffee, Daddy and Gil were poring over photography books with vintage photographs of Harlem. As Mama set the coffee tray down, I warned Gil in Spanish, "My mother's coffee is extra strong."

"She's talking about my coffee, isn't she?" Mama asked. "No fair. Speak English."

"She's just telling me that you make an excellent cup of coffee," Gil said as he winked at me.

"No coffee for me," I told the others. "I'm going to bed." I wondered if they would talk about me once I had left the room, but I was exhausted from the long day of travel. I gave everyone a peck on the cheek, and headed upstairs. I wanted to make love to Gil, but not when I was this tired. It had to be right. It had to be special. I fell asleep the second my head hit the pillow and I didn't even hear Gil come in later.

The next morning, I slipped quietly out of bed without waking Gil. I knew I was avoiding the whole issue of our attraction to each other by leaving the bed early, but I didn't want to seem too forward and I was generally anxious about how I should behave. He was, after all, as he had said, old-fashioned, and he was Salvadoran. I didn't feel comfortable taking the lead when it came to sex. In his culture, that was the man's role. I would wait for him to make the first move.

When Gil finally came downstairs in the late morning, Mama and Daddy were in the studio working and I was on the sun porch reading. He helped himself to coffee and a bagel from the large butcher block stand in the kitchen and I sat with him while he ate. I liked to watch the clean curve of his jaw as he chewed. He was compact and muscular, and he moved with a restrained gentle power.

"What is that satisfied smile about?" Gil asked me, as he took a deep sip of Mama's Kenyan coffee.

"I was noticing how handsome you are," I said quietly.

His face became serious. "If I pay you a compliment now, it will sound like I'm just returning a favor." He reached across the table and held some of my braids in his hand, then brushed my cheek and let his hand come to rest on my neck. "But it is not a favor when I say that you are so beautiful that sometimes I wonder if I am dreaming that you married me." I covered his hand with mine and held it against my neck for a minute before releasing it. It was a miracle that the two of us had found each other at all in the wide world, and an even greater miracle that we were married.

"You aren't dreaming," I said.

In the afternoon, Grandma Ruth came into the city to see me and to meet Gil.

After introductions, Gil said, "So, Grandma Ruth, half the Salvadoran community of Tucson is waiting patiently for your chocolate-chip-walnut cookie recipe."

Grandma laughed with pleasure.

"We had the most delicious Salvadoran food last night," I told her, "at this restaurant that Mama found. We have to take you there sometime."

"OK, if it's not too spicy," Grandma Ruth said. "I can't handle those hot chilies."

"But you're not shy when it comes to butter," Gil noted. "I can tell from those cookies."

"If you put enough butter in anything, it will taste delicious," Grandma Ruth said.

I had briefed Gil on how much Grandma Ruth loved to cook and I could tell that he had deliberately chosen to talk with her about food since he knew it was a topic dear to her heart. He was that kind of thoughtful.

Mama and Daddy had suggested a trip to the botanical gardens for the afternoon because they thought that Gil would find them particularly interesting. While we walked through the gardens, Grandma Ruth took my arm and leaned close to my ear. "I like him very much," she said. "He seems kind and smart. He is soft-spoken like you, Miriam. I was worried that you had rushed into something that wouldn't work, but this is good."

After Grandma Ruth went home, the rest of us went to Margaret and Gloria's for Christmas Eve dinner. It turned out that Gloria had spent time in the area of Mexico where Gil's family lived. They spoke together in rapid Spanish and I could barely keep up. We returned home on Christmas Eve fairly early because we would be going to Big Momma's house first thing in the morning. Mama and Daddy went straight to bed.

So there we were, Gil and I, on Christmas Eve, with that big bed in the middle of the room staring at us like a baffled elephant. Gil removed his shoes and lay fully clothed, straight as bamboo, on top of the blankets. I put on my nightgown in the bathroom and slipped into the other side of the bed where I, too, lay tensely on my back.

"I'll see you at Christmas," Gil said.

I didn't trust my voice. I turned off the bedside lamp. We stared with wide-open eyes at the ceiling in the dim glow of the streetlamps that crept through the windows. I imagined my eyes were fluorescent and as large as tennis balls as I attempted to calm myself. I wondered if Gil could hear how heavily I was breathing. Try as I might, I could not slow my breathing down. Our relationship had begun so abruptly. Our work together in Sanctuary had immediately been so intense. Then all those evenings at Pedro's, getting to know each other, almost a systematic education in one another. Now here we were, side by side in the dark, in my girlhood bed. I wanted to place my palm on Gil's smooth chest and run my fingers down the length of his body, to touch the firm muscles on the back of his thighs. And I wanted to touch him between his legs. I could not bear the wild swirl of my blood beating within me and I drew a word up out of the dreadful well of silence.

"Gil?"

"Mm?"

"Have you ever . . . ?" I started but did not finish.

He answered quickly, "No, never."

"Me neither," I confessed. I felt like we were speaking a forbidden language.

"Do you want to now?" Gil asked.

I steadied my voice to answer over the din of my pounding heart. "I want to with you."

Gil leaned across me and turned the bedside lamp back on. The pressure of his chest against mine as he reached for the lamp made my blood rush with wanting him. His lips were tender and luscious, like a ripe mango. Our hands sought each other with hungry discovery.

Christmas morning dawned like the golden Aztec culture dawning on the Americas. Under the tree, I found my gift from Gil in a small blue velvet box. It was a gold wedding band, engraved inside with FROM G. TO M. 1986.

Eight

 UPON OUR RETURN TO Tucson, we looked for a place to move in together. The tragedies experienced by Gil and the Central Americans whom I met through him were so dramatically different from the lives of my peers on campus that I felt like I didn't fit in at school anymore. And besides, I was married. Gil found a double-wide trailer for rent on three acres of land. He wanted to keep chickens and a goat and he wanted his own garden. When I called my parents and told them about the trailer and the land, Daddy suggested that he could help us buy a piece of property in the Tucson area. "Why throw your money away on a rental? It makes more sense to invest," he said.

I was lucky to have parents who could help us out with such a generous offer and I trusted Daddy to advise me so that I would make good decisions about my finances. While we started looking for the right parcel to buy, we moved into the trailer.

Gil and I were grateful for the life we had together. It was a far sight better than the lives of other refugees we knew. And much better than the circumstances under which Gil's family lived in that railroad car in Mexico. Gil hadn't seen his family in three years and he wished that he could get his mother into an apartment. Aunt Soph was an immigration lawyer and we called her to find out what Gil had to do to be able to visit his family and still be able to return to the U.S. afterward. She started working with us to help him become an official U.S. citizen.

When we began sleeping together, Gil alerted me that he had nightmares, so I was forewarned the first time a moaning rattle coming from deep in Gil's throat brought me out of sleep to find him sweating and disoriented. In sleep, Gil was stripped of his defenses and the images of death and torture that he had witnessed were able to enter his subconscious. I held him until he stopped trembling. He lay awake staring at the ceiling for the rest of the night. I put my head on his chest and he stroked my hair until eventually I fell asleep, just as the sunrise spread a pearly film across the sky. Whenever Gil gave testimony for one of Sister Marianne's recruitment meetings, we could depend on a sleepless night.

It made sense that Gil would have nightmares. But when I started having nightmares soon after we moved in together, it took us both by surprise. I dreamt that I was sitting on a prison cot, listening to the screams of children.

"I wonder if your nightmares are because of me," Gil said. "You didn't have them until you started sleeping with me. Maybe we should sleep in separate beds," he suggested, halfheartedly.

"Never. I want to be next to you all night long," I said, as I curled against him. "Just in case something comes up," I added, with a smile.

He laughed. Then he said, seriously, "I think you should stop going to hear testimony. Your dreams might be your way of processing information you hear about what we suffered in El Salvador. If the stories disturb you so much, then you should stop listening to them."

"I don't think I'm dreaming about El Salvador. My nightmares are about somewhere else. I don't know where they come from, but they're mine, not yours. The worst part is that I'm afraid that in one of them I'll see what makes the children scream."

"You've never experienced torture, yet your psyche behaves as if you had," Gil observed. "Don't you find that strange?"

"Very strange," I agreed. "At least we know exactly why you're having nightmares."

"You're the psychologist," Gil pointed out "What do we do?"

"You could start by trying not to blame yourself for surviving when they shot your family," I told Gil, gently. "You didn't do anything wrong."

"I survived because I showed no compassion. If I had cried as my brothers had, then I would be dead," Gil said.

"None of you would have wound up there in the first place if you hadn't done the decent thing and buried the dead," I reminded him. "And where would your family be now if they had shot you too? Maybe it would help if you saw a therapist."

"A therapist?" Gil scoffed. "And what would I say to this stranger? Even if I tell a therapist my story, what can he do to help? He'll just tell me that I'm suffering because of what happened to me and my family. I know that already. If just knowing why I have nightmares would make them go away, then they would already have disappeared. You could dig up your past, and examine all the things that happened to you, and say this is the reason for this and this is why this bothers you or why you like that. But, guess what? This will still bother you and you will still like that. How does therapy change anything?"

I wanted to explain the positive impact of therapy while at the same time honoring Gil's perspective. "Therapy helps some people and doesn't help others, depending on the person and the circumstances and, of course, the therapist. A good therapist can help a person accept that a difficult experience happened and then find a way to move past it. I think people need a safe and private place to talk about their experience and sort it out in their mind. To try to make sense out of it."

"You can't make sense out of torture," Gil replied emphatically. "That's the most frightening thing about it, that it doesn't make sense."

I propped myself up on one elbow; the cascade of my hair, woven into tiny braids, slapped against my pillow. "I hope I'm a safe place, out of harm's way, where you can make sense out of things."

"What are you trying to say?" Gil asked.

"I'm trying to say that I love you."

Nine

TO BEGIN WITH, MY Sanctuary work took the form of helping acquire services for the refugees, but by the time Gil and I celebrated our first wedding anniversary, I had decided that I wanted to do something to express my anger at the failed politics of the situation and to defy our wrongheaded U.S. government. In El Salvador people risked their lives every day to perform ordinary, decent acts, like burying the dead. I wanted to take stronger action.

"I want to become an activist," I told Gil in Spanish, for we had become accustomed to speaking in Spanish together most of the time.

"Like what? What do you want to do?" Gil asked, his dark eyebrows pinched together with worry.

"I want to lay down in front of a truck taking refugees to the airport for deportation," I told him with resolve.

"What if the truck runs over you?" he asked.

"It won't. I'll just get arrested, that's all. In fact, it will probably not even stop the deportation, but at least I will have done something," I said.

"How do you know? It could run over you."

"I'll do it with a lot of other people."

"What if it runs over all of you?"

"We live in the U.S.A. They can't do that," I assured him with growing impatience. I was a little surprised that he was trying to dissuade me.

"They can do that anywhere."

"They won't."

"You can't predict what they'll do."

"I'll take the nonviolent civil disobedience training course at Sister Marianne's church and I'll choose the right time. I'll be careful. Getting arrested here is different from getting arrested in El Salvador," I reminded him. "And there's something else we can do that's important. We can take in refugees and give them a place to live," I continued. We would have the space to make this offer soon enough, for Gil had found a piece of property for us to buy and, with financial help from my parents, we were in escrow. Soon it would be ours.

The property was a dusty twenty-acre farm with a rambling house, a barn, chicken coops, and run-down orchards begging for attention. The house needed repairs, but nothing serious, nothing Gil couldn't handle. The main attraction was the twenty acres and a good well. A substantial portion of the property was graced with an excellent irrigation system and Gil had pronounced it arable. With some hard work, Gil believed he could develop the property into a functional and possibly lucrative business. We named it Esperanza Farm.

When I started talking about taking in refugees, Gil worried that friends, acquaintances, and complete strangers would soon be camping in shanties all over his beautiful land and sleeping rolled up in rows in his living room.

"I'm not opposed to helping others who have nowhere to stay, but I don't want to have a tent city," he said.

"For starters, what about bringing your family here?"

"Here?"

"To Esperanza Farm. We could get them out of that railroad car."

"It's too dangerous. They could be caught and returned to El Salvador."

"How safe are they in Mexico?"

"Safer than they would be here."

"If they're caught, can't they just go back to Mexico?"

"If they're caught, they won't have any choice about where they're sent. The INS will decide that for them. It's way too risky."

I scrutinized him. "There's more to it than that, isn't there? What is it?"

"It's not a straightforward issue. Even if it were safe here, it would be a huge culture shock. I wish my father was still alive; he would know what to do. I miss him every day." Gil contemplated his folded hands as if they held an answer for him.

I kneeled at Gil's feet and leaned my arms on his knees. I looked up into his face, which so often opened for me like a flower. "If we can ever find a way, if the obstacles can be removed, then it's an option that I would welcome."

As soon as we moved to Esperanza, I befriended our neighbor, a Pomo Native named Annie, who had moved to Tucson from Northern California to live with her husband, John, a Navajo horse breeder. The first time I saw Annie, she appeared in my yard on horseback, with the sun tangled in her hair. She handed me a bag of apples as a housewarming gift before she dismounted and accepted my offer of a cup of coffee.

"Don't ask me what a Pomo is doing living by the desert," Annie told me. "My tribe is on the Redwood Coast, by the Pacific Ocean, the land of the giant trees. But here I am." Annie was short and wide and firmly centered on the earth. She had thick wavy hair, a broad nose, and small, dark eyes that didn't miss a detail. Contrary to the image of Natives as nonverbal communicators that was perpetuated in the mainstream media, Annie talked incessantly and shared her opinion on every subject. She worked in Tucson as a physician's assistant at a low-income health clinic, and once we started to get to know one another I was able to catch a ride to campus and back with her three days a week, which saved Gil from having to take me and made it easier for him to get to his gardening jobs on time.

A man of few words, Annie's husband, John, talked more to horses than to people. He towered well over six feet. Spending time around Annie and John and their horses made me want horses of my own. Gil was accumulating a variety of livestock, but no horses. He said they were too expensive to care for until I graduated and started to earn an income. Gil did most of the work around Esperanza because so much of my time was taken up with school and the work I did helping Sister Marianne. But I was eager to learn about how to care for livestock and plants, and he was willing to teach me.

I didn't bring up the issue of Gil's family coming to Tucson again. I left it up to him to proceed if he chose to do so, recognizing that it was no small matter and might not even be possible. But I did pursue my plan to provide shelter to other refugees. The first person who came to live in our house was Alejandro, who had grown up in San Salvador, the capital of El Salvador, and he was a poet and had been a political activist in El Salvador. He knew nothing about gardening when he came to Tucson, but Gil befriended him and taught him enough about gardening to be useful. Gil hired him to help in his larger gardens.

"Where I plant, concrete grows," Alejandro would say.

He and Gil called each other City Cousin and Country Cousin. Alejandro was living in the basement of Sister Marianne's church when I suggested to Gil that we offer him a room in our house. We had not been living at Esperanza Farm six weeks when Alejandro moved in.

As a native New Yorker, who grew up without so much as a pet goldfish, I never could have anticipated how much I would love our farm animals. We adopted a border collie, whom we named Paz. Gil took him to obedience school and trained him in over forty commands. Gil said that if we had a herd of goats and sheep eventually, as he anticipated, then he would need Paz to know those commands. Paz made us laugh whenever he attempted to herd our three cats, who were supposed to live in the barn and work as mousers. But my favorite, Bella, a petite black cat with green eyes, figured out that if she snuck into the house, I wouldn't put her out. She liked to install herself in my lap while I studied at my desk in the evenings.

I decided before we moved in that I wanted to bring the orchards back from their decline. Although my spare time was limited because of my studies, I made the orchard my first priority at the farm. I took a work-shop in tree pruning and then I put what I had learned to good use by doing some work on the existing fruit trees. I planted more bare root trees during our first winter on the land. It was inexpensive to buy the trees as bare root. I put in Bing, Rainier, and Royal Anne cherry trees. The existing orchard had several mature cherry trees already, and when they flowered in the spring, they took my breath away. I erected elaborate scarecrows, posted plastic owls with giant yellow eyes, and hung shiny Mylar strips to protect the fruit from marauding crows, jays, and other winged thieves.

Annie grew about a million pumpkins during that first autumn after we moved to Esperanza. Over the winter, she taught me how to cook pump-kins into soups, pies, puddings, muffins, and breads. When my orchard began fruiting in the spring, Annie gave me a crash course in canning and preserving and I enlisted Alejandro to help me. What he lacked as a gardener he made up for as a cook. He knew how to prepare many tradi-tional Salvadoran dishes, and Gil and I reaped the rewards.

As I settled into country life, I discovered that digging in the soil, put-ting up jam, walking Paz, and collecting warm eggs from under the chick-ens renewed my spirit and helped me cope with the often difficult work I did to help the Salvadorans. From our first week on the land, I began the habit of lighting candles on Friday night. Although Mama performed few Jewish customs, she had lit Sabbath candles every Friday night at sun-down while I was growing up. I followed in her footsteps. I didn't know the correct Jewish prayer for candle-lighting, so I said my own prayer, thanking the spirit that permeates all things for the good fortune I had received in my life. As often as possible, I tried to make time to sit on the bench on our porch and watch the sunset on Friday nights. Sometimes Gil and Alejandro came home in time to join me. On a clear night, after the sky faded to rose, orange, and finally the deep cobalt blue of oncom-ing night, I loved to watch the stars appear, gradually at first, and then bursting across the sky all at once, like iridescent confetti. Watching the Friday sunset centered and focused me for the weekend.

Ten

ONE DAY, WHEN GIL had no work for Alejandro, he went to pick fruit with some day laborers. He didn't show up that evening for dinner and we were immediately worried. Gil called Sister Marianne. By the next day, she had determined that the INS had picked up Alejandro along with the other day laborers. They were being held at an INS detention center. Naturally, Alejandro did not divulge any information about where he had been living because he didn't want us to be arrested for harboring him.

Alejandro's father had smuggled him out of El Salvador at great expense after a comrade, under torture, identified Alejandro as a Sandinista rebel. Alejandro's father tread carefully to maintain his position in El Salvador and to keep his family safe. He publicly disowned Alejandro to protect the rest of the family, even while he secretly arranged for his son's escape. Alejandro was the genuine article, a true revolutionary whose life would be in danger should he be returned to El Salvador. His poetry was widely known in El Salvador and was heavily rooted in the liberation theology that Duarte was attempting to suppress. Yet when the INS detained him, they seemed oblivious to the danger he was in and determined to make an example out of him by sending him back. Gil said that if Alejandro was sent home, he would face charges of treason. He would certainly be beaten, probably tortured, and it was likely he would be executed. Alejandro spent four months in an INS prison while Sister Marianne and her legal consultants tried to have him granted political asylum, to no avail, despite the fact that he was exactly the sort of person for which political asylum was created. The date for his deportation was set. He and twenty-two other refugees, including three children, were slated to be returned to El Salvador together.

The INS wanted a showdown, and some of us Sanctuary workers were preparing to give it to them. The time had come for me to sit in front of a truck. I attended a meeting at Sister Marianne's church where those of us planning to disrupt the deportation were briefed on the latest developments. The INS had announced the deportation date, but Sister Marianne warned us that it might be a ploy. The INS might ship the deportees out on the day before, when no one was looking. It became increasingly challenging for me to concentrate on my schoolwork with this life-and-death situation unfolding in my personal life.

Gil had gotten into the habit of coming by the campus at the end of the day in his battered Ford pickup to collect me. Then we went home, where we fed the animals and milked the goats, and ate dinner. After Alejandro's arrest, we often went to the prison in the evening to try to see him. Sometimes we were allowed in and sometimes not.

Two days before the deportation, as we drove home, Gil announced, "It's no good, Miriam."

"What do you mean?" I asked.

"The INS wants to make an example of him. Sanctuary wants to make an example of him. But in the end, the INS will send him home to Duarte, who will murder him."

"Not if enough of us go out there on Thursday and blockade."

"Do you think you can stop the bus or the airplane or whatever will carry him? You? A pesky flea? They will swat you aside and make the deportation."

"You know how much I have wanted to take action, and this is a moment that feels right to me. I refuse to sit idly by on this one. If the eyes of the world are on him when he returns to El Salvador, how can the government harm him? We must turn a spotlight on him to protect him. Then the Salvadoran authorities will look like monsters to the rest of the world if they harm him."

"Do they care? Not at all. The U.S., the most powerful nation on the globe, is their ally no matter what they do. Killing Alejandro will have no consequences. This time next week he will be dead in my country. The INS either doesn't believe this or doesn't much care. You and Sister Marianne will hope. Alejandro thinks his father will protect him. But Alejandro has one foot in his grave," Gil predicted bitterly.

The night before the deportation, we couldn't sleep, which was just as well since we both probably would have had nightmares. We lay together, entwined, talking softly in Spanish. I planned to blockade in the morning and would likely be arrested. Gil was terrified of watching me taken off to prison.

"We live in the U.S.A. and I'll go to jail with many other people. There are at least six hundred people who plan to demonstrate. There's safety in numbers. Our arrests will be publicized. I won't be tortured," I reassured him.

"Be realistic, Miriam," he replied. "You are placing yourself in greater danger than your white friends because of your color."

"When I did my nonviolence training, the trainer spoke about the dangers for people of color, gays, and the disabled in prison. We did a role-playing exercise around protecting and shielding those more vulnerable among us. I trust the others who will be there with me." But even as I reassured Gil, I took his words to heart and knew that I was indeed in greater danger than my white counterparts.

The INS conducted the deportation as scheduled. They loaded the deportees on a bus at the detention center and prepared to shuttle them to the airport. Starting before sunrise, Sanctuary workers sat down in teams in front of the bus that carried the refugees as it attempted to make its way to the airport. It was a brisk, spring day that smelled vaguely of fresh soil. When I arrived at the detention center, a group of fifteen people, many of whom wore nuns' habits or the brown robes of Buddhist monks, sat in the road, arms linked at the elbow. The police proved respectful and controlled, the arbiters of a surprisingly civilized scene. The police announced through megaphones that the demonstrators were blocking a public road and would be forcibly removed and arrested if they did not disperse.

When the group did not disperse, the police systematically lifted and handcuffed each person and led them to a waiting bus. I watched as a bus of protestors filled and the police brought another bus in. Every time a line of protestors was removed, the bus loaded with the refugees to be deported inched forward a few more yards. A new line of protestors sat down. The police arrested them. Standing by the roadside, I chanted "*The whole world is watching*," while Gil's grim words about Alejandro's fate echoed chillingly in my mind.

The sun had risen high in the sky by the time my group of Sanctuary workers sat in the road. Sister Marianne was in my group, and as we settled ourselves on the hard pavement, I heard her say, "This is God's work." We linked arms, as did the whole line of protestors who sat in front of the yellow deportation bus. My heart hammered in my chest and I was too filled with emotion to join in the chanting. I was proud to see how many demonstrators had turned out, waves upon waves. I imagined the waves would never stop, as many waves as the ocean, enough waves to prevent the bus from ever leaving. My jaw clenched. "We must stop this madness right here," I said to no one in particular, but Sister Marianne squeezed my hand, so I knew she had heard me.

A young policeman grasped my upper arm and lifted me off the ground. I looked into his sea-blue eyes. "Do you think these people should be sent home to certain death?" I asked him.

He suppressed a paternalistic, smug smile. "They're completely safe. They're here to take our jobs and cash in on our welfare system."

"Did you know that one of the men on that bus came here to escape execution?" I asked.

"I think you're mistaken," the policeman replied.

My arresting officer and I walked over to the waiting bus, which was already half filled with protestors, as if we were out on a leisurely stroll together, old acquaintances. No one would have suspected our conversation from appearances. I remained polite and cooperative and the policeman handled me gently.

"You seem like a nice young lady," the policeman said to me. "I'm sorry to have to arrest you, but you have broken the law," he said, as he snapped the metal handcuffs shut behind my back.

"Don't believe everything they tell you," I told him. "Ask questions. Find out the truth." My eyes locked with his for a long moment. Then I looked back at the bus of refugees. A new group of protestors had seated themselves in the road. I searched for Alejandro's face in the bus windows. And then I heard his voice calling to me: "Miriam, Miriam, I see you!"

"I see you too," I shouted to him, and then my eyes filled with tears, which I couldn't brush away because my hands were cuffed behind my back.

"*Adios*," Alejandro shouted in Spanish, "God bless you. We will see each other again soon." His familiar smile broke my heart.

By this time next week, Gil had predicted.

"*Gracias*," Alejandro called. "*Gracias por todo!*"

"*De nada*," I called back. It was nothing. Could I have done more? The policeman guided me onto the prison bus, which drove away to a clean, well-lit jail.

The police arrested over eight hundred of us that day; nearly six hundred were women. They did not have sufficient space in the local prison to house us protestors and they had prepared in advance for this situation by setting up red and white striped event tents on the prison grounds. When my bus pulled into the facility, they unloaded us, removed our handcuffs, and led each person through a fingerprinting and photographing process. After this, each protestor checked in with a nurse, who asked about any medical conditions that needed attention. I get a free health screening, I thought, with dark humor.

We were taken to a yard strewn with straw where we were each given a blanket, a bar of soap, and a toothbrush (though no toothpaste to go with it). Then we were assigned to one of the tents where we each claimed a cot. My co-demonstrators, determined to make good use of our time in jail, proceeded to organize workshops on a host of topics; each workshop met in its own area inside the tent. Guards stood at the tent flap doorways.

In the evening, after a supper of greasy sauce flecked with mystery meat poured over toast and accompanied by an extremely salty coleslaw, the lawyers on the legal aid committee for Sanctuary visited us and met with chosen spokespeople from our group. According to the lawyers, the judge planned to hold a group arraignment in the morning and to sentence us with a stiff fine as well as community service. We chose not to cooperate with an arraignment if the sentence included a fine, since many among us didn't have much money. We instructed legal aid to return to the judge and request a sentence of community service only. We agreed on a policy of noncooperation until assured of an acceptable sentence.

I stayed close to Sister Marianne, who was a seasoned protestor. Her proximity steadied and comforted me. Exhausted, most of us women went to bed early, despite the late evening light that clung to the day. I dropped into a deep sleep. In the early morning hours, I had one of my nightmares. I woke drenched in sweat, remembering only the tail end of the dream, when I had turned to a child sitting next to me and asked, "Are they taking you from me to torture you in real life or just in this dream?" The child answered, "Just in this dream."

From my cot I watched the sunrise wash layer after layer of gray-blue light into the tent of sleeping women. As the women began to stir, a wispy voice from the cot next to me said, "You didn't sleep well."

I turned on my side and propped my head up on my hand to stare into violet, faded eyes under a fleece of disheveled white hair.

"I have bad dreams sometimes," I said quietly.

"You were speaking in your sleep."

"What did I say?"

"I couldn't make out any of your words," the woman said.

"I have a hard time hearing stories about torture." I sighed.

The woman nodded. "We all do."

"I have dreams in which I have children and they are being tortured. I don't have any children in real life."

"Perhaps you're experiencing flashbacks to a previous life in which you and your children were tortured."

Her words gave me pause. It had not occurred to me that my dreams could be memories. If that was the case, what was I slowly remembering?

"If something happened to me in a previous life that was so horrible that it stayed with me across another lifetime, I hope I don't remember any more of it," I told her.

"Understood," she replied simply.

I took my turn with the others getting cleaned up quickly in a chilly communal bathroom and standing in line for cold cereal and milk. Our decision-making body was called the spokescouncil, and they met with legal aid right after breakfast. The spokescouncil reported back to us that the judge would not relent on his intention to fine us and that the plan was to stand firm in our resolve to refuse to go to arraignment until he agreed to community service only. We thought the judge would not opt for the bad press of having us physically dragged into court. It looked as if we would have to dig in and face a standoff with the judge. But the worst news of the day was that the INS had successfully deported the refugees. No information as to their fate had emerged from El Salvador yet.

During the day, we had access to an exercise yard, our sleeping tents, and a row of Porta-Potties. Although watched by many guards, both male and female, we were left undisturbed. We conducted workshops to make good use of our time. I had a chance to call Gil after supper, when they allowed us to use a bank of pay phones. He said he was going to Annie and John's for supper. After we hung up, I remembered that march that Daddy had taken me to when I was a little girl. When this was over, I would tell Daddy about it. I knew he would be proud of me, and it made me proud of myself. I'm your daughter, Daddy, I thought.

The following day, legal aid brought news of the deported refugees. All of them had been detained for questioning in the prison in San Salvador, all except for a woman named Maria and her children. Those of us who knew about Maria wept at this news. I had known her personally and remembered my last glimpse of her through the window of the deportation bus. She had an abusive husband who was a high-ranking official. She had likely been released to him and he would probably beat her to death sooner rather than later. In El Salvador, there were no women's shelters or safe houses. There was nowhere for her to seek refuge. What would become of her children?

Sister Marianne told me that as far as she had heard, no news about the deportees had appeared in the media, which focused on us protestors instead.

We jokingly referred to our tents as the Juliana Peace Camp because we were on the grounds of the Juliana Correctional Facility. Some of the women spent that whole second day organizing a talent show to raise our spirits. We needed something to take our minds off the fate of the deportees, and the fact of our imprisonment reminded us constantly of those other quite different imprisonments in El Salvador.

I sang in a gospel choir at the talent show. After our choir sang, a Jewish choir performed. They sang a couple of Ladino (a Judeo-Spanish language) songs from the Sephardic culture and I could understand the words because of my knowledge of Spanish. They also sang an Israeli song in Hebrew. I had never heard either of these types of music before and the songs sounded ancient and exotic to me and gave me goose bumps. Afterward, I sought out the choir leader, a professional cantor named Sherri. I complimented Sherri on putting together such a beautiful performance on a moment's notice.

"We cheated," Sherri confided. "The people who sang are in my women's chorus already and we perform together all the time."

"I'm half Jewish," I told Sherri, "but my mother doesn't practice anything Jewish except for lighting candles on Friday night and going to a Passover Seder every year."

"If your mother is Jewish, then you too are Jewish according to Jewish law," Sherri said. I had never heard of that before.

"You have a Jewish name," Sherri continued, as she studied me through candid, bright-blue eyes, her head tilted slightly to one side. "You know who Miriam was in the Bible, don't you?"

"She was Moses' sister. My father always told me she played the tambourine by the waters of the Red Sea during the Exodus from Egypt."

"That's right," Sherri confirmed. "Have you ever heard the midrash of Miriam's well?"

"No, what is that?" I asked. "What's a midrash?"

"A midrash is a story, actually a better translation is that it's a teaching, that grows out of the words in the Torah, the Old Testament. It's a teaching sprung from an interpretation of the meaning of the rich text of the Torah."

"And the midrash about Miriam's well?" I asked.

"Have you ever wondered where the Israelites found water while they wandered in the desert for forty years? The Torah never says they're thirsty, not once, until after Miriam dies. Right after Miriam's death, the Torah says the people of Israel were thirsty. For this reason, scholars of Torah conclude that Miriam had a well that followed her around. Wherever the Israelites set up camp in the desert, they had water because of Miriam's well."

"And that's called a midrash?"

"Yes, a midrash."

I had so much to learn from the other women incarcerated with me. Having the common denominator of our shared convictions about the wrongheadedness of government policy toward the Salvadoran refugees helped us cut across cultural and religious differences. I reflected on the fact that Sister Marianne, Sherri, the Buddhists, and I, although so different, shared certain common beliefs and that we all answered to a higher law than the law of the land.

A routine of sorts developed as we waited for our attorneys to negotiate the terms of our release with the judge. We understood how things worked in our temporary and artificial reality. Usually we had access to the exercise yard and the portable toilets during the day, but after dark we had to request a guard to escort us to the Porta-Potties, which stood in a neat row across the yard from the tents. By the third evening, the lousy food caught up with me. I tried to rest on my cot, but I was having vicious cramps. About half an hour before lights-out, I decided to make a trip to the Porta-Potty. At the entrance to the tent, I met a middle-aged guard with a potbelly and an orange mustache that resembled the bristles on a push broom. I had not seen him at Juliana before. In my line of sight, several women drifted back from the Porta-Potties across the yard.

"May I please use the toilet?" I asked. Respect played an important part in nonviolent protest tactics.

The guard curled his lip and rocked back on his heels to look me up and down from head to toe. "Potty visiting hours are over," he informed me in an amused voice.

"We have another half an hour before lights-out," I said, with a note of desperation in my voice. My stomach was churning.

The women returning from the yard sensed something wrong and lingered at the mouth of the tent.

"Guess your little Black ass will just have to hold it until morning," the guard chuckled, his eyes squinting to mean slits. I got a sick twisting feeling in my gut that had nothing to do with my indigestion.

One of the women standing at the opening of the tent turned and called into the tent, "Circle up the wagons, ladies. We have a problem here." The woman who had called for reinforcements was large and had short, straight, graying hair. She was an outspoken lesbian feminist, and I knew that she would not tolerate the guard's attitude. Instantly, twenty or more women stood at the ready to protect me. They surrounded me, so that the guard could not reach me. The woman who had called for help asked me what had happened.

"I just wanted to use the toilet," I answered shakily. "This guard apparently thinks the toilets at this prison are 'white only.'"

The guard who had harassed me called to a group of guards standing nearby to back him up. Meanwhile, the women escorted me en masse to the toilet across the yard. A guard's voice rang out loudly, "Leave the girl go, Bob. Don't mess with these ones. They could make a heap of trouble for you."

Bob called viciously after us, "Lesbos. You bunch of Lesbos."

When the women escorted me back from the Porta-Potty, Bob was no longer at the entrance to the tent. I thanked the women who had come to my aid and went directly to my cot. A few Black sisters were waiting for me there. They wanted to know if I was all right and to find out which guard had bothered me so they could be prepared. One tall sister in a yellow dress shook her head and complained, "Sometimes I wonder when I'll get out from under."

I replied, "I hear you."

The lights went out and I was left alone with my thoughts. Although I knew that I lived in a racist country and that my daddy's family and I were often viewed as second-class citizens because of our skin color, I was rarely confronted by it on a personal level. But then something would happen to remind me, like that guard, and the hard truth would be lit up for me with vivid clarity. Usually, like just now, it happened when I was least prepared to deal with it. Even the large woman who had come to my aid had called out, without realizing the underlying prejudice in her words, "Circle up the wagons." I knew how painful that expression would have been for Annie had she heard it, with its inherent image from countless Westerns of circled wagons, shots fired, and dead Natives: for many people the quintessential image of the extermination of the indigenous tribes of North America. Racism was so ingrained in our lives that the very language we used to communicate with one another was heavy with it. Would we ever outlive our horrific history?

Once, when I was small, I had awakened in the middle of the night and gone downstairs. In the living room I had seen my parents. They had candles lit and soul music playing softly. They looked elegant. Mama wore a strapless black gown and Daddy wore a white dress shirt. I noticed the contrast of their skin colors. Daddy, so muscular, his dark-brown hand on Mama's bare alabaster back. Mama's dark curly hair tumbled down the white sleeve of Daddy's arm as she rested her head on his shoulder. They slow-danced to the music. Dressed up only for each other. They spoke so quietly that I couldn't hear the words, just the soothing murmur of their languid voices. I did not disturb them. I watched them dance for a few minutes and then I crept quietly back to bed. On my prison cot, I clung to the vision of my parents and their slow dance that transcended race. The lullaby of my parents' love rocked me to sleep in that safe place of memory.

After a long six days, the judge relented and agreed to sentence us to a choice of community service or a fine. This made it possible for those among us who could not afford to pay the fine to elect to do the community service, so we agreed to cooperate. We attended a group arraignment, and the Juliana Peace Camp dissolved. As for the refugees, no word came from El Salvador regarding their condition. The INS had forgotten about them. The press had never noticed them in the first place.

We were allowed to use the pay phones to call for rides from Juliana back to Tucson. By the time my immensely relieved husband arrived in the pickup to collect me, the luster of having done the right thing and belonging to a group of dedicated activists had worn off and I was simply a weary and fragile young woman who longed for the comfort and safety of my own home.

"So what did you learn while you were in jail?" Gil asked.

"That I've been there before and last time I didn't make it out," I answered.

Gil threw me a puzzled look. It would be several days before I shared with Gil the insight of the old woman who had observed me having one of my nightmares, and my sense that she was correct in her interpretation.

I had dropped far behind in my studies while I was in jail. Struggling to catch up, I stayed late at the library every night. I usually called Gil when I was ready for a ride home and he would come to get me. One night when I called Gil for a ride, Annie answered the phone.

"Gil's not feeling well; I'll come," Annie said.

I knew immediately that something was wrong.

By the time Annie pulled up at the library, I had imagined so many tragedies that I was just this side of panic.

"What happened?" I demanded.

Annie pulled out of the parking lot in silence.

"Annie? What is it?"

She gazed straight ahead at the road as she told me flatly, "Your friend Alejandro has passed into spirit."

"No, no," I moaned as tears sprang to my eyes.

"Sister Marianne drove out to the farm to bring Gil the news in person."

Annie dropped me off and didn't come into the house. I found Gil sitting on the couch in the living room in the dark, staring out the window at the milky moonlit yard. The whole house remained enveloped in darkness. Gil must have sat through the sunset, not bothering to turn on a light. I touched his shoulder. He turned to me, his eyes feverishly bright. I sat on the couch next to him and my gaze followed his out the window. I pulled the afghan off the back of the couch and wrapped it around my shoulders. Gil endured, motionless as a stone statue. We said nothing. Eventually, exhausted, I curled up with my head resting on his thigh and fell asleep.

In the wee hours of the morning, I woke with a start. The nearly full moon had moved to the other side of the house, but the fields remained lit up in its phosphorescent glow, which also reflected in my face. Gil, who had been studying me as I slept, stroked my hair absently, more to comfort himself than me.

"Annie told you," he said.

"Only that he's gone," I replied.

"They claim he was found dead in his cell and they called it a suicide."

"No investigation?"

"Of course not."

"What leaders deliberately destroy one of their country's finest?" I said in fury.

"A writer is more dangerous to them than a terrorist. Even if you lock up a writer, he still has power. Even if you kill a writer, he still has power. I have some of his work and I'm going to print it," Gil vowed. "I have some of his poetry and even a few essays he wrote on revolution. I'm going to have his words published. I won't give them the satisfaction of silencing his voice."

"Tinajero," I whispered.

"Tinajero," Gil echoed.

Tinajero was a revolutionary who had been locked up for two years and then executed. While in prison, he had written, in his head, beautiful, moving, and inspiring essays on political transformation. He had his fellow prisoners memorize individual passages of what he wrote and those who regained their freedom wrote these passages down and put them together. His essays had been smuggled out of the country and printed in the United States. Some of the passages were lost when a few of Tinajero's comrades were executed with him. Nevertheless, his essays stood as a monument to the persistence of the human spirit in quest of freedom and justice.

After Alejandro's death, I called a half dozen newspapers and magazines to try to convince even one of them to print a story following up on the deportation of the refugees and their subsequent fates. No one would touch it. It occurred to me that perhaps they had been forbidden to write about it because of the politics of the people who controlled the media. What we needed, it seemed, was a good investigative reporter, but I didn't know how to find one.

That summer, the last before my senior year, I didn't go to school or work or even remain involved in Sanctuary. I felt bruised by my experience in jail and my failure to make a difference for the deportees. I went to New York for a couple of weeks, where I had a satisfying visit with my parents and spent time with Grandma Ruth, Big Momma, Granddaddy Pete, and a lot of my aunts and uncles on both sides of the family. Grandma Ruth was moving more slowly and showing signs of age that I had not previously noticed, and I resolved to spend more time with her. Daddy and I talked at length about the demonstration and my experience in jail. (He had insisted on paying my fine so that I didn't have to do the community service hours, which would have made it difficult for me to make enough time for my studies.) He told me I needed to give myself permission to take a vacation from the world and I took him at his word. He suggested that I "go on a media diet" and avoid reading the news for a little while.

When I returned to Tucson after my visit with my family, I rarely left Esperanza to go into town. Under Gil's expert guidance, I grew a wonderful and prolific vegetable garden. I adopted a black Labrador and named her Sadie. Sadie and Paz instantly became the best of buddies. Annie taught me how to ride a horse. I wore Gil out making love to him. I read humorous, light novels, no psychology books. In the fall, I started my senior year of college, harvested a heap of pumpkins, sat with Bella when she had kittens, put up twenty quarts of applesauce, planted flower bulbs in front of the house, and became pregnant with my first child.

Eleven

I MET SILVINA AT Sister Marianne's Christmas party. I liked her right away, largely because I was drawn to her children, who attached themselves to Silvina and went with her wherever she went. Three small ones, wide-eyed, silent, with delicate features and angelic faces. They never left their mother, they never said a word, they avoided eye contact with strangers. Silvina carried the youngest on her hip and, although he was old enough to walk, she never put him down in the four hours that she stayed at that Christmas party, not even to eat the plate of food that someone brought to her.

When I sat next to Silvina and spoke to her in Spanish, she was friendly to me but had little to say. I tried to talk to the children, who hid their faces in their mother's skirt. I liked her gentle patience with the children as I watched her sing along wistfully to the Spanish Christmas carols.

The next day, I wondered out loud to Annie, "Have you ever seen children who say nothing? Won't leave their mother? Don't want to play?"

Annie was grooming her horse, Yokayo, while I kept her company. She stood up on a wooden box and stroked so broadly with the brush that each pass nearly knocked her off her box. "They're sick," Annie said unequivocally.

"I don't think so. I don't think Silvina would have brought them to a party if they were sick."

"I mean their spirits are sick," Annie clarified. Then she added, "Something happened to them."

I watched Annie as she hypnotically curried Yokayo, the smooth chestnut hair of the animal shining in the morning sunlight.

"Now you're scared to find out what happened to those children," Annie said without looking up from Yokayo.

"Get out of my head," I ordered her with a quick laugh, as I hopped off the fence. Annie grinned at me.

A few weeks later, I went to the Sanctuary office to fold flyers and found Sister Marianne on the phone trying to arrange for a ride for Silvina to go to the doctor. I thought Sister Marianne could do anything, but she had come up against a logistical problem she couldn't solve. Silvina insisted on taking the children with her to the doctor and Sister Marianne couldn't find anyone available that afternoon who had a car with enough seat belts for all of them.

Annie had a big old Chevy station wagon that I could borrow, so I offered to give Silvina a ride. I went over to Annie's for the wagon. When I picked Silvina up later, we drove to the clinic in uncomfortable silence. Silvina was having migraine headaches. She looked pale and worn.

At the clinic, I sat on the floor next to a table full of Legos. I built a car with the Legos and handed it without a word to Silvina's eldest, Marco, who took it from me and examined it. Then he tentatively joined me at the Lego table. His sister, Soledad, followed him. The children said nothing, but they became engrossed in building Lego cars with me. Before long, I discovered the baby, Paco, at my elbow watching the activity intently. I handed him a small Lego truck and he ran the wheels over the palm of one hand. After a couple of minutes, he began to play with me too.

When the nurse stood in the doorway and called Silvina's name for her to see the doctor, I looked up from playing with the children to find that Silvina's cheeks were wet with tears. I wondered what it was about our Lego play that had moved her so profoundly. The baby ran back to her and she took him with her into the examination room, but the older two children chose to stay with me to play with the Legos.

The doctor prescribed a medication for Silvina, so we proceeded to the pharmacy. While I drove, Silvina spoke to me in English so her children would not understand. In a hushed, quavering voice, so quiet that I had to strain to hear, Silvina revealed that her children had been tortured in an effort to gain information from their father. She said that as far as she knew, her husband didn't have the information they sought. He had been killed in front of her and the children. When they were released from the prison, she and the children fled the country. Since that time, the children would not leave Silvina's side. They never played. They usually clung to Silvina, except if she turned on the TV. They would sit by themselves and watch cartoons. Her youngest would not speak.

"When my children play with you, I cannot believe my eyes. I don't see them play like this since the . . ." her voice faltered and then she continued, "since the time their father die. And you are a stranger. I am surprised. *Gracias.*"

I thought about what Silvina had said and I thought about my conversations with my aunt Sarah and Jade about their work with troubled children. Then I thought about the things I had learned in college and how I could put my psychology training to good use. Before I dropped Silvina and her children off at their home, I said, "I'd like to spend more time with your children if you don't mind. I'm studying psychology in college. I'm learning about how to help people recover when they've been badly hurt."

"Of course," Silvina answered without hesitation, "I am grateful."

I began to read research that pertained specifically to working with children who had suffered trauma. I read about abused children, homeless children, and children who had survived the Holocaust. I read anything I could find about therapy for emotionally and psychically scarred children. I was particularly interested in a technique called play therapy that helped children work out their overwhelmingly distressful feelings through the make-believe situations of imaginative play.

I explained to Gil, "If I can water down the children's memories of brutality with memories of kindness, beauty, laughter, and fun, then eventually the brutality becomes like one drop of blood in a giant pitcher of Kool-Aid. It's still there, but so diluted that it doesn't hurt so much."

As I played with Silvina's children and struggled to find ways to help them recover from their pain and loss, I became convinced that the way to defeat the torturers was to undo their handiwork, to unravel it, to heal where they had harmed. And I believed that my work would endure far longer than theirs.

I applied to the counseling program through the graduate school for social work at the university. Because I would have a new baby to care for beginning in June, I would have to take my time completing the program. While I prepared to earn my license to practice as a therapist, Sister Marianne found a grant writer to help her secure funding to open a health clinic for the refugees. The clinic would offer medical services, dental care, and mental health services. Sister Marianne and I shared a vision with other Sanctuary workers in Sister Marianne's church. We wanted to provide the type of counseling services necessary to help refugees who had experienced torture and witnessed violence to recover from the trauma, at least enough to lead a functional life, and hopefully enough to move beyond despair. My dream was to one day work with children in that clinic.

Twelve

IN FEBRUARY, SILVINA AND her children moved to Esperanza Farm. Those children remained so subdued that living with them was like living with mice. Gil said he wished the children would trample the corn or track mud into the house or do something that healthy children do. I said I was hopeful that one day they would be active and noisy, and that I was convinced that it would simply take time and hard work to bring them back to the wonder of childhood.

The doctor had put Silvina on a strong multivitamin supplement with iron and she was regaining her energy. If she felt a migraine coming on, she had a medication she could take that usually prevented it. She seemed more hopeful and the children perked up a bit with their mother's improving health. Silvina enrolled Marco and Soledad in the nearby school on the Navajo Reservation. The tribal medicine woman assisted in the classroom and she did wonders with Silvina's two older children. Silvina took Paco, the baby, outside with her most days and worked for us in the gardens and orchards. The fruits, vegetables, herbs, flowers, goats, cats, and dogs did for Paco what no person had yet done. They brought him out of the anguished place to which his brief experience of the world had exiled him and the child began to show noticeable glimmers of recovery. He didn't cling to Silvina as much, laughed now and then at the antics of the dogs or cats, and even said a word or two in Spanish from time to time.

Aunt Soph had helped guide us through the process of having Gil become a U.S. citizen and he was "sworn in" that winter at a formal ceremony at city hall. After that, he was able to obtain a U.S. passport and it was safe for us to travel to Mexico at last. He had not seen his family in six years. His little sister was planning to be married and she had waited for Gil to get his passport to set the date. So, during spring break, Gil and I left Esperanza in Silvina's care and traveled to Mexico for the wedding.

Two of Gil's sisters, widowed by the tragedy that drove Gil from El Salvador, had remarried and moved to homes in town with their new husbands. Gil was delighted to see them and their children happy in their rebuilt lives. Gil's oldest sister remained unmarried, but she had five children, and the oldest two, both boys, now worked. She had moved into an apartment with her children, and her sons supported her and the younger ones. This left Gil's mother in the railroad car with a teenaged son (her youngest) and the daughter who was married the week that we visited. While in Mexico, Gil rented an apartment for his mother and we moved her out of the railroad car. We offered to take Gil's teenaged brother back to the U.S. with us, but he didn't want to leave his mother. He said he liked living in Mexico.

When I watched Gil with his nieces and nephews and his teenaged brother, it broke my heart. It was as if he was trying to make up for all the years of his absence by packing one week with as much time as he could with the youngsters. Gil's mother told me that she felt fortunate to have at least one of her sons escape the clutches of Duarte and that she was so pleased that he had found happiness in the arms of a beautiful American who spoke Spanish so well. Gil's mother patted my round belly and predicted that I would have a son. "More men restored to the family," she said, confirming my own belief that I was carrying a boy.

A great weight lifted from Gil as a result of our visit. He had seen his family and they were not merely surviving but in many ways, they were thriving. He was less worried about them after our trip.

Annie noticed the difference instantly when she picked us up at the airport. She brushed off Gil's shoulders with her hand and commented, "Must feel good to unload."

When we arrived at home, Silvina's children insisted on giving us a tour of Esperanza Farm to show us everything they had done in our absence. They had assembled a small greenhouse from a kit Gil had bought before we left for Mexico, and they had planted vegetable starts, which lined the shelves in the little greenhouse. They had planted a bed of purple, red, and pink petunias by the kitchen door. After being away, I saw them in a new light and the contrast between what they had been like when I first met them a few short months before and what they were like now astonished me. Paco shyly held his thin little arms up to me and I picked him up. His small hands reached around my neck and tangled affectionately in the new baby dreadlocks that I had recently started to grow when I let my hair go natural. "You missed me?" I asked him. He nodded.

"I'm so sorry," Silvina apologized. "Marco trampled some of the baby corn while chasing Soledad. But we replanted."

Gil laughed joyously at this news. "Thank goodness," he exclaimed, slapping Marco on the back. "I was waiting for Marco to trample that corn!" Silvina looked puzzled as Gil winked at me. Then he smiled with that sparkle in his eye that never failed to make my pulse quicken. He had suffered, he had survived, and he had demanded that life give him the joy that he deserved. How I loved him for it.

At the end of May, my parents, Grandma Ruth, and Aunt Sarah flew to Tucson for my graduation. My parents planned to stay at Esperanza Farm until the birth of their grandchild, but Aunt Sarah had only a few days off from work, and Grandma Ruth said she didn't want to be underfoot at the birth, so they planned only a short visit. Grandma Ruth promised to come back again when the baby was big enough to smile at her.

I had not yet told my parents about Silvina. I met my family at the airport in Annie's station wagon and on the way to the farm informed them that Gil and I had an illegal Salvadoran refugee and her children living with us. Mama obviously didn't understand the ramifications of this, but Daddy did, and he asked, "Do you think it is wise to have this woman living with you? You have a baby to think of now."

"I don't understand," Mama said, looking questioningly from Daddy to me.

"It's against the law to harbor or aid illegal aliens," Aunt Sarah told Mama. "Although it also happens to be a family tradition," she added.

"What do you mean?" I asked.

"Well," Aunt Sarah elaborated, "during the Second World War, your Grandpa Nate worked for an organization . . ."

"He founded that organization," Grandma Ruth interjected.

"There you have it," Aunt Sarah continued. "He *founded* an organization that brought Jews out of Europe to save them from Hitler. He and Grandma Ruth took many of them into their own home to live until they could make a start for themselves in America. I remember some of them because they returned for Shabbat dinner from time to time." Aunt Sarah asked Mama, "Do you remember Chaya and Dave?"

"Of course," Mama answered.

"Did you know that Papa rescued them from Europe?"

"I didn't remember that," Mama replied.

"I just had dinner at Dave's house a couple of weeks ago," Grandma Ruth said.

"Your grandpa Nate would have approved of your refugee housemates," Aunt Sarah told me.

"Perhaps not," Mama said evenly. "Silvina isn't Jewish."

"Your father was generous to many people who weren't Jewish," Grandma Ruth said quietly but firmly, as she folded her arms across her chest.

"As long as they didn't marry his daughters," Mama muttered.

"Enough," Aunt Sarah commanded, and Mama and Grandma Ruth fell silent.

Pulling up to the house with my family, I saw Esperanza Farm through the eyes of a visitor. Our large sprawling wooden farmhouse with its faded blue shutters at the windows looked welcoming and homey. I saw Paz and Sadie in the yard wagging and wiggling with excitement, Bella perched on the roof of the barn, the geraniums, petunias, and nasturtiums casting their bright streak of color across the front flower beds, the goats chewing crookedly in their pen, the decorative wagon wheel leaning against the porch. How had a cosmopolitan girl like myself wound up here?

Daddy had been thinking about building a cottage for him and Mama to stay in whenever they came to visit and he took a walk down by the seasonal creek to look around for a potential building site. Aunt Sarah struck up a friendship with Silvina's children instantly. That evening, we ate a large family dinner of traditional Salvadoran food, including both meat and vegetarian *pupusas*, which Silvina and I had cooked in the sunny country kitchen with Grandma Ruth's help and her questions about our preparations at every step of the way. Annie and John joined us at the table. Annie brought fry bread that melted in my mouth.

During dinner, Daddy spoke at length with John. I couldn't hear what they said to each other at their end of the table because I was surrounded by Silvina's children, who chattered at me in Spanish. I don't think I had ever seen John carry on such a prolonged conversation with anyone.

After dinner, I moved to their end of the table to listen in as Grandma Ruth, Gil, and Aunt Sarah cleared and began to clean the dishes.

". . . a historian, I suspect," John said.

"Why that?" Daddy asked.

"To retell the history correctly."

"Including the omissions," Daddy added.

"Especially the omissions."

It was as if they were speaking in shorthand.

"It's painful to lose the memory of it," John continued.

"Infuriating," Daddy agreed, focusing the intensity of his brown eyes on John, "to be lost to memory. Misremembered. Forgotten. Viewed as absent. It's a conspiracy to erase all the work of our hands. As if we had no significance and never left a mark."

"Unfortunately, Natives often respond by withdrawing, a passive-aggressive thing. We withhold our greatest gifts. The culture, wisdom, healing, our spirits. We keep these to ourselves where they are appreciated, and escape desecration. It's a sad defense mechanism. If the white man says 'look, they have nothing,' then we can say to ourselves 'he says that because we have not revealed to him what we have.' Everyone loses," John explained.

"Everyone loses, but doesn't a part of you still say 'he got what he deserves'?" Daddy asked.

"Of course," John answered, "but that's not the point."

"What boils my blood is what happens to the children," Daddy told John. "Our children begin to believe that their people have made no contribution to society because of what is taught to them in school. They learn that they are invisible and that, quite possibly, any contribution they make will also be invisible. How confusing for them to try to make sense out of the discrepancy between what they know as true from their home and their culture on the one hand and the messages about themselves and their people that are foisted on them in school on the other."

"Many tribes keep their children at home to school them for that reason," John replied. "To protect them from the lies of the outside world. But most of our children go on to public school eventually, and of course a large number drop out because of the cultural disparity, difference in values, lack of support from the education system. Experience teaches them to distrust what they hear in the outside world. Then many of our children who succeed by the measures of the dominant culture (and you will notice there are disproportionately few) have had to subvert their own values in some way to do so."

"The same thing happens in Black culture," I interjected.

"You're right about that, baby girl," Daddy agreed. "These Black and Native children are pressured to suppress and deform themselves in order to succeed on white terms. And white people wonder why I am enraged. They want me to 'put the whole race thing in the past,' as if it's over, as if the culture has changed and erased racism when in fact the culture is built on racism. As if Black infants were not dying at twice the rate of infants in the general population. As if Black young men were not dying of homicide at quadruple the rate of young men in the general population." Daddy was breathing fast, his voice sharp. He was riled up. I had figured he and John would hit it off, but they had more to talk about than I had imagined.

"As if the life expectancy for Natives was not fifteen years shorter than that of the general population," John said. "As if Natives were not exiled from the rich soil of their homes and forced to live on ruined land incapable of producing anything other than substandard housing."

"Don't get me started."

"Keep my feet from that path."

"I hear you, brother, I hear you."

"Un-huh."

I looked back and forth between Daddy and John with affection. They were two gentle, mighty men who most likely could, between them, push down the wall of a barn with their bare hands if they put their will to it.

"I obviously can't speak for all Black men, of course, but for many like myself the fury manifests in not letting society off the hook. Insisting on recognition. Insisting on inclusion. And it's an exhausting and frustrating struggle because the society has effected an intentional cultural amnesia. To be truly free, a people must have the freedom to remember and celebrate the truth about their history, their culture, and their accomplishments. But remembering can be a challenge."

John bowed his head as if in prayer. "That is precisely why I returned to the land of my ancestors."

"Rina and I illustrate children's books," Daddy said. "We just completed a series of biographies of Black scientists and inventors for grade-school children. Ask your average third-grader to name a Black scientist. Maybe, if you're lucky, he'll name George Washington Carver, but then he won't know any others. We want to bring the history forward, to let it shine. It has been popular to publish multicultural folktales and legends lately, and that serves an important purpose in educating children about culture and values, but we want to do biographies, histories, facts; to tell the truth."

"In Indian country, we wonder what happened to the value of speaking truth. I don't think we can ever recover from being the brunt of lies," John said sadly.

At that moment, Mama called from the kitchen doorway, "Coffee? I brought a Dominican blend that will knock your socks off."

"Who can say no to an offer like that?" John replied, as he rose from the table and stretched. Daddy did the same, and their tandem large frames suddenly filled the room.

That night, in bed, I reran the conversation between Daddy and John in my mind. I thought about the degree that would be conferred on me the following day. I had learned so much since I first arrived in Tucson, and most of that learning had not occurred in a college classroom. Yet my college education had equipped me with the tools I needed to make a difference in the lives of others. I thought of the various kinds of education that people receive, the different pathways to learning, and the particular pathway that I would be concluding in the morning. I was proud of myself for completing college.

Thirteen

IN MY CAP AND gown, I hardly looked eight and a half months pregnant. As our department walked in to be seated for the ceremony, I saw Daddy at the railing of the bleachers taking pictures. Next to him there was a Latino man who held a camera in his hand, but instead of taking pictures he was crying uncontrollably into a large white handkerchief. I wondered which graduate was his child. The significance of this moment for him and his family was written all over his face and it made tears start to my eyes as well. I thought for a moment of the hundreds of years of deferred dreams of Black people living in America, young people who had been denied the opportunity to attend college, and I was filled with emotion at my accomplishment.

Daddy shouted and pointed until I caught sight of Mama, Gil, and the others. We waved at each other. Daddy wanted to make sure that I saw where they were seated, but by the time I took my own seat, I was too far away to see them anymore. After the speeches and the music, we filed up to the stage to receive our diplomas and a handshake from the dean. It took me a while to find my family in the crowd afterward. Gil was glowing.

"I have a college-educated wife," he pronounced happily.

The psychology department held a modest reception for its own graduates following the larger ceremony for the entire graduating class. We attended this reception, where I introduced Daddy and John to the professor who taught a class called Psychology of Cultural Identity, and the three of them were soon deep in conversation. One of my former professors came over and patted my pregnant belly and talked with me about the baby. I soon had to sit down. I had been on my feet long enough for one day. Grandma Ruth sat next to me, holding my diploma and cap in her lap. A few classmates drifted over and spoke with us. Annie brought us cookies. After I ate my cookie, I leaned my head on Grandma Ruth's shoulder. Mama noticed that I was fading and rounded up the family so we could leave. I fell asleep in the car on the way home.

With graduation behind me, I turned my full attention to preparing for the birth of the baby. Thank goodness he had not decided to make his entrance early. Grandma Ruth and Aunt Sarah returned to the East Coast, while Mama and Daddy settled in to stay until the birth. Mama and I went shopping for a crib, dresser, and changing table as well as many little things the baby would need. We set up the baby's room, even though he would sleep with me and Gil at first. Then we waited.

Daddy and Mama sketched and painted. I worked in the gardens and played with Silvina's children and the dogs. Daddy rented a pager for Gil so we could reach him when I went into labor. I planned to have the baby at home with the assistance of two Navajo midwives from the Rez. I could not imagine going to the hospital to have my baby. I was born at home myself, and that seemed like the right place to give birth. Besides, I had a pervasive fear of going to the hospital to have the baby. At the hospital, I imagined, I would lose control of the situation. They might force me to allow them to do things I didn't want, like starting an IV drip with Pitocin in it. I didn't want that kind of a birth. The thought of having complete strangers exercise so much power over such an intimate experience frightened and repulsed me.

The last few days before the birth were peaceful and lovely. Silvina and I played with Marco, Soledad, and little Paco. We ran the dogs around chasing sticks, balls, and a beat-up Frisbee. Silvina cut some of our abundant spring flowers and brought them inside where we could appreciate them while going about our daily chores. We had spectacular roses, and I arranged them into vases, then Mama painted the arrangements in vivid watercolors. Daddy set up his huge easel in the yard and painted the distant view, which was actually Annie and John's horse ranch. Annie stopped by each evening and usually stayed for supper.

The cherries had come ripe the same week as the baby. Silvina and I spent hours pitting cherries, the deep red juice running down our hands and dyeing our fingers purple black. We froze cherries, made cherry jam, and put quarts of them up in wide-mouthed Mason jars. Silvina made cherry pies, and her children gobbled them up. A slice of that cherry pie with a dollop of vanilla ice cream was heaven on earth.

One night, during the hour before dawn, in the height of cherry season, I went into labor. At first I didn't get up. I measured the time between contractions with the bedside alarm clock. When the sun began to peek over the horizon, I woke Gil. He wrapped me in his arms and we whispered to each other excitedly in Spanish, his work-worn, gardener's fingers gently resting on my stomach as it grew taut with each contraction.

As the intensity of the contractions increased, Gil telephoned the midwives and woke Mama and Daddy. Marco appeared in the kitchen, rubbing his eyes sleepily, and Gil sent him to wake Silvina, who immediately busied herself preparing for the birth. She set water on to boil so the midwives would be able to sterilize the scissors that would be used to cut the cord. She fetched receiving blankets, towels, and newborn clothing from the nursery and put them into a bag, which she placed in the oven to warm. She stacked spare receiving blankets on the changing table. Bunnies and bears blowing rosy-pink and blue bubbles peeked at her from the blankets. Humming to herself, she made breakfast for the family. I paced through the house.

"I always wanted to ride to a birth on horseback," Annie greeted Daddy breathlessly as she tied Yokayo's bridle to the hitching post in front of the porch. Not long after Annie, the midwives arrived. Silvina took her children up to the barn where they wouldn't be disturbed by my screams or moans.

My labor progressed rapidly for a couple of hours, but when I reached nine centimeters I stopped dilating. The midwives wouldn't allow me to begin pushing until I reached ten. The contractions were so intense that I began to flounder, like a tiny boat in a hurricane. I was unable to catch my breath as each contraction followed quickly after the previous one.

I heard the midwife, who listened to the baby's heartbeat between contractions, say to Gil, "I think we ought to think about moving your wife to the hospital."

"No!" I screamed in terror. "I'm not going to the hospital!" Back-to-back contractions seized me in great shock waves, washing me under with their force. I could not stay on top of the pain and I became disoriented. I kept thinking about the children in my dreams, who screamed in the distance. "Don't let them take him from me," I begged Gil.

"Take who?" he asked. "The baby? No one is going to take your baby."

"It's those people in the dream," I gasped between contractions. "They want him."

"I think she's hallucinating," one of the midwives said in alarm.

"No. I know what's going on. Leave me alone with her," Gil entreated the midwives.

"Two minutes, not a second more," the primary midwife told him as she closed the door behind herself.

Gil had recognized my terror and understood what I meant when I said that the people in my dream wanted to take the baby. He held my face between his hands and said, "It's safe. This is safe. You can let the baby out. No one will take him away from you. You can keep him with you this time."

Together we repeated the word *safe*. We repeated it like a mantra until I found a rhythm for my breathing, until I breathed Gil's reassurance. Together we chanted: *safe, safe, safe*. And I surrendered to the force of the labor.

I felt an overpowering urge to push and I obeyed my body. I was standing facing Gil, who did not, at first, realize what had happened. I hiked up my dress and, unable to speak, motioned Gil to my aid. His hands met mine between my thighs as the baby's head cradled into our open palms.

Gil called out hoarsely, "Help, help."

The two midwives flew in the door as the shoulders appeared between my legs. The midwives rushed to us, but we didn't need help from anyone else to catch the rest of our slippery boy. And then everyone was fine and everyone was laughing and Mama was opening Champagne and I was in the bed with my son on my chest and Daddy cut his grandson's umbilical cord. My baby had such black hair and such toasty brown skin.

Annie said, "My goodness, he looks like a Pomo baby."

Only Gil and I understood that we had escaped by a hair's breadth the long arm of the torturer as it grabbed for us from beyond the imagined fortress of time and space.

We named him Alejandro.

Silvina burned sage in every room of the house.

Mama cooked chickpeas, a Jewish tradition to avert the evil eye.

Daddy and Gil called a priest and arranged to have the boy baptized.

Annie hung a dream catcher over the baby's cradle.

I appreciated the protections showered on Alejandro, but I knew in my heart that Gil spoke the truth, that this baby would not be taken from me; he was mine to keep and to raise straight and tall to manhood.

Fourteen

DADDY HAD OFFERED TO fly Big Momma and Grand-
daddy Pete to Arizona for my graduation, but they agreed that they wanted
to wait until the baby arrived. When Alejandro was a couple of months
old, they came for a week. Big Momma made herself at home in our large
country kitchen, where she "threw down" as Daddy would have said; and
Lord knows she must have been sweeter than sweet after all the "sugar"
she collected from Marco, Soledad, and Paco. Paco called her B-Momma
and followed her around as if he were her shadow. Granddaddy sat on the
porch and smoked his pipe, as much at home on an Arizona farm as in the
depths of bluesy-black Harlem.

I was amazed by the intensity of the love I felt for my son. I spent hours
watching him sleep and admiring every flawless detail of his little being.
His superb fingers, toes, and ears. I did not have a single nightmare for a
long time after he was born, and neither did Gil.

In the fall, I tore myself away from my consuming love affair with
my baby boy to go back to school part-time. Aunt Soph flew out with
Grandma Ruth in October for a visit, and Alex smiled for my grandmother just as much as she had hoped. She brought Alex a nightlight in
the form of a framed five-by-seven photograph that had been transferred
onto glass and that was illuminated from behind. It was a photograph of
Grandma Ruth when she was much younger, before I was born, and with
her was the grandfather I had never known. Their smiling faces lit up
next to one another when I pushed the button to turn on the light. I was
startled by the brilliance of Grandma Ruth's smile, which revealed how
much she loved Grandpa Nate. Lit up like that, my grandfather looked
more alive than I had ever seen him and the photo made me cry for the
loss of him, for never having known him. I put it in Alex's room, on his

dresser. It would keep the darkness of night at bay for him for many years to come.

After Alex was born, I never wanted to be apart from him, but at the same time I had things I wished to accomplish out in the world that could not be done with a baby in tow. Whenever I was away, Silvina cared for him as if he were one of her own. I returned to school to complete my master's degree and I continued to help Sister Marianne raise funds for the clinic. By the time I earned my license in counseling, the clinic had opened its doors and I went to work. Meanwhile, Gil enrolled in college part-time to study agriculture.

Silvina had become my closest friend and I couldn't imagine life on the farm without her or her children, whom I also dearly loved; even so, I hoped that Silvina would remarry one day and leave the farm for a life all her own. But she showed no interest in finding a new husband. Perhaps she thought her contentment at Esperanza was a fragile peace, and so she treated it gingerly, not wanting to break it. We took in other Salvadoran émigrés to live with us from time to time and they stayed until they could establish themselves on their own, but Silvina and her children remained through it all and we were glad to have them.

The more I loved my little Alejandro, the more I wanted more children. Lots more children. Gil made me wait until I finished graduate school to get pregnant again. Then, when Alex was three and I was five months pregnant with my second child, Mama called with the sad news that Grandma Ruth had been diagnosed with late-stage pancreatic cancer and she was dying. Soon afterward, Alex and I left Esperanza Farm and flew East to be by Grandma Ruth's side.

PART FOUR

Rasunah

ONE

Rivka

I COULD NOT REMEMBER the last time I had seen such plump, fluffy clouds. They spread out from the airplane like a field of woolly sheep. Below the clouds, it was raining. Above the clouds, I hurtled through sunshine toward America, now that the Cold War had ended and the country would admit a former card-carrying Communist such as me. Yakov's heart was too weak for him to make the trek with me, so I traveled solo. I kept forgetting that the strapping husband of my youth had become medically fragile. The months he had spent in Auschwitz had certainly contributed to the heart disease with which he struggled in his old age. Yakov was staying with Zac while I was away, and I didn't have a date of return yet. The length of my visit would depend on how long Ruth lasted.

It was Sophie who called me with the news when Ruth was diagnosed with inoperable cancer. She had precious little time left. "Will you come?" Sophie had pleaded.

"Of course." The instant the words flew from the perch of my lips, I began to prepare myself for the fatigue of traveling and staying in strange rooms and the exhaustion of grieving in public with young people who would look to me for answers.

"She needs you here to go in peace," Sophie said. I heard the desperation in her voice.

"I will come." I made no further promises than my presence. I wanted to be there for my sister, to speak with her in person again before we lost each other across the great divide. Once in America, I would also find a moment to slip away to see Avram on his farm in Vermont. Although Ruth and I had corresponded regularly over the years, I had received hardly any mail from Avram. He had sent an occasional photo. Most recently, the year before, he had sent one of himself standing in front of his barn. He looked fit and strong in his sun-faded overalls as he leaned on a shovel. His hair had gone gray. Deep lines creased his face. I recognized his eyes and his mouth; otherwise I could not have picked him out in a crowd. Casting my mind back to those tenuous war years, I marveled that in the end we had lived such long lives. Soon all those who had survived the Holocaust would die off. How well would the young folks remember us and what had happened in Eastern Europe during the war?

I did not care for flying. It seemed unnatural and I had done it only once before, many years earlier, when Shayna and I went to Israel to visit Papa at his home on the kibbutz by the Sea of Galilee. Ruth and her sister-in-law, Ida, had joined us there, and we had done some sightseeing together after visiting Papa. Although Ruth and I spoke by telephone several times a year and exchanged frequent letters, we had somehow not managed to orchestrate any visits to see one another outside of that one trip to Israel. It was hard for me to believe that so many years had slipped past without Ruth returning to Paris, but it was so.

Meir was no longer living by the time we made that trip to see Papa. The kibbutz was beautiful and the younger residents clearly looked up to Papa, treating him with kindness and respect and taking care of him in his old age. He lived modestly in one room in a residence for the community elders. I did not allow him to engage me in any conversations about politics. I was well aware of his commitment to a Jewish homeland, and although I believed in the need for such a place as well, I took exception to the kind of country that my people had created. I wished that we had proven ourselves to be better than the other nations of the world, that we had been capable of creating a state where all people could live in peace and no race suffered state-sponsored oppression. Secretly, I asked myself, if we Jews could not do it, was there any race that could? But there was no point in aggravating my aged father with my doubts and disappointments about the land he loved, the land that he believed in so strongly that he had sacrificed his only son for its survival. Instead, I stepped back behind Shayna, who flooded him with questions about my mother, about Papa's early years in Russia, and about my childhood in Palestine. He answered her questions with great sweeping stories and a light shining in his eyes. Ruth and I were deeply grateful for that visit, since he passed away peacefully in his sleep the following year.

On the night approach to JFK, I felt a flurry of excitement at the sight of the dizzying fling of lights beneath me. I looked forward to the prospect of seeing Rina again and meeting Sarah and Sophie in person, of being present for Ruth's beautiful girls who had grown up without me. I had completely missed the childhood of these women, who possessed a history vastly separate from mine. The best we could hope for was to imagine each other's lives the way a reader imagines the lives of characters in a storybook. All those letters over the years from Ruth, loaded with written stories, fell short of shared daily living. Even so, I had made do with those letters, since they were what I had. I was delighted that Miriam wrote to me so often, and I welcomed this unexpected opportunity to see her, now grown up, as well.

After navigating customs, I passed through the opaque double doors into the waiting area, where I was engulfed in a warm embrace by a carbon copy of Ruth in the form of Sophie. Sophie introduced her husband, Max, a handsome man with piercing blue eyes and an air of confidence. I kissed him on both cheeks and observed, "What a fine husband." Max laughed self-consciously as he hugged me.

"Are you hungry?" Sophie asked. "We have a long ride ahead of us."

We stopped at a deli, where Sophie ate a giant kosher dill pickle, Max had a pastry and coffee, and I worked my way through a magnificent Swiss on rye. Sophie filled me in on the details of Ruth's illness.

"She's not in pain," she reassured me.

I insisted on sitting in the backseat on the drive to the house so I could rest. I felt infinitely tired, infinitely unprepared to face the ordeal ahead, and uncomfortably alone without Yakov. I nodded off to sleep for most of the drive. After we left the highway, we wove through a maze of streets, turning finally down a tree-lined boulevard with a center island and large well-maintained homes set in well-manicured yards. Max parked the car and then he and Sophie peered into the backseat. "Aunt Rivka, we're here."

"What a beautiful avenue. I love the canopy of trees."

"I grew up on this street," Sophie reminded me. "Back then the trees were not as big."

We stepped out of the air-conditioned car into a sultry June night. The crickets greeted us with their lively racket.

Max took my bag from the trunk. "You travel light," he commented.

"Can I get you to put that opinion in writing for my husband?" I asked with amusement.

Just then a dim light appeared in an upstairs window of the house. Sophie glanced up. "That's Mama's room. She must have been listening for the car." She turned to me. "She'll want to see you before you go to bed."

As I stepped into the entranceway, I recalled the pictures and diagrams Ruth had sent me when she and Nate were designing the house. How thoughtfully and conscientiously Ruth had chosen the wallpaper patterns, molding, and carpeting. Sophie took me into the kitchen and offered me a drink. I accepted a glass of water while I admired the yellow ruffled valance above the window over the sink, the dark wooden built-in benches in the breakfast nook, the glass doorknob on the door to a spacious walk-in pantry that stood ajar, and other artfully selected features of the room. Every detail spoke of Ruth's precision and impeccable taste.

Max disappeared upstairs, carrying my bag.

I finished the water and Sophie said, "I'll show you to Mama's room."

We passed under a teardrop-shaped crystal chandelier glittering above us in the high-ceilinged hallway, which opened out on one side to the living room cloaked in night and on the other side to a formal staircase. We mounted the carpeted stairs that were bordered by an elegantly turned oak balustrade.

"This room is yours," Sophie said at the top of the stairs as she waved toward a door to the right. "And here is the bathroom. There are towels at the end of your bed." The scent of rose soap drifted faintly from the bathroom. I smiled to myself as I recognized that scent, always a favorite of Ruth's. Sophie knocked softly on the door to the left of the stairway, then she opened the door and popped her head in. "Mama? Aunt Rivka has arrived." I followed her into the room.

Ruth lay propped on an avalanche of pillows. Her room was framed in shadow and rich with the history of a life well lived, hovering beyond the small circle of light cast by the bedside lamp. Sophie slipped back out, leaving us to our private reunion.

I sat on the edge of the bed and wrapped Ruth's frail upper body in my arms.

"At last," Ruth choked, her tongue stumbling over the unaccustomed Yiddish as we blinked back tears.

"At last," I echoed, in the language of our childhood. Ruth asked about the flight as we held each other's hands, basking in the delight of one another's presence.

"Your house is beautiful. I'm so glad to finally see it. What fine craftsmanship."

"My Nate's handiwork," Ruth replied, proudly.

"But your design," I reminded.

"We designed it together."

Ruth was thin, her hair gone white, wispy, and brittle as it fanned out on her pillow. Her eyes were yellowed with jaundice. She wore several delicate necklaces and a number of handsome rings. Even though she was tucked snugly in her bed, the bed looked as though it was still made, folded in immaculately at the corners. The bedspread, turned back, matched the wallpaper, the pillows, and the quilt, all with large floral designs of forest-green background and large, pale-pink flowers outlined delicately in black. The heavy furniture guarded the edges of the room. An elaborate emerald-green glass lamp stood on the nightstand and next to it an intricately carved chair with an upholstered seat in the same shade of green as the lamp. I imagined I was attending a queen in her chambers.

"You should probably get some sleep," I said, worried that I would tire her.

"I slept plenty this evening. Now I'm wide awake," Ruth reassured me. "I have a lot to think about these days."

"And what do you think about tonight?"

"I have been considering what I leave behind when I leave this life."

I plunged my hand deep into the barrel of time and came up with the memory of a similar conversation with Miriam. "Miriam spoke about that the last time I saw her," I said.

"What did she have to say about it?"

"As I recall, she said she would leave behind her love for the children and her husband."

"She certainly did that."

"She also said she would leave behind the orchards. They were remarkable orchards and she took excellent care of them. The townsfolk of Crevecoeur claimed that her orchards were enchanted because the birds and insects didn't bother her fruit, and when the fruit came ripe, well, it seemed to have an ineffable otherworldly flavor. Father Charles used to say her cherries tasted celestial."

"Trees. Now that's an admirable thing to leave behind." Ruth pinched her eyebrows together. "I'm not sure I have left anything that valuable behind."

"Of course you have, dear." I patted her hand. "What about that precious granddaughter of yours with the bright eyes, and your success in raising your three remarkable daughters? Not to mention all the beautiful things you have made, the dresses, the hats, and designing this house."

"My children," Ruth sighed. "Three beautiful, smart, and talented women, no doubt about it. I love them each, but I sometimes wonder if they would be happier or more successful now if I had done things differently while raising them back then. I realize that every parent could do a better job, that raising children is a potentially infinite activity. Still, I wonder and I worry about them. Sophie will never admit how painful it has been for her to not have any children. She lives with that enormous regret in her life. Rina is happy and is an accomplished artist, but I did not do the best job of managing the discord between her and her father. Then, after all, she didn't raise Miriam Jewish, and she has never married Arthur, so Miriam is illegitimate. Being illegitimate isn't the healthiest situation for a child, in my opinion. And Sarah, well, she's quite discreet, but the truth is that she's a lesbian."

I was surprised that Ruth did not give herself more credit for being a good mother and I told her so. "You're too hard on yourself, and on your children. First of all, it's quite acceptable to be a lesbian these days, even fashionable in some circles. You make it sound like leprosy. Sarah is a highly respected educator and she has found a lifelong companion, which is more than can be said for many women. As for Sophie, well, I know how it disappointed you when she discovered she was barren, but I think she has accepted it better than you imagine. She has a fulfilling career that engages her and she made a happy marriage. And your Rina is not so indecent for not marrying. Yakov and I were only legally married about twenty years ago."

"I thought you married in Paris before the war," Ruth replied.

"We had a religious ceremony but no civil ceremony. We finally did the legal version to make sure I would receive Yakov's retirement pension if I outlive him."

"You weaseled out of the original question," Ruth said pointedly. "You haven't said what you will leave behind."

I offered my standard answer. "I survived the war, didn't I? After that everything else is icing."

Ruth refused to buy it. "Survival is not enough. Do better than that."

With a smug smile, I told her cryptically, "A statue stands in Crevecoeur."

"A statue stands in Crevecoeur? Well, that is crystal clear," Ruth responded with mock annoyance.

"I will tell you the story."

"I'm in the mood for a story." Ruth settled deeper into the wall of pillows supporting her back.

"When I lived in Crevecoeur, I worked in the vineyards with a young woman named Nicole. Nicole did not know how to read and write, so I offered to teach her. Others who wanted to learn saw me teaching Nicole and asked me to teach them too. I subsequently taught many of the villagers how to read and write. Through the experience of teaching them, I discovered how much I loved to teach and that was how I found my vocation."

Ruth smiled with satisfaction. "I like this story so far."

"You haven't heard the best part yet," I continued. "Many years ago, the Ministry of Education decided that France needed a university located somewhere close to the farms and vineyards in the south of France where students could study agriculture and horticulture as well as liberal arts in a region that held many possibilities for field study. A committee conducted an extensive site search, investigating various possible locations. In the end they chose Crevecoeur. This was an enormous economic boon for the village and the entire region. My friend Catherine sent me a newspaper clipping describing how the search committee made their final decision. In the article, the ministry spokesperson revealed that the deciding factor, all other things being relatively equal, was that the literacy rate in Crevecoeur was unaccountably high for a rural area."

Ruth clapped her hands in glee. "Oh, Rivka, it was because of you!"

"Just so. Then, recently, the university regents commissioned a statue for the campus quadrangle. They hired a sculptor who is quite well-known in France. He is old-fashioned, and heavily influenced by the work of Rodin. He wanted to capture an inspiring image from the history of the area, one that would resonate with the local people. So he talked to people living there. When he talked to Catherine, she suggested he contact me. He interviewed me in Paris and he recorded the interview. I felt like a celebrity. I told him about the years I spent in Crevecoeur during the war. I told him about Father Charles and Miriam and about how the village grieved when we lost her and her brave children. He took photos of my photos of Miriam."

"From speaking with others, he learned that I taught many people to read. He interviewed Nicole, who has published some well-received books of poetry over the years and now lives in Nice. The townsfolk also spoke about Miriam and Father Charles and the children they rescued. So what do you think? The sculptor sculpted a statue of Miriam and Father Charles for the campus. A few weeks ago, Catherine and I went to the grand unveiling of the statue, which is a beautiful tribute to their courage. It stands on the quadrangle at the university, in front of the administration building, surrounded by gardens."

"What does it look like?" Ruth asked, wanting to see it in her mind's eye.

"I have photographs in my suitcase that I will show you tomorrow. Two figures, Father Charles and Miriam of course, reach out and hold each other's hands. Both hands, as if dancing. Miriam's body also serves as the trunk of a great tree, her feet spread into roots. Her hair flows out from her head and forms thick branches that reach upward above her. From the branches swing children of different ages and sizes. And they are stuffing themselves with cherries, which they have picked from the branches of Miriam's hair. The sculpture is life-sized and a good representation of Miriam and Father Charles. Seeing it was like recovering them in a small way. A plaque stands on a pedestal near the sculpture and it explains the story of how they tried to protect the children and that they perished. Our sculptor did a good job of collecting the memories and locking them into that statue for safekeeping. To go back to your question, when I wonder what I did with my life, I tell myself that a statue stands in Crevecoeur because I taught some peasants to read."

"What a good thing to leave behind, Rivka. A very good thing." Ruth's eyes sparkled and she sighed contentedly. "That was a wonderful bedtime story."

I patted her papery hand. "Go to sleep, little one," I said, using the Yiddish words with which Mama had always tucked us in. "I will be here in the morning."

"And so will I," Ruth replied. "For now."

The heavy blinds in my room prevented the sun from entering and I slept late the next morning. As I finally hauled myself stiffly out of the bed, I thought about how the force of gravity never ceased to amaze me as it challenged my back and knees with that first step each morning. I crossed the room to open the blinds and then slipped back into bed where I propped myself up on the fleet of pillows behind me and gazed out the window at the branches of a grand old oak tree in which a multitude of colorful birds perched. Two cardinals chattered at each other. I could not remember having seen a real live cardinal before. The sky beyond the tree blared Technicolor blue and sported tremendous sugary clouds.

As I stretched my old joints and woke to the day, I felt cheerful, and then guilty for feeling so. But how often does an old lady have the opportunity to go on such an adventure? Ruth seemed bound to the earth for a little while longer, and after taking the plunge and getting on an airplane, I could afford the luxury of a vacation in America. The enticing smell of strong coffee drifted up the stairs. I untangled myself from the bedclothes, visited the rose-scented bathroom, dressed, and headed to the kitchen.

Ruth's home shone in the daylight. The shelf in the stairwell window was laden with colorful bottles and crystal artfully placed, a set of elaborate silver candlesticks atop a lace table runner graced the piano in the living room, the knickknacks were tastefully arranged on tables and shelves. I entered the bright kitchen. A Japanese woman in khaki shorts and a green T-shirt that said MICHIGAN WOMEN'S MUSIC FESTIVAL stood slicing fruit on a wooden cutting board on the countertop.

"Good morning," the woman said as she dried her hands on a yellow dishrag and extended both hands toward me. I took them in both of mine. "I'm Jade. So happy to meet you." She flashed a deep smile. I cast around in my mind for an instant and then remembered that Jade was Sarah's partner.

"Pleased to meet you too," I responded. Then I noticed Ruth, Ida, and two other women sitting in the breakfast nook, peeking out at me. I went to Ruth and gave her kisses on both cheeks and then greeted Ida, whom I had met in Israel many years before. Ruth slid down the bench to make room for me as she introduced her other two friends. I knew from Ruth's letters that Ida and Ruth had morning coffee together regularly and had done so ever since their children were toddlers. I tried to imagine having the luxury, while raising children, of being able to stop in the middle of the morning to drink coffee with women friends.

Although frail, thin, and jaundiced, Ruth was still well enough to have coffee with these women. Every hair was in place as always and her jewelry was carefully selected. We chatted while Jade made a fried egg and toast for me, after which she retired to the den to do some paperwork. The ladies enjoyed their coffee and conversation into the noon hour, when a gray-bearded man knocked twice on the kitchen door before letting himself in. Ruth introduced him as the rabbi. He had brought three fat smoked turkey sandwiches from the deli for the women to divide between themselves for lunch.

The rabbi's eyes twinkled as he leaned close to tell me confidentially, "Ruth's favorite. I tempt her with it every day. Have to keep her strength up." He did not stay long.

After lunch, Ruth's friends left and Ruth went upstairs to take a nap. I decided to go for a walk and Jade asked if she could join me. We proceeded down Ruth's shaded street and Jade led the way to a small municipal park where we walked around a bike path bordered on either side by tailored lawns and gardens. Jade said that she and Sarah had moved in with Ruth temporarily. Jade worked as a family therapist. She saw clients four days a week and set aside one day for paperwork. This was her paperwork day, when she stayed home with Ruth. Ida came every morning on the other weekdays and spent the whole day with her ailing friend. Sophie lived nearby and frequently came over for dinner, but she always came over on Sundays for the whole day. Ruth certainly didn't suffer for lack of companionship from other women. I felt a brief pang of regret that I had not had more daughters myself.

When I asked Jade about Avram, she said she had never met him and she knew little other than that he lived in a remote area of rural Vermont.

"And what about Rina?"

"She comes to see Ruth on Thursday afternoons and stays for dinner." I remembered that Ruth had established those Thursday dinners with Rina and her family even before Miriam was born.

I studied Jade briefly as we walked toward a small duck pond loaded with mallards. "Do you like being a therapist?" I asked.

"Of course," Jade replied.

"And it doesn't depress you too much to listen to the sadness and abuse that people have suffered?" I asked.

"I empathize with them, but I do what I can to help them recover, feel better, and function at a higher level."

"You must be good at what you do," I said.

"I hope so," Jade responded humbly.

That evening, Jade and Sarah cooked enchiladas and Spanish rice, which they served with shredded lettuce and a spicy guacamole. Everything tasted delicious and wholesome. Sophie regaled us with anecdotes from her women's book group, which had met the previous evening. After dinner, Ruth and I retired to the living room while the others cleared the table and cleaned up. We sat side by side on the sofa beneath a large portrait of our parents, painted in oil, that Ruth had commissioned an artist to render from an old photograph of them in their early years in Palestine.

"You seem to have done everything within reason that you wanted to do in this life, my dear," I said quietly. "Is there anything more of import you would have liked to do?"

Ruth glanced at the kitchen to make sure her children were out of earshot. "The one thing I would like to do before the end is quite impossible," she whispered, with an impish glint in her eye.

I imagined my sister wanted to skydive or travel to Brazil or something outrageous. "What is that?"

"I would have liked to make love to my Nathan one more time," Ruth confessed. "Not the routine sort of evening, but one of those special evenings that come along from time to time in the course of a long marriage. You know what I mean."

"Yes, I do." I nodded, feeling grateful as I so often did that my husband had lived into old age with me. I wished that he had been able to make this trip. He would have liked to pay a visit to Ruth and Avram. That would have to be one of his regrets.

Ruth sighed. "I have missed him."

I covered her hand with my own. "Tell me about him," I said.

So Ruth thought of a story about Big Nate. And then another. And when her children joined us with a tray of tea, they picked up the thread and spent the evening telling stories about their father until they had to take down the shoe box from the shelf in the front hall closet to get at the really old photographs that showed him dressed up in his suit and posing next to his first Plymouth and all the rest.

On Tuesday, I took the train into the city to visit Rina and Arthur. I felt like Alice walking through the looking glass upon entering Rina's house, which contained the most marvelous chaotic jumble of wonderful and beautiful objects.

They took me to a Russian restaurant for a dinner that featured a rich borscht topped with floating islands of sour cream, and afterward we returned to the house for slices of store-bought peach pie and Rina's forty-weight, high-octane coffee that somehow did not prevent her or her husband from sleeping at night. I opted for chamomile tea. I would hazard the coffee in the morning.

Arthur brought out photographs of a dance production on which they had collaborated with my Shayna when she had done a residency as a choreographer in New York. Rina and Arthur had built masks for the dancers to wear. Shayna had shown me a few photographs, but nothing like the collection that Rina and Arthur had on hand. While we were looking at the photographs, Miriam called from Arizona to let us know exactly what time her flight would arrive. After her conversation with her daughter, Rina reported to me that Miriam remembered the last time she had seen me, when she was a child visiting in Paris, with surprising clarity, and she was quite excited at the prospect of seeing me again.

"She's bringing Alejandro with her," Rina told us. "She says she hopes that he will at least retain a little memory of his great-grandmother."

I wished he could have more than just a little memory of Ruth and wondered what bits and pieces of her presence would remain with him in all the years ahead without her.

The day I returned from visiting Rina, Ruth stayed in bed. Some days were better than others for her. Sophie brought her a tray of soup in the afternoon, and Ruth, disoriented, called her "Mama" by accident. When Sophie came back down to the kitchen afterward, she sat in the breakfast nook and wept while I rubbed her back in an effort to comfort her. But the next day Ruth woke up feeling more energetic and clearheaded and even took a short walk with me on her street.

Meanwhile, I had sent a telegram to Avram, who had no telephone. When he received the telegram, he phoned from a pay phone in front of the grocery store in the town nearest to his farm. His voice sounded rusty and he spoke in clipped sentences. I made arrangements to visit him in Vermont in a few days. After I hung up, it suddenly occurred to me that it might be awkward to see him again after so much time had elapsed. That evening I wrote a letter to Yakov to let him know about my arrangements to see Avram. Yakov would certainly be eager to hear how his old Resistance buddy was doing.

A couple of days later, on the day before I planned to take the bus to Vermont, Miriam and Alejandro, who were staying with Rina and Arthur in the Village, came to see Ruth, whom Alex called *Abuelita*, or "little grandmother." After Ruth and I had laid our hands on Miriam's pregnant belly, I sat with Miriam across the dining room table from Alex and his abuelita. Ruth had produced a stack of old magazines, paper, scissors, and glue, and then she and Alex had commandeered the table where they made collages, bent over their work like two brilliant scientists unlocking the secrets of human physiology. Alex's high-pitched voice rang out excitedly as he found just the right picture and put it in just the right spot.

Once they tired of their collage project, Alex led Abuelita to the sofa where he insisted that she read some of his books to him. He giggled and pointed at the characters and explained to Ruth what was going on in the stories. He patted her knee and held her hand with unreserved affection.

Miriam and Alex were spending the night with us at Ruth's house and when Ruth went to bed early, I seized the opportunity to have Alex to myself. I filled the bathtub with rose-scented bubble soap and showed Alex how to "shave" with a smooth-edged butter knife, holding a mirror for him to see his bubble beard disappear. Then we launched a fleet of kitchen equipment vessels on the high seas, where we encountered a band of bloodthirsty pirates. Alex demonstrated his backstroke, which emptied a good deal of water on the black-and-white tiled floor. When the bubbles had melted completely into the warm water, I noticed Alex's foot. A vivid pink line encircled the ankle of his left foot.

"What happened to your foot?" I asked him.

He looked puzzled.

"What is this scar?" I pointed to the line.

"That's my birthmark," he told me.

As I wrapped him in a fat thirsty towel, I peered intently into his earnest brown eyes. Why hadn't I seen it earlier? Akiva. I rejoiced at the recognition and pulled him close, kissing him enthusiastically in the crease of his neck with noisy kisses that made him laugh.

Cozy in his jammies, Alex sat in Miriam's lap and the two of them sang Spanish songs for me, Sarah, and Jade. Then we tucked Alex in bed and

I stayed to tell him a story, kind of like the ones Mama used to tell, that went on for years and years, about the children who traveled around the world having adventures, but instead of making the children continue to wander at the end, I brought them home to their beds. Miriam sat at the end of Alex's bed and listened. Then we kissed him good night and tip-toed out, leaving the door to the hallway slightly ajar to let in some light.

After settling Alex for the night, I went to my own room, where I packed my bag for my imminent journey to Vermont. I organized my things and prepared for bed, and then, because I couldn't resist, I crept down the hall to Alex's room, where I quietly gazed at the sleeping child. I gently brushed his forehead with my lips.

"Our little angel," I whispered in Yiddish.

As I stepped from the bus, I swept the antique, rural bus station with my gaze. The building appeared on the verge of collapse. The roof was missing more shingles than not and the wooden siding had weathered too many harsh winters. I half expected Avram to arrive in a horsedrawn buggy to pick me up.

There was no buggy, but I spotted Avram immediately. He was the only other person at the deserted station. He had gone gray. Not just his hair, but he himself had gone gray. He had faded. I slowly walked toward him, carrying my bag in one hand and my hat in the other. Avram stood frozen to the spot. I became light-headed as I saw in my mind's eye that other Avram approaching me across the field with the news that Yakov was captured and Miriam lost. My lame leg buckled briefly and I nearly stumbled.

Then Avram was directly in front of me, close at hand, in the flesh. I wrapped him in my arms with unabashed joy while, by contrast, he hugged me with careful reserve.

"I'm sorry," he muttered hoarsely, "I have grown unaccustomed to . . ." He trailed off, leaving the sentence dangling like the last dead leaf on a tree. He held me at arm's length and studied my face, as only Avram could. Deep wrinkles carved by the sun furrowed his brow.

As I processed the Avram who stood before me, with all that had changed, I pulled him close and hugged him again. This time, he responded with more ease and surrendered to the pleasure of reunion. We swayed briefly in each other's arms, as if dancing to music only we could hear. But all we heard was the call of the hawks that circled overhead in the dry blue sky. When he stepped back from me again, his awkwardness had dissipated and his mouth shaped the little half grin that I remembered so well.

"You have become an old man, Avram," I teased, in Hebrew.

"Does that surprise you?" he asked, also in Hebrew. "You, on the other hand," his eyes sparkled mischievously, "have not aged. You are a flower untouched by time."

"You have apparently gone blind in your old age."

Chuckling, he picked up my suitcase and led me to his truck. "How is Yakov?" he asked.

"Unfortunately, his heart is too weak for him to travel, which is why he is not here," I answered. "He takes medication for it, but even so, he tires easily. You know he would have loved to see you and would have come if his doctor hadn't forbidden it. He sent you a message; he said to say 'remember the dissolving bridge,' whatever that means."

Avram smiled. "It refers to one of the stunts we pulled to stymie the Nazis."

"I guessed as much," I said.

He lived half an hour's drive from the station and the town. The last five miles took us down a dirt road that degenerated into more of a footpath than a road in places. Along the drive, I shared the news about Ruth's illness, Ruth's children, Miriam and Alex, my Shayna, Zac's family, Micah's girls, Catherine and Christian in Crevecoeur, and Yakov's continued, though limited, activities. Avram nodded and smiled faintly as he listened to the fullness of the lives from which he had exiled himself.

When we arrived at his modest white wooden farmhouse with black shutters, perched on the edge of expansive fields and lush gardens, he turned off the engine and shifted sideways in his seat to look at me. "I can't remember the last time someone said that many words in a row to me," he informed me.

"Then you should get out more."

"I hope you didn't come up here to nag me about my preference for a reclusive lifestyle," he cautioned.

"I'm concerned about you," I said.

"Well, I've managed just fine for nearly five decades. It's time for you to stop worrying. Perhaps when you have had a look around my farm you'll be less concerned."

"Then how about a tour, for starters, before it gets dark?" I had bombarded him with the fullness of my life and Ruth's and I needed to give him a turn to show me what mattered to him in his life.

Avram went around to my door and gave me a hand down from the high front seat of the truck. "I need a moment to change my clothes," he said. Avram put my things in a sunny, scrubbed room with honey-colored wooden floors. The room was furnished with a tall, bird's-eye maple dresser; a ladder-backed chair; a small, hooked wool rug; and a bed covered with an orange, yellow, and white hand-pieced quilt with a sunburst pattern. Although much simpler and vastly more spare than Ruth's house, Avram's house was equally pleasurable to the eye. I changed my shoes and proceeded to the airy country kitchen to wait for Avram, who appeared almost immediately in worn denim overalls. It occurred to me that he had dressed up to meet me at the station.

"Are you hungry?" he asked.

"I could use a glass of water," I answered.

He filled a glass from the tap. I was used to drinking only bottled water and eyed the glass hesitantly.

"Go on, it's from my well," he said, with an amused expression. His water tasted purer and more satisfying than any water I had ever tasted. "This is marvelous water," I announced with delight.

"My three-hundred-foot well. Best water in the world," Avram said proudly. Then he took my arm and led me out to the gardens. He had one large barn, a few smaller outbuildings, and a chicken coop. He also had a pond and an aviary. He kept ducks, geese, chickens, pheasants, and peacocks. "They make a terrible racket," he commented about his fowl.

He had two horses and a small herd of goats. He explained that he bred the goats for sale. He also kept several sheep, one cow (named Daisy "because the secret name of every cow is Daisy," he said), a family of pigs, three dogs, numerous cats who patrolled the barn for mice, and a family of rabbits tucked away neatly in their hutches.

The dogs and a huge orange tabby cat followed close behind us. "I want to show you the orchards," Avram said as he knelt to stroke the dogs behind the ears. "They are over this way." The significance of his orchards hung unspoken between us.

As we set out across a hay field, I noted Avram's agility. For as much as his face had aged, his body retained the strength and endurance of a younger man. He walked me to a hillside that sloped gently away from us. We descended into row upon row of fruit trees.

"My apples and pears," he indicated with a wave of his arm. "And down there . . ." My eyes followed his gesture and I saw the cherry trees glistening silver green and splendid in the evening sunlight even as the word fell from his lips, "cherries. They're hers," he said simply.

"Dedicated to her?" I asked gently.

"No, quite literally. They're Miriam's. I had Christian send me grafts. Many of these trees were started from the same trees she cultivated."

"Now she has orchards on two continents," I said.

"Quite so," Avram confirmed, with a note of satisfaction in his voice. Then he continued, confidentially, "It's actually illegal to bring an agricultural product like a tree graft from another country. But we managed to do it. Sometimes you have to break a few rules to satisfy your heart."

I walked down the slope and brushed the leaves of a tree with my fingertips. Avram pointed out other fruit he grew in the orchards, including blueberries and raspberries. Then we returned to the house, where he gave me the tour of his vegetable patch adjacent to the kitchen. He picked herbs and tomatoes for our dinner. Beyond the kitchen garden, he had much larger gardens where he grew far more vegetables than he could eat and he told me that he sold his produce and then donated what he couldn't sell to a soup kitchen in town. He canned and preserved a great deal of produce to see him through the long Vermont winter.

"And you're able to support yourself with this farm?" I asked.

"Absolutely. I sell the goats (they're well-bred). I also make cheese from their milk and sell it. In the summer I sell vegetables and in the spring and fall I sell the fruit. I put up preserves and jams and sell those at the local cooperative market. I make cider. I don't require much money. I can trade for many of my needs. For instance, I trade vegetables and jam with my dentist for my dental care."

"What about feed for the animals?"

"I grow it."

"What a lot of work."

"This is what I do," he said with understated pride. "This is what I love." I could see that he had made a life for himself on this farm that was every bit as full and satisfying for him as my busy life in Paris was for me.

We prepared a late, light dinner together. The food was simple and delicious, mostly fresh tomatoes, squash, peppers, thyme, and basil from the garden stewed together and some of his goat cheese spread on home-baked whole-wheat bread. We ate and then cleaned the dishes in the darkening kitchen, just as we used to clean up after dinner for Mama as children when we argued about who would wash and who would dry. Avram waited until the last shreds of daylight disappeared to turn on the fluorescent light over his sink.

In our youth, we discussed politics for hours, but Avram had no television and did not get a newspaper. He told me that he rarely listened to his radio. He had insulated himself from the events of the world, placing the demands of his farm between himself and the bulldozer of history.

"I'm comfortable with the animals and the gardens. It's peaceful. No people, except for the seasonal hired hands I employ to help me with a harvest or a heavy job, and the occasional visit from one of my neighbors."

"You don't feel like anything is missing?" I pressed him.

Avram shrugged. "Like what?"

"People to share it with? And what of the life of the spirit that you used to talk about in Paris?"

"It's chauvinistic, and condescending, to imagine that human beings exclusively own the life of the spirit. In my experience, more humans than not are devoid of spirit. To fully appreciate the life of the spirit, one must turn aside from the world of humans."

"Surely you realize that I'm not implying that the natural world lacks a spiritual core," I replied with a touch of impatience. "I suppose I'm just disappointed that you've given up on the human spirit."

Avram snorted, "Given up on the human spirit? Well, that's an understatement."

"In the old days, you were driven to contribute to positive change and the improvement of society."

"That was the old days. I think mankind is dying off. Humans are beyond hope. I'm not pretentious enough to believe that anything I do can make a difference. I could quote you statistics on how many children in this country live in poverty, go to bed hungry each night, die before the age of five, and are victims of child abuse. Humans are no better than the fish who feed on their own offspring. Our systems are collapsing. We're cutting down so many trees that soon we'll no longer have air fit to breathe. Our fuel supply is dwindling and we have been too slow about developing energy resources with which to replace petroleum. We are destroying the ecology of the planet and rendering it unfit to support life." Avram paused in his gloomy litany. But in his tirade, he had revealed that somewhere, from some source, he did seek information about the progress of the outside world. He had read and noted these statistics that he recited.

"So says the sayer of doom. Enough already. I once knew another Avram who believed in working for change, for healing. The old Avram had faith in the capacity of the human spirit."

"Get used to the new Avram. The old Avram witnessed firsthand the human spirit that brought us the *Shoah*. The human spirit brought millions of Africans to this country and murdered them or enslaved them for hundreds of years. The human spirit annihilated the intricate indigenous cultures on this continent. What you see today is the ruins of the human spirit, the consequences of the human spirit. The human spirit tortured and killed our Miriam and her children. No, I have no faith in the human spirit." He spat his words out like poison.

"Miriam and her children were the human spirit and they were murdered by the forces that work against its survival. There is a spiritual force in the universe that is greater than human comprehension," I said firmly.

"Then explain Auschwitz."

I sighed wearily. "Of course I can't. I don't know why we suffer. I don't know why some people make others suffer. I can't imagine any useful purpose to human suffering. But my understanding is limited. I'm just one ordinary person. I will tell you what I do know. I do know that the spirit has a life of its own that transcends this life. The energy of the spirit is like any other force of energy in nature and the laws of physics demonstrate that energy can't be destroyed but rather is converted into other forms of energy. The spirit in each being is an energy of its own and at death it does not go poof and disappear. It is converted, transformed, no longer housed in matter."

"We live, we die, we turn to dust; don't glorify it, Rivka. It's a straightforward and brutal process."

I did not pursue him further into the sheltered shadow places where he dwelled. I was well aware of the depth of the pain he had suffered. And I understood that the true Avram had not entirely survived the war, but the Avram who remained had found peace in this beautiful place. "What if something happened to you out here, how would you get help?" I asked.

"Spoken as a true Jewish mother," he said with a slight grin. "Don't worry. I have neighbors who look in on me from time to time. Someone stops by at least once a week to swap local gossip. You'd be surprised how many geezers hide up in these hills. I have a few friends, young as well as old. I sometimes visit my neighbors on my horse. I reckon someone would find me eventually if I had a mishap." His words failed to reassure me.

"You should at least think about getting a telephone now that you're getting older," I told him. He shrugged.

We lingered over a cup of mint tea as we sat on the screened porch to watch the night sky fill and brim over with a bounty of dazzling stars. I asked Avram about his daily activities on the land and this brought him more out of himself as he shared some of the details of his country life. Before long, however, he yawned and admitted, apologetically, that he rose early to feed and milk the animals, and so he needed to go to bed. I, a dyed-in-the-wool night owl, lingered on the porch after his departure, stargazing, with my face upturned to the clear darkness of the sky unadulterated by the interference of city lights. I rarely had the opportunity to see so many stars. I had read that there were stars that had transmitted their light back when dinosaurs walked the earth and it took millions of years for that light to reach the human eye on Earth. Facts like that made me wonder what the difference was between physics and magic.

As often happened, I had difficulty falling asleep that night without the comforting presence of Yakov next to me in the bed. So I awoke later than I would have liked the next morning. The sunlight poured into my room, which opened onto a view of Avram's iridescent gardens. A peacock shrieked madly across the pond. I padded to the window where I spotted the noisy fellow glinting turquoise, green, and gold, his thin black headdress like an ink mark sprouting from the top of his head.

Downstairs I found fresh ground coffee in a filter set inside a drip cone atop a glass pot. I boiled water and poured it through the cone. Avram had also set out peaches and blueberries, homemade butter and jam, and a partial loaf of uncut brown bread. I sat down to breakfast, missing only the newspaper. The breakfast was, without a doubt, delicious. After I ate and cleaned up after myself, I put on my walking shoes and stepped out into the humid day. I found Avram at the barn milking goats.

"Good morning," he greeted cheerfully between pulls.

"Good morning," I said back.

"Don't come closer. You'll spook her. She's not accustomed to company." Galvanized metal milk cans with tightly screwed lids stood in a neat line along the wall.

"What do you do with all this milk?" I asked.

"I make three varieties of superbly tasty goat cheese and sell it. I have no trouble keeping up with the goats. It's that damn cow that nearly does me in," he said, not missing a beat in his milking rhythm. "I'm on the last goat, be done in a minute."

"What is on the agenda for today?"

"You. I'm trying to keep the chores to a minimum while you're here. But traditionally this is my apricot season. I also put up zucchini relish this month. And I have grapes that need attention at this time of year."

"Grapes used to be my specialty," I reminded him. "What type of grapes grow in this climate?"

"Concord. Most types of grapes can't tolerate the cold temperatures here in New England. The Concords are cold-hardy; they remind me of France, and they make a robust juice." Avram stood up from the low milking stool, unfolded to his full height, and proceeded to formally introduce me to the goats. He talked softly to the animals as he released them to the pasture. Then he took down gloves, copper wire, and crimping shears and led me to his grape arbors. We worked side by side, while I chattered on about Catherine's grandchildren, her twin boys, and Isabel.

As I worked, I remembered the grapes of Crevecoeur. And here I was, an old woman, helping Avram train his grapes in Vermont. It was rather remarkable what could happen if one only lived long enough. The knowledge of working the grapevines returned to my hands of its own accord. Unfortunately, my back was suffering from amnesia and would not cooperate. I soon confessed to Avram that I couldn't continue.

He led me to a vegetable garden near the house and opened a folding chair for me, then he fetched my hat from my bedroom to protect me from the sun.

"Sit here for a few minutes," he said. "This won't take long." He picked squash and peppers, tumbling them into bushel baskets. Then we went inside where we chopped and grated the vegetables for relish and packed them into canning jars. The mouth-watering scent of peppers, onions, and celery seed filled the kitchen, which soon felt like a sauna. Avram turned on a floor fan and I stood in the breeze it created.

In the afternoon, Avram made a picnic lunch and we carried it to the pond where he spread an orange tablecloth on the ground. We ate in the shade of a tall and stately weeping willow while gazing at Avram's ducks and geese playing on the water. As children, we had never run out of things to speak about and this had not changed. We swapped recollections about our parents and the family we had shared, so that our childhood rose to the surface and we could almost taste Mama's lentil soup or hear Papa and Meir discussing politics over a game of chess.

After lunch, we sat by the water and talked through the afternoon, grateful for a cooling breeze. "What about the relish?" I asked. "And the apricots?"

"The apricots can wait and I'll boil the relish later today after it cools off."

In the evening he set the jars of relish to boil in two vats on the stove and then we sat on Avram's screened porch and sipped ice water with peppermint floating in it while we watched the sunset creep into the fields.

"Would you take me to town tomorrow to call and check on Ruth?" I asked.

"Of course," Avram replied.

"What would you think about inviting Rina's daughter, Miriam, and her son to come up here to meet you?" I nearly held my breath while waiting to see if he would agree to this proposal.

Avram stopped rocking in his chair. The silence between us filled with the sound of the jars of relish rattling in the processing vats boiling on the stove in the kitchen behind us.

"She's Miriam's namesake, isn't she?" Avram asked.

"Yes." He seemed suspicious, even threatened. I wondered if he feared he might feel something, if he feared becoming attached to another Miriam who might cause him pain.

"She has a little boy?"

"Alejandro. He's as bright as a freshly minted dime. They live on a ranch in Arizona and her husband is a farmer. An immigrant like us, he fled a terrorist regime in El Salvador. Would you give me the pleasure of introducing you to Miriam and Alejandro while I'm here?"

Avram hesitated.

"What worries you about it?" I asked gently.

"I'm not used to company," he reminded me. "Especially children."

"I promise you'll be glad they came. They could drive up and spend a couple of nights and then drive me back. Alejandro would love it here." I longed to see Avram standing next to this Miriam, to see Alex sit in his lap and pat Avram's gray-whiskered cheek. Perhaps if Miriam and Avram met, then he would have a continued connection to the family after Ruth passed. Possibly I had the ability to arrange for someone in this vast country to care about him and maybe even look after him if he became incapable of looking after himself on his solitary farm. I hoped that Miriam, who had that ranch in Arizona, would pay attention to his well-being in the future.

"OK," Avram agreed.

"Then it's settled. Tomorrow we'll drive into town and call to check on Ruth and I'll invite Miriam to come."

The next morning, after milking and chores, Avram loaded jars of zucchini relish into crates and secured them in the bed of the pickup truck. We struck out down the driveway and onto the dirt road and finally the highway that led into town. Avram dropped me off at the grocery store where I used a pay phone to place my call. Sarah answered at the other end.

"She has had less energy these past couple of days, but hasn't visibly declined more than that," Sarah told me. "Sometimes, when she's tired, she's disoriented. But it seems fine for you to spend a few more days in Vermont. We'll wire if there's a sudden change."

I thanked Sarah for the report. Ruth was asleep and I didn't want Sarah to wake her. "Let her know that I'm looking forward to telling her all about Avram's farm when I get back," I said. I hung up and then dialed Rina and Arthur's number. Alejandro answered.

"Hello?" he chirped in his singsong voice. I imagined the child peering at Avram with those intent eyes.

"*Buenos días, mi angel.* My little Alejandro. This is Tía Rivka."

"Where are you?"

"I'm visiting my friend Avram in Vermont. He has a wonderful farm with lots of animals like your papi."

"Does he have an almond tree?" the little one asked.

"I'm not sure. I will ask him."

"The almond tree is my favorite."

"Is your mami at home?"

"Yeeees."

"Can I speak to her?"

"Yeeees."

I heard shuffling and banging and then Miriam's bemused voice. "Hello? Aunt Rivka? Are you still there?"

"Yes, I'm here."

"Alex dropped the phone. But he told me it was you. He did well."

"Very well indeed. Listen, I'm calling to extend a special invitation. I would like you and Alex to join me here in Vermont. You would adore this farm and I want to introduce you to Avram. He's the brother of your namesake. Please say you'll come."

Miriam paused while she considered my invitation. Then she said, "I have often wondered about him. I'd like to come, but I would have to find someone to travel with me to keep Alex entertained since it's such a long drive."

"Bring your mother," I suggested. "You can stay for a couple of nights and then drive me back to Ruth's."

"That sounds lovely. I'll ask her. We could drive up tomorrow."

I waited while Miriam discussed the trip with Rina and then returned to confirm that they would come. I gave Miriam the address for the farm and the name of the road at the highway turnoff. After hanging up, I felt elated. I went into the air-conditioned store, where I bought several bottles of red table wine imported from France, salmon, two limes, and a jar of Greek olives. I could not buy anything much that would taste better than the fresh, homespun food Avram produced from his own land. At the little post office inside the store, I picked up a stamp and a postcard with a picture of a covered bridge, and I wrote a short note to Yakov on the back, then I dropped the card into the mailbox. I sat on a dark-green wooden slatted bench underneath a maple tree in front of the store to wait for Avram to return and unfolded a newspaper I had purchased out of a machine.

Yakov would probably take me to task for meddling by inviting Miriam to Vermont. He thought I had a tendency to be "too busy" in the lives of others. Well, dear, I said to him in my head, it's an aging auntie's prerogative to meddle a little.

Before long, Avram pulled up in the truck. He had a roll of fencing in the back and he had unloaded the relish somewhere in his travels.

"So? Are they coming?" he asked.

"Tomorrow," I replied with satisfaction. "Miriam, Alejandro, and Rina."

Avram remained silent and contemplative until I prodded him back to conversation by asking him what had become of the relish we had put up. Then he chuckled. He said that when he dropped his relish off at the local co-op market, he heard a rollicking story about a pair of escaped cows. One of the fellows living up at Mountain Meadow Ranch had lost his cows when a fence blew down. He had been chasing his cows around trying to catch them for weeks. He had caught all but two wily, wary cows. He would sight these two renegades, but could not get close enough to catch them. The fellow said that if he didn't catch those cows by Labor Day weekend, there was going to be one heck of a hamburger barbecue at his place.

Upon our return to the farm, we ate a lunch of bread, goat cheese, tomatoes, and some of the Greek olives I had bought at the store. I sampled Avram's excellent relish. After lunch, despite the heat, we decided to pick apricots. I probably ate more of the plump golden fruit than I should have. They tasted divine. I dripped with sweat from the humidity. Avram sang a racy French drinking song from our early years in Paris. I marveled that he remembered the words to the many verses. The sensuality of the afternoon reminded me of how good it felt sometimes simply to be alive.

I declared, "I worship at the temple of biting-into-an-apricot-on-a-summer's-day, and let all the philosophers and theologians sit around in their dusty rooms puzzling to eternity."

"Amen to that," Avram said. "I rest my case."

"Meaning?" I asked, for further clarification.

"About life on the farm," he replied. "You know, our conversation last night." He did have a point. I wondered what Yakov would have said to him about his self-imposed isolation. If he had come with me, I thought, Yakov would probably have approved of Avram's choice for himself.

We watched storm clouds gather on the horizon while we loaded apricots into the back of Avram's truck in the late afternoon. And, as I boiled eggs and prepared a large salad for our dinner, the scent of approaching rain filled the house. Just as we sat down to eat, the storm broke. Avram left the door and windows open to grant the moist breeze entry through the screens. We worked our way through a bottle of wine while we listened to the rain pound the roof and yard.

Sitting across the table from Avram in the dimly lit humid kitchen, I felt a small, tightly coiled spring within myself bounce open. I felt electrified by the storm.

Perhaps Avram was pelted by my energy because he jumped to his feet, grabbed my hand, and commanded, "Come."

"Are you drunk?" I asked.

"No," he laughed, "well maybe just a little."

What happened that night? Perhaps it was the wine. Perhaps it was the rain. Perhaps it was the inexplicable energy that saturated me and radiated from me, from both of us, during the storm. Perhaps it was the sensuous apricot-picking. Perhaps it was the sheer momentum of the intersection of our lives catching up with us. Avram pulled me out the door and we ran through the warm rain to the pond. The drops cooled my skin. My drenched hair slapped my cheeks. What was I doing? An old lady running in the rain? We stopped in the thick grass by the willow tree. Avram threaded his arms firmly around my back and kissed me. He brushed my wet hair from my face. Lit by the moon, he tipped to me a face filled with desire. His chest rose and fell with his rapid breathing, his powerful arms tensed. My heart raced. My mind dashed through moments we had shared as children, teenagers, idealistic youths in Paris. I had thought of Avram as a brother, but in fact he wasn't now and never had been, despite our having grown up together in the same house. There had always been another edge to our relationship. Always. Here, on his land, at the other end of our lives, with all the years separating us from our childhood together, I saw him as a man whom I had loved. The view looked different from this direction.

"If you had not met Yakov, would it have been me?" he asked fiercely. It was a question that had burned in him all his life.

I did not love him more than I loved my Yakov and I would not have wanted to make a life with him; definitely not this life, in the wilderness, no matter how beautiful the landscape. But I certainly did love him. If I had not met Yakov, would it have been Avram? What would our lives have been like if Avram and I had married? I could not imagine it.

"That is an impossible question to answer. Who can know such a thing? But I can truthfully say that I have always loved you." That much I could give him wholeheartedly.

Avram took my words to mean what he wanted them to mean and he kissed me again. After that we surprised ourselves. We made love on the soft bed of grass, damp with the warm summer rain that continued to caress us. Our lovemaking was not the sort that springs from the wild passion of youth as the moment attempted to dictate, but it was deliberate and slow to build, as if we had been married for many years and would have many opportunities to make love again in the rain under this willow tree. Our lovemaking became a continuation of the afternoon picking apricots, the delicious dinner, our lifelong friendship, and even our childhood in that sunlit house in Palestine. We made love to each other while at the same time making love to the moon, the night, the rain, and the earth beneath us that yielded Avram his livelihood. I had always imagined

I would feel embarrassed and awkward making love to anyone other than Yakov, who knew me so well. But Avram made me comfortable. It was something we both needed to do, an act of fidelity to our true selves that Yakov would never have understood and therefore (I vowed) would never discover.

Lying on the grass in the dark, rain-drenched and satisfied, Avram whispered to me confessions he had carried through his years in Vermont. How he had forsaken the world and finally made a truce with his soul. He had not sought a partner or marriage but celibacy and solitude instead. He had learned to still the voices that haunted and hunted him, had wrestled with his demons, had carved a place of peace at last. Neither one of us hurried to leave our warm nest on the ground under the summer rain and the night sky.

"I liked to imagine that one day you would visit me here and that this might happen," he said as he ran his finger lightly down my cheek, my neck, shoulder, and along my side to my stout waist, then up the hill of my well-padded hip, as far as he could reach. "Just once. To tie up this strand of my life. Not a day has gone by that I didn't speak to you in my mind, if not right out loud."

We whispered together until we floated off to sleep, cradled in the rain-soaked grass and each other's arms. When we awoke, we picked up our scattered clothing and drifted back to the house where we dried off and nestled into bed.

We slept late the next morning, loath to leave the comfort of each other's embrace. When he awoke, Avram went directly to the barn, where the animals blasted at him with disapproval at his tardiness. I cooked a breakfast of pancakes and fruit, which we shared after Avram had finished milking.

"You realize," I told Avram at breakfast, "that if I had come to America in my youth, as you and Ruth did, I would probably have spent a great deal of time in jail and would have been blacklisted during the McCarthy era in the fifties and all the rest. Yakov as well. You know they wouldn't even let us into the country as tourists as recently as 1962 because we were former Communists. We had turned in our cards years before that, but because we had once carried cards, they refused us visas."

"The Communist threat," Avram grunted as he waved his arm. "Such foolishness."

"I could never feel at home in a country that allows such pervasive poverty, that isolates and ostracizes those who have nothing, and does so while the poor live next door to such obscene wealth. It seems to me that your American political system is more about preserving your economic system than about protecting the rights of your citizens, or improving their quality of life. Just think how many hungry children could be fed on the annual income of one of your celebrities or corporate executives. Communism is not workable, but clearly neither is capitalism, and on top of being unworkable, it's offensive in my opinion. Yakov calls it 'corporatism.' If I had spent my life in this country battling corporatism, I would certainly have become bitter."

"However, it sounds like you no longer support Communism as a viable economic system," Avram said, choosing not to comment on my tirade against capitalism, most likely because he agreed with me.

"Of course not. How could we possibly support it after what history has revealed about Communism in the Soviet Union? We turned in our party cards after the truth came out about Stalin. Yakov is now active in the Socialist Party. I have no party affiliation, although I have marvelous young friends in the Green Party and we do political work together. I vote for individuals these days, not 'isms.' And I'll let you in on a secret; sometimes I don't vote at all."

"Doesn't bother me. I've never voted," Avram boasted, with an air of superiority that irritated me. "Politicians are all the same," he said disdainfully.

"Well, I can hear what Yakov would have to say about that," I told him. "He still believes in the possibility of positive social change whereas you have given up on the idea." I wanted to tell him that he had given up on ideas altogether, but I regained control before blurting that out.

If he had been hurt by my outburst, he concealed it. "He and I are different," he said simply. That difference had never felt more acute to me. I thought back to our decision to leave the Communist Party.

"Do you know what it did to us when we learned the truth about Stalin?" I asked.

"I don't suppose I do," Avram replied with infuriating lack of emotion.

"It was devastating," I told him heatedly. "Absolutely devastating. It forced us to realize that humans are incapable of practicing Communism correctly. Yakov said at the time that there is only one way for Communism to work. That everyone in the entire country, from the workers to the bosses, every single person, must have a pure heart."

"Any economic system would work under those conditions. He can't possibly imagine that's possible," Avram said, with incredulity.

"Of course not. How could he? He came out of Auschwitz. But he does believe that if you are bothered by the way things are, then you must work to change them."

"So what do you think?" he asked, as he gathered our breakfast plates and took them to the sink.

"I think that a great many good ideas cannot be translated effectively into practice. True Communism can never exist because of the fallible relationship between men and power. So one must be careful with theory because much of it leads absolutely nowhere. Unfortunately, I'm married to a theorist who develops political abstractions." I shrugged. "Sometimes he comes up with something practical."

"So I suppose that you and Yakov approve of the politics of France?" Avram baited me, but only halfheartedly. His apparent indifference annoyed me more than anything else.

"I'm not sure I approve of any country. I approve of communities. I do think France is an improvement over America, however," I responded. At least I had managed to budge him, even if briefly, from the topic of the wonders of nature.

We lingered over our coffee and conversation until Avram kissed me and drew me to him again. The youngsters would arrive that evening, and I knew that we must stop carrying on like this, but why not just one more time? We made love wistfully and rather delicately and in farewell. And since we really were too old to behave like this, we fell asleep afterward.

I woke to the sound of the geese squawking at the pond. Their racket rose above the whir of the floor fan that sent a breeze across the room. I felt a little dizzy and lay in the bed for a while looking at Avram's face in repose. Our lovemaking had been necessary as a healing act, a closure. I felt as though we had mended a tear in our souls.

Miriam would arrive soon. I gently shook Avram awake. We spoke softly, deciding what to cook for dinner. I admired the traditional quilt spread beneath us on Avram's bed.

"What is the name of the quilting pattern?" I asked.

"It's called House on the Hill," Avram said. Like Avram's house, I thought. Distant and away from the world. Safe on high ground. Avram stretched like a lazy tiger, hauled himself out of the bed, put on his overalls, and went out to finish his chores.

I took a shower, and by the time Avram wandered in from the barn, I had tidied the bedrooms, set the salmon in a lime juice marinade, and nearly finished putting together a quiche with Avram's farm-fresh cheese, eggs, milk, vegetables, and herbs. He put the kettle on for tea and then we heard the car coming down the drive. I laughed out loud in anticipation. "That must be my dears," I exclaimed, as I hurried out to the front porch.

Miriam emerged first, jumping out of the passenger side of the car with her characteristic vivaciousness. She wore her usual farmer's overalls, which bulged out over her pregnant belly. Her large silver hoop earrings glinted against the mocha brown of her neck. Her dreadlocked hair bounced about her head and shoulders. She smiled at me.

"Hey," she called, "what a fantastic place."

Rina emerged from the driver's seat, smoothing her flowery purple dress down against her legs. Spaghetti straps crisscrossed her back in a fancy pattern; her thick, dark hair, flecked with gray, fell just past her shoulders in curls.

I sensed Avram's discomfort in the presence of these two vibrant, beautiful women. He'll get over it, I thought, as I stepped off the porch to embrace my nieces.

TWO

Miriam

AFTER KISSING EACH OF us on both cheeks in that European fashion that I so loved, Aunt Rivka immediately asked, "Where is my little jewel?"

"He's asleep in the back," I said, gesturing toward my son. Aunt Rivka peered into the backseat, where she saw Alex's sweet little face through the window, nestled in the crook of the car seat. "He did surprisingly well on the long drive. We stopped a few times to stretch and I sat in the back and played with his trucks with him for quite a while. We sang a lot of songs."

"I believe I have listened to every Spanish 'I-Can-Read' book ever recorded on tape," Mama groaned.

Aunt Rivka turned toward the porch and introduced us to Avram, a vigorous, weathered fellow in faded overalls.

Mama shook Avram's hand and told him that she vaguely remembered coming to his farm as a youngster. "I remember playing in the hayloft and feeding the animals," she said.

I scrutinized Avram through squinted eyes. "You look like someone I know, but I can't think who. Give me a minute; it'll come to me. Probably in the middle of the night, you know. Is there a movie star or someone that people say you resemble?" I asked gaily.

"Mr. Green Jeans," Avram quipped.

Mama laughed.

"Who's that?" I asked.

"A character from an old children's TV show," Mama explained. "It was before your time."

"I'm going to wake Alex. May I take him to see the animals?" I asked Avram. "He misses his animal buddies from home." More than the animals, he and I both were missing Gil. Alex called Gil every morning to give him the report on our visit. I had alerted Gil that we were going to Vermont for a couple of days and that we would be staying with someone who had no phone.

"I need to bring the livestock into the barn for the night. Would you and the boy like to come with me to fetch the animals?" Avram offered.

"Alex would love it. Thank you. Just give me a minute to rouse him," I said. After I woke Alex, Mama carried him on the path to the barn while he swam back to consciousness. When he was completely awake, he clambered down from her arms and shot off like a bursting comet. I never ceased to delight in seeing evidence of the power and energy of his little body.

Aunt Rivka dropped back to walk more slowly with Mama so she could ask for an update on Grandma Ruth.

Mama said, "She has plenty of visitors. I think it's good that you came up here for a few days. It seems to me that sometimes she feels like everyone is sitting around waiting for her to die."

I didn't hear what they said after that, because I bounded ahead with Alex into the pasture to admire the goats and pet the horses. Then we returned to the barnyard, where Alex chased the chickens, squawking louder even than the terrorized fowl.

"We have chickens too," I told Avram, "but that's it as far as birds go. You have a lot of work here."

"It's my full-time job," Avram said.

"I know how that goes," I replied. I was impressed that an old man like Avram could manage such a large agricultural operation on his own.

Avram secured the animals for the night and then Rivka alerted us that dinner was almost ready. She turned back toward the kitchen to check on it while Avram took me for a quick look at the gardens that were closest to the house. Just outside the kitchen door, I pinched a sprig of lavender between my fingers and called to Alex, "Come here, hijo, smell this."

He smiled as he sniffed. "It smells like your garden, Mami," he said.

When we went inside, we all helped get things ready for dinner. Alex and Mama set the table. I asked Avram if I could pick a few flowers for a centerpiece. "I don't have a vase," Avram apologized. "I don't usually pick the flowers and bring them inside." I arranged a bouquet of purple delphiniums and red and orange alstroemeria in a canning jar.

"Not picking the flowers is one school of thought," I said to Avram. "I'm of the opinion that they grow more blooms when you cut them, though. They like to replace what has gone. You must spend a lot of time outdoors. I spend too much time doing indoor chores or away from our farm because of my job, so if I don't take my flowers inside, then I don't appreciate them enough."

Avram seemed to weigh my words, but did not reply.

We sat down to a superb country meal with salmon, quiche, and salad. When Mama congratulated Rivka on her quiche, she reminded us, "Avram's homegrown."

So then we complimented Avram, who remained reserved and quiet. I caught him stealing surreptitious glances at me, which made me feel self-conscious.

After dinner, the light stayed with us in the long summer day, so we wandered further afield to view the "commercial gardens," as Avram referred to them. Alex bounded back and forth between us like an exuberant puppy. Gil would have liked to see these gardens. Avram had fields of corn, and he grew several different varieties, including blue corn. We didn't grow blue corn at Esperanza Farm.

Mama took photographs as she voiced her delight in the streaks of pink and violet that appeared in the sky at sunset. I drew Avram into conversation as I tried to coax him to emerge from his shell. I was trying to figure him out. There was a reason why Aunt Rivka wanted us to meet each other, and it was more than just our shared affection for rural living. But if I couldn't get Avram to talk with me, then I doubted I would discover what it was.

Aunt Rivka chased Alex, tickling him when she caught him, and listening to his squeals of delight. We meandered back to the house, in no hurry, enjoying the twilight.

After I put Alex to bed, we adults sat on the porch. Mama and Aunt Rivka sipped Burgundy. Avram made tall glasses of ice water with peppermint floating in them for himself and me.

Aunt Rivka said, "The distinctive intensity of green in Vermont just about makes my eyes pop." Then she added, with a laugh, "I need sunglasses here so I don't get a headache."

We proceeded to compare landscapes. Mama and I shared some of the things we loved about Kenya.

Mama said, "The light in Kenya has a certain quality to it that you see nowhere else. It casts a sandy orange glow. I think it has something to do with the dust in the air."

Avram warmed instantly to our description of Kenya, and it did not require much encouragement for Mama and me to share stories from our sojourn in Africa. We always remembered those years with affection. I told the story about Loud Mouth and the trouble we ran into before we understood how to live in harmony with a community garden.

"I would have liked to visit Africa," Avram told us.

"Arthur and I went to Jamaica last spring and it reminded us of Africa. It's closer and a less expensive trip. You might think about taking a vacation there," Mama suggested.

"I might," Avram responded.

But I got the distinct impression that he didn't intend to go anywhere. I wondered what happened to him during the war. Aunt Rivka had told me that Avram fought in the Resistance with her husband, Yakov. I wondered how close he had been to his sister who had died trying to save all those children and how he wound up on a farm in Vermont. I was sure there was a story there, but it didn't seem likely that I would get it out of him. He was so unreadable.

I asked him about his dogs, who were sleeping curled at his feet, and he talked about them with some enthusiasm. So I launched into a description of our Sadie and Paz, and then I told him about Annie's newest dog, Hambone. "Annie brought him home from the pound last month," I related, "and John has disliked him from day one, but Annie won't give him up. He's goofy and adorable. John doesn't like him because he's so destructive. Hambone chewed up several lawn chairs and he chewed the wood around the hinges on their woodshed door, so that it fell off. Annie and I thought it was funny, but John was annoyed. Hambone's still a puppy and not fully trained. He'll outgrow the chewing."

"I sympathize with John. I wouldn't keep a dog like that either," Mama said.

"Two nights before I left to come here, he got skunked and crawled under their car. It made the car smell god-awful. And Annie drove us to the airport in that car. I swear when we got on the plane people were sniffing us and moving away."

Avram had a couple of skunk stories of his own, which gave us a good laugh. As much as I wanted to stay awake to continue our conversation, I soon became too sleepy and was forced to say my good nights and head off to bed.

It was not long after midnight when I awoke sweating and shivering from one of my nightmares, a particularly vivid and terrifying one. Without Gil to calm me, my heart racing, I impulsively slipped into Aunt Rivka's room and crawled into bed with her. I didn't want to wake Mama, who had spent the whole previous day driving. I felt sorry to wake Aunt Rivka, but I needed her. I was trembling so hard that my teeth chattered. Poor Aunt Rivka woke to find me sitting with my knees drawn up under my chin beside her in bed. She lit a candle on the nightstand. "What's the matter?" she asked.

"Please let me stay for a few minutes. I sometimes have nightmares. Gil usually helps me through, but he's not here. I haven't had them nearly as often since Alex was born. But once in a while they still come, and I had one tonight." I continued to shiver, despite the heat of the summer night.

"Do you want to tell me about it?" Aunt Rivka asked.

I weighed my options and made the choice to confide in her. "I dream that I have a lot of children and they are being tortured," I began.

Aunt Rivka raised a shaky hand to her throat as a wave of fright crossed her face.

"Are you sure you want to hear this?" I asked.

"Yes," she said quietly, "absolutely."

"Not Alex. Other children. In the dream someone takes these children from me one by one and . . ." My voice faltered, Aunt Rivka waited, then I continued. "They maim them and they kill them. One of the children, I recognize him as mine, a toddler, has one of his, one of his feet . . ." I bit my lip and put a hand on Aunt Rivka's arm. Forcing her to listen to my nightmare was not fair. "I'm sorry, I shouldn't subject you to this."

"One of his feet is missing, isn't it?" Aunt Rivka asked.

"How did you know?" I demanded, stunned.

"Because Avram told me about it one night in a field such a long time ago that it often seems as if it happened in another lifetime. But tonight I can see it and touch it, as near as if it happened yesterday. The miserable iron taste of it fills my mouth."

I stared at Aunt Rivka in astonishment. "What are you talking about?"

"I'm sorry, my dear. You have no idea. I will tell you, I promise. But first, tell me what else you dream."

"Usually, I just dream about those children, but tonight, for the first time, I dreamed about cherries too. They were growing on a tree branch. They were full and ripe, deep burgundy, but then they dried up. To see them wither like that made me so sad that I woke sobbing."

Aunt Rivka searched my face with her eyes. "What have you been told about your namesake, Miriam, who was Avram's sister?"

"That she was a heroine in the war, protected many children, and eventually lost her life, murdered by the Nazis."

"Your dreams will make sense once you hear her whole story." Aunt Rivka proceeded to describe for me a farm in the south of France, where my namesake, Miriam, lived with her husband, Robert. The farm sounded like paradise, with its orchards, gardens, vineyards, and fields of wheat. She told me about the livestock they raised; about their big farmhouse with a warm kitchen always full of wonderful smells of cooking and baking; about Miriam's passion for her cherry trees; about Miriam's little boy, Akiva; and about Babette's children who came to live there. She spoke about Father Charles and the children whom he and Miriam rescued and nurtured. At one point, Aunt Rivka remarked, "I wish I could tell you this story in Yiddish. It's a bittersweet story and would do well told in Yiddish." But she told it in English, because that was the language we had in common. She described the vibrant home in Crevecoeur and Miriam's desire to give the children what she called "an enchanted childhood." Then she related how Miriam was captured and told me about the night that Avram came to her in a field with the horrific news of Miriam's torture and murder.

The moment each sentence fell from Aunt Rivka's lips, I recognized each piece of that other Miriam's life as if I had always known it. It belonged to me. No longer dreams, nightmares, and intuitions, the truth of that other life became real, and I possessed it.

As Aunt Rivka finished, she said, "I believe you have her returned spirit and that you will build your farm and family again, that you will have many children and delight in raising them. I believe that Alejandro is Akiva returned. And I also believe that your children will not be taken from you this time. You are owed happiness. It was paid for many years ago."

By this time, we were both weeping. I wanted to tell Gil about all this but knew that it would have to wait because it was not the sort of thing I could share with him on the phone or in a letter. I wished he had come with me on this odyssey. Aunt Rivka held me until the storm passed and we could wipe our eyes and speak again without breaking down.

Then she said, "A statue stands in Crevecoeur."

"What do you mean?" I asked, mystified by her words and still processing all that I had just learned.

In reply, Aunt Rivka went to her suitcase and took out photographs she had brought of a statue of the other Miriam that stood at the university in Crevecoeur. As we passed the photos back and forth, she explained to me about teaching people to read during the war and how the statue came to be there in the town that had sheltered her.

"You can keep these," Aunt Rivka offered. "I have more copies."

"This helps me understand why it's so important to me to heal people who have suffered trauma, particularly children," I said.

"Important work," Aunt Rivka replied. "What worries me is how to heal the ones inclined to inflict the pain so that they cause no further suffering."

"I have come to think that the only surefire way out of the vicious cycle is to prevent anyone from choosing to hurt others in the first place," I told her, with conviction.

"How do you propose to do that?"

"Only one way, Aunt Rivka. Raise the children well so that there are no torturers among them. Each child. One by one."

She smiled. "That's a tall order."

"One worth devoting one's life to."

"Certainly one worth devoting one's life to."

The rising sun began to lick the edges of the morning sky and I rose with it to return to my own bed. I kissed Aunt Rivka on both cheeks. As I tiptoed out the door, she called softly after me, "You are owed, my love, remember that always."

THREE

Rivka

EXHAUSTED FROM TELLING MIRIAM'S story, I fell into a deep sleep. When I opened my eyes a couple of hours later, I found a little boy in bed next to me humming an aimless tune. The instant he saw my eyelids flutter open, Alejandro pounced, hugging me with his firm little brown arms, his wide-set eyes sparkling with good cheer. He smelled of rose soap.

"Tío Avram is making a big breakfast. It's going to be yummy. He let me milk the goat. The milk came out. Squirt, squirt." He demonstrated his milking motion with his hands. "You can drink some. And I gave the grain to the chickens. Mami is still asleep. She's missing everything. Should I wake her up? Grandmama says let her sleep. What do you say?"

"I say you are a chatterbox." I tickled him under the arms and in the crook of his neck. He rewarded me with an infectious belly laugh.

"I guess I had best get up and prepare myself for this big breakfast." As I washed, I reflected on the incomprehensible pathways of life that brought a little boy to refer to Avram as "Tío Avram."

My stomach growled ravenously as the most wonderful smell of muffins baking greeted me from the country kitchen. I wondered how many pounds I was gaining on this vacation.

We eventually allowed Alejandro to wake his mami so she could breakfast with us. And breakfast we did. Avram produced blueberry muffins fresh from the oven slathered in butter and raspberry jam, fried eggs with yolks that stood up and saluted from the pan, sliced apricots in yogurt, apple cider, and strong coffee with fresh cream.

After we cleaned the dishes and Alejandro picked a bouquet of flowers for the table, we set out for the orchards at Miriam's request. She and Avram swiftly fell into a highly technical discussion about cultivating fruit trees. Miriam said that Gil was teaching her how to graft. Avram offered her grafts from the cherry trees he had brought over from France. I would find a time to tell her later that the grafts he offered were from the same stock that Miriam had grown in Crevecoeur. Avram clearly felt a kinship with this young woman, who appreciated the work and rewards of running a farm. I wondered if he sensed any deeper connection with her.

In the afternoon, Avram took Alejandro out on the pond in a beat-up canoe while we women chatted and watched from the porch. Rina had brought handwork for a textile project. She was making pillows and she had brought the front squares, onto which she embroidered details that added to various grasses depicted on them, in order to give the grasses more depth. Before long, Miriam went inside to take a nap. When we were alone, Rina looked up from her embroidery and cast a smile in my direction.

"You look disgracefully content over there in your rocking chair, Aunt Rivka," she said.

"I feel disgracefully content. I am enjoying this time with the family immensely. Particularly this brief respite in Vermont before returning to say good-bye to your mother. I'm gathering my inner resources to support me for what lies ahead."

Rina bowed her head again over her work. "I understand completely. When we return, we'll be there until the end. This little trip is the last respite we'll have. I must say that it feels weird to have you right in front of me doing ordinary things. I tend to half imagine you in legendary proportions."

"I'm only a person, like everyone else."

"You and Mom both seem legendary to me. I feel as though when Mom passes and when you return to France, the legendary ones will have left and only us ordinaries will remain." Rina looked into the distance where the purple peaks of Vermont's Green Mountains stood out like the hooded heads of elders gathered in palaver.

"You and your sisters are each extraordinary in your own right. And one day your grandchildren will view your generation as the legendary ones," I replied. I doubted that Shayna would ever describe me as a "legendary one." She was the famous dancer, and her father was the legendary Resistance fighter. But I understood what Rina was saying because I sometimes thought of my own parents in legendary proportions.

"But you, look at the trail you blazed," Rina pressed on. "You made changes in the way people live their lives. My daughter does that. She has greatness in her."

"Your daughter possesses a mighty spirit," I agreed.

"I've spent my life in the ivory tower, making my art, on my own and also with Arthur and our colleagues. No one can accuse us of squandering the talent that we have been fortunate to possess. We've had the rare opportunity to use our talent to delight others and perhaps make a difference in their lives. But I often wonder what I have done or could do that would make a change for the better in society."

"There's much to be said for bringing more beauty to the world. That's one of the things your mother did, with her clothing designs and other projects. And in your case, those books that you and Arthur have illustrated are no small accomplishment. They're not only beautiful, but they also preserve and promote important legends and stories. Besides that, you have lived a life that serves as a model," I said.

"What do you mean?"

"I mean that you have demonstrated in the most intimate and challenging relationship on earth that race does not have to divide people or nations. It's not the big guys in power who will ever make deep and lasting change in the world. It's the people. When the hearts of people change, then the world will change. That's what Communism was originally about before it was corrupted by power-mongers."

"My daughter believes in changing the world one person at a time."

"Where do you think she learned that? You're already the stuff of family legend, Rina. You're just not old and creaky yet."

"You're not creaky," Rina protested.

Finished with their expedition, Avram and Alejandro were turning the canoe over and tying it to a tree by the pond. Alejandro's shrill voice rose high and unintelligible from the distance. Avram's deep rumble answered the little one's questions.

"You have a precious gift in that child," I said as I watched Alejandro.

"You don't need to tell me that; I already know," Rina assured me as she followed her grandson's movements with her eyes, her hand that held her embroidery needle poised above her work.

"I suppose you do."

Alejandro scrambled up the path to the house from the pond and breathlessly informed us, "The duck caught a fish, right in its mouth, while we were watching." As he continued to talk about the duck, Rina led him inside to read a story to him in the hopes that he might take a nap.

Avram and I wandered into the garden to pick vegetables for dinner. I removed my shoes so that I could feel the earth between my toes. Avram put his arm around my waist while he pointed out a family of bluebirds perched in the willow. Then he said, "I'm glad you brought them to the farm."

I studied his sun-leathered face. "You don't recognize her, do you?"

Avram appeared bewildered.

"Miriam. She is ours. The same spirit."

Avram threw his head back and laughed. "Stop. You're scaring me with this hocus-pocus. I'm going to pretend you're joking," he said as he kissed me quickly, surreptitiously, on the lips. "Thank you for coming, and for giving me all of yourself while you were here."

For an instant, I looked into the face of the Avram of my youth. Then it dissolved and we went inside to prepare the evening meal.

We ate a leisurely family dinner that evening. At the table, Rina told Avram, "If it's all right with you, I want to get back up here to your place with Arthur. I want him to see the scenery around here, your trees and those mountains. We're working on a storybook about a Mohawk legend and I want to use this scenery in it. I'd also like to do a tapestry of the view from your porch."

"You'll have to come back soon," Avram warned. "Winter comes early and lasts a long time in Vermont."

"I'll take photographs while I'm here and bring Arthur back in the autumn," Rina decided.

"Autumn is a good time for city people to come to Vermont. Not too hot, not too cold, and spectacularly beautiful. Come in October."

"Is that an invitation?"

"An open invitation," Avram offered, with an oddly formal bow.

I was pleased that I had initiated the connection. The children were reacquainted with him. Rina and Miriam would likely stay in touch with Avram and perhaps look out for him if necessary after Ruth passed on and I flew back across the ocean. Miriam was bound to come back to Vermont because she was drawn to Avram's farm and because her Alejandro would insist on seeing "Tío Avram" again.

We turned in early after a long day in the fresh air. Everyone slept peacefully right through the night. In the morning, Miriam whispered to me in the hallway that she had dreamed only of ripe cherries glistening on the tree.

After breakfast, we reluctantly prepared to leave. We had removed the weight of Ruth's approaching death for a few days and we would soon take it up again. Miriam went with Alejandro to the barn to say good-bye to the goats. Rina busily shot photographs. Avram's farm would no doubt turn up in the illustrations for a children's book before long. Avram and I walked to the willow by the pond to take our leave.

"You've found a clear and safe shelter, away from the confusion and lunacy of the world. I'll carry Vermont with me always in my heart and imagine myself in the house on the hill when I need respite."

"Maybe you will come back," Avram's voice was hoarse and hopeful.

"I'm getting too old to travel like this," I said regretfully. "And I hate to fly," I added. He took my hands, kissed me.

"It has been good," he said.

But I thought, no, it has not been good for you, Avram. You deserved more. He clung to his love for me because it was the central attachment that remained for him from before we lost Miriam; but if there had been no war, he would have had a completely different life, full of possibilities, and he would have made a marriage of his own that was strong enough to eclipse his love for me.

We walked slowly back to the house, hand in hand.

The distraction of Alejandro saying good-bye and trilling his abundant questions helped me get through the final parting. I knew I would never see Avram again in this lifetime. As we drove down the dirt driveway, I turned to take a mental snapshot of him standing on his porch, hand raised. I hoped I would find him the next time around.

Upon my return from Vermont, I learned that Shayna had telephoned from Paris to say that she had rearranged her schedule in order to join us at Ruth's bedside. She would arrive the following afternoon. As an adult, Shayna had become more like a younger sister than a daughter to me in many respects. We fussed over Yakov's health together and she often went with us to the doctor so that she could hear firsthand what he had to say. If we wanted a second opinion, it was usually Shayna who called Micah to find out what he thought. Then she would call me to explain. She and her husband, Pierre, frequently came over to our house for dinner or went with us to Zac's, especially on the weekends. I met her at a restaurant for lunch a couple of times each week. She came with me to rallies and demonstrations once in a while and consulted me about the choices before she voted. We spoke by phone practically every day, even if briefly. I was relieved that she would soon be by my side.

My first night back from Vermont, I ate a quiet dinner with Ruth in the breakfast nook. I assured her that Avram had made a comfortable life for himself in Vermont. We reminisced about our childhood, filling in the blanks in each other's memories as no one else could. "I'm surprised that I remember such details from the past when I can't remember where I put my glasses fifteen minutes ago," I joked. We talked until after midnight, holding back the curtain of sleep in order to share one more conversation.

In the morning, I immediately sensed something wrong in the house. Jade met me in the kitchen with the news. Ruth had suffered a series of strokes during the night. The doctor had come and gone in the wee hours. Sophie and Sarah had tended to Ruth while I slept through the entire thing.

"How bad is she?" I asked, anxiously.

"She is partially paralyzed and having great difficulty speaking," Jade answered. "She's sleeping right now. Sarah is in with her."

I was shocked that she had deteriorated so quickly and felt a pang of guilt for having taken time away from her to go to Vermont. I had thought we would have a little longer than this to be together.

After breakfast, I took a walk in the neighborhood to clear my head. I once again admired the graceful trees that arched to meet each other above the yards and houses. Some of the trees in these yards were hundreds of years old and had likely planted themselves. Others, such as the trees that lined the street in a row, had been planted by a human hand, someone long dead who had left their handiwork for future generations to enjoy.

In Vermont, Alejandro had told me, "I wonder what will come after people."

"What do you mean?" I had asked.

"First we had dinosaurs and then they died. Now we have people. I wonder what comes next."

Perhaps after people there would be just trees, a species that could live for hundreds or thousands of years. I was sure that trees contributed to the planet in ways that humans failed to comprehend. We humans are so preoccupied and self-important that we could easily miss the impact of another species entirely. What if we have overlooked one of the most vital lessons of our existence, that we are not top species?

Late in the morning, when Ruth woke, I slipped in to see her. She seemed to be partially elsewhere and at last I fully believed that she was dying. Her eyes were a bit glazed and she was turned inward as she collected herself for the journey ahead. She was noticeably detached from her earthly relationships and I understood that I would not have another conversation with her in the flesh in this life. Many of Ruth's frequent visitors stopped at the house, but her daughters turned them away, except for the rabbi and Ruth's dearest friend, her sister-in-law, Ida. News of Ruth's condition spread in the community and the phone began to ring. Jade fielded the many calls from concerned friends, neighbors, and members of Ruth's synagogue. In the evening, Max collected Shayna from the airport and drove her to the house.

When Shayna arrived, I fell into her arms tearfully and thanked her for coming. Once I had calmed down, we sat in the breakfast nook together while she ate some cheese and crackers with an apple and she caught me up on the family's comings and goings in France. Zac was taking good care of Yakov. Micah felt that Yakov should be walking to strengthen his heart and Zac's wife had him out every morning for a turn around the block. Yakov was up to a mile each morning and feeling more fit. The big news was that Zac's eldest, Sebastian, who had married a little late in life for Zac's tastes, had just announced that his wife was expecting a baby. Shayna saved the best, about herself, for last. She had not danced professionally for many years, but she worked regularly as a choreographer. With excitement, she told me that she had just been hired as the artistic director for the National Ballet's experimental studio lab.

It was not yet nine o'clock when Shayna, who was jet-lagged, turned in for the night. After that I went into Ruth's room and sat beside her for a while with Ida, who quietly told me stories from the many years that she and Ruth had spent raising their children together, years that I had read about in letters from afar. We could not tell if Ruth was asleep or not, as she rested with her eyes closed. I hoped that she heard the lull of our voices and was comforted. Ida left at about ten-thirty and Sophie slept in the bed next to her mother in case Ruth needed anything during the night. I lay awake in my bed next to my own daughter, wishing I could freeze time at that moment, before Ruth left us.

FOUR

Miriam

THE DAY AFTER MY cousin Shayna arrived, we women planned to spend the afternoon together at Grandma Ruth's bedside. It would be me and Mama, Aunt Soph and Aunt Sarah, Aunt Rivka, Shayna, Ida, and Jade. Uncle Max had offered to take Alex to the park.

When Mama and I arrived at the house, just after noon, Jade and Aunt Rivka were in the kitchen preparing lunch while Ida and Aunt Sarah sat with Grandma Ruth. Jade had just rinsed a heap of purple-red cherries and put them into a bowl. Aunt Rivka was slicing cheese on a cutting board. When Jade saw us enter, she squatted to Alex's eye level to greet him.

"Do you have a hug for Auntie Jade?" she asked Alex.

He had a little plastic airplane and he flew it in his hand across the room until he reached Jade and then hugged her roundly. Jade kissed his cheek.

"And what are you up to today?" she asked him.

"Uncle Max is taking me to the park. I brought one airplane for me and one for Uncle Max. Mami says I can play with the water. I brought my Mickey Mouse towel," Alex replied excitedly. "Look," he continued as he brushed his hand across the top of his head, "I still have my haircut."

"He loves this haircut and every morning when he wakes up he asks if his haircut is still there," Mama told Jade.

Shayna entered the kitchen and greeted me and Mama each with a warm embrace and, of course, kisses on both cheeks. I motioned proudly to my son by way of introduction and told Shayna, "This is my Alejandro."

She turned to Alex with her hand outstretched as if to shake his. He beamed up at her, with that impish, infectious smile of his, and she seemed to think better of the handshake. Instead, she dropped to her knees in front of him and gave him a delighted hug.

"You smell good," Alex told her.

But I barely registered what he had said because my attention had shifted from Shayna and Alex to Aunt Rivka, who stood by the sink sobbing. I went to her and put my arms around her. "What is it?" I asked.

She wiped her eyes and shook her head. "I'll tell you later," she said, as the other women in the room turned their concerned faces toward her. "I'm OK," she reassured us. "I just had a moment, but I'm OK now."

Perhaps I would have questioned Aunt Rivka about her "moment" if not for the fact that Uncle Max and Aunt Soph came in just then.

Alex jumped up and down shouting to Uncle Max, "I brought you airplanes and I have my baby suit and my buckets and shovels!"

"He means his bathing suit. He calls it a baby suit," I explained.

"Then we're good to go, buddy," Uncle Max said.

I handed my uncle the Mickey Mouse towel, the "baby suit," and Alex's sweatshirt.

"Come give Mami a kiss," I requested. He ran up and wrapped his arms around my neck. "Be a good boy for Uncle Max," I instructed, then he was out the door with Uncle Max hurrying to keep up while clutching a plastic bag of toys and snacks that I had thrust into his hands.

We ate lunch hurriedly together in the kitchen, eager to get up to Grandma Ruth's room but not wanting to bring the food up there. It didn't seem right to eat in front of her when she clearly had no appetite. She had not eaten anything since she had the series of strokes. We had barely been able to get her to drink a little water. When we entered, we found Ida attempting, unsuccessfully, to coax Grandma Ruth to sip a little orange juice through a straw.

The room brimmed with flowers and sunlight; Aunt Sarah had opened the wide double doors to the screened sun porch that my grandfather had built off the bedroom, and a slight summer breeze drifted in. I hoped that when it came time for me to die, I would go during the winter. It would be so much harder to leave during summer's bounty.

Ida gave up on trying to get Grandma Ruth to drink the juice and went to sit on the love seat against the wall by the closet, where she took out her knitting. Aunt Rivka sat down on the chair that Ida had vacated next to Grandma Ruth and took her sister's hand. Mama sat on the end of Grandma Ruth's bed and bent her head over an elaborate embroidery on which she was working. Shayna settled in a spot in the middle of the carpet, where she occupied herself with an intricate series of leg stretches. Jade, who had brought a baby blanket that she was hand quilting, shared the love seat with Ida. Aunt Soph had mountains of papers spread out on a card table. It was some type of paperwork that did not require much concentration and she plowed through it, methodically sorting things into piles and circling items on long lists. Pruning shears in hand, I meticulously worked my way through the cascade of flowers in vases and jars crowding virtually every surface as I removed the dead blooms and rearranged the live ones. There were dozens upon dozens of roses, in every hue. Aunt Sarah sat on the other side of Grandma Ruth, opposite Aunt Rivka, and held Grandma Ruth's other hand.

"Aunt Rivka, what was it about Alex and Shayna meeting that set you off a little while ago?" I asked. Perhaps I should have let it drop, but my curiosity got the better of me.

"It was moving for me to see them together," Aunt Rivka replied. "I had not seen them together for fifty years."

"What do you mean?" Mama asked, as all of us abandoned what we had been doing to stare at Aunt Rivka. I wondered if the stress of Grandma Ruth's impending death had made her a little crazy. But then I recalled our conversation in Vermont and the pieces began to fit into place.

"I am occasionally able to recognize the spirits of people who have returned, who have been reincarnated. I recognize Alejandro. He has the spirit of Akiva, the son of my sister Miriam." Aunt Rivka and I exchanged a charged look and she nodded to me ever so slightly, as if to alert me that she was about to share her recognition of me and my son with the others, but I had already realized what was coming. "Shayna and Akiva played together when they were small and the emotion I felt when I saw them together again took me by surprise," Aunt Rivka explained in a no-nonsense tone that dared contradiction.

"She recognized me," I said softly, as I inhaled the scent of a deep-red rose. I gazed intently at the layered petals of the rose, worried that if I looked up I would discover the others staring at me in disbelief in the same way that they had stared at Aunt Rivka. One could not disbelieve the truth of a rose. Then I added, "I can remember things from a previous life as the other Miriam, in France." I glanced at Mama, who was wearing a curious and faintly hurt expression. I could tell that it bothered her that I had not confided in her before telling the rest of the family about this. I would have to talk to her later and explain that I had not sorted it out in my own mind until that moment, in that conversation.

"I'm a little lost," Aunt Sarah said. "Help me out here because this sounds kind of eerie to me. Like a conversation we ought to conduct in a tent in the graveyard by flashlight or something."

"Do you think that you and Miriam know each other from a past life?" Mama asked Aunt Rivka.

"We knew each other before in this life. It's complicated," Aunt Rivka said. "I believe that our Miriam here is the reincarnation of my adopted sister Miriam, and that her son, Akiva, who perished when he was two years old, has returned to her in this lifetime in the form of Alejandro."

Shayna added, "The last time I saw Akiva was at a birthday party for me at Miriam's farm in Crevecoeur. Miriam hitched a donkey to a wooden cart, and Akiva's father took us children for rides. The cart was decorated with flowers."

"It was for Shayna's third birthday. Miriam threw a big party for

Shayna," Aunt Rivka told us, and then she said to Shayna, "The best birthday present she gave you on that day was a magnificent memory to keep."

Mama returned her attention to her handwork, bending her head over the violet, mauve, and sky-blue threads. Without glancing up from her flashing needle, she cocked her head to one side and collected her thoughts, the way a storyteller might gather listening children to her skirt for a story. And then she said, "It makes total sense to me. I've never recognized a person as a returned spirit, but I'm sure I can remember my own past lives. Sometimes when I see a particular object or have a certain experience, it triggers a past-life memory for me. I feel as though I recognize something that I have no reason to recognize. I have a sort of flash or vision, which has no easily explained relation to my present life, yet it feels so familiar that it is as if I am taking a walk in the woods that I have taken over and over again along the exact same path."

"Give us an example," Aunt Soph said.

"OK. Say that I see a pattern in a Navajo woven blanket; well, it might cause me to feel a particular emotion, such as contentment, and I just know that I have worn a blanket like that once long ago, even though I have never seen the blanket before in this life. One time Arthur played me a piece of music that began with the sounds of people moaning and a ship creaking and I was suddenly there, inside a slave ship. I experienced the overwhelming terror, grief, and disorientation of a person trapped on that ship and I nearly passed out. I'm convinced that I was an African slave in a previous life, maybe in more than one previous life; and that I also lived many lives long ago on this continent as a Native."

I had never heard Mama talk about this before. I was grateful for the convergence of women in my family that had prompted this conversation.

"Have you ever had experiences from a previous life come to you in dreams?" I asked Mama, thinking about the memories that had pursued me in my own runaway dreams.

She turned her embroidery over, tied off a thin thread, and cut it with a tiny pair of scissors. "It's interesting that you should ask that," she said. "I haven't thought about it in years, but there was a time during my twenties when I had a recurring bad dream that could have been a past-life memory."

I had never told Mama about my nightmares. I found the fact that she had experienced a recurring bad dream a bit unnerving.

"What was the dream?" Shayna asked.

"It would usually start with the scent of flowers," Mama said, and she described her dream for us. It was nothing like my dreams. She said that she was in love with a gardener in her dream and that her parents in the dream didn't approve of him. Her mother was submissive and afraid to defend her or stand up to her father, who sent the gardener away and forced her to marry someone else, a horrible man.

"The dream usually ended with the man I was forced to marry raping me. It was pretty awful. I haven't had that dream since I got pregnant with Miriam," Mama said thoughtfully. "And, as I recall, the very last time I had it, the submissive mother finally stepped up and intervened between me and the domineering father. In fact, the last time I had that dream, I was reunited with the gardener whom I loved and the dream ended happily. I haven't thought about it in a long time. You know," she added as she concluded, "there was this one sort of odd thing about it. We were all Chinese people in the dream, even me."

FIVE

Ruth

I CANNOT SPEAK. I want to, but I cannot. My voice has fled already onto the path ahead of me. I want to tell my daughter. I think for a moment that my sister will say something. She knows. I told her once about it. She studies my face closely. I can feel her decide to hold her tongue. I understand. It is not for her to tell. It would have been for me to tell and it is not her place. She steps back from it and does not touch it. Quite right. It does not matter that my daughter will never know this time around. It matters to me that I know that I did the work that needed to be done and because of it my daughter and I are clear, are free, and therefore we are able to move forward.

SIX

Miriam

GRANDMA RUTH SQUEEZED AUNT Rivka's hand ever so slightly and Aunt Rivka murmured to her, "I know, I know, my dear." Then Aunt Rivka said, "She still hears us. Tell the others about your dreams, Miriam," she urged me.

"Sometimes," I began, "I have vivid nightmares. I dream about children who are being hurt." Mama looked up in alarm. I didn't want to cause her to worry, but I had opened the subject and would have to finish. "I won't tell you what happens to the children in the dreams. It's pretty horrible. I've had the dreams much less often since Alex was born. When I first started to have these nightmares, Gil thought it was my way of absorbing the stories about the violence experienced by the refugees that he and I help. But I became convinced that I was remembering something from a previous life. I had one of my nightmares while we were in Vermont and I told Aunt Rivka about it. As it turns out, she recognized some of the details from my dreams. They correspond to real events in the life of the other Miriam, her sister."

"The first time that I met Miriam, when she was a little girl, and Rina and Arthur brought her to visit me in Paris, I recognized her," Aunt Rivka said. "So when she related what happened in her nightmares, I decided to tell her about the other Miriam. It seemed like it would help."

"It did," I assured her. "I'm glad that I know." I put the pruning shears down on the nightstand and tapped Aunt Sarah's shoulder. "May I hold her hand for a while?" I asked timidly.

"Of course," Aunt Sarah replied as she stood. She went to the doors that led to the sun porch and looked out at the oak tree in the front yard. I took Grandma Ruth's hand, light as onion skin, light enough to float into the clouds on the slightest breeze.

"My past-life memories are sometimes pleasant and sometimes not, but either way I welcome them," Mama said. "They have become an important part of my creative process."

Shayna stood in the brightness of the windows at the end of the room, where she was silhouetted against the windows. She said, "I wonder how much of my inspiration as a choreographer comes from my imagination and how much is a form of deep memory."

Mama caught Shayna's eye and said, "I think a lot of what we call 'creative process' is simply an extension of the connection between us and the many spirits who have gone before us."

The thought of Annie's mother popped into my head and I was eager to share her story with the other women. "We remember the transcendent elements," I began. "We remember what matters. It's like my friend Annie's mother who has Alzheimer's. Annie and her mother are Pomos. The Pomo tribes of Northern California are known for their brilliant basketwork, which is tightly woven, so tight you could carry water in some of the baskets and so firm that some baskets are used for grinding grain. Pomo basket weavers make gift baskets that are tinier than thimbles, and giant feast trays as big around as a kitchen table. The culture of the Pomo would probably have remained obscure to all but their own people and a handful of anthropologists if not for the baskets. Because of the baskets, many anthropologists and historians have studied the Pomo culture and history and written about it. Annie's mother is one of the last great Pomo basket weavers. Younger women are learning and practicing the craft, but Annie's mother is a master. She lives in a nursing home and she doesn't recognize her own children and grandchildren when they visit her. The only thing she remembers is how to make baskets. Her daughters collect the grasses and roots she needs and they bring them to her. She weaves every day. A few of her baskets remain on display in the Smithsonian. The people in her life have become no more than passing spirits to her while the knowledge of the baskets has endured. So here's the thing: What if we remember the essential, timeless elements? Even if we don't understand the significance of these memories."

"I like that idea," Aunt Sarah said.

"What do you think is the purpose of your unique gift?" Aunt Soph asked Aunt Rivka.

"It's not unique," Aunt Rivka answered. "More people than you might imagine can remember. It's not something people normally talk about in ordinary conversation. And then there are those who just don't realize they're remembering. More people would soon discover that they could remember if they were open to the possibility."

"But what about Soph's question?" Jade asked. "What do you suppose is the purpose?"

"Does it have to have a purpose?" I asked.

Aunt Rivka answered, "I think the purpose is related to the evolution of the human spirit and of all spirit. I believe that all beings living and no longer living, seen and unseen, known and unknown, has spirit within them, that a rock, a person, a cat, a tree, or a bracelet has spirit, and that all things and all beings, both seen and unseen, are interrelated and have an impact on one another. I think that people know each other from past lives and that all of us have functioned in the world in many different personifications. Every spirit breathing now, in the past, or in the future exists in profound relationship to every other spirit."

Mama put down her handwork. "I recently read that scientists have been discovering links that lead them to believe that individuation is not the key to evolution. The key lies instead in the ability of organisms to function as part of a community and to contribute to the greater whole. Darwin had it partially right when he linked mutation to survival, but it's not the fittest that survive best; it's the individuals who develop the ability to cooperate with others in community who have the best chance of survival. It's that profound relationship you just mentioned, Aunt Rivka. People who develop their ability to cooperate and connect with others, resolve conflict peacefully, and collaborate stand the greatest chance of prevailing in the course of nature."

"Your philosophy supports the trend in cooperative learning to which I have subscribed since before it became popular," Aunt Sarah said with satisfaction. "Basically, we must learn to work together or we'll become extinct."

"Exactly. And people who have a more fully developed spiritual sense have the greatest chance of survival on the planet," Aunt Rivka said. "Those deep memories of incarnations spent within different cultural contexts contribute to the overall evolution of a spirit, so that more fully evolved spirits are fundamentally multicultural."

I laughed out loud and the others turned startled faces toward me. "Sorry. You just reminded me of something," I explained. "You know how you often have to identify your race on standardized forms? Well, one time I was filling out a form for school, and I was required to check only one box to identify my race and, I couldn't resist, I checked the box for 'Caucasian.' I mean, why should I always check 'African American' when I'm half white?"

"These days they usually have a box for multicultural. You can check that one, baby," Mama suggested.

"Everyone should technically check that one," I pointed out. "Latino people are combinations of indigenous people and Spanish invaders. Many Asian Americans are a mixture of more than one Asian culture, like Chinese and Korean. Most African Americans are actually a variety of races, like Daddy, who has European, African, and Native American blood. Even white people are a mixture of different cultures, like Italian and Scottish or something, so that the term *white* is, in fact, meaningless."

"It's true," Mama agreed.

"Then there's this little girl in here," I patted my belly. "Jewish, Black, Native, Latina, and who knows what else thrown in from Daddy's lost past. She'll have to check every box available on those ethnic identification forms."

"She'll mark the 'all of the above' box," Mama said, laughing.

"Now that one in there," Aunt Rivka leaned back into her chair like the words of a poem leaning back into their deepest meaning. "We have been waiting a long time for the evolution that brings us that one in there."

"That one in there is beyond evolution; that one is revolution," Mama said.

"That one will save us from extinction," Aunt Rivka declared with satisfaction.

"Do you have a name picked out?" Aunt Sarah asked.

"I'm sure she's going to be a girl, so we only have a girl's name," I replied. If I was wrong, and it was a boy after all, we had many names to choose from on Gil's side of the family. The others turned their faces to me expectantly, waiting to hear the name, and I suddenly felt shy about saying it out loud for the women of my family, almost as if I should have said the name to them for the first time within the context of a religious ceremony. And yet, this gathering at my grandmother's deathbed felt like a ceremony. I released the name to them, like a dove let loose to the sky. "We're thinking we'll call her Rasunah."

SEVEN

Ruth

"RASUNAH," I WHISPER. IT is the last word I ever say. Daughter of my daughter's daughter. I turn the name Rasunah over in my mind. I will never see Rasunah, except perhaps in another life, another context. Will we recognize each other? My life has gone by in the time it takes for a bird to chirp. So swiftly. All of it so swiftly by. The choices, the complexities, the struggles, the successes, the moments of pure and resonant beauty. Everything seemed so urgent at the time, so in need of doing to get to the next thing. Like stones in a river that one must step on to get to the other side. One stone at a time. And I stepped on all of them and here I have arrived at the other side. Or perhaps my whole life was just one stone in a river and my next life will be the next stone. Too vast to grasp. I hear a clacking sound. I recognize it as the clacking of chess pieces. Papa and Meir playing chess in the late evening, their muffled voices rumbling in the front room. I can see Mama's golden apricots swimming in a jar of honeyed water on the windowsill, the late afternoon light fixing a numinous glow on the preserved fruit. I can taste the salt air as the ship that carried me to America pulls into the harbor beneath the towering figure of the Statue of Liberty. I feel the weight of Nate's hand against the small of my back or resting on my waist and I lean into him, remembering that Count Basie number (what is the name of it?) that we so liked to dance to together. Nate's touch, just his proximity, could sometimes make the hairs on the nape of my neck stand at attention. I smell the sweet clean fragrance of my babies as I lift them one by one out of their baths and nuzzle them and wrap each in a thick fluffy towel. Those perfect babies who came from my own body so many years ago that I can hardly believe it ever happened. Those wide-eyed babies who grew into competent women; my baby who had a baby of her own; whose baby grew up and carried other babies. We are like nesting dolls. And the tiniest little nested doll curls its perfect form within the daughter of my daughter here in this room. Rasunah. I float lightly on this bed

and listen to the voices surrounding me, wrapping me in their vitality of energy and motion. Who are these people? In one moment, I will summon my strength and rise from this bed and make breakfast for the girls. I look to my left and my right. Rivka on one hand. Miriam on the other. My sisters. Mama tells me to call Benjy for dinner. I will do it shortly. With Rivka on one side and Miriam on the other, in the room my Nathan built for me, the room where I conceived each of my splendid daughters, I breathe in and out, in and out, and then, I stop.

EIGHT

Miriam

I CAUGHT IT IN the silence of her pulse immediately and looked, through my tears, at Aunt Rivka across the bed, who realized at the same moment as I.

"Her pulse stopped," I told the other women. "She's gone."

Aunt Rivka began to hum the Russian Yiddish lullaby that her mother had sung to her and her sisters as children. And of course we all knew it because we had drifted off to sleep to that tune as infants and then as toddlers and still again as youngsters until we outgrew such childish practices and the tune became a part of our deepest remembrance and then, years and years later, some of us sang it to our own children in the dusky twilight. Our voices intertwined, like the intricate threads of Mama's embroidery or the complex movements of Shayna's choreography or the many ingredients that I mixed together to make good soil for growing vegetables, as we sang Grandma Ruth to sleep across the river.

NINE

Rina

AFTER MOM PASSED OVER, Soph, ever the expert organizer, made the arrangements for the funeral, which, in accordance with Jewish law, took place within forty-eight hours of Mom's passing. I felt sort of like I had drifted to a place on the edge of reality. I felt disintegrated. I watched my body perform everyday tasks from a great distance.

The memorial service took place at the synagogue, conducted by the rabbi who had visited Mom every day during her last illness. He had been a good friend to her and knew her well. His words provided comfort. The synagogue choir sang. A few friends and family members spoke, reminiscing about Mom. Listening to their stories brought her back to us in a small way. Many of her friends wore dresses and hats that she had made. Ida's anecdotes made us laugh. She had known Mom so well and she skillfully captured her personality in her stories about her. She told us about a time before Mom and Nate were married, when they had gone up to the racetrack in Saratoga one weekend with Ida and Uncle Izzie, and that once they got there Mom had been shocked to discover that Nate and his brother were placing bets on the horses.

"I wondered what she had imagined we were going to do at the racetrack," Ida said. "She was so absorbed in making hats to wear for the trip that she never once stopped to think about where we were going. But I can testify that those hats were gorgeous."

I sat in the first row of the synagogue with the rest of the immediate family, my focus on the service and the people who spoke. When, at last, we rose to leave, I turned to discover that not only was the large synagogue packed with hundreds of people, but the lobby held many more people who could not fit in the room. And as the sea of people parted to give our family room to exit, I saw beyond, into the street, where others who could not fit into the building, or even onto the grounds, stood, fill-ing the street. The police had closed off the entire block to cars. Where did all these people come from? Who were they?

Eight uniformed policemen had to clear a path for the two family limou-sines and the hearse to exit the street. Arthur held my arm as I walked slowly through the crowd. The people reached their hands out to stop me and my sisters, to touch us in consolation, and say a few words. I listened carefully to the soft-spoken heartfelt messages delivered to me, Sarah, and Soph.

"Your mother and father brought our family out of Europe during the war. My father, Yossel, was quite a character. He sponged off your parents for years, but they were patient with him. Your parents saved my life. My daughter is a pediatrician in Great Neck. My son is a biochemistry professor. This is my grandson. I brought him with me to honor your mother's memory."

"During the Depression my father could not afford to pay for his oil to keep the heat in our house. Your father let us buy on credit for two years. We paid back every penny, but it took a long time. Such generous people, your parents."

"When my mother lay dying, your mother brought hot food to our house every evening. For five weeks she brought food. Such a thoughtful woman."

"Your mother helped found the Sisterhood in this synagogue. They don't make them like your mother anymore."

"Your parents allowed my two aging great-aunts to live rent-free in an apartment that your family owned when my aunts' eyesight failed and they could no longer support themselves making lace. They lived rent-free for years until their death. Your parents were so kind."

"Your parents brought our family out of Hungary during the war. They encouraged my grandfather to go to college. We owe our success in this country to your mother's generosity."

"Your parents rescued us from the *Shoah*."

"Your parents brought us out of the eye of the Holocaust."

"Your mother saved our lives."

Everyone who reached out to us had a story, an appreciation, a mem-ory of good deeds done and not forgotten. I had not fully realized how generous my mother had been. And my father. My image of Nate was so different from the one painted by the words these people spoke. If I allowed myself to dwell on thoughts of my childhood, I would surely surface many memories of my father that I had fastidiously hidden or shunted to one side, memories that would make me miss him and wish for more than the failed relationship for which we had both settled.

I paused, standing close to Aunt Rivka, and together we looked out over the sea of mourners. I heard Aunt Rivka speak, not to me, but to my absent mother.

She said, "This is what you left behind, my darling, all of this."

TEN

Miriam

AFTER THE FUNERAL, WE returned to Grandma Ruth's house to begin the ritual week of sitting in mourning, or *shiva*, during which friends and family visited to offer their condolences. Aunt Sarah and Jade planned to move into the house and maintain it much as Grandma Ruth had left it. They were thinking of taking in a foster child, a troubled teenager whom Jade was counseling.

"In a big house like this, we could take in several children," Aunt Sarah said. It seemed that the people in our family would continue the habit of taking in those less fortunate than us to live under our roof.

As we sat in the living room waiting for guests to return from the cemetery, Mama said, "I never knew how many people our parents helped. All those people who came to the service. It took me completely by surprise."

"It surprised me too," Aunt Soph said.

"And such a variety of people," Aunt Sarah remarked. "I mean, not only Jews. I know that Papa believed in taking care of one's own and that he gave a lot to the synagogue and the Jewish community, and I knew about the European refugees he brought over during the war. But I never knew how much he gave to anyone in need, like those people who couldn't afford fuel to heat and cook with during the Depression. He just gave them free fuel."

Grandma Ruth's house soon swelled with guests, food, talk, and laughter. Alex had fallen asleep on the couch in the midst of the activity. That child could sleep through anything if he was tired enough. Gil had not been able to book a flight out in time to make it to the funeral. I felt as if I had not seen Gil in years, and Alex was showing signs of stress from being separated from his papi. I couldn't wait to return to the familiarity of daily life at Esperanza.

The seven days of mourning had just begun, but the ingathering of women was already dissolving. Shayna and Aunt Rivka had booked their return flight to Paris. I knew that Mama had fallen behind on a big project spread out in her studio at home. Aunt Soph and Aunt Sarah would finish the traditional mourning week in Grandma Ruth's house after the rest of us left.

As the last dusting of evening light brushed the treetops, Aunt Rivka walked us out to Daddy's car to say good-bye to my family. Daddy buckled Alex into his car seat, and Aunt Rivka gave him several sloppy kisses that made him laugh. She hugged Daddy and Mama, and then she turned to me. In the morning we would travel in opposite directions. She put one arm around my waist and patted my belly with the other. It had been an emotional day, especially for a pregnant woman, and I started to cry.

"Don't fret," Aunt Rivka soothed me. "I will write to you. I plan to be around for a few more years."

I nodded, brushed away my tears, and offered her a watery smile.

She held my hand as I eased into the backseat next to Alex.

She started to close the door and then stopped. "Oh wait! I have a question I wanted to ask you," she said. "Right before Ruth passed over, you said you planned to name your baby Rasunah."

"Yes, Rasunah," I replied.

"I wanted to ask you what the name means."

"It's a word in a lost Native American language that is no longer spoken. It means something like 'spirit memory.'" I remembered Aunt Rivka's words at Grandma Ruth's bedside: every spirit breathing now, in the past, or in the future exists in profound relationship to every other spirit.

A subtle, satisfied smile graced Aunt Rivka's lips and the corners of her eyes as she closed the car door and raised her hand in farewell, or perhaps in blessing. Daddy backed the car out of the driveway and we carved our path down the tree-lined street.

ELEVEN

Rivka

 RASUNAH ARRIVED DURING THE autumn pumpkin harvest at Miriam's farm in Arizona.

She telephoned me on the day of the birth and in her euphoria promised to bring the baby to France so I could see her. I told Miriam I wouldn't hold her to such a grand promise. But she kept it.

"I want to stand before the statue of the other Miriam," she wrote to me, "with my children and my husband. I want to visit her orchards, to walk where she walked."

So, on an overcast spring Sunday, Zac drove with me to the airport to pick them up in his family van. We arrived early and walked to the waiting area for international flights, where we found seats facing the windows. Zac opened a newspaper while I gazed at the clouded sky until an earnest young voice next to me interrupted my thoughts.

"I don't believe the stars created the Earth," the voice announced.

I peered into the intent face of a girl eight or nine years old. The child's dark eyes approached black and her straight hair, which flowed past her shoulders, was the color of a raven's wing.

"Pardon?" I asked, although I had understood exactly what the child had said. I wanted a moment to gather my thoughts.

"Martin said the stars created the Earth, and I don't believe him," the child stated quietly.

"Who's Martin?"

"Maman's friend. He said the universe used to have gases and matter until it exploded and some of it became the stars and some of it became the planets and one of it became Earth. He said the explosion of the stars created Earth."

"That's called the big bang theory," I told her. "Because everything supposedly exploded with a bang. Many scientists teach that theory and many people believe it. Other people believe that a god created the world. Those people don't believe about the big bang. Different people believe different things."

"I don't know about god theory," the child responded, skeptically. I wondered about her ethnic identity. She had honey-colored skin and almond-shaped eyes. She could have been Philippine, or Latina, or a member of an indigenous tribe from anywhere in the world. Perhaps she was multiethnic, maybe part Asian and part African.

I said, "Some people think that living things started as tiny creatures in the water and that they changed, over many long years, into other beings, that changed into other beings again and again, that finally became humans." The teacher in me was gratified to have spontaneously simplified the origin of species.

"That's evolution, right?" The child hooked her curtain of hair behind her ears. She tipped her head slightly to one side and studied my face. "I don't believe the big bang. I don't believe evolution either. And I think people made up God to explain things they don't understand."

"What do you think created the world, then?" I asked with interest. This conversation with this unusual little girl was like a gift that had dropped in my lap.

The girl's mother appeared and tapped her daughter on the shoulder. "Have you made a friend?" the mother asked.

I addressed the mother: "We were discussing the mystery of creation."

The mother laughed lightly. "That sounds about right," she said.

The girl stood to follow her mother, but before she left, she leaned in close to my ear and whispered, "I don't know how it was created or why it was created, but the world wasn't created by accident."

I followed the girl with my eyes as she took her mother's hand and disappeared into the crowd. The image of that enigmatic young face lingered in my mind even as Zac and I greeted Miriam and we met her Gilberto, a compact man with intense eyes and a winning smile. The child's words clung to me as I bent down to allow Alejandro to wrap his arms around my neck and as I marveled over how much he had grown and the fact that he was now a big brother.

"I brought my baby for you to see," Alejandro announced.

Zac proclaimed enthusiastically to the world at large, "Look at what a beauty my cousin made!"

"She fell asleep just before the plane landed," Miriam informed us.

"Isn't she exquisite?" Zac boomed.

I would have liked to agree, but I couldn't get a good look at her what with the commotion of Miriam and Zac handing the baby back and forth between the two of them.

"Is he always like this?" Gil asked.

"He's incorrigible," I replied, patting Zac's shoulder with affection. "You look well, Miriam," I told her. "You are so svelte already after having the baby!"

"Oh, I'm not," Miriam replied mournfully, "but thank you for saying so."

We made our way through the crowded corridor and down the steep escalator, which thrilled Alejandro. Standing behind Miriam on the escalator, I got a better look at Rasunah, who slept blissfully on her mother's shoulder. Zac and Gil waited for the bags at the carousel while Miriam and I parked ourselves at a row of plastic molded chairs.

Alejandro informed us, "I have to go to the bathroom."

"Would you take her for a moment?" Miriam asked. I reached for the sleeping baby. "We'll be right back," Miriam said.

I cradled her in my lap and looked into her mocha-brown face.

Rasunah's eyes fluttered open. She was instantly alert and cheerful. Somehow the combination of Latina, African, and Semitic blood gave her eyelids a delicate fold that made her appear almost Asian. It occurred to me that Rasunah looked as if she could have been related to the culturally ambiguous youngster with whom I had exchanged such deep thoughts about creation. The baby peered at me curiously with her bright eyes as she attempted to stuff one chubby fist into her mouth.

"Welcome back," I said to her.

She studied my face. Then she gave me an enormous smile.

"Rasunah, Rasunah, Rasunah," I crooned.

I cuddled her close and rested her against my shoulder, nestling my face in the creases of her neck, breathing in her sweet baby scent. I pressed my lips against her soft skin, felt her hair tickle my nose, and kissed her little cheek, then I launched a question in Yiddish down the corridor of her perfectly coiled ear: "And who in the wide world might you be?"

Acknowledgments

[*Spoiler alert: Don't read the Acknowledgments until you have completed Part One of* Memories from Cherry Harvest.]

I AM GRATEFUL TO Frances Fabri, who has been my spirit guide for the past couple of years as I have completed my journey with the story I have been carrying in me all my life and which evolved into *Memories from Cherry Harvest*. Frances was a Holocaust survivor, born in Hungary in 1929, who passed away in San Francisco in 2006, leaving a bequest to Matt McKay. Matt and his wife Judy chose to use Frances's bequest to create the Fabri Prize and I thank them for selecting *Cherry Harvest* as a winner. I have been actively working on this book for the equivalent of twenty years or more and I probably would have spent my entire life rewriting it if the McKays and Tom Southern had not mercifully rescued me from that fate by awarding *Cherry Harvest* the Fabri Prize and thereby ensuring that it would be completed and published.

I so appreciate my early readers, who plowed through the first draft of the book back in the 1990s, when it was an epic tome, too heavy to lift, and more like an elephant than a novel. My earliest readers included my parents Eugene and Natalie Wachspress, my husband Ron Reed (who, such a *mensch*, has read the book several times), and my friend Carol Williams. I am grateful to other readers over the years who contributed to the development of the book, including my brother Dan, Linda Sobolewski, Nanette Tver, Elena Castañeda, Stan Janiak, and Judy Corwin. I have been blessed with the ongoing support and encouragement of all those mentioned above as well as other family and friends, most notably my children (Yael, Akili, and Sudi), my brother Bill, many Reed and Grant family members in Chicago, and "the Milvioids" from back in my Berkeley days; all of whom have believed in me and my talent for years and years and years as the rejection letters accumulated in my file cabinet and the unpublished manuscripts piled up under my bed.

Words cannot express how grateful I am to have worked with the amazing Liz Parker at Counterpoint and my brilliant editor Anika Streitfeld. Thank you Charlie Winton for your vision that brought Anika to this project. The love, thoughtfulness, and care with which you read my words, Anika, came through in every minute of our discussions and every edit you made.

For seventeen years my husband and I lived on forty acres of remote forest in northern California, where we raised our three children. Just down the dirt road from our house was the Butler Cherry Ranch, owned by George and Ella Butler. I never met Ella, who died in 1985, but our family knew George well. He passed on in 1996. For half a century the Butlers opened their orchards every year in June for any cherry pickers who wished to harvest cherries. George charged a dollar per pound for the cherries and promised not to weigh anyone on their way out (good deal because we ate our share). The Butler Cherry Ranch was sold in 1998 and the cherry trees were removed and replaced with private vineyards by the new owner. I am grateful to the Butlers for the many magic hours that my family, friends, and our rural community spent in their cherry orchards; and for inspiring the central symbol of life's abundance and beauty that found its way into my book.

Cherry Harvest is my creative transformation of the lives of many members of my family, most notably my French cousins Yael and Joseph Wachspress. Joseph (my father's first cousin) fought with the French Resistance until he was captured and sent to Auschwitz, where he spent eighteen months. He survived and returned to Yael, who remained hidden in the French countryside with their baby for the duration of the war. Yael and Joseph lived well into old age and I visited them in Paris on several occasions. This book is especially for them, to honor their memory, and to share with others the story that has been passed like warm bread from hand to hand around dinner tables in the Wachspress family for as long as I can remember. I thank Yael and Joseph as well as my other ancestors who inspired this story for having lived the lives, persevered, made the sacrifices, and put forth into the world their many good deeds that grew from the values of our shared Jewish tradition and culture.

I stand in awe of and remain ever grateful for the mysterious well of memory from which I have had the privilege to draw abundantly. I am thankful for the gift of creativity that is my constant companion, my comfort, and my delight. And thank you, Dear Reader, for welcoming my imagined characters into your own imagination to dwell there for a time.